TWELVE STORIES HIGH

BEVER-LEIGH BANFIELD

ISBN: [978-0-9986348-3-8] (ebook)
ISBN: [978-0-9986348-6-9] (paperback)
ISBN: [978-0-9986348-1-4] (hardcover)

Cover by 100 Covers (100covers.com)
Author Photos by Kevyn Major Howard (headshot-photography.com)
Interior design by Stacey Blake (champagnebookdesign.com)
Proofread by Anne Victory (victoryediting.com)

First printing edition 2023

Published by Twinkle Entertainment

Visit www.beverleigh.com

12 women of color.

A dozen whodunits.

Which girls will survive?

Long story short—they're in deep trouble.

The sheroes of *Twelve Stories High* are suspected of murders they didn't commit. Hounded by dangerous unknown forces. Entangled in secrets and lies. And because they're Black, they're on their own—accused, abused, and on the run from cops as well as killers.

When Florida's hubby demands a divorce and suddenly disappears, relocating seems her only choice. Until her newfound land is cursed, starts growing enemies like weeds, and begins to unearth a deadly mystery buried in her past.

For Cherrie, who's catering boats to fund free meals to feed the homeless, being suspected of killing a media mogul on his to-die-for yacht is poisoning her future—and threatening to starve the hot new love she's stirring up aboard.

Willow is having a nervous breakdown. Haunted by the spirit of a grandmother who exhorts her to hunt for long-lost wealth, she jets to the Caribbean on a genealogical quest for a fortune in hidden family treasure.

From a southern small-town scandal to a seat on the Hollywood casting couch to a seven-year-old in the hot seat and four amateur painters finding their artwork hung beside their nemesis, these stories and more unfold as Trouble gets spelled with a capital TEA.

For My Angels
Leo Banfield, my adored daddy, buddy, protector
and always biggest fan
and
Theresa Banfield, my beloved mom, who loved me unconditionally
and blessed me with her love for books

CONTENTS

TRIPPING THE FLIGHT FANTASTIC

SHE HAD NO IDEA OF THE MORTAL THREAT THAT leaving her Brooklyn home would pose until she was looking up at it from over six feet under.

Florida Homer Freeman hopped in the back seat of the spit-shined Lyft, clutching her fifty-years-new train case. The treasured piece of paisley luggage giddily purchased on layaway five decades before she left her man today felt like a talisman. When she'd bought it when she was a twenty-year-old, she'd worked as a promising placement rep at Reliable Temps in downtown New York, helping people find good jobs. It was during her lunch break one fine day that, rather than grabbing her usual tuna on rye at the deli downstairs from the agency, Florida made up her mind to explore the neighborhood around her.

Smitten by bright spring weather and rounding the corner from Forty-Sixth Street to Fifth Avenue, hobbling along in too-tight shoes, she spotted a baggage shop and noticed a sign that seemed to call to her. THE ADVENTUROUS WOMAN ON THE GO, it read in a shiny golden script above a swank suitcase display. It ignited a blaze of wanderlust that continued to burn within her heart, making her yearn for exotic ports. She paid for her case on layaway and, six months later, wore its key on a gold chain hung around her neck and hidden inside her buttoned blouse.

From that day, foreign travel became her dream, and the quest saw her gathering slick brochures about cruises, airlines, grand hotels, and interesting people she might meet. But the dream remained just that until now, for the spritely septuagenarian had just pennies she'd saved in a brown glass jar, not even a week of vacation time, and little encouragement from her nearest and dearest to indulge herself. And so it was that fifty years had elapsed before she hit the road.

"If I knew then what I know now," she reflected on the tragic event that transpired on that windy day she finally took the train case home and hid it under her bed. But Florida couldn't indulge regrets. She kept moving with hope in her heart. The pilgrimage she was embarking on this day would right an egregious wrong, and that was what mattered. Nothing else.

The lumps in the Lyft's back seat tortured Florida's aching back and booty, seeming to punctuate the bumpy ride. But the white baby shoes that bobbed in the windshield and pink foam rubber dice that swung from the rearview mirror made her smile. The driver had a family, she concluded. Driving came with risks. Maybe the man who was shuttling her to the airport had his own big dreams. She decided to overtip. The Lyft lurched to a halt at the terminal by a United skycap podium. Running late, she avoided the skycaps, as her loving daughter Madison, excited by the notion of her mother taking her maiden voyage at seventy, had bought Florida two large rolling cases and an instructive Fodor's guide detailing her destination in Fort Lauderdale, a popular tourist spot in the state for which Florida had been named.

The grinning, Armenian-accented driver hopped out and ran around the hood. He opened Florida's door with a bow and took her arm to help her out in the way her three grown daughters did on occasions when they visited.

Florida's eldest, Keys, lived on Cape Breton Island in Nova Scotia—divorced, broke, sad, and isolated—raising an autistic son, the sweetest grandchild in the world. Her middle daughter, Ocala, was a stay-at-home mom who was wearily wed to a pedigreed investment banker, Sturges Poole, who'd moved his bride to Winston-Salem, North Carolina, on a whim. It was ostensibly done to be nearer his parents after the couple's fourth child was born. *His* parents. Well, ain't that a kick in the head. Florida was an afterthought to her son-in-law, a selfish man, so she seldom heard from Ocala, but she constantly worried about her well-being and happiness so far away. Ocala was not the most stable girl, and she tended to be emotional, whereas Florida's youngest, Madison, was much more levelheaded. The successful TV commercial director was happily married to Broadway producer Armbruster Kane, a real fat cat. Madison phoned home every day and resided just up the I-95 in Connecticut, in suburbia, in a massive coastal mansion.

But none of their problems took focus today. For once, they were not to be top of mind. This wasn't the time to think about kids or grandkids. This was her moment now. Florida's era had finally come, her chance to let go of sacrifice and dive into her passions.

The traveling mother of three paid the fare and included a generous tip for the driver, who told her about his twin toddlers while he rolled her belongings up to the ticket counter to "fly the friendly skies." As Florida waited in the check-in line, an old gent pushing an empty wheelchair winked, took his hat off with a nod, and eyed her with approval. She adjusted her neckline, averted her gaze, and presented her printed ticket to the girl behind the counter.

At seventy, Florida still was a showstopper. Looking to be in her 50s, she was statuesque, stylish, and ladylike, with translucent amber skin. A perfect size ten with a short, natural hairdo and chic, upscale, and trendy style, she was once a showgirl and would always turn heads. She was eye-catching in the yellow dress the kids picked out for Mother's Day. Only her custom-made shoes belied her age, those bulky oxford flats that comforted corns and calluses and soothed her fallen arches. Her feet had hurt since childhood, but even so, Florida loved to walk. She adored getting out to breathe fresh air. It made her feel liberated. Liberation was what she needed now, on the heels of her recently broken marriage.

"Free at last," she muttered, quoting Dr. Martin Luther King. New freedom preoccupied her mind. She was learning the meaning of the word. This trip represented a breakthrough into independent life. Other orientation consumed her whole adulthood for so many happy years. But things abruptly changed, and now she had to change herself.

The plane was packed to nearly full, but it took off just ten minutes late. Madison had booked the flight online, nabbing Florida a window seat in a short and cramped two-seater row. It seemed Florida had it to herself when the doors at the front of the plane were closed, and that caused her to relax. She snuggled up in the orange cardigan sweater she'd knitted for the trip and lost herself in a gothic romance novel, eventually dozing off. When she woke, the plane was airborne, and three flight attendants were serving soft drinks, wheeling a cart along her row, and offering minuscule bags of pretzels. As she snacked and attempted to choose a movie, fumbling with her earphone jack, she noticed the very same gentleman who was ogling her figure earlier was seated aboard the airplane too. Interesting. When she'd seen him in the airport, he was wearing a ratty blazer she assumed to be a uniform and pushing the empty wheelchair that she figured was for passengers. Back then he had looked like an employee. Now he was dressed in a three-piece suit with the look of a designer cut. Oh well, it was none of her business. But the man kept staring at her.

Well, turnabout was fair play, right? And she didn't have anything else to do for the next few hours. What the heck. She shifted in her seat to get a better look and check him out as he chatted up a flight attendant hovering near the restrooms. Now was as good a time as any to learn to evaluate strangers if she was going to see the world, she thought. She appraised him to be in his eighties and just above her height of five feet nine. He was skinny, a fetching cocoa brown, with a full head of salt-and-pepper hair, reptilian eyes, a long, sharp nose, and lips the size of hot dogs, which were slathered with shiny lip balm or zinc sunscreen, she could not tell which. He returned to his seat and sat stock-still by a window with the shade pulled down on the opposite side of the airplane, almost inanimate in a creepy way. He was one row up from Florida, beyond a long center five-seater and two nearly impassable center aisles, penetrating her with a disconcerting glare behind bifocals. Was he leering, sneering, making a pass, or wondering what was in her purse? He tipped his hat and winked again. She pretended not to see him.

Sage ought to get a load of this, mused Florida as she turned away to the clouds outside her window. Maybe he'd try to get some sense and realize there were other men—albeit likely ancient and infirm, on the prowl for a live-in nurse—who might desire the wife he'd dumped. The great Sage Freeman was her wayward, seventy-seven-year-old spouse, who'd returned from his weekly Tonk card game last week, trudged into their kitchen door on their golden anniversary and—not with cards, gifts, candy, flowers, a ring, or a bottle of French champagne, not even with a hug or kiss—announced his dissatisfaction and his plan to depart to the Harlem YMCA to begin their estrangement. The breach was unanticipated—well, at least by Florida—and a rancorous break-up ensued to such a degree that Florida no longer cared about her husband's whereabouts or if and when he might return.

Their children were undone in a week of utter pandemonium resulting in the current trip.

"Do you mind?" asked a woman of Florida's age, who gestured toward the empty seat and legroom next to Florida.

Florida snapped out of her reverie and shifted her train case back to the space beneath the seat in front of her. "Not at all," she replied as she tried not to show her reluctance to relinquish both the privacy and roominess.

"What are you reading?" the woman asked, plopping down in the adjacent seat, her ample girth spilling from it onto Florida with an unpleasant whoosh of air.

"Into the Arms of Love," was Florida's answer as she pried her sweater out from under the woman's hip.

"I only read the scandal sheets." The woman giggled, jiggling.

"I like romances," Florida said. "They're fun. I can't put this one down. The author is African American and so is her heroine, Angelique Browne. She's a private eye who falls in love while investigating an anthropological dig in southern Egypt. Her lover's a hunk who plunders tombs, but Angelique doesn't know it yet. It's not often I find a Black romance with characters like these. Don't you think it's a shame there's so little diversity going on in publishing?"

"We need more diversity everywhere," the new seatmate said and popped her gum. "Except in morgues and prisons. No one bars our path to those. Inclusion would be a joke if it was funny. I've had it with being harassed. I protest with these kids. Thank God for them; they give me hope. We're going back, not forward. If you can't drive, walk, stand, or breathe without some nosybody trying to act like you dare not belong, it's time to exercise your power. My son saw on the internet that if African Americans were a country on their own, we'd be the fifteenth biggest damn economy on the planet. Ain't that somethin'? Makes you think. Black women command the bulk of it. But if some of these haters had their way, they'd send us off to Mars."

"Not even there, if Mars is free and all the Martians live in peace," said Florida. "But you're right. We're shrewd. We're innovative. We work hard. And we each have a vote, if we don't let them take it away, because they know they'll lose if we show up in numbers."

"I'd *walk* to Mars to cast my vote."

The ladies slapped high fives.

"Where are you headed, Fort Lauderdale?"

"If I'm not, then I caught the wrong plane." The woman guffawed and slapped her knee. Her laugh was infectious and musical, and it lent her dark brown face a glow and dimpled both its smooth round cheeks. A long scar ran the length of her plump left jaw. Her earlobes were laden with earrings so heavy their piercings were short, deep slits. "Are you connecting or destinating?" she asked. "You never know these days. I can't stand to be on planes too long. I'm happy I got a direct flight and I don't have to land in Miami. Takes forever to walk to that baggage claim."

"I'm heading outside Fort Lauderdale. To a suburb," Florida chirped. "Can't wait."

"I wish I could say the same," the seatmate countered, mouth turned down. "I wish I didn't have to go… You got family there, some friends, or what?"

Florida leaned on the woman's plumpness, lifting her hand to the side of her mouth as she lowered her voice and confided, "I inherited acres of property from an uncle several years ago. Never seen it, but when the lease ran out on the couple I rented to last week and I found I had a little time, I figured why not check it out? It's now or never, don't you think?"

"Uh-huh. You got that right. What a blessing. If you live long enough, you find out good is everywhere. You just have to take it by the hand when it pops up and be grateful." The lady looked up at the top of the plane, closed her eyes, whispered softly, crossed herself. She caught Florida's hand in her fleshy palm and pumped it like a well. "Hey, my name is Willa Rhodes."

"Florida Freeman. Nice to meet you. You have family down that way?"

"Yup. Attending my little grandbaby's funeral, unfortunately. My son lives down there with his wife." Willa extracted a tissue from her pocket, sniffled, rubbed her nose.

"Oh heavens. My condolences," Florida offered with a moan. "Bless his soul. Did he have a disease? What happened?"

"Raven happened," Willa answered with a twisting nose and mouth. "Raven. My boy's wife's a plague. A pox on my house, that girl has been from day one. Something's wrong with her. No brains and no home training. I have just the one son, and he's such a good boy, but he up and married this Florida girl from the hood down there Miami way. Got a long hair weave, all kinda bling, fake fingernails, thick makeup. And the skimpiest clothes you ever saw. You can see what she had for breakfast most days. Just this side of nakedness. A schemer, that's what that one is. She wound him around her pinky, yanked him way down south to be with her, and the next thing you know, they was havin' a baby. Poor fella. Two months old. Tiny darlin' got all shot up in a drive-by last weekend. It's all her fault."

"That's horrible, Willa," Florida said. She patted Willa's fleshy arm. "These guns. And folks without a hope. They need to do something about it. Uh-uh-uh. I'm sorry, Willa. Hard to imagine how that must hurt."

Willa lamented, "She's on drugs. When I catch her, she's goin' to rehab, or I'll ring her scrawny neck. And I'm bringing my boy back home with me if I have to hogtie him and stuff him in my suitcase under my underwear. That gal is…" Willa stopped midsentence, pointing across the aircraft toward the staring man. "You know that guy?"

Florida quickly shook her head.

"Well, I hope you're single, girlfriend. You have an admirer. What's his story?"

"Beats me, girl," said Florida as she primped her hairdo. "Stalker."

"Wish I had me one."

"A stalker?"

"Any man!"

"Watch what you wish for. They're a job. My husband wears me out. If he were a dress or a pair of shoes, I'd take him back, I swear I would. And not to exchange, for a total refund."

Willa cracked up and slapped her knee. "You're funny. I like you. I like your style… Say, where'd you get that snazzy bag?" asked Willa, admiring the old train case.

"Manhattan. I've had it for years."

"Oh yeah? It still looks spanking new. They don't make 'em as good as that nowadays."

"This is my first time using it."

"My goodness. You're a saver, huh? You saved your land, your bag, your trip. Shoot, as soon as I get a thing, I seem to wear it out. Maybe that's why I don't get so much."

"I wore my husband out, for sure. He left last week to who knows where. I haven't heard a mumbling word." Florida dropped her news deadpan.

"Mine went out feet first last year," said Willa. "In a box. My hero one day and gone the next. Left nothing but a stack of bills and a stink in our apartment. But I sure did love that man."

A pall draped over the chitchat, and the two women sat in silence for the remainder of the flight, Florida gazing out the window and Willa watching the staring man watch her new friend like a new TV. When at last the plane landed, Willa stretched, and Florida, whose ankles were swollen like two tree trunks, wrestled her shoes back on.

"Here's my cell number. Call me," Willa invited. "Since you're here alone, let's try to get together. I'll be needin' a break from Raven, and I can help you sort your new place out."

They finished exchanging phone numbers and addresses and vowed to have some fun. They thought to do lunch, get mani-pedis, hang at the beach, or go sightseeing. They trudged through the airport running their mouths, Florida dragging her carry-on, Willa complaining about the distance, declaring her bad knees felt like bricks. As they collected their checked bags, Willa's son and half-dressed daughter-in-law showed up to pick up Mama Will.

The daughter-in-law was surly and unfriendly in the brief exchange. *Willa was right about her vibe,* thought Florida when she was introduced. "Judge not, lest ye be judged," was her conclusion as they parted.

When she stepped out into the white-hot sun and the suffocating humidity, perspiring, mopping her brow with a hankie—one she had had for fifty years—unbeknownst to Florida, the staring man was skulking, keeping an eye on her from close behind.

The land was more than Florida dared to dream. The house was sprawling. It was homey, quiet, handsomely furnished, surrounded by nature, pristinely kept. All ten acres of farmland seemed to thrive. The orange orchard. Grapefruit trees. Queen, king, date, and coco palms that flourished nearby myrtle trees and leafy Tabebuia plants. Traveling bougainvillea, bottlebrushes, and hibiscus flowered endlessly around the yard. There were lavender jacaranda trees, azaleas, crocus, dahlias, oleanders, and caladiums. Daylilies in full bloom. There were berries enough to live on, even sell as jams and jellies.

In back of the house, a shack leaned like the tower of Pisa near a fence surrounding a well-tended vegetable garden brimming with corn, tomatoes, string beans, peppers, broccoli, cauliflower, lettuce, and zucchinis. Wide melon patches overflowed. Florida ventured through her fields in a fog, unable to comprehend the place was actually hers to keep, that it had been her land all these years and she had never claimed it. She could've raised her family here, and now it could actually change her life. She had marshes and a big man-made lake that was home to herons and egrets, mallard ducks and Muscovys, and cormorants and anhingas.

Why didn't I come here sooner? Florida sighed. It was a paradise. All she had to do was come out of the tiny box she was living in for a whole new world to open up. But of course, if she had done it then, she couldn't do it now. Now when her marriage was falling apart and she needed to start life over again. All over again, and at her age. She never thought it'd happen. But there was some measure of peace in it, and in seeing that the Dernieres, her former tenants, had revered the place, keeping it painted inside and out and the farm in tip-top shape. They'd even been kind enough to leave some gadgets behind for her to use, most in the kitchen and the barn.

On the counter next to the stove, she found a landline phone with an answering machine still hooked up with a dial tone. A blinking light indicated eight new messages, unanswered. And though Florida wasn't sure they'd be for her, she stopped to play them back.

The first was a digital welcome note. "Hi, Florida. Maidie Derniere. Thank you for all you've done for us. We hope you enjoy your home as much as we did. Let's keep in touch." But no phone number lingered on the screen. The number was restricted.

The next message tore at her heartstrings, pushing her homesick button, fear response, and maternal instincts all at once. "Hi, Mommy. It's me, Madison. Call us as soon as you get there so we know you arrived and it's all okay. And text us pictures right away, 'kay? Kisses. *Xs* and *Os*!"

The third was another love note from a daughter who was missing her. "Hey, World Traveler. This is Keys. I'm calling so you don't forget your superhero grandson and his mother while you're on the road. We're sending you love to the moon and back. Talk to you soon. Have a fabbo trip."

Florida's spirits were up in the sky when the fourth message played and brought her down. "Please, Mommy, call me. It's Ocala. Something's happened. Buzz me back." Florida shrank and her heart skipped a beat as the next message pleaded, "Mommy, I need you. Call right now. It's urgent. I need help." The next was from Ocala too. The sixth alert was hostile. "How dare you leave town without telling me first. I hate to get news from Madison. You always tell her everything. You never consider my feelings, like you failed to inform me Daddy left. Well, I'm hoping you're having a horrible time. I'll never forgive you for leaving me hanging. You neglected me. Remember that. But what do you care? Forget it now. I'll handle this myself."

Leery of using the landline phone, Florida fished for the cell phone Keys bought, keen to return Ocala's call but dreading what her child might say to her. The remaining two messages, probably from her, were no doubt full of fury too, but Florida played them anyway.

"Hi, Florida. It's your new best friend. It's Willa, ready to have some fun. I'd love to hang out tomorrow, and my son can pick you up. I have an exciting girls' day planned. Gimme a ring. Let's set a time. Hee-hee-hee. We'll live it up."

The thought of good times brought a moment's relief. She might take Willa up on that. But she played the final message and it stood the hair up on her head.

"Mrs. Freeman, you don't know me, but I have some information that you have to act on right away. The truth about your family. The one you had then and the one you have now. You only get one chance. Meet me at nine tonight at Flamingo Gardens. Don't be late. Come alone, or I'll come after you." An icicle slithered up Florida's spine. *What in the world was that about?* Her family. What did he mean by that? Who'd leave such a terrible message? A lawyer? Maybe about the estate? But the will was settled years ago. She owned the property free and clear. She had every right to be where she was. And why would a lawyer address her that way or meet in that strange location? His voice was bone-chilling. He knew her name. It sounded like a threat. Her stomach began to gripe and churn. First Ocala and now this. It wasn't what she'd planned.

She wrung her hands, looked out the window. Starting to feel too warm and faint, she flopped into a kitchen chair. Maybe it was a prank call. Sure. A kid or a telemarketer setting her up to buy a security system. Might not be a bad idea. But later when she got settled in. Right now she had to control herself. Why should she give a man she'd never met permission to rattle her? Particularly with Ocala running around in such a state. No. First things first, which wasn't him, whoever he was and whatever he wanted. He'd caught her alone for the first time in years, that's all. She'd block the call.

Florida dialed Madison, got no answer, hung up, dialed again. She called Connecticut three more times. They all went straight to voice mail. Deflated, she left a lengthy message, aching to hear her child's kind tone, hoping to be reassured and get an idea what Ocala was tripping on in advance of phoning Ocala. She was reticent to hear bad news on top of her marital quagmire now, particularly if it concerned her kids. The girls were her life, her heart and soul.

She felt guilty about procrastinating, but she had good reason not to call. Ocala was a job. Ocala was heartless and hateful, but that didn't stunt Florida's love for her. It meant Florida had to love her more in order to help Ocala feel her love and try to love her back. The process was a drain. She'd thought young Ocala would outgrow all her adolescent hurtful ways. But

Ocala got meaner and terribly cold. Her words could wound like bullet holes. She enjoyed hurting others, that much was clear from the look of elated contempt on her face. She especially went for her family members, trying to tear their bond apart. She was always upset about something. It didn't matter what it was. Ocala's neurotic demands perennially cut through Florida's sense of peace, and with Sage incognito since he left, Florida had no backup means to quell Ocala's anger. Only Sage was able to calm her down. Ocala was a daddy's girl who wore her daddy out.

Florida's feet began to ache. All of a sudden, the strange, airy space of her uncle's home turned spooky. Florida tried to ring Keys next, but her oldest daughter didn't answer either. What was going on? Florida sneezed and blew her nose. She had only one way to find out.

Florida called Ocala and was relieved to record a message and hang up with no harangue. Ocala was mistress of false alarms, and maybe her messages only meant more manufactured drama. But then even the boy who cried wolf eventually had dire need for help. The thought made Florida shiver in the heat and made her blood run cold.

She couldn't just sit on her hands and wait for the man on the answering machine to call and harass her again. She had to move. That guy sure didn't sound like a random bot, and how did he know she was there and not in Brooklyn? Maybe he just lucked up. Maybe he'd found the number listed in a random queue somewhere. Who cared? She was tired of stressing out.

"I'm going to enjoy my trip," she said. "I'll have a blast no matter what."

Uncle Buzz's green Chevy Impala cranked right up when Florida turned the key. She'd figured it might need servicing, so the roar of the engine, as loud as it was, presented a surprise. Uncle Buzz always bragged about the car. He'd willed it to Florida in his estate. She then rented it to the Dernieres in a package deal with the rest of the property until the young couple was able to find an affordable ride to call their own. The old vintage clunker, in A-1 condition, was cherried out and looking good, and it boasted a full tank of gas the Dernieres had thoughtfully left behind.

Young Baron Derniere was the serious type. His wife, Maidie, appeared to be his match. And, if anything, smarter than Baron, though she had only culled that impression over the phone when they called to report the rent was late or the ancient furnace died. Baron was cordial but spoke few words, whereas Maidie was blunt, ambitious, and resourceful, and she spoke her mind. Baron worked hard but was always broke and talked only of finding a way to survive, whereas Maidie hinted at big dreams. They both knew Uncle Buzz for years. In fact, they called him Uncle Buzz, and Buzz all but adopted the couple, such was the family bond they'd formed. That's why Florida felt it a shame how she had to displace the Dernieres the way she did in order to reclaim the farm, but as Baron and Maidie reminded her, millennials like them moved so often it was no big deal. They considered themselves "vacation movers" with zero intention to put down roots. They moved where they could find a job or gain a better lifestyle.

Florida drove five miles to get some toiletries from CVS. She bought groceries at Publix and pie at a bakery and loaded it all in recyclable bags.

A bony teenage box boy, featuring sprigs of fiery-red spiked hair, a sprinkle of freckles, and conch-pierced ears, loaded the bags in the Chevy's trunk. "This is a real cool car you got, ma'am. I'm gonna get me one like this," said the boy as he peered inside the car and rounded it to pat the hood.

"Young man, I do believe you will," said Florida. "Keep your sights set high. Keep learning. You can do anything." She attempted to tip him but he refused.

"Thanks, but we can't accept no tips, ma'am. Have a good day now. See you next time. Take care where you go down here. Not everyone's as sweet as you."

She wondered what he meant by that but let it go and drove away. From there, she rode on to the independent bookstore, Reading Write. Once inside, she admired the romance section, choosing *A Dangerous Passion* and *What He Really Wanted* from some shelves inside a pink endcap. The novels had steamy covers and were published by a new imprint that featured strong Black heroines embracing bad boy suitors. Florida advanced to a checkout line roped off with a wine-colored velvet cord beside an expansive wall of glass. As she handed her credit card to the clerk, she glimpsed someone out in the parking lot in the corner of her eye.

It was him. She saw the staring man. Florida blinked and turned to look, head snapping around in his direction, but the man had vanished.

Jittery, Florida paid the bill and exited onto hot concrete, deciding to zip to a kosher deli two doors down to get a snack. She purchased bagels, cream cheese, blintzes, matzo ball soup, and pastrami on rye. She bought a knish to nibble on as she hoped to feel better once she ate. But the image of the man remained, the weird phone message threatening her. Maybe jet lag or dehydration made her see the staring man and make more of that call than was warranted, her imagination playing tricks. After all, she was out of her element, and Ocala's rant unnerved her. There were too many recent events unresolved, like Sage vaporizing the way he did. She hurried to the Chevy, clutching the paperbacks, checking the space between parked cars.

Once in the Chevy, she took deep breaths and tooled beyond the strip mall lot, allowing the bright beams of sunlight dappling the roadside as they swept through trees to dampen her anxiety. As she calmed, she became more curious, taking in pleasant surroundings and heady scents and wondering who her neighbors were while she cruised back via the scenic route, feeling her way home street by street, meandering past big comely nests. Homes burst with pride of ownership, for as many Black families as for white, she observed as she watched them trim their lawns, walk dogs, and play catch with their kids. Others—many whose ancestors owned their land for several generations—rode tractors, picked citrus fruits, or played basketball, guitars, or chess. Sprawling, secluded lots lent loads of space to growing families, newlywed couples, artists, entrepreneurs, hermits and ne'er-do-wells, migrants, relocated workers, transients and younger folks migrating back into the South to regroup and recoup after tragedies and disappointments in the North. The area held an illusion of safety for elderly pensioners, retirees, and empty nesters craving change.

Landscaping was lush and colorful, edging fences and dotting front porches furnished with wicker lawn furniture, sisal hammocks, children's Big Wheels, slides, and swings. That was, when you could see the houses. Many were cloistered behind tall, flowering bushes, gates, or wooden fences, recessed off the road and hidden from prying eyes that mightn't mean them well.

Florida pulled the Impala into her driveway. Hers. It was hard to believe. All those years they had rented when she owned this and Sage was none the wiser. She wondered what other amazing opportunities she'd let pass her by. What jobs. What money. What men. What trips. What far-off magic queendoms.

The old kitchen was more than quadruple the size of Florida's kitchen in Brooklyn. She imagined the meals she could cook in it. And for whom.

The girls would love it here. And the grandchildren. She could plump them up. Most of them ate like birds and still had energy to burn. She organized her haul in a walk-in pantry as big as her New York bedroom, setting a kettle on for tea.

The doorbell rang. *Who could it be?*

Heart pounding, brow breaking out into a sweat, Florida tiptoed past the sunroom, crept across the spacious great room, secretly peered out through a sidelight, halfway expecting to see the staring man's eyes glaring back at her.

Instead, it was Willa who filled the doorway. Rocking a size twenty-two flamingo-pink-and-turquoise bathing suit that valiantly strained to cover the subject under a nylon cover-up that hid a multitude of sins. Willa barged in with an oversized purse, jiggling more bumps and curves than graced the Harlem River Drive. "Last one in's a rotten egg! Grab a bikini, girl, let's go," she encouraged, laughing loudly.

Florida sighed relief and clapped her hands, escorting Willa in. "Willa, I haven't owned a swimsuit since before Jesus parted the sea."

"Well, we gotta get you one. I'll add the big mall to our shopping list. We ain't got time to fool around. My son's out in your driveway waitin' to drop us off out by the beach before he goes to work. Let's move it, slowpoke. Life is short."

"I have a car. I can drive us around... except I don't know where I'm going."

"No worries. We'll take the water taxi if we want to galavant."

"I'm expecting a call from my daughter Ocala."

"That's why you have a cell phone, Flo. C'mon, party pooper, make some waves."

"But Willa—"

"But nothin'. Live your life. Besides, if I hang with my daughter-in-law, I'll straight up go off on the girl."

"Okay, you're right. It's our time now," Florida agreed with a wink and a nod. "Give me a minute to grab a few things." In a flash, she snatched her books, her keys, two towels she found in a linen closet, cash, a bottle of suntan lotion, and baggies full of sugary snacks. She dumped the whole trove in recyclable bags and plopped a straw hat on her head. "Off to adventure." She chuckled, sliding her feet into flip-flops and closing the door with a clack of the lock.

As soon as she latched it and walked to the car, the landline next to the cell phone she forgot to take began to ring.

The phone jingled four times before answering itself, recording the message: "Mom, you were robbed, and Ocala has gone missing."

Willa's son, Justin, was six feet five, decked out in trendy rap couture. He was dark and lean, in his early twenties, wearing baggy cargo pants, diamond-like studs in both his ears, a grill inlaid with emerald chips, and a pair of purple running shoes that looked to be brand-new. A tattoo of an avenging Black angel rippled on his right triceps, visible due to his sleeveless tee with a picture of Tupac on the front. Mandalas were shaved through his faded hairdo, one on top, one on each side.

With Willa and Florida riding shotgun, Justin drove his teeny car like the vehicle was a loaded weapon, stabbing and shooting through traffic at life-threatening speeds and rattling fellow travelers, unconstrained by lights or stop signs, lurching and revving and blaring his horn. Florida white-knuckled the passenger door as the compact sped over boulevards, its stereo system blasting hip-hop tunes whose pulses beat so hard they vibrated Florida's seat like the chairs that massaged her during manicures. At first the music felt assaultive, but as Florida often did, she adjusted, rocking to the rhythms, finding herself in the flow of the lyrics, captured by their poetry and plaintive, mournful cries for help.

One rapper extolled from a radio station: "They killin' your grandmama, jailin' your dad. They paintin' your future with nothin' but sad… baboom-baboom, baboom-baboom… You been givin' respect but don't get none, y'all. Yo, bump that, make them suckers crawl… da-doo-dadoo, da-doo-dadoo… When another baby gangsta dies… cavoom-cavoom… for the money and lies… sha-toom, sha-toom… Turn the White House red… kapow-kapow… 'fore we all be dead… bang-bang, bang-bang… Fight back, no slack… man, learn to hack, or you gonna stay hungry as long as you Black…"

Justin's front tires popped onto the curb at the shoreline with a disturbing whomp that rattled beachcombers and passersby. He waved at a gaggle of giggling coeds craning their heads and waving back as he whizzed past plaid Bermuda shorts on seniors hitting golf balls. Three toddlers building a sand castle broke into tears as he braked onto the beach. Every sunbather turned when they made their entrance, Florida sheepishly piling out and catching a glance of what proved to be herself in the passenger window, regarding with horror the punk-rock style of hairdo napped up on her head like a thrift-shop woolen hat. No measure of raking her fingers through it seemed to restore its former coiffure. It looked as if combed with an egg-beater now, and the ocean breezes made it worse.

"Thank you," she managed to wheeze to Justin.

Justin grinned, and in that moment, charmed her irretrievably. "I'll pick you guys up when I get off work," he assured them, loudly screeching off.

Florida and Willa set up towels, umbrellas, books, and food enough to feed the sailors manning the battleship floating through whitecaps off the coast. They kicked back on white sand and enjoyed the view.

"A slice of heaven," Florida mused while people-watching, taking dips, reclining into a peaceful afternoon of reading, munching, laughing with Willa, viewing the shifting sky, and walking along with her feet in the cooling waves of the Atlantic.

When she woke from a nap to the sound of the sea, she blew kisses to a pudgy infant frolicking under a rainbow-colored beach tent with its parents. Then she chatted with her newfound friend and applied more suntan lotion. "Thanks, Willa, for getting me out and about. I'm so happy you came to bring me here. This beach is like a paradise."

"That land you got is paradise. Why didn't you say you was Buzz Homer's niece?" Willa chided.

"You knew Uncle Buzz?"

"Everyone in town knowed Buzz," claimed Willa. "You'll be welcomed here."

"That's really good to know."

"Buzz was a powerful, rich old coot. He was humble, though, and kind. He had juice, but you never would'a guessed by the way he gave and cared for folks. My daddy played Tonk with him every Tuesday night for thirty years. That is, until it… well, you know."

"Know what?" asked Florida, shading her eyes.

"That mess what happened up in there." Willa searched Florida's face for any hint of recognition. "Honey, you really don't know what went on in that house you're livin' in?"

Florida's tummy balled into a fist. All the junk she ate congealed. "No, but I wish you'd fill me in."

"But I shouldn't be the one to tell you. I should mind my business, Flo. Don't you got family you can ask? I figured you bein' his heir and all, you knew what you was into."

"No. And you're giving me goose bumps. Spill it. Is there something I should know?"

"Let's drop it. Talk about somethin' else. Forget what I said and enjoy your trip." Willa cast her eyes down, tugged at her visor, trailed off, closed her eyes.

Florida brushed sand off her legs. "Well, don't leave me hanging. What's the deal?"

"You sure?" Willa leaned with a look of reluctance, glancing around with her hand to her mouth. "You can't never un-know what you know, you know, regardless to how much you think you'd rather *not* know what you're findin' out."

"Quit talking in riddles and spill the tea," said Florida, flipping the brim of her hat up, batting away a mosquito that was trying to sting her shoulder.

"Honey, I'm sorry to tell you this, but your Uncle Buzz made the best moonshine south of the Mason-Dixon line, out there at the back of your house. Rumors ran wild about it too, how he made the still from scratch himself. They said the old man was rakin' in money hand over fist and bur-yin' it in them walls you got out there to keep it safe."

"The walls of the house?"

"That's what they claim."

"Ain't that a blip," said Florida. She jostled to pull her towel closer to Willa's, flipping her brim back down. "Did they say what became of the money? Did somebody find it?"

"That's a mystery. Can't tell if it got found or not. That part of the story gets real bad, according to my daddy. See, one Tuesday, whilst they was pla-yin' Tonk… if you can believe the tale they tell, considering how they love to brag, and ain't none of this gossip true for sure, but the way the story went back then…" Willa disclaimed without taking a breath.

"Spit it out," begged Florida, trying to swat the mosquito again with no success. It was buzzing even louder.

"Anyhoo, you got a right to know if anybody does. Especially now the place is yours. But the scandal ain't about the cash. That moonshine money. No sirree."

"The scandal? Tell me what you know. I won't hold it against you. Seriously."

Willa seemed to mull it over, trying to decide what she should say, mushing her lips together to try to keep from unleashing a hornet's nest. "Well, it seems old man Derniere and Buzz got into a pissin' contest over a particular set of hands they drew in the weekly Tonk game way back when. That's how it started. The terrible rift. Bet came to bet, and it all went sour. Your Uncle Buzz lost his whole farmhouse to Pappy Derniere right on the spot—his money, land, and everything—but Buzz refused to give it up because he claimed the game was rigged. He refused to fork over because he caught Pappy Derniere red-handed, cheatin'. Pappy had swindled the regulars and several other players too, once folks began talkin', comparin' notes. Pappy was holdin' an extra deck in his sleeve and pullin' cards from it. Your Uncle Buzz caught on to him, called Pappy out, and things got rough. When the other Tonk players backed Buzz up, Pappy got scared and pulled a knife. My daddy claimed to see what happened after that, but…"

"What?" asked Florida. "Don't stop now."

"My daddy was one to stretch the truth, so I never was able to verify…" Willa mashed her lips together. "Daddy was a liar. He lied to my mama somethin' fierce, so I take the whole thing with a grain of salt, but the rumor's still alive today with other folks around these parts. Most of the Black folks anyway. And some of the white folks know the truth. They say it's the night Pappy disappeared without a trace. For good. Plus, if you buy the ol' wives' tale—"

"Which is?" asked Florida.

"Well, you asked. They say Pappy Derniere put a whammy on Buzz Homer's future generations. They say he cast an evil spell. A curse. With a voodoo doll and all. And chicken blood and other stuff. He conjured that any bad happened to Pappy's folk would double happen to the Homers through eternity. Spooky, ain't it? Superstitious. People say that house is haunted. Rumor is there's ghosts in there. That anyone touches the money, dies."

Florida shivered in the sun, her goose bumps rising on tanning arms. "*My* house?"

"Uh-huh. Ain't it wild? Your uncle got a reputation then on in, as damaged goods. Nobody messed with him or his kin. As a matter of fact, we all was stunned when we found out Buzz's heir—that's you—went and rented the place to Pappy Derniere's great-grandson and his schemin' wife. But now I see you didn't know… Life sure is strange, Flo, don't you think?"

"I didn't have a clue." Beads of cold sweat erupted like popcorn stippling Florida's upper lip. She dabbed her mouth and mumbled low, "I wonder if Baron and Maidie knew."

"You kiddin'? Sure they did," said Willa. "It can't be no happenstance. They know what all went on back then."

"Maybe they didn't. They're so young."

"They're millennials, not babies. They didn't fall off no turnip truck."

"Now I wish I'd never left New York."

"You can't blame yourself for all of that. You pretty much live a world away. The story is local gossip, that's all, girl. Tongues waggin'. Period. And as far as you rentin' to Baron and Maidie, how could you suspect those two had any ulterior motives? You can't go around thinkin' the worst of folks, no matter how much bad faith you see or how your heart gets trampled on."

Florida, lost in her own thoughts, said, "What deep, dark secrets families keep."

"Especially deep, dark families. We keep secrets to deal with all kinds of crap. Every family has a history, Flo. And secrets and lies are woven in. Secrets are like our family photos. Heirloom trinkets we pass down generation to generation. They get stored in the veins of our ancestry. They fester and invade our genes. They help us store our ancestry because it's been stolen away from us and we need it to tell us who we are and how we can move forward. But the past needs to stay in the past sometimes, so we can envision the future… It's like your pretty little train case," Willa observed. "It has its place. You saved it for a rainy day. Now you're puttin' it to good use to write another chapter in your life. It didn't have much value till you traveled here to see your land. But your daughters will treasure that case someday, and they'll pass it on as life goes on. They'll find belonging packed inside. And wisdom. And connection."

A gray cloud formed on Florida's face, and a bellow spewed forth from her diaphragm. "The day I bought that train case, Willa, that was the worst day of my life. That's why it took so long to use. It was filled up with my guilt." It erupted from Florida like a volcano, sad memories flickering through her head like a black-and-white movie out of sync. "Till now, I never admitted this. I've never told anyone else but you. I never could stand to recall it. My baby was kidnapped on that day." It came out in a growl. "Oh, and it was all my fault. While I was being selfish, living a daydream, purchasing that case, indulging in my fantasies with a salesman in a luggage shop, the babysitter stole our infant. Snatched him right out of his crib in broad daylight and spirited him away. Vanished and never reappeared. And I never once cuddled my baby or even laid eyes on him again. I'd give anything to get him back. But I can't. I can't, and it pains me so." Hot tears burned a trail down from Florida's eyes to her cheeks and pooled beneath her chin. "That case got packed up with my grief, and nothing else fit in."

"Oh my gracious. I'm so sorry. That must sting you awful bad." Willa reached out with a motherly hug. "There, there now. You let it out. More room on the outside than within. Let go. All these years you been carryin' that? Lay it down now. What a burden." Willa rubbed Florida on the back and softly whispered in her ear. "I don't know what it's like to lose a child, but my grandbaby goes to his grave tomorrow, and that don't make no sense at all. It hurts so bad I'm 'bout to scream." Willa's head jerked, and her hat fell off. "I'm 'bout to blow my top."

Florida pulled back, rubbed her eyes, held Willa's gaze, and sighed. "It's a different world from ours now, Willa. We were brought up to imagine a person's morality made them who they were. Nowadays it's like anything goes out here. Nobody wants to take responsibility for what they do. Right is as wrong as good is bad. The Golden Rule is out the window. Lies travel fast as the speed of light. Life isn't as sacred as it was. The rich get richer, the poor get screwed. Little kids and we seniors get kicked around, and the bad guys get all the publicity."

"But it isn't as bad as it looks. Can't be."

"I believe that too. But it's taxing maintaining that positive view with so much negativity. Good folks may toil in obscurity. Still, there have to be many more good than bad, or the world would not keep turning. We just have to keep moving and changing the world with our unique and special gifts. We matter. The throttle is in our hands. We're as powerful as this sea and sky."

"Amen," Willa averred, tearing up. "People are much more important than things. My daddy loved to quote the Bible. Mark 8:36, I think. 'For what shall it profit a man, if he shall gain the whole world and lose his own soul?'"

"Money and power don't make you a better person, they amp up who you are."

"Yeah. If you were an ass before you got rich, then you're an ass*hole* now."

They cackled, and Florida slapped her knee. "Be cool. We don't want to pee ourselves out here where everyone can see." They slapped a high-five and laughed harder.

"So, what are you gonna to do about it?" Willa inquired, sobering.

"What?" asked Florida.

"All that money. What if nobody found it yet? It might still be inside your house."

An imaginary arctic freeze cut through the subtropical sunshine, icing the shore as if it were mounds of snow. They simultaneously shivered.

A loud horn honked, and Willa turned. "Let's hit it, Flo. It's Justin."

Florida treated Willa and Justin to dinner at a stone crab joint, after which Florida filled up Justin's gas tank and they headed home. As Justin pumped gas, Florida checked her purse to see if her cell had messages.

"Oh no. I think I lost my phone!" She rummaged through her purse again.

"Are you sure you brought it out with you? I saw it in your kitchen, but I don't recall you taking it."

"Come to think of it, I don't remember either. Oh well, you must be right. It must be where I left it then. On the counter by the landline. I guess it's a really good sign that I didn't even think to check till now. I'm enjoying myself too much to worry."

"Then I've done my job," said Willa.

But all of a sudden, the trouble back in Brooklyn nauseated Flo. And when she got back to the house to Madison's frantic message, she was shocked.

"Mom, where have you been? I've been worried sick," said Madison in a trembling voice when Florida quickly returned the call.

"What happened? I was at the beach," said Florida. "I forgot my phone. Everything's fine here. I'm okay. Did you find Ocala?"

"No, she's gone. She left yesterday morning about six thirty to take the children off to school, but she never came home, Mom, and what's worse, she never picked them up. You know that isn't like her, as difficult as she can be. It's not like Ocala to blow them off. You, me, Sturges, Keys, okay. But never her kids, you know that. The school called Sturges's office, and he claims he rushed out to retrieve them as soon as he could, but the kids are so upset he has to keep them home today. And she's always on the telephone or Facebook, you know how she is. Spreading gossip and lies about everyone. But she hasn't called anyone I could find, and she hasn't logged on in a couple of days."

"Sturges says he hasn't heard from her?"

"But you know we can't trust his word. She and Sturges fight like cats and dogs."

"Has he called around? Did he look for her?" asked Florida, sounding unnerved to herself.

"According to him, he called the cops when she didn't arrive home late last night, and the nanny called his job today to say she wasn't home. And you know how Sturges hates the cops. He has to be totally terrified to call them up for anything. They told him they can't even look for her until she's been gone for a couple of days. She's not a missing person yet. They say people take off all the time. They say she could've run away. And it's true, Mom, you know how she is. So crazy and quixotic. No telling what's going through her mind. I mean, she could be throwing a tantrum somewhere, messing with everybody's head. If anything's happened to her though—"

"Don't even think it," Florida shouted. *Oh please, God, not another child.*

"You're right. She's fine. She'll turn up soon… and blame us all for what she did," said Madison. "It's exhausting. Now I'm sorry I even bothered you. But I'm completely worried."

"Sweetie, I'm coming. I'll book the next flight."

"Don't ruin your vacation, Mom. You haven't had one ever. Ocala could just be playing hooky, freaking out as usual. It's not like she isn't miserable. She could've run off with another man."

"I hope she did," said Florida. "Well, not really. That marriage is toxic though."

"I wouldn't blame her if she did. Her husband is a wacko. But she could have run off without scaring us half to death, you know. That's possible. She's probably enjoying the drama. She's only been gone for a day and a half. I'm sorry I overreacted and called hysterically the way I did. Sturges is home with the kids by now. They're his responsibility. I would've flown down, but with work and the robbery—"

"Oh my gosh! Our house was robbed. Good gravy, I forgot. When it rains, it pours. Does your father know? What did they steal from us?"

"Nothing, Mom. It's stupid. That's what's weird. There's almost nothing gone. I mean, I don't know everything you guys have—"

"Well, you certainly have a good idea. Just tell me, how does it look to you?"

"You and Daddy will have to check it out, but it's fine as far as we can tell. The TVs are in the living room and your bedroom, along with the stereo and your other electronic stuff. The Blu-ray player. Both computers, your printer, and your laptop too. And tablets and MP3 players, and your jewelry is in the bedroom safe. Some bracelets are on the dresser, and I saw some credit cards and checkbooks in a desk drawer, undisturbed. I even looked in that empty ice cream box in the freezer where you guys keep the household cash in case of an emergency. There was over five hundred bucks in it. Whoever broke in there tossed the place, but as far as Army and I can see, all your valuables are accounted for. Except Ocala, obviously… And that ancient address book you keep on your nightstand. We can't find it anywhere. Isn't that weird?"

"But pretty lucky. If that's all that's missing. It might've been teenagers out for a lark."

"See? You might as well hang in there. Daddy's not back. We changed your locks. We're here now cleaning up the place. There's really nothing you can do, so let's not spoil your fun."

"At least I know what's up, up there. You did the right thing. I'm sorry you're stressed. I guess I'll just wait to hear from you before I make a move. Call me the minute Ocala gets back."

"I will," said Madison. "Honestly. First Daddy goes. Ocala's next. You travel to check out your house down there and your home up here gets vandalized. What's up with that?"

"I'm not quite sure. But trouble comes in threes. That's three. It should be over now."

"I love you, Mom."

"I love you too. To the moon and back. Remember that. Hug Army and tell him thanks for me." Florida waited to hear the click that said Madison had hung up first. "What the heck is going on?" she mumbled. *Isn't that weird*, she thought she heard Madison's voice reverberate like a warning afterthought. "Something's making things go wrong, and I don't know what it is," she pondered as she left the stove, the conversation boomeranging, making her feel uneasy.

The sunset from Florida's Florida room, the screened-in back porch with a view of the stream, resembled a watercolor painting, she observed as she stepped out on the tile. Florida wrapped her delicate hands around a steaming cup of chamomile and sipped the herbal blend, its warm brew coursing through her veins and bringing with it calm. But alas, her taste for tea was gone. Gone like Ocala. Gone like Sage. Gone like her sweet-smelling baby boy. There wasn't a single day she lived that she didn't ache to snuggle him or wonder if he was still alive, leading or being a follower, wealthy or living destitute, fat or skinny, lonely or loved, cowardly or confident. She never had closure, never knew. And where was Ocala? What was she doing? Would Florida have to endure the unbearable torture of losing a child again? This time without a husband. She didn't believe she could bear that cross two times, and even pondering it, her nerves wound as tight as new violin strings, and she fidgeted, kneading her hands.

A hot-pink-amber sky lit like a fireplace in wintertime, painting the distant horizon into enchanting shades of lavender. A sliver of silver opalescent moon hung like a pearl within a diamond-studded sky of stars, forming a gloaming celestial umbrella so clear it took Florida's breath away. Crickets chirped street corner songs accompanied by Southern chorus frogs in heat, their rattled tunes mixing with horny toad mating calls in the orchestral sounds of night. Sweet scents of magnolia and jasmine danced in the air and waltzed into Florida's senses, dizzying and narcoleptic. Nature seemed to rule here more than anywhere she'd ever sat. And yet there was something unnatural, something or someone that didn't belong in such serene surroundings as this land.

Trouble was brewing like scalding tea, and Florida yearned to root it out.

What if the recent events were related, as Madison suggested? Sage. Ocala. The trip. The break-in. All just synchronicity? Florida's life wasn't ever eventful. It was *too* routine, in fact. But now, all of a sudden, tremendous excitement. Florida's musings examined the shape of the puzzle pieces gathering, assembling them into a larger picture forming in her mind. Recalling the tall tale Willa spun, she couldn't help but wonder if the horrible curse that Pappy Derniere once laid on the Homers might be coming true in a series of odd events. Why didn't Baron and Maidie Derniere ever mention it while they were living here? Didn't they know? Of course they did. Willa had called it right. It was the reason they had rented.

As darkness wrapped its cloak around her, Florida started to feel her answers deep in the roots in this hallowed earth, though she didn't exactly know why the land beneath her feet was trembling, making her feel like it was under siege. As far back as the time her baby boy was kidnapped, she'd dreamed of this trip. She'd ached to return to her family ties, but she couldn't see past her little life in Brooklyn. She saw past it now. And she sensed her family needed her more than ever. Not just the girls and Sage. Her ancestors. Guardian angels too. She felt their presence keenly.

Rambling into a restless sleep, she visualized the staring man who followed her all the way here from New York. She was sure of it now. There was little doubt. He represented danger. It was possible she was imagining it, but he seemed to be turning up everywhere she went, even briefly at the beach. She was certain she saw him on the bridge at the 17th Street Causeway. He was following cars behind Justin's car and got caught on the bridge when it opened up. Then she spotted him nearby the sand at the gas station, pumping air into a tire ostensibly, turning away when she stared at him. The next time she saw him, she'd confront him, get to the bottom of why he was there.

Was it him who had her home ransacked? But why? What was he after? Why was her tattered old address book the only item burgled up in Brooklyn? It was nothing one could sell. It had no intrinsic value. It had zero meaning to anyone but her. And maybe Sage. Was Sage involved? Ridiculous. What would he get out of it? But then why would he abandon her and not even call or say goodbye before his quick desertion? What had gotten into him? Another woman probably. Or maybe he got into her. That thought was so revolting. But even at his stage of life, he was still quite sexy in his way. Black men were at a premium. Her grandmother, who'd once farmed this land, had a habit of saying, "Breath and britches is all a man needs to get a good woman, even with one foot in the grave and the other foot sliding on bacon grease."

But Sage? He had never behaved like that. Or she had not found out. He was always so reliable. Why would he want to flake out now? Sure, it wasn't easy getting old—losing hair and mobility, eyesight, hearing, family, friends, your memory and your independence—but they had each other, right? Why throw that away? Didn't other folks long to grow old together, steeped in their love and belonging? She'd counted on him all these years, and in the end, he let her down. On their fiftieth anniversary, no less. What'd she do to deserve that treatment? Nothing. Had he lost his mind? What was it, Dump on Florida Day? Or week. Or whenever hard times might end.

The message from the anonymous caller streamed into her mind again. Who left it? What did he mean to meet him tonight or she'd regret it? What did the caller know about her family? Was it to do with Ocala? She was a constant tribulation. Florida rocked in the wicker chair, pumping in hypnotic rhythm, drifting into fitful dreams.

She awoke with a start at eight p.m. to the comforting sound of gentle rain and went into the house to call Madison, her youngest, who was raw energy and answered with a breathy gasp. Without any word from her middle sister, Ocala, and with her oldest sister, Keys, her houseguest in Connecticut along with her eight-year-old nephew, Nile, Madison sounded more harried than before and on the ragged edge.

"Talk to Keys, Mom. Please. She's going nuts. She feels responsible. She got a whole bunch of messages from Ocala a couple of days ago, but Nile was being a handful, and she didn't take the time to call her back until yesterday morning. Ocala was already gone, and Keys feels really bad about it all. Maybe you can chill her out… I'll let you know when we get news."

Florida heard a shuffling noise, and Keys came on the telephone. "You all right, Mom?"

"I'm fine. And the farm is amazing. I think I ought to come home though."

"No way. We're not letting Ocala trash another special time for you."

Florida bent to rub her ankle. "No point in us taking this personally. Try to relax at Madison's, okay? We'll find Ocala. We were aware she wasn't well and we tried to address it, but we failed. This is a serious wake-up call. The minute she's back, we'll intervene and finally find the help she needs."

"Unfortunately, now we all need help because she puts such strain on us. She loves to stress us out. We walk on eggshells all the time, and look at the drain on you and Dad and how it hassles Madison." Keys began to cry. "But the truth is, Mom, with all of that, I'd rather know she's playing us than that she's in some trouble. I think we need to call the cops."

"Sh… It's going to be okay. If she doesn't get home by tomorrow night, we'll hire a private detective. If she got herself in trouble, the police will only make things worse. If they find her, who knows what they'll do. She's liable to wind up jailed or dead. Have you considered that? Give her a little room. Her and your father. Let them breathe. We all need space from time to time. Let's not go off half-cocked… Besides, I may be onto something down here. Let me dig around."

"In Florida? Why would she be down there?"

"I didn't say she came down here. It's only… Sweetheart, never mind. You'll have to take my word for it."

"Mom, take care. Be safe, okay? We're all concerned about you too."

"Well, don't be. I can handle this."

When the call ended, Florida roved like a zombie through the gloaming house, checking the door locks, battening the windows against the howling wind and rain. As she snapped the kitchen window shut, she spotted a stream of light, a flashlight beam in the pitch-dark pasture, far off, out in the orange grove. She opened a drawer, pulled out a knife, peered through the gossamer curtained window, tried to detect where it emanated from and who was producing it. It swung in an arc toward the swamp and disappeared behind the lemon trees. "I have the heebie-jeebies," Florida admitted to herself. She looked at the clock above the sink and hustled up into the master bedroom, opened her suitcase, rifled through it, donned a pair of denim skorts and a sleeveless, off-white eyelet blouse, then shuttled her suitcase to the attic, and ventured into the night.

Thunder clapped and lightning flashed, splitting an inky navy sky. It was eight thirty p.m. by the Chevy's clock—half an hour until the appointment she felt terrified to keep.

Florida thought about turning back when, according to the map in the Fodor's guide, Flamingo Gardens was approximately a half mile south. It was already quarter after nine, and the ride in the storm was harrowing. With every drop of rain that fell, Florida birthed another doubt regarding the wisdom of the move. Second-guessing herself, she determined she should've told Madison where she was meeting the man, but she didn't want to worry her. This meeting was likely a setup, but the caller knew something clandestine about her family. It was worth a shot.

The last streetlights petered to pinheads on the deserted road behind her. She slowed the Impala the minute she saw the sign for Flamingo

Gardens. Dousing her headlights, she veered off the road and splashed into a minor sinkhole, spinning two wheels and churning mud until she could crunch a path through gravel on the darkened shoulder. Rattled at how she so easily could get stuck out here in no man's land, she stopped shy of the entrance by a hundred yards and hid in a fold of banyan trees. Maybe from this vantage point, she could spot him before he spotted her. Or maybe she ought to get out where she was and hoof it the rest of the way to the meet so the guy couldn't see her car approach before she checked him out. Wild animals lived in the sanctuary. Likely in its surroundings too. And the night was so foggy one couldn't detect an elephant herd stampeding by, far less a wild man hidden close. It was so densely foliated only a flamboyance of flamingos would dare rendezvous. No one in their right mind would reconnoiter at this hour. But then no one but her would venture out to meet a stranger making threats.

Florida, weighing alternatives, reconsidered bailing out when a pair of high beams blinked three times in a corner of the parking lot. Did somebody see her? Was it him? She dug in her handbag, fingered her wallet, pens, a coin purse, lipstick, tissues, and a small vial of red pepper spray. It was pink and looked like a lipstick tube. She held it tightly, popped the cap, released the safety, touched the trigger, and ambled the Chevy toward the blazing lights, its wipers scritching.

The car was a late-model Porsche, silver and black with tinted windows. Florida couldn't see inside. She pulled parallel, keeping her distance, leaving the engine running noisily, keeping the shift in drive, left foot on the brake, right on the accelerator.

The Porsche blinked its lights again.

All of a sudden, a rap on her window made her jump and turn, confused.

On the other side of her window, the large man's hand that was knocking banged again. It bore Ocala's wedding ring on a knuckle of its pinky, clacking loudly on the glass. The hand-crafted style of the diamond setting was unmistakable. It blinged in the Porsche's headlights, causing Florida to scream. Florida slit the window open. "Where is she? What have you done with her?"

"Whatever I felt like doing with her, Grams. Be cool and listen closely," hissed a disembodied voice in a vaguely familiar acid tone. The man tugged at his ski mask, breathing hard. His hand not wearing the ring was holding a gun, directed at her head. "If I wanted to hurt her, she'd be dead. And the same goes for you, Grams. Do like I say."

"Please. I'm begging you. What do you want?"

"Everything, Grams. The American dream. The money, the car, the props, the land. You're hogging my homestead. That ain't fair."

"How's that?" stammered Florida, gripping the spray can, cracking the window a little bit wider, listening, trying to place the voice. It was muffled behind a ski mask.

"That farm belongs to me," was the disconcerting reply the man growled back.

"What farm?"

"The one you're squatting on. Don't act stupid. You know what."

"I don't. I don't know why you called me here, but my daughter has nothing to do with it. You said you had information. That's why I came, to hear you out."

He emitted a derisive laugh, coughed, drew a sleeve across his nose.

Florida didn't move a muscle, frightened of making him angrier. "Who are you? If the land is yours, then prove it, and I'll let it go."

"Aw. It hurts me, Grams, that it don't mean no more to you than that. I paid you rent for years on a house that's mine, and you're willin' to let it go without puttin' up a fight."

"Baron? Baron Derniere?" guessed Florida, thinking how different he sounded now.

"Uh-uh, Grams. It's Robin Hood. I'm'a take from the rich and give to the poor."

"Only nobody in this car is rich. You're nothing but a common thief." His contrivance was coming clearer now. Baron was Pappy Derniere's grandson, and Pappy had disappeared. Baron was likely Pappy's rightful heir, convinced he owned the land. How far he was willing to go for it was the question at the moment. "Put down the gun. We can work this out."

"I'm already working it out. My way. Maidie convinced me that home title fraud would work, but we got caught. We got all mixed up with a nosy clerk and almost got busted when we filed. I'm tired of taking chances now. I'm taking the property free and clear."

"Where is my daughter?" Florida shrilled, one hand on the cell phone propped in the well of the car door handle, trying to dial, the other hand grasping the pepper spray canister, ready to squeeze the trigger.

"Your girl is with Pops, and they're both safe now, but that won't last forever, Grams."

Florida gasped convulsively. She gulped and tried to suck in air. "Stop calling me that. You're not my grandson. None of my children behave like this."

"You'll never see father and daughter again if you don't get out of that car right now and follow my orders to a T. I could shoot you, you know. I ain't playin', Grams. It wouldn't be the first time." His silver gun beckoned her out of her car.

Florida quavered, opened the door. "Don't hurt them. I promise I'll do what you want."

"You bet you will. It's all on you. Sign off on the farm, and they'll both survive."

Florida's brown eyes flooded, and her chest clamped like a vise. She wavered as she left the car, heart beating like a snare drum.

"Don't croak before the reunion, Grams. It's only a bunch of signatures. Be done before you know it. Get away from the car. Stand over there." He pointed toward a queen palm tree.

Florida thought of Ocala and Sage, composed herself and breathed in deep. "You got it," she managed to warble, wiping her eyes in a bid to collect herself as Baron barked instructions.

"Wait for the papers tomorrow. Immediately sign them in front of a notary. No lawyers, no cops, or the deal is off. Put the documents in your mailbox when you leave the house. Do not return. You'll get on a flight to New York tomorrow night and not look back. You're like Lot's wife now, you'll turn to salt and your sexy brat and weak old man will be heading from ashes to dust before you know it if you stay down here. You do like I say, there'll be no harm done. But don't get cute. Don't blow this, Grams, or I promise you, they're luncheon meat. Get it right, and as your parting gift, I might let you retrieve your long-lost son."

"My son? You know about my son? My infant?"

"He ain't no infant no more," Baron slurred. "He ain't yours neither."

"He's alive?" she screeched. "Do you know where?"

"I know lots. And you better not follow me when I leave you here, you get me?" Baron backed away from Florida, scanning the parking lot, training his gun on her chest. He rattled like a snake as he slithered back into his automobile.

"Where did you get the car?" asked Florida as he fired his engine up.

"None of your business. You're so square. I keeps me a fly whip all the time. Your ass is so damn gullible." He slid in the Porsche, flipped her the bird and, whooping cusses, sped away.

The next morning whizzed by in a frightening blur. Florida's head was pounding. When Keys and Madison called from Connecticut, Florida didn't have the heart to pick up and relay the dreadful news. She hadn't slept a wink all night while fretting over what to do. The storm got worse on her way back home, and the farmhouse creaked and moaned as ill wind blew through clapboards, shingles, stucco, and its aging windows, single-paned and showing signs of wear.

The paperwork arrived at noon when a FedEx truck pulled up outside. Florida opened the envelope to briefly skim the documents. She had thought she was ready for anything and yet was astonished by what she saw. She'd been totally committed to signing the agreement when the sun arose—no matter what details it held—but the contract was worse than she thought. What Baron proposed as a property transfer in that darkened parking lot was far broader than he'd divulged. He was demanding the farm for a dollar sealed inside the envelope and extorting her for everything. His ransom not only required that she relinquish the groves and farm to him but everything else she inherited from her uncle's estate as well. All that, plus every bit of Florida's savings accounts, and Sage's too—along with their earnings, investments, assets, annuities, IRA balances, and even their monthly pension checks for the rest of their natural lives.

This was a shakedown of epic proportions, but hard as she thought, she saw no way out. After Baron got through with them, they would be homeless, penniless, deep in compounding debt, with nothing to leave for their kids or grands. Not that they had all that much saved, but they'd scrimped and put it all to work, studying up on retirement issues, eating on less than ten dollars a day with a wardrobe older than the kids they'd sacrificed for all these years.

What little remained of Buzz's stash could possibly see them through old age. And if Sage divorced her, more than that. As a single, she could afford a little apartment in a senior village. Maybe one of those snazzy assisted-living condos by the beach. She never could know when her health might fail and refused to be a burden. That was swirling down the drain though.

Nothing was worth more than family, and she longed to reunite with hers. If it cost her every dime she had, so be it. It was a price she'd pay.

She scanned the rip-off docs again and hustled to get to the notary at the copy shop in town. For a chance to see the child they'd lost, she'd succumb to extreme extortion now and have Baron arrested later on when Sage and all her kids were at her side and safe and sound. Baron might get away with his current gambit, but he'd suffer.

Against the advice of the notary, Florida signed the property transfer papers and rushed upstairs to pack. The train case, she would leave behind because it brought bad luck. If Sage or Ocala remained a hostage or got hurt at Baron's hands, Baron would wish she'd called the cops. She'd tear him limb from limb. At seventy, that would be difficult and a blight on her ledger this late in life, but she sure could put a hit on him. Some of her nephew's friends would kill for a date with a hooker, a bag of weed, and a bottle of Ace of Spades.

Her stomach was curdling like sour milk as she climbed the attic stairs to where she'd stowed her luggage earlier, her feet protesting heartily. She wondered if Baron staged the break-in just to snatch her address book to find out where Ocala lived and maybe her other two daughters too. If so, he'd have gotten the names and addresses of all her loved ones in one swoop. After he cleaned her out this time, there was nothing to stop him from coming back and trying kidnapping again or blackmailing her or anyone she knew. The shakedown could go on and on. The nightmare might not ever end.

The pain in her feet snapped her out of that thought, and something else occurred to her.

The notion that Sage didn't leave but was taken had her rethink their relationship. Might Sage still be in love with her? The epiphany, coupled with his situation, made her start to cry.

Her tears brought another revelation. She wasn't hopeless or helpless at all. Ocala and Sage were somewhere, right? And probably together. Could she find them herself and bring them home? That was the only real way to ensure their safe return from Baron. Baron could kill them once he got it all, if he hadn't done so yet. If Florida didn't deposit the envelope in the mailbox like he'd said, he'd have to keep at her, wouldn't he? He wouldn't just give up. He'd push until he got his way. He'd keep them alive as leverage. While he did, she could launch a search for them. Not through the cops. They wouldn't care. Ocala and Sage would be just another Black girl on a flyer and an old Black man who'd wandered off. How much energy would they exert to get them back to their family? Zero. It was up to her, like Baron said. And maybe Madison and Frank. But what if Baron caught them too? Or Keys. Or what if they called the authorities? Baron might exact revenge. No way, she had to work alone, act fast to find Ocala and Sage while each of them was in one piece. Either way, she had to leave the house, make Baron think he'd conquered her. She had to play along.

The train case was perched on an attic shelf. Florida reached for it, lost her balance, toppled, and sent the train case tumbling. She grabbed the shelf from which it dropped to keep herself from falling forward. The train case bounced and took a roll. It landed by a brass owl doorstop holding the hatch to the attic ajar. Florida dusted off her hands and went to pick the train case up. As she bent, a floorboard under her left foot squeaked and slid about an inch, making her teeter a second time. Struggling for balance, she broke her fall by grabbing the brass owl door stop. But it shifted and tipped her off-kilter, and she heard a faint clink and a sliding sound, and before she determined the source of them, the end of the floorboard lifted slightly, making her heel dip down as if on a tilting miniseesaw.

Balancing, she peered at it, one corner of her mouth turned up. She lifted the end of the plank and found she was staring down into a black hole that appeared to be several stories deep. She couldn't see a bottom, but a rush of air came whirling up. It was stale but cool, invigorating. Kneeling, she peeled the floorboard back. And another. Then another. Until she could see a black circular staircase bolted to a sheer rock wall. Her mouth fell open, and she wheezed. *Why was it placed there, and where did it lead?* She doubted it would hold her weight but decided it would have to. Placing her right foot tentatively, she descended, cautiously grasping a rail, the rickety staircase swinging and swaying, slamming her into the cold rock wall. When she recovered, she took another step down into a narrow space, forging into a gap below a ledge that led to musky gloom. She hit bottom in an antechamber. It was cramped and close and musty, dimly lit by a bare bulb Florida tightened, making its pale light brighter. It blinked and made a sizzling sound.

The weird glow made the chamber look more like a room than an underground catacomb. It was lined with Victorian rose wallpaper on all sides and the ceiling too, a first layer peeling, revealing another layer of paper. Midnight blue. The space was empty of furnishings except for an antique cedar chest that sat on a lengthy slab of concrete block with letters carved on top. It looked like a crypt from an ancient Egyptian tomb in the Valley of the Kings. Hesitating and breathing in shallow gulps, Florida moved through the tomb as if compelled, cobwebs attacking her about her face and hair. She peered at the top of the crypt-like box. It read Rockabye, baby, on the treetop. When the wind blows, the cradle will rock. Odd, thought Florida. What does it mean? Florida, frozen, stared wide-eyed. Hot pain shot up from her ankle into her thigh and caused her to double over. Bending to rub it, she tweaked her back as she slowly advanced for a closer look at the chest, her sore back stiffening. The scent of the cedar chest filled her lungs.

The front of the chest had a rusty lock that swayed a little as she watched. *Did it dangle, or did she imagine it?* A chill ran up her aching spine, but she couldn't turn back now.

Using the hem of her blouse as a grip, she yanked on the lock. It failed to give. A rat ran over her foot. It squealed. She kicked at it, hobbling, yelping, heaving, backpedaling into a wall behind her, whooping, placing a hand on her chest, her heart beating like a hip-hop tune. Clutching her breast, her left hand found her necklace, fumbling the silver chain and the pendant train case key she'd worn since she'd bought the train case in her youth.

Eyes twinkling, Florida surveyed the trunk, the rat and the rust forgotten but her back and neck complaining as she examined the keyhole of the lock. On an instinct she could not resist, she pulled her key chain necklace out and shimmied her key at the aperture. To her delight, it sort of fit. She jiggled it in. The lock gave way, the lid of the trunk lifting up on its own.

Florida peered inside the trunk.

Within was another flight of stairs. Another room. Another trunk. The route down was like Russian nesting dolls, one fitted inside another.

The third level's trunk was moldy green. Freeing it from a spider complex, Florida dared peruse it but was reluctant to touch its mildewed skin. Using the hem of her blouse again, she pushed the red button it had on top. The lid opened. There was no fourth staircase. Instead, a hand-tatted lace wedding dress with a high collar studded with pearls lay folded, its bodice covered with hundreds of rhinestones sparkling like diamonds, keen as knives. Florida eyed it with wonder, unfolding it, stippling her fingers over its delicate contours, holding it up to her body, marveling at its fine details. She placed it aside and continued to search.

Underneath the wedding gown was a picture of her with her long-lost son. The image almost knocked her off her feet, it felt so visceral. Had Buzz taken it all those years ago when he came to New York to meet the new arrival? Why'd he hide it here? It filled her with ennui. She slipped it in her pocket when her eye caught a sepia picture of Uncle Buzz with his breathtaking wife. She picked up the photo. The love of his life. Ah, yes, her name was Eva. Eva tragically died of consumption, according to notes on the back of the photograph. The sight of the couple made Florida sigh. Their haunting wedding portrait depicted the heartrending reason Buzz never remarried after he shared a life with her. The couple looked head-over-heels in love. Loss of such passion could break a man, thought Florida as she stared at them. Or a woman. Or both lovers.

Beside the silver-framed photo of the lovebird bride and groom was a painted tin with a decorative design like a Christmas cookie box. Its lid read "Lancer's Soda Crackers—every bite a sheer delight." The tin was dented on one side, so Florida forced her fingertips under the lid to pry it up. As she gripped it, she broke a fingernail at its base, and it began to bleed. She sucked it then wiped it on her blouse before wrenching the tin with her other hand, determined to yank it open. When she finally did, she held her breath. Secreted in the tin was a diary fashioned of well-worn leather binding. Sneezing from dust, she brushed it off and, squinting, saw two gold initials, *B* and *H*. Buzz Homer. She recognized the monogram. She opened the book, and its yellowed pages fanned to reveal a set of drawings, maps, old photos, one pressed rose, and handwritten notations of the family history running through Florida's veins and impacting her life that very moment.

Uncle Buzz's entries told a tale that hinted at hidden dangers Florida feared her family had to fight against or die—the ruinous curse of Pappy Derniere and the progeny he spawned.

Ten p.m. and Florida launched her plan of action with precision.

The whirring of an electric drill was silenced as the crunch of the Porsche's tires rolled up the Homer gravel driveway at a stealthy speed. The irregular trill of Florida's heartbeat raced in her temples and thrummed in her neck as her ears inclined to the syncopated clomp of a pair of beat-up Jordan Airs and a couple of Payless pumps cutting a path across the creaky porch to collect ill-gotten gains.

"I *still* say we should scout the airport. Are you sure she caught a plane?"

"Maidie, the old crone's all freaked out. Believe me, babe, she's in the wind."

"So the land is finally ours?"

"This big house too, with Buzz's greenbacks. Just because we didn't find them yet don't mean them boys ain't here. Now we can tear out the walls to the studs and get to them for sure."

"I ain't holdin' my breath to find that cash," said Maidie in a bitter tone. "It's a fairy tale. Ain't no cash in there. We searched every wall inside this house and didn't find nothin' but rags, asbestos, tons of those stinkin' Confederate flags, and dead mice, dude. The money's gone. That is, if it was ever here. I ain't spackling and painting one more hole."

"You don't have to, babe. I got you, girl. I scared the old biddy half to death. Believe me, she did like I said. You'll see. I got it all worked out." Florida watched from a foyer window as Baron reached inside the mailbox, snatching the envelope Florida left. "She did it! Look. I told you. This is just the start. We'll find his stash. In the meantime, we got all of this." He kissed the large envelope, pumped his fist. "It's plenty. We can do what we want. Check it out. We got money to burn."

Maidie jumped and clapped her hands. "I knew it. It was my idea, remember? I thought the whole thing up. You and me renting. The blackmail trick. I planned all of it, and it's paying off. Oh, what would you do without me, boo?" She grinned and grabbed the envelope.

"I don't know and don't wanna find out," said Baron, kissing her, lifting her into his arms and twirling her around. He snatched the big envelope back from her, and the smack of their lustful tongues in full-lipped kisses joined the cricket chirps and the frenzied rustle of heated, caressing bodies in cheap rayon clothes.

"Not here. What if somebody sees us," Maidie cooed. "Come on, let's go inside."

Florida heard the dead bolt click. *They copied the key,* she thought. But they're not going to get away with it. She took off a clunky orthopedic shoe and held it above her head.

When the door scraped open, Baron lifted Maidie like a blushing bride and slung her into the vestibule, pinning her up against a wall, his back to Florida's heavy shoe, his hands exploring Maidie's thighs and wandering into her panties, pulling her thong aside and plunging in.

Florida leaped from the shadows behind the door, cold-cocked him on the head, and then pummeled him with her corrective footwear, raising a lump on his scalp with the steel shank built inside its custom sole. She socked him again on the temple and thrust her knee into his groin. Baron fell forward into a face plant, hitting his brow on the edge of the console table, spurting a geyser of blood and dropping Maidie on the polished surface of the parquet floor.

Maidie scrambled to her feet, fled out down the driveway to the Porsche, extracted a gun from the glove compartment, cocked its hammer, and headed back, determination in her eyes.

When Baron came to, he was strapped with duct tape pinning him to a kitchen chair, a buzzing drill bit at his ear. "Be cool, Grams. They're both fine, okay? I'll tell you where they at."

"You'd better tell the truth," warned Florida, pressing the trigger of the drill and causing it to grind. "I'm all out of patience. Your wife's locked out, so nobody can help you now."

Bang! A bullet pinged into the rear of the house and shattered the kitchen window. Glass peppered Florida's back and arms as she stood facing Baron, her back to the porch, ducking and hiding below the sink.

Maidie fired five more shots outside on the veranda.

The third caught Baron in his chest, the last two in his eye and throat.

Florida heard her scream and saw her scurrying into the grapefruit grove.

Florida took off after Maidie, barefoot, holding the whirring drill, her face awash with tears for Baron, tears for Ocala, tears for Sage, a river of tears for her baby boy, and more rage than Florida had ever felt. Maidie made tracks like a hungry bloodhound. Florida chased her, zigging and zagging through the grove and racing toward the giant cornfield, swarms of mosquitoes eating her alive and raising angry welts. She tried to keep up with the younger woman, but found her feet and ankles hollering, swelling like parade balloons as she slowed to a trot and ran out of breath.

"Leave me alone!" Maidie shouted. "Let me go! They're in the moonshine shack!"

The last image Florida saw of Maidie before she collapsed into the grass was a silhouette of flailing arms disappearing in the distance.

The reunion was joyous. The farm was lit up. At dinner, Sage's prayer was even longer than the usual eternity his family felt before they could dig into any meal. Nobody beefed it this time though. The whole family was too grateful. Even Ocala wore a smile.

"So, Mom," asked Madison, "is it true? Pappy Derniere conned Uncle Buzz?"

"Yes, sweetie," Florida answered. "And the repercussions were immense. Pappy was a card shark in the North, but no one here knew that. Pappy was a grifter. When he heard Uncle Buzz had a fortune and he learned there was a weekly Tonk game every Tuesday night in town, he figured it'd be like taking candy from a baby if he played, so he conned his way in with a bunch of lies and proceeded to rob the players blind. Uncle Buzz only bet so much each game. One particular night, when his cash ran out after Pappy ripped off everyone, since Buzz had quit the moonshine game, he bet the moonshine shack. When Pappy supposedly won the game, he claimed he won the entire farm and spread the lie clear to the county line. He thought he could steal everything Buzz owned."

"Guess it runs in their family," Keys chimed in.

"Just ask *me*," Ocala said.

"Running does too, apparently. Pappy escaped when Uncle Buzz told him he'd call the cops to turn him in. Uncle Buzz didn't kill him; he left on his own, but the fact Pappy suddenly disappeared made neighbor folks suspicious. It's a small world in a Southern town—a whole lot smaller in those days. All kinds of rumors swirled. See, Pappy ran off with Uncle Buzz's wife, and it was scandalous. Uncle Buzz held forth that Eva died because he was embarrassed. But he wrote the truth down in the diary I found in the attic, and that's where the secret stayed."

"Until now," said Sage. "Truth will come out. Girls, that's how your mother saved the day, and that's why I'm so proud of her." Sage took another heaping bite, his chest protruding as he did, a wink of his eye catching Florida's own.

Florida watched her family gobbling seconds and thirds of the meal she'd cooked, unable to reach any peace because of the son she wished were there with them. *Count your blessings*, she intoned more inwardly than outwardly. Be happy with the kids you have instead of upset for the one you don't. That lent her a bit of serenity, but the words Maidie spat like poison darts as they hauled her off to lock her up ricocheted in Florida's consciousness: "You'll never see your son again. Not ever. Your whole family's cursed."

Ding-dong! The farmhouse doorbell rang and shook her from her reverie.

"I'll get it," said Florida, doffing her apron and wiping her mouth of candied yams.

It was Willa, ever the buxom beauty, hugging Florida to her chest, her spandex leggings tight as sausage casings, blouse ablaze with sequins, feather boa at her neck.

Justin stood out on the porch near the doorjamb, wearing a tasteful, crisp, beige suit.

Florida waved to catch his eye. "Justin, come in. I'm glad you came."

He regarded her with a sheepish smile. "Gramma?" he uttered, looking up.

Justin's birth grandmother, Florida Freeman, fainted where she stood.

"I get it, Flo, it shocked us too," Willa confided around a fire as everyone drank mulled cider and gathered around to listen to her yarn. "We only just found out ourselves. See, Justin and Baron Derniere was close from the time they was friends in grade school. Maidie was in their class then too. Justin visited Maidie out to the lockup yesterday afternoon. She's havin' a real hard time and decided to cough up what she knew to try to shave her sentence down."

It got so quiet in the room that the ticking of the mantel clock was deafening as they listened hard while Willa broke it down. "When Pappy blew town, he vowed he was gonna make good on gettin' revenge. He didn't get the farm, and he was mad as heck Buzz stood him down. Never mind he ran off with Buzz's wife and broke Buzz's heart to pieces. Pappy still wanted all his wealth. So Pappy rode north to pull off his blueprint to kidnap your baby boy for ransom. He figured to get the land that way. He found out you was Buzz's heir. Buzz raved about you all the time, and he didn't have no one else he loved the way he seemed to worship you."

"But Pappy had kids. Why take my boy?" asked Florida, holding Justin's hand.

"He didn't want your baby boy. He just wanted to hurt your uncle. He knew hurting you would hurt Buzz bad. And he wanted Buzz's moonshine money more than he wanted Buzz's wife, as gorgeous as she was. Only, Pappy got scared to get caught with the kid. He got paranoid Eva would find him out and hurry back to Buzz. So, one evenin', seems like yesterday..." Willa misted over. "Pappy shows up on my doorstep, cradlin' the cutest, loudest cryin', tiny crumb crusher you ever saw. Claimin' the baby was his by a gal in Mobile who ran away from him. The ploy was a lie, but it sounded real. What he actually did was bed your babysitter so she'd snatch your boy. But it sank in how much trouble he was in when the babysitter balked when he dumped her. She said she'd turn him in. He came cryin' to me then, lyin', pleadin', beggin' me to raise *his* kid. He knew how I desperately wanted a baby and couldn't have none of my own, because I confided in Eva and she let on while the two of them had their affair."

Willa stopped for a moment and wiped a tear. "Me and my husband tried for kids, but we miscarried over and over until he warned me to let it go or he'd divorce me and move on. He told me he couldn't take no more, that he couldn't keep hopin' and gettin' let down. Then a few days later, the baby came. I thought it was a miracle. I felt it was how it was meant to be. My Buster fell in love with him, and our marriage got better than ever before... Oh, I swear to you, Flo, on Justin's life, I never woulda took him if I knew the child was yours."

"I believe you, Willa," Florida said. "And I don't even care how we got to this point. I just want to know where my boy is now."

Willa looked down and wrung her hands. "I'm sorry, Flo. He passed away. He was in a car crash when he turned thirty-one. Both he and Justin's mother died."

A mournful wail issued from Florida's lungs. Unnatural sounds gushed from all three of her girls, and they rushed to her like a cresting wave and threw their arms around her.

"Oh, I'm sorry it happened. It's okay," said Madison, patting her mother's back.

"You still have us," Ocala cried.

"And look, God gave us Justin. We have him to love. That's such a gift," Keys added.

"Yes, it is," said Florida, wiping her eyes and taking deep breaths. She smiled and held out her arms, and Justin quickly rolled into the warm group hug and nuzzled his face in her neck.

"I promise to love you till death do us part," Sage vowed. "And stay right by your side."

"It's true we're all a family now," said Florida, tears running down her cheeks. "And that feels so good to finally know. I'm not saying I'll ever forget the son I lost, or I won't need time to grieve, but I'm blessed and I'm thankful to God for you all. You mean the world to me."

"And let's all be grateful the worst of the past is over and can't bother us. Baron is buried right here on the farm, and Maidie will be in prison for more years than she can count. We might not forget what was done in the past, but we can build a future here together. All of us."

"You got that right," said Florida. "I guess I always knew I'd never see my boy again. But I see his likeness here right now... Hey, Justin, why don't you turn that old still shack into a music studio?"

"Can I?" asked Justin, popping up. "That'd be a dream come true."

"We have enough land to make everyone's dream come true. For us, a retirement home. For the girls, a swell vacation spot. And for Willa, a rent-free guesthouse you can visit anytime."

"Well, I better go buy some overalls," joked Willa, pretending to grab her purse.

Everyone laughed, and the tension broke.

"Let's head in for dessert," said Florida. "We've worked up an appetite."

They prayed, ate peach pie, and joined hands by the fireplace, turned on the lights in the grapefruit grove, and drank wine from the fridge in the moonshine shack under a harvest moon.

When the drama was over, the Freemans and the Rhodeses melded their family ties.

Justin and his wife moved in with Sage and Florida on the farm, working the land and innovating ways to profit from the crops. The gift shop they started sold jellies and jams and a cache of local arts and crafts. Madison, Keys, and Ocala embraced their young nephew and his industrious wife and treated them like solid gold. Florida's granddaughter-in-law was so much kinder and smarter than she seemed once her aunts-in-law accepted and mentored her and gave her a fighting chance. Raven, once a runaway, was really quite a gem.

Willa could not believe the change in Raven and started to like the girl, which came as a welcome surprise and kept the peace, at least most days. And Willa became a fixture in the new guesthouse built by the grove. She was dating a man who purchased a neighboring farm to create a summer camp for poor and underprivileged youths.

Justin returned to school part-time, studied, and earned his GED.

Sage bonded with his grandson, fishing and helping him renovate the still shack, tinkering with construction tools, recording equipment, acoustic foam, and audio production software suites. He even began to rap to beats.

Ocala returned to therapy and, on meds, began to heal herself. She managed her anger a day at a time, still a handful but much less so.

Keys found the courage to file for divorce and moved her son to Florida.

The train case, after its big adventure, escaped the attic frequently to explore distant ports of a wondrous world with Florida and Sage. The train case proved to be good luck, and Florida Homer Freeman was perhaps the luckiest one of all, with her family, friends, a happy life—and the cool thirty million bucks she found underground in the house her uncle built.

A
SPICY
BROWN
MYSTERY

L ET THAT BE A LESSON TO YOU I'm named after a spicy brown mustard, and I've been trying to cut it ever since. Cut the mustard, that is. And it's challenging. Who set that standard, anyway? Certainly not one of a darker hue, systematically precluded from "making the grade" for that one reason. When you look at it philosophically—rather than letting it piss you off—whose concept of you really counts? Who's the arbiter of your value? You, I would say. And your higher power. Not others' self-interested beliefs, opinions, and projections. If you leave your self-worth to the whims of others, you might as well only eat sugar and salt and wait to see what happens.

Little children are even more vulnerable to what others think than are adults, and that can cause them injury. I know, because of what happened to me as a kid with brown skin and a sense of self-respect no one could steal from me. And that, my friend, came at a cost. A price I first paid in second grade. When I learned to do me, and to do my best, and to learn from my every experience and pass my lessons on.

LESSON #1 ~ *One has to do one's best in life and let the chips fall where they may.*

As long as you do your best, there's nothing more anyone can ask of you. And as long as your best keeps getting better and you grow, your life improves. Life reflects your patterns. You think and say and do your life, and as you evolve into higher self, some people will feel you and some will not. But that's on them and not on you. As long as you're reaching for the stars with an open heart and open mind, evolving to who you're meant to be and doing what you're meant to do, only heaven can judge your progress.

That's my perspective anyway. If it makes me a Pollyanna, fine. You have to believe in something, right? And I believe in goodness. Everywhere and all the time. There's always a plus in a negative. In even the most bizarre downturn, there's an upside if you focus on the positive and chart your path. You may have to strain to see it, but as my parents always used to say, "You have to take the bitter with the better." I'm convinced of it.

My life isn't always easy, but I sure enjoy the ride. And I love to help others find happiness too. It may sound like a syrupy tweet, but everyone's life should be filled with joy. Life really is wonderful, after all, and that's largely due to people. Positive folks like you and me who choose to lead an upbeat life, press on like life is always sweet, and believe all things do work for good. The universe is on our side, and miracles really do grow on trees. Dreams come true for those who see them long before they materialize. We see what we believe and not the other way around. We choose to know we matter and can make the world a better place.

Now, I know not everyone gets the same or equal opportunities. Fair and unfair are at constant odds. Unfairness is perennial. Inequality is a morbid fact. The scales of justice lurch one way and not toward the side of the poor or underserved or very young or old or those with deeper shades of skin. All but the most dishonest have to admit these hard, disturbing truths or resolve to lie to others just as boldly as they deceive themselves. The rich get richer, the poor get poorer. Some of the best of us lose their freedom or lives in throes of silent pain, and some of the worst behaving among us rise to heights beyond their worth or even their imagining.

It has already been a four hundred-year wait for little girls like I once was to be treated like we're precious. I've come to know there's strength in that and all things work out in the end.

The little girl that lives within me still is strong and kind and filled with hope and light and endless love. The vision she saw remains intact, more vibrant than it ever was, despite the obvious pitfalls and the burdensome necessity that women like me run faster and jump higher to compete. The rat race, for some, is designed as a one-yard dash on flowery beds of ease, and for others it's a marathon of hurdles and long-distance runs. We suffer invectives, violence, hiring and housing discrimination, hatred, health that fails for lack of care, income disparities, low expectations, high interest rates—and the harmful list goes on and on.

We deal with this in different ways. And as I look back, I find my repose in things that occurred in my childhood, the way I responded to those events, the self-respect they birthed in me, and how I survived when some did not. At the root of my accomplishments as a writer and a politico—and there have been many, I'm happy to say—grows more than the simple need to excel, the burning desire to change the world, or even the imperative to fulfill the spiritual sense of purpose and mission at my core.

The seeds of my will to overcome less-than-great expectations grew because they were fertilized not by children but by elders I encountered. By men and women entrusted to nurture my delicate sensibilities, who spoke "you can't," "you're not," and "you won't" into my fledgling consciousness, punctuated by "don't dare be you." By adults who orated virulent, negative words as a curse on my innocence as casually, assuredly, or forcefully as one utters "please" and "thank you." By instructors who dared permit themselves to strive to negate my potential and to limit my possibilities without any basis for doing so in my character or intellect.

They did so for one reason.

As I said, I'm Spicy Brown.

The ebb and flow of my life, therefore, my adventures and bouts with outrageous fortune seem at this point to issue from my first response to oppression at a very early age, at a moment of dangerous childhood—in a matter of life and death.

I should have known the fix was in, but I was just a kid.

It was second grade, and Miss Folley, my teacher, was arranging our classroom seating chart, presumably according to how well we fared on our standardized tests and assignments. I started in the third seat, setting my mini-sights on the coveted desk adjacent to Miss Folley's.

I immediately sensed how my opening spot was irritating Folley, who appeared to be barely able to conceal her consternation. Mean-spirited, cross-eyed, vengeful, crass, she was feared by everyone in the school, including our timid principal. Nobody ventured to challenge her random edicts, rules, or dictums. The students were too terrorized, and the faculty shrank from acknowledging her bad energy in their midst. And no one dared to question her. That is, no one but me. I thought answering questions was her job. She thought it was making life miserable.

Perhaps that's the reason she couldn't stand the sight of me moving from seat to seat, progressing as she should want me to. As counterintuitive as it was, at my tender age, it baffled me. I was too young to see racism driving her hostility, but as I advanced to the second and then the first seat, tension mounted. Visibly. Verbally. Violently. Viciously.

Why was she displeased with me? It was terribly confusing. Her anger seemed so odd to me. Didn't she praise my bud, Bianca Stewart, every chance she got? Crawford McKenzie, Jason Schmidt, Lane Filmore, and Billy O'Toole weren't treated badly, nor was Roger Hayes. Why did they gain her increasing admiration and gold sticker stars while she relegated *moi* to the darkest dungeon of her fiefdom? I was posting solid As. Mightn't it have a chilling effect on my grades were I a more timid soul? Back then, it never occurred to me that that might be her goal. My parents would never stand for it, and knowing her treatment would outrage them, I struggled by myself. Poor Gerald Singleton had it worse. The only other Black soul in the class, he sat in the very last seat by the closet, having to smell the gerbil cage—and he even won the science fair.

Complicating the situation was my witnessing, with no small frustration, Stacey Short, a bold, blond classmate, praised for all her failures. Even her most pedestrian efforts garnered her the green hall pass, though she occupied the nineteenth seat. She never approached the top five. Folley's praises only made things worse. She now resides in a penal institution in Manhattan. The media dubbed her "Scamming Stacey, the Baby Bunko Queen of Brooklyn" when she got busted at fifteen. The girl pirated child pornography she and her boyfriend stole in Queens and later became a Wall Street siren bedding felonious bankers helming the 2008 stock market crash. She dealt in home foreclosures with her "inside" information. All the signs were apparent in second grade that Stacey was on the prison path, and yet Miss Folley favored her, commenting on her big blue eyes when she pilfered a series of library books and sold them on the street. And so it went for other fair-haired students while I, on the other hand, got beaten with textbooks, whiteboard erasers, the wooden hall pass, and whatever else Miss Folley had at hand.

I couldn't put my finger on the problem, but I smelled a rat.

LESSON #2 ~ *When things don't seem right, rout them out. Always trust your instincts.*

Fortuitously, my struggle with Miss Folley mercifully took a turn, interrupted by a quirk of fate. After torturing most of her second graders, Folley up and disappeared. They initially said she took off on a short sabbatical to parts unknown to marry the mirthless music teacher—hapless, toothless Mr. Stafford, the unsuspecting tuba player she stumbled upon at a Bingo game and from thence began to manipulate into an object of her affections. He was at least a head shorter than she and weighed a jillion fewer pounds, but they managed to turn their Jack Sprat status into a badge of honor. This spouse would be her second, and her fellow instructors wondered why any man in his right mind chose the shrew, far less two males in succession.

The announcement came early one morning when our beleaguered principal, Mr. Beagle, dubbed by the students the Bald-Headed Eagle, arrived with breaking news. I guess, as second graders go, our class was restrained—or rather repressed—on the average matriculation day, but the cheer that went up when we learned Miss Folley was gone was swift and thunderous. Not unlike the Munchkin chant when the house fell onto the Wicked Witch. Mr. Beagle, tall and ghostly pale, had a face as long as our summer vacation and ears as large as an elephant's. In a baggy suit, a wide red tie, a mixed-gray handlebar mustache, and lace-up shoes with ribbed silk socks, he shuddered and wrinkled his nose.

"Let's get maintenance up here immediately to deal with that putrid odor. It smells like skunk spray in this room. What is it, that rodent over there? Did one of you bring in chopped liver for lunch? Or perhaps a bad egg salad?"

With a flourish, a bow, and a wave of his arm as he backed toward the door in squeaky shoes, he introduced our substitute, a short, plump, soft-fleshed, white-haired woman sporting a flowery granny dress, black nursing shoes, a soothing voice, and only three fingers on each of her hands. Ms. Adwell. Her, I was happy to see. She was nice. She appeared to love teaching. She encouraged us and wore a smile. Miss Folley never, ever smiled. The entire class was so relieved we remained on our best behavior even when Adwell left the room.

Ms. Adwell's intercession taught me several things, but mostly this:

LESSON #3 ~ *Something good always happens when they try to screw you up the worst.*

Avoiding one odious fate only plunged me headlong into another.

The trouble was Ms. Adwell stank. Mr. Beagle was right. She did have a foul smell. Not just any old body odor stench—an oppressive, persistent, malodorous funk that fouled up the air so badly even the boys could hardly breathe. Because we liked her very much, we imagined the stink was there before and she just made it stronger. We were sure we'd smelled it earlier, but after Ms. Adwell closed the door, the dreadful effluvium worsened. We kids had to hold our noses, but as far as the class was concerned, any fetor was preferable to Folley's wrath.

That was until what happened next.

It transpired as I was stapling craft paper onto our long wooden table at the back of the classroom that afternoon, tucking neat hospital corners at intersections as I went along. I was given the chore by Miss Folley before she left, and I was proud of it. Thanksgiving was a week away, and we were assigned to illustrate the lifestyle of the pilgrims, a task we decided to undertake by erecting a model village with construction paper, popsicle sticks, brightly colored squares of felt, Styrofoam shapes, pipe cleaners, glue, foam core, and clumps of modeling clay.

I was left alone to do my work of prepping the table for the display as the rest of the class clattered into the hall and blustered through the stairwell door to descend to the gym for PE class and a spirited round of kickball.

No sooner were they out of earshot, I ran out of staples.

I had to reload the stapler. What could I do? The sub was gone. Surveying the scene, I observed Ms. Adwell left the supply closet key in the lock, which seemed to be a sore misstep. Miss Folley hoarded school supplies as if her pension rested there, or an enemy nation might invade and chalk might be the only ammo saving her from certain death. Miss Folley guarded that key with her life, but Ms. Adwell, seemingly trusting of us, apparently didn't see the need.

I set down the stapler, crossed to the built-in, gazed up at the huge brass key ring dangling way above my reach, mulled over whether to go for it, my mouth as dry as desert sands. Was it better to stand by impotent, awaiting my fellow students' return with the knowledge I disappointed them or to opt for the risky alternative of going where no kid went before?

Hmm… It was a conundrum.

I could follow the class, interrupt PE, engender the ire of my peers, and trouble arthritic, sweet old Ms. Adwell—who'd then be obliged to hobble all the way back up the hall to 201—or I could simply turn the key and find a box of staples. I was capable, wasn't I? Better to take the initiative, climb up on a stool like I had good sense, open the cabinet, retrieve the box of staples, load the stapler, and complete the awesome job. I was O Sole Mio. Who would know?

I settled on the latter course. It was the most efficient, least embarrassing choice a girl could make. I had to come through. It had to work. This was our first history project since we sculpted all those dinosaurs and turned the whole school on its ear. It was my responsibility to get a table up to speed to erect our model pilgrim village. It was a test of leadership. I had to be on the case. When I set a goal, I went for it. After all, I was in the second grade. Heaven help any force of nature trying to come between me and my big-girl panties. I sprang into action.

I ran to the door of the classroom, stuck my head outside, and checked both ways for traffic, especially the angry teacher kind. I was committed at this stage. Once I determined the coast was clear, I shut the door and locked it. Hurrying back to the rear of the room, I shimmied a tall metal stool to the cabinet, coaxing it with all my might. It was labeled with red magic marker warnings: Stop! and Ask permission first! My knobby knees rattled. I disobeyed. I was flaunting a written order. Theoretically, I was a good girl, and to disregard Miss Folley's rules never boded well for anyone. She could waterboard a kid for this if she ever got wind of what went on. She probably would. With a grin on her lips. On stage in the auditorium.

I mounted the stool, my breath loud gasps, my heart thrumming in my size-six chest. My anklet socks, bunched up in loafers, dug into my heels. My fingers, tiny as they were, reached high up toward Ms. Adwell's key chain, Folley's menacing alto protests ringing in my nervous ears.

I flashed on the witch in the *Wizard of Oz* pedaling at me furiously.

Standing on tiptoes, grasping the key, I defiantly turned the lock. It clicked.

The door creaked open.

That's when I saw it.

The corpse in the cabinet.

Crammed, like a crabapple inside a straw.

Boy did it stink, and man did I run.

Miss Folley—Mrs. Stafford now?—was in there, stabbed in both her eyes with a sharp pair of #2 pencils.

No one believed a word I said. Not the janitor. Not the school secretaries.

No teacher I approached. The only response to my cries for help came from Mr. Garofolo, the handsome young assistant principal, who in less than one semester, dated a path through the kindergarten teaching staff and broke five hearts. Mr. G palmed me off on Mr. Copley, the African American Harvard grad who, at just twenty-six years old himself, was the sole guidance counselor in the joint. I could hear them talking through a door.

"Tom," Mr. Garofolo said, "why don't you people teach your nappy-headed kids to tell the truth? This one is smart, but she doesn't know fact from fiction. Lies get girls expelled. We can't tolerate this kind of thing. Are you aware, if I had a gun, there's nothing in the department rules to stop me from shooting the little bitch?"

I stopped crying and started hiccupping as I processed Garofolo's words. Would he kill me for telling him what I knew?

"That's grossly inappropriate," Copley said with a strained and weary voice that revealed volcanic anger. He opened the door and looked down at me. "Spicy, wait for me up the hall," he instructed, guiding my shoulders north as I hiccupped and tried to catch my breath. When the door closed behind him, I turned back around to listen to them arguing as their volume grew louder and more intense. The next thing I heard was a swack and thud.

Mr. Copley emerged with hasty strides, shaking his hand and murmuring, "Mr. Garofolo needs the nurse… Ms. Rainier, please call Ms. Plack," he said, addressing a teaching assistant.

Garofolo rushed past me, whimpering and clutching a fistful of bloody tissues, holding a Coke can to his jaw and shielding a would-be shiner.

Mr. Copley winked at me and said, "Don't worry. It's going to be okay."

He reached for me, but I saw blood on his hand, so I ran for a higher authority. Not Ms. Adwell. Not Mr. Beagle. I ran down the hallway wailing, "Fire!" and set off the fire alarm.

From my vantage point near the administration office, I saw a hectic scene. I marveled as all the doors flew open, kids and teachers flooded forth, and each classroom emptied out in turn, spilling onto Perille Street in the Bronx in a blustery New York snow. It was bitter cold when they filed us out. The weather was icy and gloomy gray. Snowdrifts topped my skinny thighs. I was the only kid without a coat. My teeth were chattering.

There was gonna to be a spanking in this for me, I just knew it.

The firemen arrived in yellow slickers, the police in their scary blue uniforms. They had guns. I was scared they'd shoot me dead. I saw on TV where they shot a kid and nobody ever went to jail or even got detention. Paramedics arrived in an ambulance and listened to my story. They expressed their surprise that no one had bothered to check out classroom 201.

A tall fireman with ice-blue eyes consulted with Mr. Beagle first then squatted down in front of me. "Hello there, Spicy. That's your name?"

I nodded.

"I cook at the firehouse. I use lots of spices there," he said as he wrapped a thin blanket around my back and over my shoulders. "Spicy. What a lovely name."

"Thank you." I politely smiled. "Do you like mustard?"

"Yes, I do."

"I'm Spicy Brown. That's on the jar."

He laughed but for only a moment. "Spicy, did you tell someone you saw a dead woman in room 201?"

"Yes, mister," I said.

"Call me Kenny, okay?"

"Yes, mister."

"Spicy," Kenny said, "can you show me exactly where she was?"

"Uh-huh," I replied as I grabbed his big hand. It was fleshy and rough, as warm as toast, and coated with sooty black stuff like my daddy's hand was when he cleaned Gaga's fireplace. But I didn't mind. He looked just like a prince I once saw in a fairy tale. I liked the brown princes best of all, but I couldn't find many books with those. Or movies. Or cartoons. Mommy told me brown princes live in real life, and when I grow up, I'll meet one. This prince had fluffy orange hair, a badge, and an earring in one ear. And freckles all across his nose. Wow, and he gave me a lollipop. Then he lifted me up and patted my back, and somehow I felt better. Not nearly as good as when Daddy hugged me, but okay enough.

When we hit the third floor, it was not okay.

It was Kenny and me in the lead and behind us folks from a big red fire truck, police people, Dusty the janitor, Mr. Beagle, Copley, and Ms. Plack, the brittle, chinless nurse who hurt me one time when I cut my hand. It bled even worse when she got through. As usual, she wore thick white shoes and brandished a giant set of teeth and a matching king-size toothbrush.

"Where?" Kenny asked, and he squeezed my hand.

I pointed toward the classroom. I was done with answering questions now, over it, ready to take a nap. I wanted to run away and hide. I wanted my mommy. I wanted my daddy. I wouldn't take another step. My pulse was racing so fast and hard I was sure adults could hear it. "There," I said again, planting my feet. The procession came to a jarring halt.

"Where?" asked Kenny.

"Right in there. In the arts and crafts cabinet. On the floor."

"Show me." He gave my arm a tug and pulled me toward the classroom.

The prospect of seeing that gruesome cadaver again made me dig in my heels. "I don't want to look. Go see for yourself. Let me go," I wailed. "She looks so bad. I won't see her again. You can't make me!" I fought to get Kenny to turn me loose.

Exoria Plack clacked the giant teeth and wiggled her wrinkled turkey neck. "Too many Nancy Drew mystery books if you ask me," she commented.

"I didn't ask you," I thought aloud. "I love reading. You can't stop me."

"The stories these kids get in their heads," Mr. Beagle responded offhandedly.

"That odor isn't in her head," said Kenny, striding down the hall. He turned to Ms. Plack and exhorted her. "You're a nurse. Don't you recognize that smell? You ought to detect it a mile away."

Ms. Plack took a whiff. Her nostrils flared. She clenched the gargantuan teeth to her breast, gasped, and fell against the wall.

"Open it!" I ordered Kenny, sick and tired of being dissed. "She's in there like I said."

When the cabinet opened a few moments later, no one expressed any further doubts.

Two grown policemen drew their guns. They crouched and aimed them straight at me. One of them yelled I should put up my hands. The other whipped out a plastic strap.

Dusty pulled me to his side.

Mr. Copley hid me behind his back. "She's seven. Have you lost your minds?"

A policewoman's radio crackled and made Mr. Beagle jump up like a jack-in-the-box.

They sure believed me now.

LESSON #4 ~ *When you know, who cares what others think?*

A female cop hurried me down to the principal's office so fast it went by in a blur. She grilled me like a rack of lamb. A male cop stood by at the door. Another beside the windows.

First came my mom, who got yanked off her job as an editor for a publishing firm. Mom had to ride three subways there, and she rushed in panting, her coat buttoned crooked, her hair in a state of wilding out, her handbag zipper open. "It's okay, baby. Mommy's here." Red-eyed, she knelt and hugged me tight. "Sweetie, are you all right?" she asked.

I couldn't reply. I was too freaked out.

"What have you done to my child?" she admonished, directing her ire at Mr. Copley, Mr. Beagle, and Ms. Plack. Lacking an answer, she turned to me. "Sweetheart, tell Mommy what happened. I'm here. It's over. Don't you worry. Mommy will straighten the whole thing out."

"Miss Folley," I whispered. "Mrs. Sta…" I tried to relay the horrific events but was too traumatized to access my words.

"What's going on here?" Mommy demanded, her voice rising up to a fever pitch. She clutched me inside her hand-knit coat. Her sweet smell made my legs give way.

"Step into my inner office. Please," Mr. Beagle invited. "We need privacy. There's been quite a serious incident," he barked. "We need to address it."

As the door to Mr. Beagle's sanctum closed behind us, I threw up, blowing chunks all over his shiny floor as Mommy rubbed my tummy. Mr. Beagle hurried to grab a trash bin, and through the barely open door, I saw uniformed cops and guys with a gurney, climbing up the steps. Behind them were rubber-gloved women mounting the stairwell, carrying cases.

"Mrs. Brown, I'm afraid there's been a… murder." Beagle finally spit it out.

"Murder? Was it the classroom gerbil? I tried to get Folley to lock that cage," Mom said as she cleaned my jaw and mouth with a wipe she plucked out of a packet.

"No, the victim was human," Beagle avowed, his dentures clicking.

Mommy's jaw dropped, and she blinked a few times. "A murder of a *person*? Here at the school? For what possible reason? What happened? Was it a parent?"

"No, unfortunately it was a teacher," Beagle instructed. "And the police are here."

"What does that have to do with Spicy? Was there a shooter at the school? Where is he now? Did he try to hurt Spicy? Answer me. Was it a hate crime?"

"Probably. No one could stand her guts," Mr. Copley said under his breath.

"Oh my, were any children hurt?"

"No," Mr. Copley said. "Mercifully."

"All the children are fine and accounted for," Mr. Beagle assured my mother.

"Then who—"

"Spicy's teacher, Mrs. Stafford." Copley broke the news.

Mommy sucked in a ragged breath. "What, she's dead? Who murdered her?"

"Policemen want to question Spicy." Beagle mopped his glistening scalp.

The good nature rubbed off my mommy's face like chalk wiped off a blackboard. "Why?" Mommy asked. "Did she witness it?" She sat and lifted me onto her lap, stroking my hair and kissing my head.

"She's a suspect. She found the body," said Mr. Beagle, staring in my eyes.

"Wait. You've got to be kidding, right? You're not seriously saying my second grader killed a teacher in this school." Mommy stood up and gripped me tight.

"She'll be taken into custody—"

"Oh, you think so?" Mommy snipped. "Well, over *my* dead body. You must be crazy, saying that. We resent the accusation. You're smearing an innocent little girl. My child isn't going anywhere but home, and you can bank on that. Tell that to whatever cops you called. Or better yet, tell the *New York Times* when they ask because I'm calling them and contacting my congressman yesterday, and the ACLU, NAACP, CNN, and every acronym except the KKK. You're not railroading my little girl, you hear? I realize she's too smart for you, but Spicy wouldn't hurt a fly. If police touch a hair on her head, I promise you we'll hit back hard."

We heard a commotion in the hall, and Daddy zoomed in, coat flying. Endeavoring to come off cool and calm, evidently more briefed than Mommy was, Daddy breezed in with the family lawyer, Attorney Archie Swipe. Mr. Swipe was a pit bull Daddy's dad grew up with in Barbados. Swipe, a gay sexagenarian ambulance chaser in danger of losing his license, whipped out his business card, cinched his tie, and limped over with help from an ebony cane with a jaguar carved on top of it to slap a manila folder onto Beagle's desk with great panache.

"My client is free to go," Swipe claimed. "From here on out, you contact me. And just between you and me, my friend, we will hold you personally responsible, along with the city authorities, for any trauma to this child. How dare you imagine this tiny girl could begin to commit such a heinous crime, logistically if nothing else, on a woman perhaps three times her size, before you even know the facts? That alone indicates a bias. I'd no longer count on your pension or one penny of savings if I were you."

Mr. Beagle's bald pate turned fuchsia.

During the resultant verbal skirmish, I could only gag and gawk, my feet dangling off the hard lip of a chair. The adults seemed large and powerful for the first time in my little life, and my mother, though clearly distraught, looked intense and prepared to go to battle. I felt dizzy and hot and overwhelmed. My gums began to tingle. I had the sensation of falling down. I felt my daddy pick me up, a darkness creep over my consciousness, and reality fade to background noise.

The following day was awesome.

I don't remember much after I fainted, neither the hospital nor the ride home.

I still only recall waking up the next morning with sun on my curtains and blankets of snow on the ground and the trees in our small backyard. And of course, I remember Thurman.

My best friend and next-door neighbor, nine-year-old Thurman Whitby, stood by me. A certified, bona fide, tested genius, Thurmie lucked up with a whole day off from school to bring me solace. "Right in the eyeballs? Man, that's cool!"

"Thurmie, this isn't a video game."

"Geez, that's got to hurt," he conjectured, shaking off the willies. "Hurts probably worse than getting shot or having your vaccination. I'll have to look into that later on… Whoa, what if she's a zombie now? Or a vampire. She could return that way."

"When people get murdered, they don't come back," I postulated to sober him though I had no idea if that was true.

"When my Nana died, she didn't come back. She said she'd look after me when she was gone, but unless I missed her when she came—which, statistically, counting my sleeping hours, could well be the case—she couldn't return to me after all. Her promise was impractical as, extrapolating mathematically, those odds are very low. Then too, Miss Folley was supermean, and Nana was an angel. So obviously Nana's in heaven, but Miss Folley might not get that far. More likely, she's a ghost."

"What a mean and awful thing to say… You think she's going to haunt me now?"

"It's possible. Face it, she would if she could."

"Oh, Thurmie, what am I going to do? I'm frightened. You're not helping me."

"I'm trying." Thurmie could act so dense.

"Try harder. You're weirding me out! Thurmie, I saw her. All that blood. I keep seeing her over and over again. Seriously, it's a nightmare. What if it never goes away?"

"Oh man, was it like a Jason movie? Michael Myers? Damien?" he asked me wild-eyed, munching chips. "I was Freddy Krueger for Halloween and I hardly got any candy."

"It's terrible. Worse than a horror flick. I'm in trouble, Thurmie. Really bad. I think they think I did it," I confessed and started bawling.

"Well, it's logical," Thurmie reasoned. "You had motive, opportunity. You discovered the body, didn't you? It would seem to make perfect sense. There'll be evidence of her animosity toward you in her grade book, right? And Beagle probably told the cops she treated you like dirt. They'll deduce you resented her abuse. They'll think you fit the profile. Only, you're not an introvert or an outcast or some kind of freak. That should weigh in your favor as murderers go. Plus, you're not a young, white male enraged because somebody told him he'd be displaced by a little girl like you. And you only killed one person, so the random shooter thing won't fit. Conversely, you're young, gifted, Black, and female, thus statistically far more likely to be suspected of almost anything. I wonder how many school days I'll get off to visit you in jail?"

"Whose side are you on?" I nudged his arm. "I. Don't. Want. To. Go. To. Jail!"

"You're a minor. You might not do much time. Unless you're not tried as a juvenile and they finger you as an adult. As a kid, you'll no longer get the chair. You won't be electrocuted."

"Electrocuted. Oh my gosh!"

"Relax, they didn't rough you up like they would if you were me. It's much more likely you'll get off. There are hate groups killing every night and twice on the weekends in some towns. They seldom do time if they get caught, and how often does that happen? And look at Wall Street banking crooks. They never get more than a slap on the wrist. And the villains in Washington. They don't do time. Spies, election fixers, tax evaders, money launderers, cheats. Most of them barely get house arrest. When they wage a fake war that kills thousands of people, hundreds of thousands, around the globe, they're not sent to those federal prison resorts for as long as it takes to cash bad checks. I saw a mass murderer on TV who they treated to burgers before he got booked. I mean, heck, you're just a kid."

"I guess you're right, but just the same, they're framing me to take the fall."

Thurman, who was twice my weight, crumpled the chip bag and glared at me like I sent him to bed without dessert. "Not if I can help it," he declared, taking on that determined look he reserved for conducting experiments in his science lab in his dad's garage. He pushed up from the floor and plopped onto my bed with a bummed-out frown on his chubby face, his Coke-bottle eyeglasses fogging. "Gee, Spice, we have to fix this. Quick. I'll rescue you. You wait and see. I don't normally consort with known criminals, but I sure am on your side." And then he took my hand to add, "I just want you to know, if you go to the slam, I'll be waiting when you get out."

LESSON #5 ~ *A true-blue friend is a wonderful thing. A loyal guy is priceless.*

"The way I see it," Thurman said, "your ability to prevaricate is your best asset at trial. Why, you're the best fibber I know." He continued to damn me with faint praise.

"What? I always tell the truth," I said on the defensive.

"You make up those wonderful stories though. It's fantastic. You're like a talking book."

"So what? That isn't lying."

"Anything lacking empirical data—"

"Thurmie, it's time for you to leave."

"But it's settled, right? You'll tell a lie." Eyes bright, he added, "Better yet, I'm thinking I'll lie *for* you. I'll give you an airtight alibi. You just tell me what to say."

I realized with a sinking feeling this was turning Thurmie on. "But—"

"Spice, what you need is an alibi, and I'm just the guy to provide it. Only, first we'll require additional facts. Let's ascertain the time of death." He inserted his honey-colored thumb in his mouth and started sucking.

"How are we supposed to find that out?"

He took his thumb out of his mouth with a smacking noise and wiped it on his shirt. "Your lawyer, for one, and failing that, I'll check for it in the paper. But of course, we'll have to be careful though. Whoever killed Miss Folley won't much like you getting off the hook. If you get cleared, the hunt is on, and that endangers them. The real killer could want to shut you up."

Thurmie always found inventive ways to totally terrify me.

That's partly why I liked the guy.

"Listen, Spicy, here's the plan," he began, but my mother showed up at the door with a tray with two bowls of tomato soup, two golden grilled cheese sandwiches, two steaming hot mugs of apple juice with cinnamon sticks and apple slices, and some mashed potatoes. *Things must really be bad,* I thought. I traditionally had to run a high fever to warrant this much comfort food. Otherwise, Mom served meat, a carb, and a drastically overcooked vegetable.

When Thurmie dug into his slap-happy meal, I could tell the brainstorming was over. There was no planning, hoping, wishing, dreaming, or anything else with Thurmie once he got a whiff of treats.

We ate in silence.

Thurmie left.

I managed to catch a little nap.

That's when the detectives came calling.

Despite Thurmie's admonitions, I resolved to tell the cops the truth, to explain how I'd found the body in simple terms, without imaginings. It wouldn't be Thurmie keeping house for some freakazoid in cellblock D if they caught me in a bald-faced lie. And telling the truth was right to do. Ostensibly anyway.

The wrong arm of the law tromped through our house, upending every speck of dust, and they weren't wearing uniforms. Instead, they wore cheap suits and shoes. A rude Detective Egan guy, a crew-cut clod with micro-lips, drawn acned cheeks, and dark circles around his glassy eyes kept looking Mommy up and down. I didn't like the *way* he eyed her, like she was a charbroiled steak. The other detective, whose name was Chen, was shorter and slighter than Thurmie was, gnawing what smelled like cinnamon gum. His thick, coercive Southern drawl kept peppering my mom with insulting barbs. I could tell by the way she fired back.

Mom measured them with an appraising gaze. Or maybe it was naked fear.

They rummaged around the dining room, mishandling the delicate china and crystal housed in the new Lucite buffet Daddy bought Mommy two weeks ago as an anniversary gift. Daddy worked overtime to afford it, letting me in on the big surprise "to teach me the value of setting goals." That and to share the excitement with me as I gleefully cheered him on. He told me she saw it in a magazine and assumed she'd never have it. He said, "It's worth working the rest of my life to help her make her dreams come true." He wanted her to know he thought his wife deserved the very best. He said I deserved the finest too, and he bought me a tiny Lucite table when he made my dollhouse. Daddy's not with us anymore, but I always remember what he said, and I know when he referenced the rest of his life, he didn't know it'd be just two years.

Egan rolled evil eyes over Mommy's slender curves and licked his lips. I ran to stand in front of her and gripped her skirt behind my back. "You and your kid better watch yourselves," he growled. "Quit playing games."

"I'm not playing games. We have our rights," said Mommy with her head held high.

"Y'all better cooperate, Li'l Miss Uppity," Chen chimed in. "We're watchin' ya."

"You have no right to search without a warrant. You can't touch our things," my mother asserted, clutching me, gathering her neckline in a bunch. "I never should have let you in. I was trying to cooperate. You said you came to ask questions. Ask them now or you can leave." She squinted. "On second thought, leave now," she bade them, moving like a dancer, crossing to the foyer door.

"What, you got something to hide in here?" asked Egan, refusing to leave us alone.

"Spicy, go get the telephone," my mother directed.

I retrieved it.

Mommy dialed Attorney Swipe.

Egan threw Mommy down onto the sofa, snatched the receiver, and tossed it away. Then he and Chen trashed our living room, dining room, kitchen, bedrooms, baths, and basement, rifling through our family photo albums, pots and pans, the pantry, laundry, Mommy's lingerie. I saw Egan sniff a pair of pink lace panties, slip it in his pocket, then upend Mommy's panty drawer. The detectives overturned my room, and I watched them destroy my dollhouse, easel, bookcase, Scooby-Doo pencil case, pink lamp, and Barbie bedding. By the time Attorney Swipe arrived and got rid of the inquisition team, our once-pristine home resembled the messy result of a frat house party.

"Don't worry, Mommy." I patted her back. "I'll clean it. Just forget those guys."

Mommy looked on in shock as Attorney Swipe asked questions of his own.

I recounted my account as best I could, and the hideous weeks leading up to it. I divulged Miss Folley hit me. I told about the desk assignments, how she got angry as I moved up, how she liked to hurt my feelings. Swipe looked sad as he took notes.

"Spicy, go upstairs," said Mommy after the lawyer bid goodbye. "I think you ought to take a nap."

In my room, I sat on the edge of my bed and took in the destruction.

I froze when I heard the front door slam.

"The place looks like a tornado hit it," Daddy hollered. "What went on?"

I sneaked to the top of the stairs, looked down.

"Sh, she's sleeping," Mommy said. "Calm down. I'm working on it."

Mommy explained all about the detectives, omitting that they manhandled her.

"We're not going to take this lying down," said Daddy. "We'll fight back. We'll ruin the bastards before they ruin us. They're trying to destroy our lives. Look at this bombshell," Daddy said as I peered down through the banister and craned my head to try to hear. He handed my mommy a newspaper folded open to an article, his chiseled cinnamon features tied in a knot as he paced the living room as if his heels caught fire. "I don't understand why they're dragging a sweet little innocent girl like Spicy into a crime it's so clear she could never commit."

Mommy responded, "I called the *Times*. Gwendolyn Farmer works there now. I edited that book she wrote, exposing the music industry and how its discrimination works, remember? She's got juice. The book's a bestseller. She owes me one, and she's really pumped up about our plight. She's starting a story about us tomorrow, from Spicy's family's point of view."

"We need it. They're casting suspicion on *us*," said Daddy, closing the curtains.

"I wondered how long that leap would take," said Mommy. "Better us than Spicy."

"Yeah, we're adults. We're equipped to fight back," Daddy said.

"Our baby's just learning how," said Mommy. "It's not fair."

"I intend to protect her, no matter what. Whatever it takes to make this nightmare go away for her, I'm down. I'll do anything. *Anything* for her, dear. I don't want you to worry."

Mommy sagged into a floral wing chair, fanning herself with the front of her blouse, her normally peachy complexion turning a sickly shade of pea-soup green. "The word's getting out, and people are talking," said Mommy. "This could ruin her reputation for a lifetime if we let it stand. We have to turn the tide right now."

"It's gonna trash us too," said Daddy, untying his tie and snapping it. "They'll be floating the theory her parents took revenge for what Folley did to her, but you and I have alibis that can put the lie to whatever they say. It's okay; we're not to blame."

"It makes me so angry I could spit. If our child was a blonde, they would call her a victim," Mommy said. "They'd be placing a halo around her head, vowing to catch the real killer and lamenting the fact that that poor little girl had to stumble upon a body."

Daddy knelt down in front of Mommy, stroked her hair, and cupped her hands. "I know it's the last thing you want to hear, but we have to absorb a financial blow with everything else that's going on. I had to set them straight at work. And I did it in spades, believe you me… I'm sorry, dear, I lost my job."

Mommy stood up, smoothed her hair, and walked off like a zombie.

"Where are you going?" Daddy asked.

"You need a cup of coffee, sweetheart."

"I need to bust somebody's—"

"Sh…" Mom put her finger to her lips as my bunny slippers trod the stairs.

"There's my princess." Daddy smiled. "Now she's feeling better. Guess who's going to the zoo this weekend. Whaddaya say?"

"I don't think it'd be good. I caused too many problems."

Daddy lifted my chin. "Now you listen to me. You aren't the problem, you understand? It's not your fault Miss Folley died. We know you didn't hurt her. You're a beautiful, kind, and loving girl. We have nothing to hide from anyone. Nothing to be ashamed of, kid. You and your mother and I are happy, healthy, prosperous people. Good people. We can do anything. Whatever we put our minds to, got it? That especially goes for you."

"But you didn't even ask me if I did it," I said, my head hung down.

"That's because we know you couldn't. It's not in your nature, Spice," said Mommy.

"Did you?" Daddy asked me then.

"Oh, sweetheart. Why would you—?"

"Honey, let her answer," Daddy insisted. "Did you, Spice?"

"No, Daddy, I didn't hurt her," I cried. "I never want to hurt anyone. I felt sorry for Miss Folley. Nobody liked her. Not one kid. And the teachers liked her even less. Nobody thought about how she was crossed-eyed. Maybe she couldn't see and that's why she was crabby. She could've got bullied too. I don't know why she hated me, but I didn't want to be like that. I want to be like you and Mommy, Daddy. I feel guilty now. If it weren't for me, we'd all be fine. How are we going to get out of this? What did I do wrong?"

"You didn't do wrong. You're all that's right." Daddy wiggled his fingertips, tickled my ribs, and made a silly funny face. "The truth will come out soon enough. Keep your chin up, hear me, baby? Lift the corners of your mouth and turn that brown frown upside down." He grinned, and we rubbed noses.

Daddy could always make things better. Daddy was my hero. Daddy was strong and sturdy, medium height with large, thick hands. He had a handsome pecan-colored face, white teeth, a trim mustache, a muscular frame, huge onyx eyes, and a short, wavy thicket of coarse dark hair. His blue-white shirt was as crisp as a cracker. His pants creased like an envelope, and he walked with awesome swagger. Everyone called him a fashion plate, like the cover of a magazine. He allowed me to tie a Windsor knot in his tie every morning at seven a.m. He would ask me which tie would go best with his suit, stand me up on the foot of my parents' bed, and patiently watch me whip the tie around and square it up. When it was done, he would cross the room and joke, "The finished product." Then we'd all laugh and start the day.

"It will always be the three of us. It's going to be Mommy, baby, and me," he said with a grin and kissed my brow.

The doorbell rang. My tummy churned.

"Not again," Mommy said and shivered.

"I'll get it," said Daddy. "I'll send them away. Whoever it is, I'll blow them off."

As Daddy marched bravely to the door, it occurred to me just how lucky I was to have such parents filled with love.

LESSON #6 ~ *Pull together in times of crisis, or you'll soon be pulled apart.*

It was Cookie Whitby at the door, Thurmie's bubbly mother. She was bearing hot tuna casserole, asparagus with Hollandaise, those cute cupcakes she loved to make, and a wealth of information. Aunt Cookie was broad, big-haired, and buxom, light on her feet and quick to laugh. And considering how often her home got disheveled by Thurmie's ambitious chemistry projects, her good-natured giggles amounted to major feats of maternal pride. She recently won the Pillsbury Bake-Off with something called "Survival Pie," and her skin was the color of fresh-baked rolls.

"Well, I guess I know what went on here," rang out in the contralto voice that starred in our church choir. "This place looks like a cyclone hit. I saw the cops comin', so I baked a cake. I should've thrown it at them. Do they all gotta show such disrespect? Y'all know they shot up Sadie's place out searchin' for some teen they say looked like her son LeKwame, right? Thank goodness he was gone to work. Her poodle caught six rounds." She handed Mom the casserole. "I figured lil Spicy could use a snack and you could use a break."

"Yum, it's still warm. You're a life-saver, Cook," Mommy said. "We'll dig right in."

Aunt Cookie asked, "How are y'all holdin' up?"

"We're hanging in here, Cookie," Daddy fronted.

"Yeah, when things get tough, that's all we can do."

"What's up?" asked Mommy, keen for gossip, taking hold of Cookie's hand.

"I got the scoop, girl, that's what's up." Aunt Cookie, who was a plus-size girl, crowded her bulk onto half the couch as the three of us gathered around her. She gazed at me with forlorn eyes and handed me some Gummi Bears. "First, my Thurman sent you these."

"Thanks," I said and took the bag. "His favorite," I said brightening. "Tell him I ate a red one first." I opened the package, found a red one, popped it in my mouth.

Aunt Cookie moaned, "He's on a tear. The boy's eatin' us out of house and home for frettin' and worryin' over you. Just since that chile come today, he done already gobbled up six hot dogs, four baked potatoes, polished off my spinach pie, and downed near half a chocolate cake. He went straight to his bedroom, closed the door, and didn't watch no science shows. And that's a first since preschool, chile. He wants to get this mess cleared up."

"Cookie," said Mommy, inching closer, "what's that scoop you said you had?"

"Oh yeah, I lost my train of thought." Aunt Cookie shuffled her bulky thighs from the back of the couch to the edge of it. It creaked as she moved, and we saw it bow. "They got more suspects poppin' up. New ones. All around. You know that Mr. Copley, right? Well, he punched Garofolo in the jaw and almost broke it. They made Garofolo press charges on Copley. Phony, but they just might stick. Copley's got a record. They say when he was at Harvard he pulled a knife on a professor there. That means he tends to violence."

"Oh no, not Mr. Copley, Mommy. Mr. Copley's really nice."

Mommy only licked her lips. "Who else?"

"Fred Beagle, honey bun."

"Beagle?" Daddy queried her. "The principal's got some dirt on him?"

"Turns out…" she started, then she stopped and jerked her head to reference me.

"Oh, lately Spicy's seen it all," said Mommy with a dismissive wave. "She's taking it better than any of us. Can't shield her from the truth."

"Them two was doin' it!" Cookie wailed. "On the daily." She guffawed.

Doing what? I wondered as she laughed. Some parents could be so obtuse.

"Beagle and Folley?" Daddy questioned. "Now I know you're lyin', Cook."

"If I'm lyin', I'm flyin'. I seen pix… Right under Mr. Stafford's nose. And during recess, for heaven's sakes. In the broom closet, as I understand. The affair began three years ago and didn't slow down when Folley got engaged to Mr. Stafford. He was still married at the time. The cops are checkin' that out too. This afternoon, they perp-walked Stafford out of the music room in cuffs and rode him to the station. Something about some threatening notes he exchanged with his ex back in the day. And of course, the husband tops the list of suspects in a murder case. Y'all might be on the back burner at this point, though not for long."

"This is fantastic," Mommy whooped. She slapped her thigh and clapped her hands.

"And that ain't all the buzz out there," Aunt Cookie said and wagged her head.

"This is just too good," said Daddy.

Aunt Cookie continued, "The dental hygienist whatshername, the chinless chile?"

"Miss Plack," I hastened to volunteer.

"Turns out slick-sly Jane Folley stole ole Beagle from Miss Plack."

"Shut up," Mom said. "You're kidding me."

"Him and the nurse was together first, but apparently Folley set her sights on him and that was that."

"Who'd peg *him* for a Lothario?" Daddy asked and stroked his chin.

"You gotta watch them quiet ones," Aunt Cookie said. "They freaky deaky."

Daddy turned to Mommy. "As soon as this blows over, we're enrolling Spice in private school. She's taking class in Peyton Place."

"At least that takes the weight off us," Mom said, inhaling long, deep breaths.

"Not quite," Aunt Cookie stated. "Them pencils stuck in Folley's eyes was just like Spicy's pencils is."

Oops. I knew that wasn't good. It landed with a thud. Like the time Thurmie farted so loud in church that even the organ player stopped and sniffed and looked around.

"That doesn't mean anything," Daddy protested, fingers drumming the coffee table. "All parents buy those cheap-o pencils. They suspect the whole damn school?"

Aunt Cookie said, "Wait. Hold on a sec. Seems Folley wrote hateful school evaluations into Spicy's records. Not for Spicy's schoolwork—Folley couldn't deny she got straight A's—but for 'attitude' is what she wrote. 'Behavioral' is what she said. 'Sassy' is what she labeled her. The deaf hear that dog whistle. Folley's prejudice was real. Y'all know I'm the head of the PTA, so certain things get back to me."

"I caught wind of some nasty remarks myself," Mom said, "and I confronted her."

Aunt Cookie frowned and clicked her teeth. Her animated breasts leaned close. "That didn't stay secret very long. It's common knowledge y'all had a set-to back on parent-teacher day. Faculty says she used the N-word, callin' Spicy out her name with awful racial slurs."

"Good thing I didn't know till now," said Daddy. "Or I might be guilty. I could wring that woman's neck."

"Don't even joke like that," said Mommy. "Let that hate speech be on her."

"You're right. She's dead. It's over with," said Daddy, "till the next hate comes."

"I asked Beagle if he knew about it," Cookie told us with a frown, "but he brushed me off and dressed me down. He told me I sounded completely absurd and I wasn't to mention it ever again. But the dude was arranging a cover-up, and now we know why, don't we, friends? The man was protecting his chick on the side."

"Where do those people get the nerve?" said Daddy. "That's corruption."

"How do we get Spicy's records corrected?" Mommy asked. "That's all that matters. They can impair her future if we let them stay the way they are. Those lies could follow her all her life. How many other kids' lives were ruined during the school years Folley taught?"

"It's out in the open," Aunt Cookie said. "It's busted. Eyes are on it now. The school board, parents, and the mayor. She called for a review of Folley's student files to see what's justified and what was blatant sabotaging of minorities at the school. You better be cool about Folley though. None of that junk don't change the fact you threatened her and people saw."

"I threatened to report her," Mommy said. "Not take her life."

"As long as your child detected that stiff, alone in the room with no supervision, y'all are in the crosshairs."

"Why was she left alone to begin with?" Daddy asked her. "That's the question."

"Spicy had no business in that classroom by herself," said Mommy.

"That's for sure. You oughta beef it. Subs aren't always qualified. Some substitutes are better than the teachers. Others stink." Aunt Cookie snapped her fingers. "Oh, I almost forgot. There's one more thing. Another kid. A girl. Her last name starts with S. Not Small…"

"Short?" I piped up. "Stacey Short?"

"That's the name," Aunt Cookie said.

"What about her?" Daddy asked.

"Dusty the janitor claims he caught her swiping Folley's purse."

"Stealing?" I choked on a Gummi Bear. I had a green one in my mouth.

"He caught her the same day Folley left."

"Well, that's a coinkydink, isn't it," said Mommy.

"What did he do?" asked Daddy.

"Same thing I would do; he buried it. He kept his mouth shut and went on with his life. The girl's father heads the city council. Dusty decided to put the purse back in the desk and zip his lip. He figured, next thing they'd arrest him for it. He didn't want to get involved."

"Did they determine when Folley died?" asked Mommy, reading my mind again.

Aunt Cookie shrugged and scratched her wig with a long, acrylic fingernail. "Far as I know, they didn't say when or where she was killed. It's a mystery. No one knows why she turned up at the school. She was supposed to be out on leave."

Daddy said, "Interesting. Doesn't add up… I wonder if someone lured her there."

"Or maybe they killed her somewhere else," said Mommy. "And they dumped her there."

"I'm keeping my ear to the ground," Aunt Cookie said. "I'll keep you posted."

"Thanks. You're the best," Mommy said with a smile.

"Ditto. And thank Morris," Dad said. "Tell him I owe him that game of chess."

"He'll sure be glad to hear it. Well, all righty, I better get back to Thurm," Aunt Cookie declared with her trademark giggle. "He might'a ate our stove by now." Groaning, she double-pumped off the couch, bent over, and gave me a bear hug.

"Thank Thurmie for the gummies too," I said and pecked her on the cheek.

"My boy would do anything for you."

TV cameras were camped out on our doorstep, blocking the streets and drawing crowds.

The scrutiny was off the chain. Not to mention our neighbors' consternation due to the noise and invasion of privacy caused by nosy passersby. Our phone kept ringing off the hook until Daddy unplugged it from the wall except for the times he conferred with Archie Swipe, who spent most of the day contacting cops about our legal status.

Swipe, admittedly out of his league, recommended we hire one of his buddies, Benjamin Robeson Fortiet, a criminal lawyer widely regarded as top dog in his field. Fortiet had a high media profile matching his astronomical fee. Daddy had to call a bank about a second mortgage. That blow sent Mommy up to bed with a hot water bottle and aspirin tabs.

Swipe was determined to get to the bottom of how my identity leaked so fast. I was a minor and that was verboten, but Daddy said to let it go. The cat was out of the bag and the horse was out of the barn, was his retort. He preferred to file a complaint against the detectives who defiled our home. Swipe agreed to draw up papers, suggesting it'd help with our legal fees if we managed to prevail, and maybe if there were a trial to come, the suit could prove the NYPD had acted out of bias.

When Daddy announced my bedtime, I was the loneliest girl in the galaxy. Up in my room, I put on my jammies, unlocked my diary, wrote a brief entry, and dozing, hit upon a plan. I wished Thurmie was with me to flesh it out, but all I could do was eat Gummi Bears, press my brow to the plaster wall, feel its coolness numb my stress, and succumb to a fitful, fretful sleep.

I issued the ultimatum to Thurmie as soon as he checked in. "Are you with me or not?"

He mashed his lips and punched my calculator. "Probability of a successful outcome—"

"Yes or no?" was my demand. "It's almost noon already."

"Okay, I will, if you insist. But what if it only makes things worse?"

"I'll blame it on you," I said and laughed.

We used Mommy's desktop computer to type six letters and six envelopes: one each to Mr. Beagle, Mr. Stafford, Mr. Copley, Mr. Garofolo, and Miss Plack. The sixth, we directed to Stacey Short. The first five letters read as follows: "I saw what you did to Mrs. Stafford. If you don't want it on the news, bring a whole thousand dollars at midnight tonight to the oak tree in the schoolyard. Be there, or else!" We signed, "A friend." Looking back, it wasn't subtle, but it certainly was provocative. To the letter to Stacey, we added this: "P.S.—Don't tell your parents."

Thurmie, the hyperintelligent son of the gossipy head of the PTA, located the targets' addresses in his mother's bulging address book. We bundled the notes in Thurmie's coat.

Lacking permission to go outside, I had Thurmie deliver the missives via bike into enemy territory under the guise of his paper route. In an effort to bring him needed luck, I tied my scarf around his neck like I saw a medieval maiden do in a book from the library. Thurmie sneaked out through the rear cellar door to avoid being hassled by the press.

He returned empowered, jazzed, and flushed. "Done," he said, and we shook hands.

11:00 p.m. that eventful night.

I awoke with a start to the clanging alarm of my Minnie Mouse clock.

I bolted up. The dark was disconcerting. Rattled, I listened for signs of parental life but heard nothing around me stir. Scrambling out of my *Jem and the Holograms* jammies, I slipped on jeans and a top. I put on a pullover sweater, donned red socks inside my orange Keds, wrapped the strap of my camera around my neck, and stripped the sheets off my canopy bed. They were harder to tie than I thought they'd be, but I relied on Girl Scout knots to daisy chain the bedding. Minnie's puffy, outstretched mitts signaled the time was eleven fifteen. Okay, it was time to make my move.

In the dark, I tiptoed to my door, placed my hand on the knob, and slowly turned it. *Click!* It opened with a creak, and the snap of the lock exploded through the silent second floor.

I stiffened, waited, held my breath, and poised to hop back into bed in case my mom or dad awoke. I widened the opening a tiny sliver, peered out to the hall.

No sound. No light. The coast was clear.

I eased the door shut and donned my coat, tiptoed to the bedroom window, unlatched it, slid it open, heard it squeal. *Quiet. Quiet. Almost there…* Raising the stubborn dry wood frame of my window upward inch by inch, I got stunned by a blast of winter wind that slapped me like Miss Folley's hand. My tummy swelled up like a water balloon. Oh no. I suddenly had to wee. I needed to tinkle really badly, but I knew I had to hold it.

I looked out the window. Two stories down. The ground telescoped even farther away. I unraveled the sheet-ladder out the window and shimmied down it, holding tight, knots stopping my feet at intervals to ensure a safe descent. I pushed against the frosty bricks and swung to the top of the mulberry tree. From there, I descended. That was fun. *Ah*, I sighed, as I touched the grass and realized I'd hit bottom.

"Gotcha!" A hand clamped over my mouth.

I tried to scream, but the hand was firm. I writhed and squirmed and kicked and bit, but an arm encircled my tiny waist, and the next thing I knew I was smothered by a thick blanket pulled over my head. I resisted by tugging against the cloth but was wrestled to the ground.

"Stop it." It was Thurmie's voice.

I struggled under the blanket and managed to surface for a breath of air. "Thurmie, get off me. You scared me to death!"

"But Spice, it's just thirteen degrees. Why didn't you bother to wear a hat? Body heat can escape through the top of your head."

"Your head is the one with the hole in it," I chided.

"What? I rescued you. Hypothermia's nothing to trifle with."

"Neither am I. I almost peed!" I admitted, spooked and furious. "What are you doing here anyway?"

"I'm saving you from yourself."

"And who's going to save me from *you*?" I fussed.

"Oh, quit being silly. C'mon, let's go."

11:45 p.m.

Thurmie and I approached school grounds. We trotted together, hand in hand, keeping to shadows that veiled the street. Thurmie's hand was sticky. The part of the yard outside the fence was eerie and deserted. I'd never considered what school was like at night, except when I played with the band, and then I had my parents and my flute to focus on. I was happy Thurmie was with me now. He had a flashlight, pocket knife, binoculars, two Snickers bars, Aunt Cookie's red pepper spray canister, a thermos of hot chocolate, and his well-worn baseball bat. His backpack was a cross between a pantry and a magician's chest. I could never be sure what would pop out next.

We hid in a bush across from the oak tree, huddling, sipping cocoa.

"Hey, what if no one shows up, Spice?"

"We retreat," I had to capitulate. "We regroup and think up something else."

Ten minutes later.

We got a nibble. Someone took the bait.

At first it looked like a homeless person appearing out of nowhere. Hunched over in a long frock coat. Creeping. We couldn't see a face. Thurmie peered through his binoculars.

"Who is it?" I asked and yanked his sleeve.

"Can't tell. Here, take a look through these."

The binoculars were so powerful they made the phantom creature seem as close to me as Thurmie. But still, I couldn't make out a face. I saw it wasn't a coat they wore but a cape with a clasp and draping hood. The cloaked figure advanced, looking back and forth, proceeding toward the towering oak with something in its hand.

Thurmie's wide round eyes swept my own. "Whadda we do?"

"Get a picture," I said.

"How?" he inquired.

"We get up close."

"Oh heck no. Nope, we're staying here. If my goal was committing suicide, I'd eat myself to death."

"Don't worry. I have a master plan."

"When do you *not* have a master plan?" he whined. "That gets me grounded."

The figure disappeared from view. All we could see was the towering oak and the trail of the phantom's dark, billowing cloak.

"Get down on your knees," I exhorted Thurmie.

"I think it's a little late to pray."

"I need to climb up on your shoulders," I whispered. "Swing your backpack to the front."

Thurmie dropped to his knees with a quizzical look, reversed the backpack, braced himself. I mounted on his shoulders. I wrapped the large blanket over my head, draping it lengthwise to cover us both, and... *Poof!* We were a grownup. Sort of. It was kinda lame.

Thurmie, moving like a panther much to my surprised delight, gripped the red pepper spray trigger and inched up on the figure from behind. I pointed my camera, prepared to shoot.

Surprise! We got the drop on it, and jamming the flashlight in its back, Thurmie, in a man's voice, boomed, "Drop the hood, you murderer. Turn around and keep your hands up."

The phantom turned around, all right. It reeled on us like a whirling dervish, snapping its cloak like a giant bat wing, knocking us kids down. We scrambled up and tried to run but got tangled in the blanket. It reminded me of the time my Brownie troop collapsed our camping tent and got trapped inside the canvas when we thought we heard a grizzly bear.

I screamed but the sound got caught up in my throat and turned muted and inaudible. I reached out for Thurmie but came up empty, the phantom's punches thrusting us apart, tattooing my head and neck. Thurmie hauled off and slung his backpack, but a swift kick knocked him cold. *Ouch!* A sharp object stuck me once, twice, three times, over and over again. In my arms, my back, my legs, my side, drawing blood I could feel run down my hip. It jabbed me like a nail or knife, puncturing me in several places. I could barely stand the pain. The figure attacked. I fell down on my back, the phantom looming over me, straddling, slashing, cutting, scraping.

Something sharp plunged toward my eyes. A pencil. A fistful of sharpened pencils. Just like the pencils that killed Miss Folley.

I raised my camera and fired a volley of blinding flashes into the darkness, catching the phantom foe off guard. It raised its arm to shield its eyes. I kicked and sent it reeling backward, spotting its clunky, worn black shoes—that looked like old Ms. Adwell's.

Afterward, everything kind of blurred. I remember twisting an orthopedic shoe and shrieking, "Don't hurt Thurmie!" There was a foot inside that shoe, and it was attached to a leg that broke and a hip that fell and fractured. I vaguely remember the wail of police car sirens, swirling fog and strobing lights, and a hairy ride home in the back seat of a squad car speeding terribly fast. Detectives Egan and Chen transported me back to the house, much nicer now. They were so eager to bust me they surveilled me like they said they would, so they saw me run away that night. It evidently saved my life. And Thurmie's. He recovered.

Thurmie is now an astrophysicist with a world-renowned conglomerate he's owned since he was twenty-one. He plans to go to Mars. He also secretly runs a Silicon Valley think tank, blogs, invents, and hosts a TV science show. He recently won a Nobel Prize.

Ms. Adwell wasn't the sub's real name. She was born Bettina Sharp. We learned she was mentally deranged, an escapee from an institute for the criminally insane. She was the sister of Folley's ex-husband, who Folley messed over years before in an earlier spate of philandering that ended in his suicide. His demise drove Adwell to our class for revenge through Folley's murder. She got Folley to meet her at school by pretending to be Miss Plack with evidence that Stafford contracted HIV in the weeks before they married. She killed her as soon as she arrived.

There were so many suspects in the case that nobody's name was really cleared and a pall hung over several lives. What with the crazy romantic hijinks going on between the Staffords, Mr. Beagle, and Miss Plack, no one shook the scandal.

Stacey, who stole Miss Folley's purse, pilfered it to purchase drugs. Her mother, chained to opioids, birthed Stacey into a life of addiction. When Folley found out she took the purse, she gave Folley our note to save herself.

Mr. Copley, who'd pulled a knife on his Harvard professor, got booted off the staff. He heads a small nonprofit now that works to help kids stay in school. It was later revealed that a rabid anti-affirmative-action crusading instructor unfairly failed Copley to sabotage his academic scholarship. Copley didn't stab the guy, only threatened to knife him to scare him into filing the real grade Copley earned, but Copley went on to teach the way he wished he'd once been taught.

LESSON #7 ~ *In the pithy words of Santa Claus, "Be good for goodness' sake."*

As for my family, Thurmie, and me, we netted a commendation from the mayor and the city council. Retractions from journalists issued next, apologies from the police commissioner, Chen, and even Egan. Then came toys, stuffed animals, college tuition, and sweet-smelling floral bouquets. We also got such epithets as "smart-mouth nigger" and "pickaninny" expunged from my school records, a process that proved "more arduous and time-consuming than it should." That's what my husband, Thurman, wrote in his doctoral thesis anyway, and his clinical studies at Harvard served to begin to change the process through which substitutes get vetted.

I learned a lot of lessons in those tough few days and passed them on. I learned that, though I was small in stature, I could be brave and powerful. That I had a mighty power of one and I could make a difference. I could change the world from the inside out in even an adverse circumstance. I learned that in a world of good people some folks chose to do bad things. I learned morality is a choice and each of us has to make that choice and act accordingly. I learned everything each of us does affects the universe and its inhabitants in awful or in wondrous ways. I understood good could come from bad and decided to always work for good at a very early age. I realized what special people my parents were, how much they loved their child, how very much I adored them both, what a magical blessing family is, and the gift of having special friends.

I learned about racism too. Firsthand. That lesson was unfortunate. But I also learned that people who might harbor a negative assumption about me and actively seek to do me harm because of the color of my skin can never diminish my destiny or who I was or could become. I realized in the second grade that only irrational fear could deter me, depress my spirit, dim my light, or repress my ardent passion. Oppression could never snatch one possibility away from me, not in the overall scheme of things. I learned the boundless miracles of my talents, abilities, dreams, potential, and endless hope inside my soul would ultimately triumph.

I was no pariah. I was a fighter, a doer, a visionary. I would achieve through amazing grace. I'd follow a greater calling to be the most generous spirit I could be.

Still, I wondered if the blessing of being an African American female in this world would always make things hard.

That, too, is settled. Now I know.

GREENES
WITH ENVY

Their start-up kicked off at nine o'clock and ended at nine thirty.

Kenishia and Kayvon Kartaway were conducting a gala red-carpet launch to celebrate their new website for merchandise liquidation. The Kartaways formed Turnover.com to compete with the likes of Overstock and other behemoth online stores. Their business was set to officially enter the marketplace in twelve short hours, and their hope for success was set sky-high. They'd invited their friends and relatives, business associates, colleagues, and the press to delight in the Kartaway story and their brand as comeback kids. Dealing in surplus goods was a breath of fresh air for the married couple, a method of reinventing what had been their prior success. Buy low, sell high, ensure good value just as they'd done as singing stars. Excellence was the core of their business plan—giving back to communities that supported their music days.

The Kartaways had topped the charts, but due to a series of downturns, hit the skids and hadn't quite bounced back. They were keen to establish an income stream to get back on their feet and move ahead, but the path had not been easy. They'd failed at a couple of ventures after their R&B career had tanked, but they'd found they were talented entrepreneurs who could spot big opportunities, act with good timing, exhibit good taste and, following the show-business adage that every performance should open and close with a bang, market with dramatic flair.

The launch was in the works for months. It was planned to go off without a hitch.

Kenishia turned heads in a pink-sequin dress, and Kayvon sported a Sean John tux as clean as 007's. Champagne flowed with hot hors d'oeuvres, and Hollywood lights lit empty shelves prepared for merchandise arrival now behind the curve. The stock was late unfortunately due to hiccups in the transportation pipeline they had put in place. The delay was a source of major stress as some orders wouldn't be coming in until after the site went live. Some products would drop-ship to buyers directly from local manufacturers, but others were meant to be kept in stock from vendors overseas. The Kartaways had the foresight to set the order arrival dates far enough in the future to under-promise and over-deliver supplies to customers, and they hired sufficient personnel to fill the pending orders. But in case the logjam stretched too far, they hoped the goodwill they'd built up as a socially responsible entity might prevail.

Kayvon and Kenishia believed in giving and helping others build their dreams, beginning with hiring practices. Their employees formed an odd-ball group they felt could use a break. Turnover's front office consisted of Trent Cunningham, an auditor and expert accountant who'd driven drunk and beaten a manslaughter charge; Nola Dunbar, a quick-witted legal eagle living down her seedy past as the madam of a call-girl ring with an international clientele; and warehouse manager, Farley Traylor, downsized from a shady firm that closed because an investigation sent it into bankruptcy. The remaining crew were part-time workers—graduate students, buyers, techs, paid interns, and ex-convicts working to assimilate into society after committing minor offenses. Those were the bulk of the employees, paid wages over minimum. Some of them manned the telephones, others kept the website live, still others maintained the computer banks or worked to manage stock. So far, the group was faring well.

Trent, Nola, and Farley helped orchestrate every aspect of the enterprise, from financing to sourcing to SEO, publicity, ads, acquisitions, deliveries, contracting, and smooth product flow. Turnover.com was competing in a cutthroat web-based ethos that could chew up and spit out faulty setups in one bite, so they had to be on their toes. The company purchased excess goods from companies that were dissolving and thus selling off their assets. Often, this happened in bankruptcies. Creditors, with a court's permission, tried to recoup whatever they could, or sometimes shareholders sought a way to convert inventory into cash. From them, one could buy bulk bargains for just pennies on the dollar if one bargained well, then resell at near market price.

The Kartaways' first big haul was meant to blow everyone away. Designed to show up at nine at night, a caravan of freight trucks would arrive at the warehouse loading dock hauling ten million dollars' worth of goods—a discontinued line of textiles purchased in China and Taiwan, a stash of computer hardware from a Silicon Valley plant shutdown, a bevy of natural beauty supplies from a Brooklyn broker Farley knew, a whole catalog's worth of close-out clothes made of cotton grown in the USA, some silk scarves bought in India, crystal jewelry made in Austria, carpeting, lighting fixtures, antique case goods, purses, cell phones, shoes, big-screen TVs, books, furniture, musical instruments, office supplies, china, flatware, boots, and wigs. At eight forty-five, a bank of rented floodlights lit the receiving bays and the lights in the warehouse dimmed to half. Kayvon and Kenishia led their guests to a platform at a loading dock to goggle at the fleet.

A live band played to build suspense. The air crackled. The show was about to go on.

At 8:51, Kayvon and Kenishia sang their hit "A Brand-New Life," and the song brought down the house. When it ended, Kenishia took the mic and spoke from the heart to delighted guests. "Our mission," she said after clearing her throat, "is to offer affordable upscale goods to low-income neighborhood residents, recycle unsold items that might otherwise overflow city dumps, and contribute cash and consumables to charities we hold dear. All this and, well… make money too."

There was laughter at that, and then Kayvon continued, "It's been a big thrill and a lot of hard work, but with all of you good friends by our sides and support from our buds in the media, Turnover can be a force for good for many years to come. And please know that my beautiful wife and I are here for you like you've been here for us. Drink up. Enjoy yourselves."

Kenishia dabbed her teary eyes. Applause broke out. Band music swelled. Hefty LED headlights lit the scene at precisely nine p.m. Engines rumbled. Pavement shook. A shiny Mack truck hood ornament caught a beam of moonlight as it rounded a corner, casting bling along its route. Guests cheered, clinked rented champagne flutes, and struck up a chorus of oohs and aahs.

Kenishia's heart fluttered and skipped a beat. Kayvon beamed beside her.

The caravan ambled toward the bay. The first three rigs crept into it, backing up one at a time beside one another like can-can dancers. The rest of the trucks—there were twelve in all—stood idling, rumbling on the street, lined up with screeching air brakes.

The lead driver, a burly blond hulk in torn jeans, leaped down from his perch behind the wheel, hocked, spit on the concrete, rubbed his eyes, and lumbered to Kayvon. Limping, he rolled up the tattered sleeves of a washed-out red-plaid flannel shirt. Upon sighting the guests, he furrowed his brow, circled his shoulders, yawned, and stretched. "Press hard, fourth copy's yours, my friend," he said with a chuckle, eyeing Kenishia. "I gotta get both signatures," the hauler barked and winked. "It says on the instructions. There." He pointed to the paper.

"Thanks," Kayvon said and hugged his wife. "We'll sign it as soon as it all checks out. We have a receiving procedure. We're a little short on staff to inspect the goods and tag them all tonight, but we can begin the review and match the loads to the bill of lading. Our crew has a checklist of the stock, and we authorized the purchase orders. There should be no problem."

"Yes, sir," said the driver, tipping his cap. "You're the boss. Come take a look."

Kayvon gazed down at his soul mate, stroked her hair, peered into her twinkling eyes, and gave her a gentle, soulful kiss. "Mission accomplished. Dream come true."

"I can't wait," she said and smooched him back. "Can you even believe it's happening?"

With a clatter, the back of the truck peeled open. Kenishia turned and clapped her hands. But instead of the crates that should have appeared, there was nothing but empty cargo space.

"Where's the merchandise?" Kenishia asked. "Is it all packed in those other trucks?"

"Yeah, what's up, man, nothing's here," said Kayvon with a chuckle.

"There was," said the driver. "I don't get it."

"Wait. Are you kidding me? Where'd it go?" Kayvon smiled toward the party guests, their faces alive with anticipation. "Let's go on to the next," Kayvon suggested. "It's probably only this one truck. Get it together, man. Seriously. Let's do this. We've got press here."

The truck driver took off his baseball cap and scratched a head of matted hair. "My rig wasn't empty. I just weighed in," he declared, confusion in his voice.

Kayvon approached the second truck, and it was as empty as the first. "What the heck is going on?"

By now, the reaction of guests was mixed. Some muttered, some laughed, some looked perplexed. Others bore that expression of wanton delight that often accompanies schadenfreude, the sometimes-unconscious pleasure derived from a setback, misfire, or failure of the aspirations of others. But all held their collective breath as they peered at the cavernous empty truck like commuters in opposing traffic, gawking at a highway wreck. Photographers shot videos and stills at a clacking, frenzied clip, their flashes flickering over the bay like an old-school Moviola. The eighteen-wheelers, parked askew, wheezed rancid black puffs of smoke and continued to chug with their trailers agape like a trio of hungry lions' mouths.

Kenishia shuddered. "Oh no, Kayvon. Tell me this isn't another fiasco."

"Let's not panic. It's a mix-up. Must be a logical explanation."

"Driver, we need our stuff right now," Kenishia carped, her forehead lined.

"You're saying you left with loads and now they're gone? What, they just disappeared?" Kayvon asked the driver.

"I don't know. I had max capacity at the last weigh station. Now there's this."

"They all got beamed up by a UFO in an alien abduction? You'd better come up with a tighter excuse," Kenishia demanded, one hand on her hip.

"I think I'll call my boss," the driver said. "Hash this thing out with him."

"I'm talking to you," Kayvon responded, fingers balling into fists. "What about the next truck? What's in there?" He stalked to the third big rig, but it too had a barren cargo bed except for a pile of padded blankets and a wooden pallet stack. Kayvon snorted like a bull. "You need to account for our merchandise, and yesterday, you hear me, pal?"

"We're not going to let you rip us off," Kenishia declared, whipping out her phone.

"Hold on," said the driver. "There's nine more rigs. I'll check 'em out and let you know."

But each in turn seemed emptier until at the end of the long parade there was only one truck left.

Kayvon exploded at the driver. "None of you realized your loads were gone?" he asked, his ire unconstrained. "Your trucks didn't handle differently? Give me that bill of lading, dude." He snatched it out of the driver's hand.

"Contact your insurance," the lead driver warned as he limped back to his rig and lamely climbed up in his cab. "Tell them your shipment never arrived. Ain't nothin' I can do."

Another barrage of pictures accompanied a swarm of reporters shouting queries, mics plunged into Kayvon's face. "Kayvon, where's your merchandise? What will you do now, call the police? Does this mean Turnover can't open tomorrow? What about your investors—won't they balk? Was this a highway robbery? Got any idea who ripped you off? How do you feel now your business has failed before it could even get off the ground?"

The first driver, looking humiliated, maneuvered his rig from the dock and split.

The last trucker inched in, in his place. As he opened his rig, a curious crush of guests scurried over to take a peek, the drama evident at this point, the stench of grand theft in the air.

The trailer door slowly rattled upward. Camera shutters in burst mode clicked.

In succession, there came a collective gasp. Screams. Groans. Yelling. A stampede.

What the witnesses eyeballed was not for resale, auction, investment, or trade on the net—but two dismembered corpses.

Kayvon immediately called the cops, his blood pressure in the ceiling. He told them what little he knew, rattled off the address, and asked them to hurry. Then he scrambled to buzz the insurance brokers, only to hear a recording say a rep would call back Monday. This was a drag that was not unexpected, considering it was a weekend night. He buzzed the insurance company directly next, hacked into a claim hotline, and via a frustrating autobot, attempted to file a claim electronically but was unsuccessful. The policy was on file somewhere, and he didn't have the number. Without that, he could only give his name, but the autobot demanded more. He had to dig up the policy, but the cops were on the way. Who knew what would happen when they alit, but if the past was an indication, it would likely not be good. Kenishia accessed the insurer's app, but they didn't remember their access code. It was clear it would take until morning to get a claim rolling with some kind of humanoid.

Meanwhile, the reporters were landing a scoop. The launch was a tragic flop, but no one could say that it was boring. It was seriously juicy entertainment news, and everyone loved that fact. Two happily married singing stars just ventured outside the music biz and not only got ripped off but straight up stumbled onto two murders. That didn't happen every day, didn't pop up in social media feeds on a regular basis, that's for sure. It was water cooler fodder that would lead to speculation. How were the Kartaways involved? They had to be mixed up in it. Why else did two corpses turn up in bits and pieces at their place?

The cops took light-years to arrive but were keen to make up for lost time. They questioned the guests like criminals rather than innocent witnesses to a crime, which wasn't exactly a huge surprise to the many minorities in the group. First came uniformed officers, then detectives, then the FBI, of course, as the trucks had crossed state lines. Next came a wise-cracking team of forensic experts wearing latex gloves. They crawled over the trucks like a colony of ants in the wake of a failed picnic, dusting for fingerprints, snapping photos, bagging every scrap they found. They interrogated every guest, recording each one's name, address, phone number, email, Facebook page, favorite color, and astrological sign. They bullied the truck drivers, hauled them away, confiscated all the rigs but one, and cordoned off the neighborhood.

When the "dicks" homed in on the Kartaways, the interrogation was harsh, unrelenting, and didn't let up until sunrise: Who did they know of that might want to harm them? Did they ever consort with criminals? Did they have enemies, launch any lawsuits, fire employees, sleep around? Could this be a warning or message from someone? Had there been phone calls, notes, or threats? Just what had they been up to? Was this a real business or some sort of front? For money laundering? Drugs? Illegals? Arms? Perhaps a slavery ring? Where did the shipments originate and with whom? Who'd they do business with? They unleashed all kinds of implications ending with an accusation. Was the merchandise insured? For how much? Implying the Kartaways hired hijackers to pull off an insurance fraud.

The Kartaways wound up shuttled away in handcuffs, suspected of killing strangers no one could identify. The police said they did it to cover their tracks. Or maybe their plot went awry somehow, perhaps in a struggle over cash, and two of their co-conspirators, as a consequence, literally lost their heads. Come on, admit it, the Kartaways did it. Why else would things go down this way? It wasn't every business got two stiffs delivered to their door. The cops continued to threaten jail and demand the Kartaways come clean, but the Kartaways' lawyer pointed out there was nothing connecting them to the crime, and the cops had to let them go their way.

"For now," an angry detective said before they headed home.

Kayvon rifled through their medicine cabinet, knocking small items down into a sink of sudsy running water. "Baby, where's the Alka-Seltzer?"

"Top shelf on the left," Kenishia advised. She heard a loud crash, an *ow!* and a moan. She shifted the ice pack on her forehead and called to the bathroom from their bed. "Are you okay?"

"I'm still alive," he answered. "Where are the Band-Aids, shug?"

"Right next to the Bactine. You need help?"

"I need some divine intervention."

"What are we going to do, K? This is awful. How can they think we did it? Us, with no criminal histories." Kenishia plucked a tissue from a box on her side of their bed. "Our lives have been an open book for over twenty years. In magazines. On Instagram. We've sung onstage around the world and never once colored outside the lines. Well, except when it came to our music, I guess. We definitely broke some new ground there. No drugs, no drinks, no shady deals. Not even so much as a DJ kickback paid out for good airplay. Doesn't that count for anything?"

"You bet it does. We're not in jail. If we didn't have any resources—even as minimal as ours are these days—we'd be under a jail and no one would know. That's if we made it to the jail without getting shot in the back. As it is, we can hire a smoking attorney and maybe have a fighting chance." Kayvon popped two Alka-Seltzer tablets into a glass of water. "We'll go on the offensive, shug. The court of public opinion could rule in our favor if we play it right."

"But why should we have to go through that? We're innocent."

"No one admits they're guilty. Criminals claim they're innocent, and innocent people get locked up. It's not fair. It's the name of the game. Look at the crooks who go from the White House straight to prison and vice versa, lying like a rug. Lying is more on-trend than dropping carbs or using gifs—deny, deflect, defame, defraud."

She snatched the ice bag off her head and popped up like a slice of toast. "I've got it! We'll get a publicist. You're right. We need some help. The more we let people hear our side of the story, the better chance we'll have. We need a crisis manager. Remember our drummer in Rio, Chico Juegas? He got a fabulous one. We ran into him at the Hollywood Bowl, and he said he salvaged his career because of a public relations wiz. He put the number in my phone."

"Brilliant. That's my baby girl." Kayvon cuddled her under the covers. "Let's hire him."

"Let's hire her. She'll probably be expensive and she may balk at the prospect of taking us on. The facts are so grisly, she's liable to pass when she sees those corpses in that truck."

"I have to admit those mutilated bodies rattled me as well. Even back in the day when my homies were banging, they never went at it as crazy as that. It's going to take a miracle to identify their body parts. Considering how chopped up they are. Like chickens in a fast-food joint."

Kenishia groaned and shuddered. She nuzzled her head on his muscular chest. "I can't get it out of my mind. It's gross. That poor woman without any arms or legs."

"The guy's privates were sliced like luncheon meat. They cut him up like a—"

"Kayvon, stop!" She swatted his stomach to make her point. "You know what creeps me out the most? The fact that they were in a truck delivering stuff to us."

"I know. But that could be happenstance," Kayvon deduced.

"Or purposeful."

"Okay, but we're not owning it. We had nothing to do with that truck or the deaths. Let's get that straight right now. They can't blame us for what went down before it got anywhere near our offices. The questions are how and why they got there. That's the narrative we'll push. Who had motive and opportunity? Not us. We have an alibi. We were wrapped up in our opening."

"Right. We're the victims. We're ripped off. The thieves must be the killers."

"We wouldn't have put them in that truck. Look how bad it's messed us up."

"Correct. But that's what's bugging me. What if somebody did it to mess us up?"

"Let's not go getting paranoid. People have killed for a whole lot less than the ten million dollars in saleable goods in those trucks, no matter whose goods they were. My cousin Makari got shot for a box of Pop-Tarts in that store he owned. For some cherry Pop-Tarts the dude is gone. Murder is a selfish crime. It's the nature of the beast."

"But why us? I can't shake that thought. Those drivers swore their trucks were full."

"That claim sounds shaky too. A truck doesn't handle the same when it's empty as when it's full. They couldn't tell? Not one of those big-rig truckers knew they were deadheading? Give me a break. And none of them saw a robbery? It stinks to high heaven, the whole damn thing."

"Those bodies sure didn't dismember themselves." Kenishia snuggled in and sighed.

"Well, it isn't on us and we're not going down. I promise I'll get us out of this."

"It makes me sick to think of it. It's like a locked door mystery, the kind I used to love to read. It's different when you're at the center, though. Who do we know who'd be capable of it?"

"Every soul we've ever met. You never know who you're dealing with. Anyone, under the right conditions—"

"Why are you being so cynical all of a sudden?" asked Kenishia. "How can relationships stand a chance if no one dares trust anyone? People are better than you think."

"But sometimes they surprise you. Faith is a dangerous thing, Miss Trusting Pants. We're trusting to a fault and look how that's turned out for us. What I can't figure is how they did it. How they pulled it off. It's like a Vegas magic act, the way all those loads just disappeared and two headless bodies took their place," said Kayvon, chugging his Alka-Seltzer. "We'd better come up with some answers. Quick. Those cops are going to keep digging, and if either of us so much as wet our pants in preschool, we'll get rolled. Maybe not you, but they'll take me down. Let's face it, guys who look like me get killed for letting their heart beat."

"Could be someone counting on that," Kenishia considered with ponderous eyes.

"I have to admit it crossed my mind."

"I don't think we have many enemies. At least not that we know of yet."

"Might be a social network troll, some racist creep, or just bad luck."

"It'd have to be very, very bad," Kenishia said with twisted lips. "I mean, think about it for a sec. Our launch and all our merchandise. This could've done us in."

"Thank goodness we have insurance, or our Turnover business

would crash and burn. We need to check our policy to be sure we're totally covered. I'm confident we'll be okay, but who knows what'll happen next? I'm beefing up security measures the first thing in the morning."

"You think they'll come at us again?" Kenishia asked with great alarm.

"No, I didn't say that, shug. I'm looking at possibilities and tightening up our act, okay? It's a matter of damage control. All this havoc is dragging us through the mud. The rumor mill's grinding overtime. It'll be in the papers and on TV. They'll be sending out carrier pigeons with our misfortune in their beaks."

"I already know. I checked our feeds. They're tweeting us to death right now."

"And let's add up the dollar signs. The lawyer plus the publicist." He counted expenses on his fingers and all ten of them ran out. "Unless we can grow a money tree—"

"We're watching our dreams go up in smoke for a crime we have no clue about. I just don't understand!" Kenishia exploded off the bed, arms flinging, hair bobbing, feet stomping the floor, her Victoria's Secret cami and panties making Kayvon tent the sheets. It wasn't only her lingerie getting him hot, it's what was in it. He thought no other woman in the world could look as fine as his did with her back against the wall. "We've tried so hard. It isn't fair. We work 25-8 to do good and be kind, and this is all that comes of it?"

"Well, you know what they always say. No good deed goes unpunished."

"I never believed that stupid phrase." Kenishia sucked her teeth.

"Babe, we're suspected of double murder, insurance fraud conspiracy, and probably kidnapping the Lindberg baby by the time all's said and done. If that doesn't constitute punishment, then I don't know what does… But you know what?" His eyes lit up.

"Oh no. I know that expression. Wait. Whenever you start to smile like that, we go from a frying pan into a fire. You're gonna come up with some crazy scheme. Forget it, we're playing it safe this time. We're in hot water as it is. I'm not letting you get us into—"

"Hold on, baby, hear me out. You said we need public sentiment on our side, and I agree. I know how we can charm the public. Or engage our fans, at least. Do it the way we always do."

Kenishia inhaled and looked down at the floor. "Why do I have this sinking feeling?"

"We can write a song about it."

"What?" Kenishia said, widening her eyes, indicating her mortification.

"Our current predicament, shug, what else? We write a hot hook and record a hit. Today. While our names are on everyone's lips. Not in a good way, I get that. This could be the upside."

"Hold on. Did you fall and hit your head? A song?" She crossed to the bathroom door.

"Where are you going?"

"For aspirin tabs. I fear you've had a stroke. Your brain isn't functioning properly."

"I'm serious."

"I know you are. That's what's so unnerving."

"Think of the headlines. Think of the cash. By tonight, all eyes will be on us, shug. We can tip the scales. You heard the lawyer; we're in deep. The guy will cost a mint. We lost our entire investment, and the insurance is going to take eons to pay us, if it ever does. We're under investigation and that's going to hold it up. The bills will just keep rolling in. We're liable to lose our home, our freedom, every single thing we've got."

"You're right." Kenishia flopped down on the bed. "But a song won't get us out of this. And think of those people's families. How do you think a song would make them feel?"

"Whatever they feel won't be our fault. We're fighting to survive."

"But we can't just—"

"Listen, sugar. We'll do everything we can to fight for justice for the folks who died."

Kenishia clasped her hands and prayed. "Oh please, God, bless those people's souls."

Seeing her eyes well up, he rushed to hold her close and kiss her nose. "What?"

Kenishia held back tears, blood draining from her smooth brown face. "What if it's more than we imagine? What if whoever killed them might've mistaken those two for—"

"Us?" asked Kayvon, holding her tighter, stroking her hair. "Don't think I haven't thought of that. Don't worry, sugar. I'll protect you. Trust me, I would die for you."

The next morning, the sky was deceptively sunny. Birds chirped in the trees outside the Kartaways' window, making the world sound gay. The groundskeeper mowed their large green lawn. The paper boy hit the front door with the *Times* as he did on normal days. If one didn't know the sky was falling, everything would seem peachy keen in their suburb of LA.

Kayvon and Kenishia showered and dressed, tried to eat something, found they couldn't, hopped in their Benz, and sped to work—well, they tried to anyway. They made it out of their garage, but they had to two-wheel it around a blind curve to get to the nearest boulevard, three motorcycles chasing them. Upon leaving their gated community, they spotted a crew of reporters who were camped out at the guarded gates, scouting the entrance to the grounds, waiting for any sign of them. It wasn't easy losing paparazzi, as they both knew well. What they didn't know was who else was on their trail, as yet unseen.

The pair didn't notice the cops on their tail until nearly ten minutes through the ride, but when a police car ran a light, they knew the jig was up. *Had cops been watching all night long?*

Undaunted, they made their way downtown in an effort to get to Turnover, but when they got there, they found the industrial complex their warehouse occupied was buzzing, besieged by not only authorities but look-ie-loos and journalists. It seemed they had no place to go.

Kayvon sped by their address. "So much for that. They're everywhere."

"Not to mention my cell phone blowing up."

"I had so many voice mails, texts, and emails I just turned mine off."

"Honey, are the cops still there?"

Kayvon looked in the rearview mirror. "You bet, shug, but not for long." He took a sudden right. By a drugstore, he swung another right and then a hard left to a parking lot beneath a skyscraper, underground. He swerved into the first empty parking space he found, the tires screaming. He quickly cut the engine off. The cop car whizzed past in a flash.

"Good going, baby, that was close," Kenishia said. "My head is pounding."

Kayvon punched the steering wheel. "Damn. I was hoping they'd get a clue by now that'd lead away from us. I'm guessing as long as we're in their sights, they're not going to try to look anywhere else." He sighed.

"There's only one way out." Kenishia dug in her handbag, swiped on lipstick, smoothed her pink lace dress, looked in her visor, primped her hair. "We have to turn the tables, like you said, and solve the crime ourselves."

One reason Kayvon and Kenishia left their high-rise New York condo was the City of Angels's shifting postcard-picture slideshow scenery. At this moment, as they rode side by side wondering what they should do next, their move to LA had seemed a perfect choice in spite of the waking nightmare. An aura of sunlight warmed LA, covering the mountains, hills, and ocean, reflecting no hint of the scandal and terror that scarred and marred the day. Only the knots in the pits of their stomachs seemed to hang clouds overhead. Santa Ana winds whipped away every layer of grayish smog and hazy mist while the panorama of Malibu Beach advertised for heaven.

The Kartaways' silver Mercedes traveled the Pacific Coast Highway on a breeze that blew in over sand and surf. Stretches of metered parking lots were scorching hot tickets on weekends, but on a Monday noon like this, they were open for resting, thinking, meditating, journaling, stealing a kiss, gobbling a lunchtime seafood snack, or in many cases, smoking grass without being busted by anyone. One could sooner win a sweepstakes than luck up on a parking spot out here between TGIF and dusk on any Sunday afternoon. But a workweek was in swing again, a time for new beginnings. Today they were scheduled to make a big splash in the tide pool of the internet, and their belly flop wasn't lost on them.

Kayvon pulled over. "Let's chill out." He put his arm around her. "We really need to think this through and figure out a plan."

"Okay, so where do we start, Sherlock?"

"The way I figure it, solving a crime isn't all that different from liquidating."

"Huh?" Kenishia kicked off her shoes, hung her feet out the window, wiggled her toes. *My Kayvon*, she thought, *can do anything.* "Look at you, getting this figured out."

"Are you kidding? I put a ring on your finger and haven't got you figured out."

"That's different. You'll never accomplish that."

"I figured out that much… Anyhoo, as I was saying before I was rudely interrupted—"

"Interrupted? I never interrupt."

"You did it again. I was—"

"No, I didn't. I listen to every word you say."

"Good, then—"

"When you're making sense."

"How am I going to catch a killer if I can't even get a word in edgewise?"

Kenishia mimed putting a key in her lips, twisting it, throwing it over her shoulder.

"The point is—"

"People get killed for a reason."

"Yeah, like cutting their husbands off."

"You said it. Anger. Let's start there. Maybe he killed her then killed himself."

"Oh sure, and cut himself up into pieces."

"You're making me see those two bodies again," Kenishia admitted in singsong.

"Maybe we shouldn't just start with motive."

"The ten million smackers they stole from us."

"Why they got killed is key, it's true, but *how* they were killed is a bigger clue," Kayvon concluded, leaning forward, wrapping his arms on the steering wheel and resting his chin on his hands. "Let's get Nola to ask if the cops know how. There's liable to be a murder weapon. Meanwhile, we'll investigate. People are likely to tell us much more than they'd ever tell a cop."

Her love came down, and she scratched his back, re-smitten by his character, his jet-black skin, his lean, hard frame, his strength, the angular planes of his face, and the sapphire glint in his solemn stare. Everyone took K seriously, but she saw humor in him too, and vision, purpose, perseverance. She saw the whole rest of her life with him. "I believe in you. I trust you, K."

"How did I get so lucky?" Kayvon asked, a love light in his eyes. "I swear I love you so much, shug. I'll never let anyone hurt you. Whatever happens, you have me." *The most beautiful woman in the world is actually in love with me,* he thought. She took his breath away with that sensual look of adoration she trained on him in times like these. Her, with her knock-dead gorgeous eyes that could freeze you in your tracks and stop your heart even when they were filled with tears. And that golden glow in her flawless face. His wife could melt an iceberg. Her curves were in perfect proportion, in the best places, wrapped in copper flesh. Her mind was as vast as the ocean before them, more powerful than a cresting wave. The lady had guts of stainless steel. She was kind, compassionate, loved everyone and made each day a joyous thrill.

His girl was relentlessly positive. Hilarious, and she thought he was too. And her faith made her so forgiving. She was the sexiest woman alive. He would fix this for her if it killed him.

Kenishia looked out to the sea and said, "If we consider *how* they were murdered and who might want Turnover trashed, the juxtaposition of those two things could net a real good suspect." As soon as she said it, her cell vibrated. "Argh," she grumbled. "Should I answer?"

"See who it is."

Kenishia looked. "It's Nola, babe. We talked her up. Her ears were probably burning."

"I hope she has an update, not a warrant or a subpoena."

Kenishia swiped the answer icon. "Nola, what's up? … They know already? That was fast. I'm glad you called. Well, don't keep us in suspense. Who were they? … What? Oh no!"

"It can't be." Kayvon started the car.

"It is," Kenishia said.

"We're screwed." He eyed the rearview mirror cam and backed out of the parking spot.

"The victims were Hank and Twyla Greene. Who would want to kill those two?"

"According to the cops, *we* would. They were our business rivals."

"But, babe, we barely knew the Greenes. Who goes around knocking off everyone in their line of work? That's nuts." Kenishia bent forward and started to moan, her head hung down between her knees. "Oh man, I feel so bad for them. I felt awful before, when I thought they were strangers. Now it's like it's ten times worse."

"You can say that again. They think we killed them. Now they can connect us. We knew them; that confirms our guilt. But why would we kill them and leave them in that truck for all the world to see at our opening? It makes zero sense. Nola said the Greenes bad-mouthed us. What did she say they claimed we did?"

"She didn't."

"Cops will say bad blood, that we got mad and killed them both."

"That's ridiculous."

"Is it? Not to them. Somebody must have told them that."

Kenishia arched an eyebrow. "Were they?"

"Were they, what?"

"Bad-mouthing us. Trying to make our business bad, assaulting our reputation."

"How would I know? They were so standoffish. Twyla really envied you."

"What she envied of me was my marriage to *you*."

"Don't sell yourself short on that account. You're everything she wasn't."

"You think they were sabotaging us and what they did backfired on them?"

"I just think their two bodies were found in a truck that was on its way to our business launch, and I saw they were supercompetitive. Who knows what they might have tried to do."

"Maybe they trashed us to ruin our deals in an effort to dry our supply chain up, and they could've been successful."

"But the drivers claim those trucks were full. That means the deals were going through."

"Oh yeah, that's right. What's up with that?" Kenishia rubbed her forehead. "But we can't take the drivers' words. If they tried to manipulate suppliers, they could corrupt the drivers too."

"Well, then let's call the sellers up and ask them all point blank." Kayvon pulled his cell phone out.

"Hold on." Kenishia touched his bicep. "Maybe we shouldn't tip our hand. They have us on thirty-day open billing. None of them got our checks yet, right? I shudder to think how they'll react if we start asking questions. We could give away more than they may know. Why should we ruin relationships by flooding them with suspicion? Calling could do more harm than good."

Kayvon put his cell phone in the holder on the car's air vent. "You're right. I don't trust the suppliers either. I don't trust anyone but you. Till we find out exactly who's working against us, all we know is those purchases didn't arrive, the Greenes were sticking their noses in it, and someone's out there killing folks."

"The cops could accuse us of hassling suppliers for a nefarious reason too. Let's lie low until we find out more. As long as we stay off the grid, it's all rumor and accusation. Once we talk, we could misspeak. For now, the police know the Greenes were up to something. That's a start. And remember," Kenishia said, "we have an alibi. If nothing else came from that grilling last night, the authorities know who was with us in the hours before those trucks arrived."

"Right. But when did the Greenes get offed? We might *not* have an alibi for the time they actually bit the dust."

"There's that." She squinted. "But then, too, the launch was not a secret." Kenishia pointed a finger to emphasize who might have known. "We did radio phoners. TV interviews. E-blasts. Invites. Facebook posts. We told the whole world a big shipment was coming. Anyone could have found out when, what route, and who'd be driving."

"Bottom line, there are only two explanations. Either those trucks didn't ever get loaded or cargo got loaded and then ripped off. Somebody knows how the Greenes got in that truck and the fate of our merchandise. I figure those truckers know more than they're telling. They have to be involved." Kayvon pulled out into traffic. "Let's get ahold of that lead trucker, shake the truth out of him as best we can, and follow whatever leads from there."

One hour later, Kenishia and Kayvon pulled into an old truck stop gas station fifty miles north, in the picturesque town of Valencia. The place had a stable and country store that doubled as a liquor barn. It sat at the crest of a sleepy suburban bedroom community lined with homes. Nestled in rolling hills above the San Fernando Valley, it was *Leave It to Beaver* country. Crime was all but nonexistent there. Except perhaps for the wads of cash lonely soccer moms spent on expensive clothes and shoes and indulgent manicures for themselves and their bratty four-year-olds. That was a crime in some folks' eyes.

A Mack truck waited near dry brush. Myles, its driver, dozed on fuzzy, cow-print covers in its cabin, steeped in swampy sweat and smoke and slumped down in his seat.

"Are you sure this is where he said to meet?" Kenishia asked Kayvon with a frown. "Who does he drive for, Pony Express?" A tumbleweed rolled by.

Kayvon laughed and pointed. "There he is. Let's get this over with."

They walked to Myles in blazing heat.

"Yup, the stuff was there all right. I checked every ounce of it myself." Myles coughed, then took a sip from a steaming cup of what looked like engine sludge. He kicked up his feet, puffed a brown cigarette, ran a grease-stained hand through his sun-bleached hair. "See, like I already told them cops, I figure some dudes hijacked our load with them dead folks at the root of it. We musta got jacked when we stopped to grab some grub and get some… rest."

"Is this where you stopped?" Kenishia asked. She shielded her eyes and looked around.

"Yes, ma'am, they got good food in there. And we was a extra-long caravan. Some guys just needs a smoke. You got dudes gotta pee, gotta take 'em a nap, gotta grab 'em a snack or blow some farts… Oops, pardon me, ma'am, but youknowwhudamean."

"How long were you here?" Kayvon inquired.

The driver mumbled. "Lemme see. Er… I'd say about three hours."

"Three hours?" said Kenishia. "With our freight? What were you doing all that time?"

"Ma'am, it's lonely on the road," Myles whined.

"What's that got to do with it?"

"Well, this gal, Portia. She's real cute. I'm single. We hang out."

"I see. You were with a woman," Kayvon posited in knowing tones.

"So, you and she…" Kenishia blushed.

"We kinda got carried away," said Myles.

"Along with our ten-million-dollar load," Kenishia said and rolled her eyes.

"She got a li'l place down the road apiece. I think she pays it by the hour. Last night she said we was there three hours when I had to give her cash."

"Did you check on the trailer before you took off?"

"No, sir," Myles whined and hung his head. "But I noticed the cab didn't drive the same, like you said. I sensed the load was lighter. We was all high as a kite by then, and the last weigh station was five miles back. I was so sleepy; I just kept movin', tryin' to make up time."

"The other drivers stopped here too?" Kenishia asked and fanned herself.

"Yes, ma'am, same joint. The Dew Drop Inn. It's right across the road. We had us a party with the girls… I didn't drink no liquor though. I only smoked four joints, is all."

"Oh? Congratulations." Kenishia huffed and crossed her arms.

"And downed a coupla Red Bull cans."

"I sure hope you enjoyed yourself." Kenishia peered across the road.

"Me and the boys all feel real bad, with them Greene folks turning up like that, all chopped up like they was. Don't none of us know how that went down."

"Somebody knows, pal. Someone did it," Kayvon said and shook Myles's hand.

"Maybe Claude has a clue in the office there." Myles pointed to the Dew Drop Inn.

The desk clerk at the Dew Drop Inn dimly confirmed Myles's tired account, and along with it, granted truckers did get ripped off at the truck stop—mostly by hookers stealing their wallets, but pimps had an ever-evolving game, as did thieves maximizing their profits. Killing was not outside their realm. Thieves repeatedly hit the convenience store, so murder, to Claude, was less unspoken than an inevitable consequence, the cost of doing business. As long as the robbers were armed, he concluded, there was always a chance someone would die. And with ten million dollars locked up in twelve rigs and drunk truckers' loose lips sinking ships, it didn't take a psychic to divine how things went bad. But Claude denied he saw the Greenes and couldn't say where they fit in.

The Kartaways sped down the Golden State Freeway, descending the I-5's curves and slopes back into the smaze of Los Angeles, wending to Treasure Trove Liquidations, the office of Hank and Twyla Greene. TTL was in beautiful downtown Burbank, housed in a stuffy storefront spot off sleepy Burbank Boulevard, where the main drag split to a five-fingered hand near Victory, by Costco. Though not a bad sales location just a stone's throw from two shopping malls, TTL was located on one of few streets untouched by revitalization.

"Treasure Trove," the pudgy receptionist said in funereal tones with a Russian accent, hiccupping into a duct-taped intercom on a crate in front of her, a relic from the Jurassic age of technology like a rotary phone or a car with roll-down windows. She peered through the bars of the grimy glass door, brushed aside her fringe of purple bangs, and pressed a rusty buzzer.

Kenishia reluctantly entered first, sidestepping the layers of dust inside that seemed to coat all surfaces. A strand of crusty, oversized jingle bells tinkled as they closed the door. The place was a musty, cluttered dump that screamed disorganization. Stock slumped in crooked cardboard boxes, protruded from broken plastic bins, and bulged out of busted office chairs not even a rat dare occupy. A stink like mold spores, rotten food, arthritis cream, and a giant foot ran into the Kartaways' nostrils as a handful of marble-eyed workers slumped over desks with a dim and aimless look not uncommonly viewed in the newly bereaved and soon-to-be unemployed.

"Uh-oh, babe, time warp alert," Kayvon wisecracked quietly.

"I hope you had your tetanus shot."

"Appointment?" asked the receptionist.

"Yes," said Kayvon. "With Ms. Greene." He knew full well that couldn't be.

"She passed," the receptionist replied, belying no hint of regret, remorse, relief, or any emotion. She hiccupped and beckoned them to her, awkwardly waddling past a beaded curtain, emitting a rancid smell of wine. "Vee are going to close up soon, but you can take the tour."

"The tour?" Kenishia repeated with dread and barely concealed revulsion.

"Who conducts it, Michael Myers?" Kayvon muttered to his wife. He took her hand and gallantly held the curtain for her with a smile, ignoring the horrified look on her face and the way she was tugging away from it, the curtain causing her to sneeze.

The warehouse was mazelike and covered with cobwebs. Kayvon and Kenishia took it in with prying, hungry eyes. Every inch of the storeroom was crammed, but their withering scan of the dank warehouse revealed no trace of their missing loot or explained how the Greenes could be involved.

Everything seemed to have been there for years, most boxes sealed with yellowed tape.

It was clear the Greene business was in the red, which explained their desperation. How they managed to keep the doors open this long was mysterious in itself.

"Are you receiving new shipments?" Kenishia asked. "We're hunting for lots of stuff."

"No vay," the receptionist replied, her accent thick and guttural. "Is vhat you see is vhat you get. Vee haven't got any new stock in months," she said in a confidential tone.

"Is Mr. Greene the buyer here?" Kenishia asked offhandedly.

"He vas, but he's deceased as vell. Vee just found zat out a half hour ago."

"So, you don't mind sharing suppliers then?"

"To tell you the troot, vee vere no longer sure about vhere he was getting zee items from. Zhere vere often shady characters. I don't ask qvestion vhere I'm from."

"I see," said Kenishia, sneezing again, beating a hasty retreat from the storeroom.

Kayvon turned on the charm as the Kartaways left. "Sorry about the Greenes, Ms.—"

"Miss Belitnikov. Katrinka."

"Thanks, Katrinka Belitnikov. For a busy woman like yourself to help customers in your time of grief speaks well of this business and of you."

She melted like Velveeta cheese and offered him her hand. "Vhat a lovely gentleman." Then she wrinkled her nose like she smelled bad fish. "Dees beezness vas no goot."

"Oh my. Well, thanks and best of luck." Kenishia waved goodbye.

The Kartaways left with a silence between them, feeling the weight of the Greenes' demise, sorrow their business went so bad, increased concern about their own, and compassion for all the employees the murdered couple left behind.

On their way to the car, something struck them as odd. A brand-new storefront two doors up incompatible with the shabby block. A sign said Import-Export, and they saw antiques inside.

"Now that we know our stolen goods aren't at the Greenes', that's one less lead. Let's go there and nose around. Neighbors may know something." They did, and Kayvon pulled the door.

Ainsley and Zartem Linx appeared like a hologram, standing side by side. The owners looked eager and intense, as if no one had been in their store since it opened and this could be their last best chance to sell their objets d'art.

Turned out, they were archeologists, unusually tall and lanky, draped in matching maroon highwater pants, a couple of button-down, polka-dot shirts, knit argyle vests, pink plaid bow ties, and identical pairs of Oxfords. Ainsley had an incessant blink, because of, he said, his cataracts.

Zartem wore horn-rimmed lenses perched on the tip of a ski-slope nose.

As the door slammed shut, Kayvon observed, "These guys should have a guard in here."

The small store was named Fair Trade Imports, and in contrast to dirty TTL, it was pristine, aesthetically pleasing, and as spotless as a cotton pad. Wildflower, lemon, and lavender scents mercifully lilted on filtered air, and clean white walls held paintings that appeared to be original. An intriguing display of bottles and oils arranged in alphabetical order gleamed in a glass hexagonal case in the middle of the polished floor, and pedigreed antiques arrayed in stately vignettes around the store lent the ambience of a sterilized museum inventory.

The brothers, conversant and energetic, welcomed Kenishia and Kayvon and responded when Kayvon broke the ice by bringing up the Greenes.

"Why, yes, we're acquainted with the Greenes," said Zartem. "What we didn't sell, we let them liquidate. A shame, what happened to them though, according to Miss Purple Bangs."

Ainsley chimed in rapid-fire. "As a matter of fact, the other night—"

Zartem elbowed Ainsley's ribs. "How did you know them? Were you friends? What did you say your name was, sir?"

"I didn't. I'm Kayvon Kartaway, and this is my beautiful wife, Kenishia."

Zartem stepped sideways and screwed up his face. "Kartaway? Isn't that—"

"Wait, they warned us." Ainsley blinked and backed away.

"Warned of what?" Kenishia asked.

"You people have some nerve coming here, I'll grant you that," snapped Zartem. "They told us about you weeks ago, about how you might try to contact us and attempt to steal our business… and now look what you've gone and done."

"We haven't done anything," Kayvon told him, moving to shield his startled wife.

"Get back. Don't move an inch," said Zartem. "We read the papers. We're informed. Don't think you can get the jump on us like you got the jump on them."

Suddenly loud, shrill, squealing sounds emitted from something overhead and bars descended from the ceiling, sectioning the store in half, walling the Kartaways off from the Linxes and, more importantly, the door. The bars were connected by chain-link fencing.

"What do you think you're doing?" Kayvon shouted with alarm.

"Let us out of here!" Kenishia screamed. "Are you crazy? You can't lock us in."

A sign on the fence winked ELECTRIFIED, lit up in hot-red neon. "We'll have you arrested," Kayvon barked, his face breaking out in a sweat. He advanced with a leap and a fearful grunt, but that only set off a blaring sound and a deafening, pulsing din.

"That's rich," said Zartem. "Call the cops? I wonder how that'll turn out for you. Call them. They'll be thrilled you did. Who will they believe? You're the ones who came to shut us up. We simply flushed you out. We might even keep you around for a while before we turn you in. It could be fun to sweat you guys and see what we can get from you. You're loaded. What's your freedom worth?"

Ainsley stepped in front of him. "What are you saying, Zartem? No. I'm not getting involved in a thing like that. Get on with it. Call 911."

"You're already involved, you idiot. Don't you realize that by now?" said Zartem. "This is all your fault. You failed to mind your business once again, and we're paying the price for it."

Kenishia spoke in an even voice as if she were talking to a child who was playing with a live grenade. "We just want to clear our names. We had nothing to do with what happened to the Greenes. We swear it, don't we, K?" She turned to her husband, who looked so fierce she didn't wait for his reply. "We were hoping you could help us out. We don't want to harm you."

Ainsley turned to Zartem. "I believe her, Zar. They need to know. He's right, they could put us in jail for this."

"Know what?" Kenishia asked, suppressing panic and misgivings.

"Nothing." Zartem waved her off. He bustled to the windows, closed the blinds.

"Zartem Linx, you answer me," said Ainsley. "What do you plan to do?"

"We'll pay you thousands. How about that?" Kayvon offered, thinking fast. "Whatever we have isn't much right now, but we'll be earning more real soon. Lots more. Guaranteed. We have a new album coming out," he fabricated. "Drops next week. You can have every dime we earn from that. Our iTunes sales alone could get you everything on your wish list, guys. We can sign it all over to you right now. This is false imprisonment. You have to let us leave."

A silence fell over the two Linx men, Zartem growling low and deep and starting to pace along the fence as seconds passed like eons. Finally Ainsley's soft voice said, "Sounds like a pretty good deal to me. What do you think, Zar? They're in trouble. This could be our answer. We can leave town for Tahiti tomorrow, sell the store, rent out Mom's house, and go. Just disappear. No one will find us in Bora Bora. Isn't that where you want to live?"

"You believe that crap he told you? You're even dumber than I thought. Now they know our destination. When will you learn to button up?"

"Listen," Kenishia interrupted. "Whatever it is you're afraid of, it's not us. We're music people. Artists. We're about the love. Why are you guys so paranoid? What happened? What do you guys know?" She quizzed them, walking to the fence, just inches from its lethal volts.

"Get back, woman, or I warn you—"

"Stop it, Zartem. This is sinful. Get ahold of yourself and quit bullying others for once in your life. I'm tired of it. Can't you tell this woman's not a threat? She hardly weighs ten pounds. Where is your sense of right and wrong? Or has it abandoned you like your husband did? Where is he now? He was a fine one, wasn't he? Following those Nazi websites all day long and half the night. That's why you're so mad and filled with hate. It's not acceptable!" Ainsley burst into a flood of tears, his ears turned as red as two pickled beets as he pleaded with the Kartaways. "I heard it all. I think he knows. The killer, I think he saw me. I can't keep silent anymore."

"Ainsley, shut your face, you wimp. You never stand your ground."

"I'm standing my ground right now, okay? I'm doing what I know is right."

Kayvon, pulling his wife back from the fence, looked wildly for escape, eyes darting around the prefab cage for any way to breach it.

"I'm not going to let you drag me down. Not this time. I just won't! Mother would spin in her grave if she saw you doing what you're doing now."

Ainsley shouted at his brother, banging one fist in his other palm. Again, he faced the Kartaways. "From the second they told us their bodies were found, I longed to speak up. We were too afraid."

"Shut up!" Zartem scolded. "That's enough. You don't know what you're saying."

"I heard them plotting to steal from you," Ainsley blurted, chest poked out.

"Are you crazy? You want to get us killed?" Zartem ran over and cracked the blinds. He peeked out, shut them, locked the door.

But the toothpaste didn't go back in the tube. The story gushed from Ainsley Linx like water over Niagara Falls. "I was tossing out garbage three nights ago."

"The evening before the Greenes turned up?" coaxed Kayvon, egging him on.

"I heard them consorting behind their place, in the alley, with some brute. I never could stand when they smoked back there. Atrocious imported cigarettes. The unfiltered kind. That awful stink. I'm allergic. I asked them a jillion times to smoke at the end of the alleyway, so I marched right down there to complain."

Zartem patrolled the locked front door and flipped the OPEN sign to CLOSED. "I told him to mind his business, but he insisted on going to tell them off," he said. "He's such a fool."

"When I spotted their visitor, I turned back. That is, until he raised his voice."

"What did he look like?" Kayvon asked.

"Rather attractive," Ainsley assessed. "In a rustic way, if you like that sort. You know, a weightlifter type of guy." He swallowed and blinked like a railroad signal. "Blond and as wide as a wrestler. Only, he was really rude. He called me a geek, imagine that. In response, I pretended to make my retreat, but I hid behind the dumpster."

"From there, you can easily eavesdrop," Zartem explained while adjusting his tie. "They didn't stop smoking. It served them right. They did strange things down there."

"Were you able to make out what they said?" Kayvon prodded in low tones.

"For sure. But I regret it now." Ainsley's visage paled.

Kenishia reached to touch him despite the fact he'd trapped her in a cage. "Don't hesitate, you might save lives," she soothed with psychiatric calm.

"And one of them could be yours. Or maybe your brother's. You don't want that, right? So tell us what went down," said Kayvon, inching along the unsafe fence.

"Hank handed him something. I couldn't see what," Ainsley continued without a breath.

"Then the guy agreed to trick the boys, whoever they were, into making a stop at some dive up in Valencia or Santa Clarita. I couldn't tell which from the way the guy described it. In those foothills off the 5 freeway. He said he'd take cash to waylay the boys in order to meet the phantom trucks. I was confused about what that meant, but that's what he called them, phantom trucks. It was spooky, I can tell you that."

Zartem shivered. "It's the truth. Ainsley stayed up all night long, so frightened I gave him a Valium. He's worried the stranger might come back. If he spotted Ains, he will."

"He was creepy, with beady, bloodshot eyes and leathery, suntanned skin," said Ainsley.

The Kartaways exchanged a look.

"Myles," Kayvon muttered. "Is that all? Ainsley, what else did they say?"

"He bullied the Greenes, demanded cash. They said it'd be no problem. They said he'd get paid at the transfer point. I couldn't figure that out either. Where were they getting their money from? It was obvious they were going bust. Just look at their place; it's a total dump. But they told him their 'partner in crime,' as they put it, could easily kick up that and more."

"What partner? Did they mention who?"

"I didn't overhear a name."

"And his ears are as big as his mouth," said Zartem. "If that guy is the killer, he'll silence Ainsley. What if he shows up here, like you?" He crossed to peer out through the blinds again.

"Well, we can't help you locked in here," said Kayvon, gesturing at the cage. "And it sounds like you need every friend you can get. I'll refrain from knocking your lights out if you open this portable prison, Zartem. We have a common interest, pal. All four of us need the killer caught. The enemy of my enemy is my friend, and you dudes qualify."

Zartem hesitated, bit his thumb. He lifted a black remote, held down a red button, and the cage rose with a screech and then a clang.

"Good luck, guys, we're out of here." Kenishia scrambled toward the exit. "Leave town. Get some therapy!" she shouted back over her shoulder.

Kayvon got up in Zartem's face, teeth clenched, eyes boring through his skull. "If you ever scare my wife again, you'll wish that dude in the alley came for you. And that's a solemn vow. I'll liquidate you both."

As Kayvon and Kenishia rushed away, him trotting as she held his arm, another thought occurred to her. "Oh wow, we should've known. Myles mentioned the Greenes when we talked to him. He denied he knew how they got killed, remember?"

"Come to think of it, he did. I slept it at the time, but how could he know the victims' names so soon if he wasn't involved in it? The pieces are coming together, shug. But we don't know who hired him, and until we do, we're on the hook."

In the car, Kenishia took out her phone and googled "phantom truck." The first result from her search was a firm called Phantom Trucking Company. She tapped the address in the GPS, and they cut across town to Miracle Mile. The lobby was spacious, with marble floors, a guard in a uniform at a desk, and an atrium with plants and trees that soared to a domed glass ceiling. The Kartaways posed as potential clients, signed in at a semicircular desk where the guard, who was reading a comic book, directed them to the elevators, told them to ride to the penthouse floor, where they then, awaiting a supervisor, sat and looked around.

"It's nice here, sugar, don't you think? Though compared to that wacky joint we left, anything's an upgrade."

"We're lucky we got out of there. The memory gives me goose bumps."

"That's how easily people get captured all around the world. It makes you mad. How simple it is for anyone to take another person's rights and freedom. It's deplorable. In that brief time we were in that cage, I felt I might do anything to get away and keep you safe."

"I've heard of eccentric office gadgets entrepreneurs have had put in, but who installs a frigging cage? Those brothers should lock each other up. They're a danger to society."

"I had a good mind to kick their ass if we weren't already in a jam."

"I can't believe I'm saying this about someone who tried to enslave us in broad daylight in Los Angeles, but I'm hoping you-know-who does not return to you-know-what them. Those guys are right to be afraid."

Kayvon's stomach growled. "I'm starving. Let's go find a snack."

"There might be a bank of vending machines by the restrooms, pook," she pointed out, indicating a nearby restroom sign. "Get a granola bar or something. I could use a bite myself." Exploring the hallway, they found machines, bought trail mix and two cold Smartwaters. Popping the caps, they each took sips and, pausing by the atrium, started to wolf the trail mix down.

"Let's get some more water," Kenishia suggested, smacking her lips as her bottle drained. "They said it's going to be a wait." As she tilted her head back to drink the last drop, there it was, the very clue they needed. Hidden in plain sight on the dome—a portrait of Phantom Trucking's owner. It was Farley Traylor. "Look!" she exclaimed. "They're Farley's trucks."

Kayvon tilted his head back, looked up, sneered. "Well, ubba dubba."

Kenishia was surfing the internet like waves on the beach at Waikiki. At her desk in her home office, she was basking in a ray of hope. She sensed they were taking their power back. At last they were onto something big. She was eager to get to the bottom of it.

Over the span of their singing careers, the Kartaways traveled like kings and queens.

They had all the best accommodations, private jets, were wined and dined, but lately all that faded out. Kenishia had a bout with cancer, their recording label bit the dust, music industry profits waned because of a wave of new technology, and the Kartaways, scrambling to reinvent and stay relevant in the industry, got stretched out keeping pace. Trent, their bookkeeper, had made good investments with their dwindling IRAs, but in 2008 when the stock market fell, they took a huge walloping hit to their savings like everybody else.

They learned a fall can happen fast and climbing back can take some time.

That's when Kenishia started to work the web. She had a gift for tech. Online, she got an email about the liquidation industry. It seemed to hold some promise. She started researching merchandise sources and took a web-based business course that hooked her up with hackers, some of whom Turnover now employed. Two were among the former inmates working in their IT room, busted for major felonies that started out as high school pranks and ended in lengthy sentences because one was Black and one was brown and neither of them had any green. What they did possess were dazzling minds, a penchant for electronics, and mad coding skills and game designs. They taught Kenishia many tricks.

Kayvon, during this period, got into videography. He bought camera equipment, green screens, lighting, videocams, new microphones, and an editing software bundle, both for audio and video. He directed their own music videos first and advanced to produce and direct creative content for musician friends. Even now, he was chasing an editing deadline in his music studio, with his door open while Kenishia surfed.

"Who knew Farley had all this going on?" Kenishia called. "It's awesome. Come take a look, K. This is wild." He saved his file and crossed the hall to find her hot on Farley's trail, digging up tons of dirt on him, information they wished they'd known before, assets they never dreamed he owned. A hefty stock portfolio, thousands of real estate rental units, Delaware shell corporations, several offshore bank accounts. "It's amazing. Would you look at this? Farley told us he was down on his luck, but nothing's further from the truth."

Kayvon rolled an office chair beside her, sharing her monitor. "Whoa, the bugger owns all that?"

"Yup, and zillions more. I only scratched the surface, but I'm setting up a spreadsheet in Excel to try to sort things out. Look what I found about how he rolls." She clicked on a link to an article that was published in the *Los Angeles Times*. "Farley executed a hostile takeover of Phantom Trucking years ago after originally being a trucker there."

"The place must be worth billions now."

"Looks like he wormed his way up through the ranks, but his climb turned into a steep decline and the board members voted to boot him out. Evidently he was the target of an FBI investigation into some massive interstate fraud involving phony applications for some loans he bartered for, for some dummy subsidiaries. They got traced to a New York conglomerate his buddy owned, called GreyRock. It was riddled with corruption too. They say Wall Street is scared of the banks and the banks are only scared of GreyRock. GreyRock dealt in illegal foreclosures, money-laundering, political lobbying for foreign interests, mail fraud, bank fraud, wire fraud, and other egregious felonies. The whole family is under investigation."

"Whoa," said Kayvon. "Scroll down, shug."

"Apparently, Farley got off by rolling over on some higher-ups."

"Who?"

"Good question. Doesn't say." Kenishia hit the Page Down key.

"Hold on, babe. What's that item there, that story about the Russian bank?"

Kenishia's eyes darted across the screen. "Looks like Farley's deep in debt." A chill ran up Kenishia's spine. "What the heck is going on?" She covered her mouth with both her hands, and they read the text with lightning speed.

"They gave him a loan for eight hundred mil. Why is a man with that kind of money messing around in our start-up business, being our warehouse manager?"

"It beats me. Maybe the money's gone."

"We couldn't spend that in a jillion years."

"Speak for yourself. I'd love to try."

"Dag." Kayvon whistled. "Eight hundred mil. That's almost a billion. That's serious dough. How'd you like to be struggling to pay that back? Farley must be tripping."

"What did he do with it? Where is it now? Did he burn it in his fireplace?"

"More importantly, what did he have to do to get it? And with Russians?"

"Oh em gee. He's up against it. Farley could owe individuals, the government, or some oligarchs. No telling who he rolled over on or what kind of folks he's indebted to."

"Hey, look, he had silent partners," Kayvon observed. "He wasn't alone. There were cosigners on that loan he got." Their four eyes searched to find the names. "Nola Dunbar?"

"Our attorney? No."

"And look, there's our accountant too. Trent Cunningham. Well, I'll be darned."

"They were in it together all this time. What in the world are we dealing with?"

"I'm not sure, but believe me, we're going to find out." Kayvon bolted to his feet and helped her slide her jacket on. "C'mon, let's go. They played us, shug."

"Well, they're not going to play us anymore," she said.

"We'll change the game."

Farley's fortress stood in Encino's poshest area of the hills. It was ten p.m. and so pitch-dark it appeared the man in the moon took off on vacation with the sun. Kayvon and Kenishia pulled their Mercedes to fifty yards up from the Traylor estate. In contrast to the rest of the street, Farley's home was lit up like a Christmas tree. Security floodlights shone on three luxury cars in its private, gated drive.

The Kartaways cut their lights and engine, coasted by azalea bushes, checked to make sure they weren't followed, donned their brand-new black ski caps, and surveyed the neighbors' driveways, windows, doors, and closed garages.

Kayvon said, "Let's rock and roll."

Kenishia wrestled a bag from the back seat, easing it into her lap and reaching inside to get a box. The Pirate Eye Surveillance Shop's apt logo picturing a buccaneer glowed blue on the recycled tote as she handed the box to her hubby. "Here."

"Let's see if this thing works." Kayvon opened the shrink-wrapped box with his car key, fiddled with molded Styrofoam, and extracted sound equipment wrapped in little plastic bags. "The salesman assured us we'd hear conversations up to a hundred yards away. I figure we're somewhat less than that. We ought to get a signal." He clipped the My Spy listening kit on the dashboard with an adapter, inserted rechargeable battery packs, and aimed the mic at Farley's door. The sound was distorted at first, but he tweaked the settings so it came in clear.

"Fine. You do what you want to do, but I could get disbarred. I warn you, leave me out of it," said a voice they instantly recognized. "I never intended to go this far. These people don't deserve it."

"That's Nola," Kenishia said, raising the volume.

"Shh. This bad boy's working great," said Kayvon.

"We should phone record," Kenishia said. "My battery's low."

"I got this." Kayvon tapped his cell, hit the icon for his recorder app.

A male voice flooded the quiet Benz. "She's right. I can't stomach this anymore. You never said people were going to get killed. I'm too long in the tooth for a prison stretch."

"That's Trent," Kayvon said. "I'm'a bust his—"

"Wait," Kenishia said, tugging his sleeve to prevent him from bolting from the car.

"You don't have a choice. We owe too much. You think they'll let us go our way?"

"That's Farley. Listen up." Kenishia leaned in, licked her lips.

"Don't act like you had no hand in this. Get over it, Trent, you cooked the books," said Farley.

"*Our* books? Wait. Oh snap." Kayvon checked the recording app. The little light was on.

"You're in it as deep as me or her. I ain't lettin' you cream puffs back out now. You don't get no do-overs."

"That sounds like Myles," Kenishia said.

Nola countered, "I. Am. Out." Her high heels clicked across a floor.

"You're out when I'm good and ready, toots," Myles blustered.

"Who do you think you are? You'll never be good, and I'm ready now."

"Whoa." Kenishia's eyes grew wide.

"They're not playing." Kayvon jerked his head. "Duck, a car's about to pass."

They leaned to avoid two bright headlights.

"I thought you was a lady. Huh!" It was Myles's voice, an angry growl. And then from the speaker came something else. A sound that was unmistakable. A shotgun cock.

Kenishia gulped. "Was that a—?"

"Gun. Oh crap. It's on."

"People, people," Trent chimed in. "How do we settle this amicably?"

"We divvy up now and press Delete." Nola's heels clacked louder.

"I'm not walkin' away with two lousy mil," Myles said.

"It's actually two-point-five," Trent reasoned. "Ten million dollars split four ways."

"Whatever. Cut the crap, Grandpa. You and I know that's chicken feed. You can't fool me. I'm hip to you. You lose two mil in a golf game, spend that much on a bad blow job. I had drivers shadow you jerks for months. I know who y'all been dealin' with in all them foreign deals. I'm takin' my fair share, is all. You lightweights need some smelling salts? Don't bother looking shocked."

Farley insisted, "Take it, Myles. It's more than you'll ever see again."

"Put down the gun; we can work this out." Trent's raspy voice was gasping.

"I'm takin' the whole ten million, egghead. I took all the risk. Y'all can split up what you rip off next. See, I got a calculator too, and I'm here to make sure I get it all."

The Kartaways turned to each other and stared, their eyes as big as traffic lights.

And then came Nola's icy shrill. "I'll explain it again for the lunatic fringe, the lowest common denominator, and this dense Y chromosome—"

"Quit with them big words," Myles said. "Or—"

"What?" Nola countered. "Don't fool yourself. This isn't some Bogart rerun airing on TCM tonight, you freak. How will it look if I disappear?"

"I won't mind findin' out! Don't tempt me, sweet cheeks, this thing's loaded."

"Time's up, kiddies. Use your heads." Trent was audibly wheezing now. "Listen to logic one more time. I didn't agree to murder. I only signed on to my part in the scam."

"Ditto. Ciao, boys, it's been real. I'm taking my cut and I bid you adieu." Nola's heels clacked on the floor again.

And that's when they heard it. *Bang! Bang! Bang!*

A thud and then silence.

"Oh my gosh. Did you hear that?" Kenishia's mouth flew open.

Kayvon gunned the engine, hit reverse, slammed the gear shift into D, and scratched the Mercedes Benz fingernails on the blackboard of the silent street. The listening device fired off of the dashboard, shot from the car through the driver's window onto the road, and shattered there as the Kartaways made their getaway.

"Well, we botched that up real good," said Kayvon, gunning it up the block.

"We have to go back. We left the mic. Someone will wonder whose it was."

He made the first right, and they hit a dead end at a sparsely inhabited cul-de-sac. Tires squealed as Kayvon whipped around, and the car fishtailed back down the street. "Too late," said Kayvon. "Let it go. We'd be in the line of fire. Forget the mic. It's yards from there."

"Oh Kayvon, do you think she's dead? We can't just leave her there like that. Let's at least call 911," Kenishia argued, trembling. "Please. Let's stop and call the cops."

"No way, babe, that'd be suicide. How would we try to explain what we were doing out there in the first place, selling Girl Scout Cookies? We'd be sunk. Those guys are in the wind by now. The cops wouldn't buy a word we said, not after what happened with the Greenes. They'd lock us in a dungeon undersea and thrown away the key. We can't get caught ten miles away."

"Quit driving around in a circle then."

"I'm not driving around. We're lost!"

Kenishia pressed her window down and let the night air hit her face. "Pull over, I think I have to pee."

Kayvon dodged into a park, underneath a tree, away from streetlights, hidden by a pile of concrete blocks in deepening nighttime shadows. The park, with its monkey bars and swings, was deserted save for a squirrel family chittering in branches overhead. "Shug, we didn't *see* the shots, we only overheard them. We don't know any more than Ainsley does. We didn't tell him to alert the cops; we advised him to mind his business. Shouldn't that go for us as well? What if Myles didn't actually shoot someone? He could've been firing warning shots. He might've shot and missed. And even if someone did get hit, there's every chance that they'll survive. It's not worth ruining both our lives reporting facts we can't back up. Still have to pee?"

"Not now. You're right. Okay, so let's get going."

They pulled out, and an amber light came on, on the dashboard. "Wouldn't you know it?"

"What?"

"We're almost out of gas." Kayvon smacked the steering wheel.

They coasted to the boulevard and pulled into a filling station, running on fumes, gas gauge on E. Panicky, Kayvon filled the tank and tried to act all nonchalant while wary of every passing car. He pivoted east to the 134, melding into traffic lanes, zooming to the 101. They took that freeway toward downtown.

"Where are we going to go from here? We can't go home. We can't just cruise," Kenishia said, her eyes bright pink.

He exited in Chinatown to a restaurant with blackened windows. Lowering their heads and hurrying in, they sequestered themselves in a booth at the back that was lit by one red candle jar. They ordered, and Kayvon dove into chow fun and an order of spicy fresh green beans once he polished off his egg drop soup. Kenishia couldn't eat a bite of her kung pao vegetable delight. She glanced around at other booths, lowering her voice to an anxious purr, her chopsticks idle in her hand.

"What if somebody saw us at Farley's? They'll assume we fired the shots. And what if Myles comes after us? Or Farley? We were at his office. What if security cameras picked us up? They'll know we know."

"Stop worrying so much and eat your food." Kayvon chewed an egg roll.

"I think we should get the next plane out. They can't kill people they can't find."

"Running will make us look more guilty. Besides, we have clues to follow up… Do you know which computer Trent used most?"

"Yeah. We gave him the old Dell laptop rig. He's not tech savvy. He doesn't have a need for speed like we do. Why'd you ask?"

"He's keeping records somewhere, right? Maybe they're longhand, maybe they're digital. Where's the laptop, at the office?"

"Yup. He locks it in his desk."

"Is it password protected?"

"Probably. I'm confident I could hack into it. If I hit a snag, I'll call a tech."

"Great, let's pick it up." Kayvon took a last big bite and paid the check and tip.

Ten minutes later, they destinated. The press was gone, and their Turnover building looked normal from outside. Of course, cops could roll down any minute and they didn't feel safe anywhere anymore, so they circled the block a couple of times to make sure the coast was clear. They sat in their car in the parking lot, her gut like she swallowed a water balloon and his blood pressure throbbing in his neck. They scoured the street and alleyway, flinching at every leaf that shook, and they finally got out and headed in.

A rat jumped off a dumpster lid, and Kenishia leaped to Kayvon's arms.

"This is absurd. Let's go inside. It's either faith or fear," he said.

"We have to believe we're in God's hands." She held on to his elbow.

Kayvon inserted his key and flipped the lock. "Wait here, I'll get the light." He strode up the hall in the darkness, reached for the wall switch, tried to flip it on… and tripped over Nola Dunbar's legs.

"What happened?" inquired Kenishia, hearing the noise out by door-way. "Kayvon? K? I'm coming in."

Kayvon scrambled, tripped again. "Don't! You need to stay out there. Go back to the car. We're breezing."

Another day. Another setup.

Two more bodies at their doorstep—this time Trent and Nola.

Kayvon and Kenishia didn't run; they decided to buy some time. Their warehouse was old and it had a dumbwaiter. They wrestled the corpses into it, slipping and sliding in sticky blood and straining to stuff them down the chute before they were discovered.

Kayvon jammed the chute door closed. "We might as well sell dead bodies now. They're all we have in stock."

"We can't afford the shipping charge." Kenishia, breathless, fanned herself. "We're running out of time. If we can't get the truth out of Trent or Nola, what's left, tarot cards?"

"Let's go get this place cleaned up and grab the laptop from Trent's desk."

"That works. If the cops don't catch us first. Or the killer. Better speed it up."

Back in the car with Trent's laptop and their offices looking presentable, they drove into a rocky lookout point at the top of Mulholland Drive. They sat on a bench with their faces lit by the laptop screen and went to work in a cutout that overlooked pinpoint lights of the rambling LA skyline.

After a half an hour or so, Kenishia told Kayvon, "That was simple. His password is barely a password at all. It's his birthday in reverse. You know, people should take more care with passwords. Otherwise, why have them?" She clicked file folders. "Here we go. I'm excited. I have an idea. I think I saw something the other day. Farley shut the computer when I came in, but I sneaked a peek over his shoulder before he realized I was there. I saw the filename he was in and thought I'd check it later on. I didn't think much of it at the time, but I figured it was a Turnover file—like accounts receivable, late or due—and the way he slammed the laptop closed was odd and a lit-tle suspicious. What if it was a Phantom Trucking file he didn't want me to see? Or part of the books they said he cooked." She clicked file folders, opened files. "Shazam!"

"They're definitely entries, shug. You might've hit it on the nose."

They cruised the lengthy Excel doc.

"Oh wow, it's here in black and white. Look, sugar, that could be us right there. KK10M. Kayvon and Kenishia. Ten million dollars. His final entry. And it's dated yesterday. What an arrogant sack of snot he was. He recorded the whole scam step by step."

"And he did it right under our noses."

"He probably couldn't help himself," said Kayvon.

"He didn't even try. His system was as sophisticated as his stupid password. What about these other entries? How do we figure out who they are with just our names to work with? With no others, where's the proof?"

"Finding them could take a while. There are thousands of transactions," Kayvon observed and sucked his teeth. "When you add them up, that's quite a sum."

"Let's take a look at Phantom's books," she said. "We could cross-reference them."

"Think you can find them?"

"If they're here."

"Myles said Trent was cooking books. We thought he meant ours, but he might've meant Farley's."

"We can try the birthday password. That might get us in." Before long, she was able to pull up a ledger. "Yass!" she said.

They slapped high fives. "My genius wife. I think I'll keep you."

"Yup, I'm out of warranty. No refunds, no exchanges. You bought a final sale, big boy."

"And I got a bargain."

"We're in!" said Kenishia when icons appeared on a home page. "One, two, three. But what do we look for, do we know? What do cooked books look like, pook?"

"Maybe they look like duplicates. A real set and a doctored set."

"I don't think they'd be in QuickBooks or a common app like that. Trent would use proprietary software he had custom made… Wait. I'll cruise the program files."

"Look for similar filenames, shug. If Farley ever turned on Trent, Trent would want him dead to rights if he had to resort to blackmail. Controlling Farley would be tough."

"If it were me, I'd hide cooked books in software only a hacker could tell was not an innocuous video game, but I don't see any games in here except for the bloatware on the drive, and those games all came preloaded. I can look but I doubt we'll find much there."

Kayvon treaded behind the bench. "His records are probably backed up too. He'd want to have redundancy. You know, backups stored on external drives, flash drives, or SD cards…" Kayvon pointed at the screen. "Look, there's a journal folder, sugar."

She clicked on it, and a list dropped down. "These filename dates go back for months. This might be what we're looking for." She opened the first file in the list. "Check out these notes. It's everything. He recorded all his dirt. Where he went, what he did, with whom he did it, dialogue, the dates and times. It's all here, Kayvon. How'd you know?"

"I took an educated guess. Trent wasn't the *gratitude* journal type."

"He should've been from the looks of it. He should've been grateful he wasn't Black or brown, if nothing else. He was leading a life of crime scot-free. He'd have probably gotten a slap on the wrist even if he eventually did get caught. If he was the color of you or me, they'd have choked him for stealing a stick of gum. Look what he got away with." She opened file after file until she had stacks of windows piled up. "See, he detailed their entire game plan. Why would he do a thing like that?"

"To CYA if things went south. For proof of his version of events. Trent probably found out Farley rolled over to Feds before. He might again. Maybe Farley planned to clear himself in case he ever needed to, with a bunch of contemporaneous notes that make others look guilty and him look like a saint. This is exactly what we need. It proves we're not the crooks."

"Only, what does it have to do with the Greenes turning up in our delivery truck?"

"Let's see. There might be clues in here… Gimme the mouse, shug. Take a break." Kayvon scanned the data log, assimilating what he could, summarizing and narrating what he learned to Kenishia, who was kicking back and rubbing itchy eyes. "Farley placed ads on the internet, in social networks, trade chats, blogs that served as hunting grounds. He targeted start-ups anywhere he could find a mark he thought might bite. When Farley got a company hooked on shipping merchandise through him, he referred them to Nola, who drew up contracts, handled their various legal affairs, and recommended Trent to handle bookkeeping and accounting."

"Sounds familiar."

"Yeah, I know. After their scam began paying off big, all three of them formed a partnership—well, more like a conspiracy—to infiltrate companies, drown them in debt, and suck out loads of borrowed cash, leaving the owners holding the bag and in a legal quagmire. They went from one firm to the next, setting up shop and moving on after draining the owners dry. They apparently did it to pay off the giant loan they owed the Russian bank. The interest was piling up on a principal that was ginormous as it was, and the hole was getting deeper. According to this, when they couldn't remit, the Russian mob collectors came. And they didn't just send out nasty letters, phone calls during dinnertime, or liens on their estates. Late payments could literally cost an arm and a leg, and that's compelling. Desperation set in and they disagreed. They needed to launder their money, and that took additional sleight of hand. They had to put the operation deeper in the hole. They fleeced entrepreneurs, celebrities—"

"And trusting musicians like us who love to do what they love to do a lot more than juggling bills and spreadsheets."

"And with GreyRock's position on Wall Street and its lobbying efforts on Capitol Hill, they offered other benefits in lieu of cash repayments—influence peddling and insider trades."

"How did they get away with that?" Kenishia asked and rubbed her eyes.

"Crooks pull off amazing crimes. The white-collar criminals usually skate. Sometimes their victims don't know they've been had until creditors start to suck their blood."

"Where do you suppose that money went? I mean, how many houses and suits and cars and jewels and fancy meals and bottles of wine can just one person want? It's decadent. It's narcissistic. Don't they have compassion? What sort of person finds happiness in valuing things above people, pook? Villages could be fed with that. Or maybe cancer could be cured. And how many kids could be educated? My goodness, how can they sleep at night? And for that matter, come to think of it, why did they steal our shipments too?"

"Greed. That's why they did it all. Not just their greed, but that Russian bank's. Or rather the men behind the banks and the government that makes them rich and leverages their power."

"What does it say about that in the journal?"

"The shipments? We didn't get there yet."

"Let's move ahead to this year's dates." She opened her eyes, saw pages turned.

Kayvon read on and grumbled, "Farley. Huh. We should've known. Farley's the one who came up with that angle. Figures. He got Myles involved. Having been in the trucking business, Farley knew the ins and outs. He taught Nola and Trent how to rip off shipments hours before their ETA. They stole and then resold the goods—three or four times when they found they could do so without delivering anything. Often, they bore no consequence as they moved whole freight cars' worth of stuff or ultimately loaded crates on planes to make another pile of dough reselling to the Kremlin at a fraction of the price. Nice work if you can get it, eh?"

"It's awesome they could jump that off."

"By switching full rigs for empty trucks, they made the cargo disappear. Drove it straight to the Port of Long Beach, *poof!* Left everyone scratching their heads. Most of those who paid for freight had insurance and didn't miss a step, but those without coverage took a bath. Nola helped the more fortunate owners file claims before they could get disgruntled and kick up a fuss with authorities. That's how they stayed one step ahead."

"What do you bet they bribed underwriters to ease the insurance pipeline too?" Kenishia concluded with a sigh. "Probably gave them kickbacks. What a funky, airtight strategy."

"And to do it, they wanted insiders like Myles to help them manage the trucking end for local shipments in the States. But Myles is a loose cannon. You gotta hand it to them though. They didn't leave a trail. It says Phantom's insurance carrier got suspicious but never dug up proof. Farley, Trent, and Nola didn't leave one fingerprint behind."

"Till now," said Kenishia.

"Till the Greenes. The Greenes got scammed the way we did. Only worse, and for a longer time. Hank told me he didn't invest his money back into his business like we did."

"It looks it, too. The place is a disaster zone," Kenishia said and shook her head.

"I remember Hank bragging at some event that their fortune was held by a savvy investor stashing it off shore."

"In Moscow?"

"Certainly looks like that. Trent was the one who wired the funds, but this says he was unaware to whom. He had an account number. That was all."

"Good luck with collecting ROI from a safe inside the Kremlin or a locker in Ukraine."

"Once there, it never existed, and they were better off not finding it. Farley was able to bilk the Greenes, but when they caught on, it was dangerous. They could've blown it all."

"What did they do, call the FBI?"

"The journal doesn't say. In fact, it appears to end right there. I'm guessing they went for a piece of the pie and demanded in on the con."

"Oh no."

"It was a fatal error. They'd have done better to blow the whistle. It wasn't a good idea to horn in on an international den of thieves. Myles is a piker compared to them, but I guess he doesn't know it yet."

"He'll probably find out soon enough," Kenishia said with goose-bumped arms.

"But he might not still be breathing."

As it happened, Myles was breathing hard.

A figure rose out of the stillness, casting a shadow over the cliff and bench, lengthening, spreading a pall on the couple, the laptop beam, and the gloaming moonlight filtering through imposing, nearby brush. A sudden chill. A dry twig snapped. The hammer of a revolver clicked.

"You two is as irritatin' as a boil, and I'm poppin' it." The business end of Myles's gun—the second from his arsenal—was pointed at Kenishia's head. "Y'all honestly thought y'all wouldn't be seen there spyin' outside Farley's crib? We got eyes and ears all over town."

Kenishia let the laptop whir.

"What do you want?" Kayvon intoned, emanating a look-I've-had-it vibe.

"That computer, for one. And your ass for another."

"I didn't know you went that way."

"Shut up and turn around!" Myles roared.

"Is this how it went with the Greenes? With Trent? With Nola? Who else did you kill?"

"Stand! It ain't no invitation."

"Aww, I'm disappointed, Myles. Why not shoot me in the back? You're not above it. You've done worse. Go mano a mano. You and me. Man up. Let my wife go."

"Boy, you must think I'm an idiot."

"No, Myles. I know you are."

Eighteen big tires crunched the gravel, slid to the shoulder, blocked the road, and a silhouette hopped from the cab of a truck as long as a railroad car.

"Nice to see you, Farley," Kayvon said, his back to Traylor. "Delivering pizza at this hour?"

Farley advanced from the rig with a Glock in his hand and a grin on his face. "Myles, put the princess in the cab." His head jerked toward the rumbling semi.

"I don't think so," Kayvon bellowed, plumbing the depths of his diaphragm.

"Nor do I," Kenishia yelled.

"Do you hear an echo?" Farley asked.

"Must be because we're so high up in the canyon no one will hear her scream."

"Stick a fork in them now, they're done," said Farley.

"I was just thinking the same about you," Kenishia said. "Guess what? I just uploaded your funky transactions and Trent's dear diary entries onto the FBI computer tip line. Right about now they'll be contacting LAPD to round you up. Which doesn't give you scads of time. Our car is equipped with GPS. It'll give them our current location. Not to mention our phones will too. And yours, of course. Did you turn it off? My phone has a po-po scanner app. You can chat with them while they're racing up. This laptop does as well. It's Trent's. Come check it if you like. There's fascinating stuff in here. Oops, and I almost forgot the recording we made of you shooting Trent and Nola. Isn't it exciting, Farley? Won't it just be tons of fun?"

"Your wife's a cool cucumber, I'll say that. It's pretty hot," said Myles, and he dug his gun in Kayvon's back. "But she couldn't play poker with that bluff. Go on, get movin'. Over there. You're gonna take a dive." He hustled Kayvon toward the cliff. "I sure hope you can fly."

Farley moved to grab Kenishia, twisting her arms behind her back. "I'm sorry, kid. I don't believe you. None of it had to be this way."

Myles said, "If you'd shut your beak, songbird, you might've been able to worm your way out."

"I'll be singing like a canary in a few minutes, Myles, you wait and see."

Out of the navy blue of night, two blinding high beams climbed the ridge, boring down on the group like UFO lights, casting a sheen on the edge of the cliff. Suddenly midnight turned to dawn as a torrent of helicopter blades swooped down from overhead, swarming, circling, swooping, darting, whirring, producing a deafening beat. A beam lit the scene like a concert key light, making Farley turn and squint.

"Who's that in those choppers?" Farley asked.

"Smoke them. Let's get out of here!" Myles shouted. "It's the cops!"

Farley yanked Kayvon by the collar, ducking and dashing off into a stand of trees and thrusting Kayvon down. Farley advanced, aimed to fire his gun, but Kayvon jumped up, whirled, kicked Farley's wrist, and slammed him to the ground. The gun fired off into a tree. Kayvon launched an iron left, a right, and then a roundhouse kick. He headbutted Farley, sending him backward, pitching him awkwardly toward the cliff at an odd and faltering angle. But Myles had Kenishia by the neck, and before Kayvon could fend him off, the trucker rammed the butt of his revolver down on Kayvon's head, and Kayvon fell. Out cold.

"LAPD!" a bullhorn blasted.

"D-A-M-N!" Myles hollered back. He snatched Kenishia by her neckline, yanked her hair, and punched her face. Blood spurted from her busted lips. Sirens wailed and choppers whirred as he dragged her toward the sharp cliff's edge, scraping her body over gravel, lugging her like a piece of luggage, flinging her like a rag doll. Kenishia bit and kicked and scratched him, digging her manicured nails into his muscle, tearing his hairy flesh. Myles hurled her to the precipice, beating her, slinging her over a boulder, dangling her over the canyon below. He hollered, "Back off, or I'll drop her, I swear!" He yelled, but the choppers drowned him out. He worked to pry free from Kenishia's grip and swung her farther off the bluff.

"Help!" yelled Kenishia. "Help, Kayvon!"

Kayvon, on the edge of consciousness, heard the call of his wife and began to rally, struggling with all his might to right himself and save his soul mate.

Kenishia clung onto a branch on the hillside, pebbles and loose dirt pummeling her scalp and sprinkling down into her eyes and mouth. The branch cracked, and Kenishia slid, Myles mashing her hand with his cowboy boot as if to extinguish a cigarette butt.

All Kenishia could say in that last frightful moment was, "K, I'll always love you."

A chunk of the hill made of solid rock broke off and tumbled onto her.

The branch gave way.

Two bodies fell—Myles darting into the mouth of the canyon, Kenishia landing safely on a narrow ledge that broke her fall twenty feet below the ridgeline.

When Kenishia awoke in a hospital bed with Kayvon alert in a chair beside her, holding her hand with both of his, the first thing she saw was a room full of flowers, the largest bouquet made of stargazer lilies, her favorites, just like her wedding bouquet eight joyful years ago that day. She lay there constrained in a body cast, and then, feeble and gentle, she squeezed Kayvon's hand and uttered a soft, "Yoo-hoo."

His eyes leaked and he wiped his cheeks. "Oh, shug, you're awake. I thought I lost you." Kayvon moved in closer.

"Ooh-ooh," she sang in a small, dry voice. "You can't get rid of me that easy. Our life's much too easy breezy."

He sang back, "I love you so. I will never let you go." He kissed her lips, let out a sigh. "Guess I have to delete my dating profiles, now you're back. I'm booked for months… Say, tell me, are you free tonight?"

"No," said Kenishia. "But if you have coupons, I'll charge you a nominal fee."

"Okay, then I'll cancel my prior engagement."

"Good. I don't want to use these casts to knock some poor girl out."

Resting with Kayvon reclined beside her, Kenishia awoke from a peaceful nap.

"See? Check it out, we're heroes now." Kayvon showed the *Los Angeles Times* to her.

Kenishia asked, "Well, what's it say?"

"How great we are, but we knew that."

"Oh cool. They finally noticed."

Kayvon read the text aloud. "In a stunning reversal of fortune today, a former *Prime* magazine man of the year, Farley Traylor, pled guilty to felony charges including at least four murder counts. The onetime trucking executive's confession admits unlawful acts undertaken with international co-conspirators over many years. Traylor admits to killing two partners in crime and Hank and Twyla Greene, whose bodies turned up in a truck last week. Sources say Traylor promised the Greenes, in exchange for monies he allegedly stole from them, a cut of ten million dollars robbed from Kenishia and Kayvon Kartaway, the award-winning pop recording artists at whose fledgling internet start-up four dead bodies were found in just three days.

"Traylor's deal with the Greenes apparently soured when Traylor allegedly laundered billions of dollars through their ailing liquidation firm without consent. The cash ended up at a Moscow bank via real estate holdings in New York. When the Greenes caught Traylor in the act, they demanded a larger piece of the pie and in so doing sealed their fate. It was due to a last-minute truck mix-up at a truck stop in Los Angeles that what was to be an empty truck delivered their bodies parts instead. A memorial for the Greenes is planned. Authorities credit the Kartaways for cracking the case and catching the killer.

"Thousands of fans keep vigil on streets near Angel of Mercy Hospital where Kenishia recovers from suffering serious injuries at Traylor's hands. Many prayers and best wishes go out to her. The world hopes to hear her sing again as soon as she is able."

Kayvon went to the window and opened the blinds. "There are tons of fans out there."

"I can't see them, but I feel their love. I'm just happy what happened to us won't have to happen to anyone else."

"We're the hottest entertainment news on every social network, shug." He returned to his wife and held her tight. "What do you say to a comeback now?"

"I'm ready to write a song."

In the crowd outside the hospital, an enforcer was holding a floral bouquet.

He was making a small delivery… to collect on a very large debt.

LITTLE

WHITE LYE

A LITTLE WHITE LIE CAN SEEM INNOCENT.
Until a liar gets caught with a lot of white lye.

Jericho Jordan was curious when he discovered that lye in Thunder's big black flatbed truck by accident. He couldn't imagine Thunder making soap or disinfecting floors or toilets, fooling with biodiesel, curing food, unclogging drains, conducting a chemistry experiment, processing metal, cleaning his oven, or doing another legitimate chore with sodium hydroxide. He *could* see Thunder synthesizing drugs, so he thought that's what was up. Thunder was doing what Thunder did—floating another get-rich-quick scheme, hanging out with hard-core thugs.

Thunder was the jealous type. Jericho knew that all along, ever since they'd got to be next-door neighbors as close as two loners could get to being friends without respect or trust. Jealousy thrived in Thunder's genes. Or *jeans*, more like it. Truth be known, his father was killed in a bed with another man's wife just a couple of years ago. And when Thunder was dating a woman, look out. He was only one perilous step from a fight in which someone would get hurt.

With guys like Thunder, Jericho figured—now Jericho had nothin' but time to think—the jealousy gene was like the sports gene. Either you got it or you ain't. And folks who got it, got it bad and just can't find no other way to satisfy themselves.

So the die was already cast when that gal came sashayin' up from New Orleans with those long, red, sexy fingernails and her tight-fittin' dresses and mile-long legs, lugging that yellow suitcase with her baby-soft, gimme-the-world-now hands and that *Help me, Daddy, I'll die without you* pout on her perfect, lip-sticked lips. Even a bat with bifocals coulda seen how things might not end well.

Jericho saw the girl walkin'—no, sidlin', no, prancin' really—up Sly Street, scopin' out the Circle K. Jericho hadn't laid eyes on so sweet a brown sugar before in all his life. The sight of her copper skin and windblown hair intoxicated him. Jericho's Mama, Lulubella—rest her palm-readin', dress-makin' soul—had never warned Jericho off such lethal creatures as this stranger. Lulubella was a church-goin' woman who didn't encounter no femme fatales in the choir at Calvary Baptist Church in Chattanooga, Tennessee. At least not that she claimed.

The prancer wasn't from 'round these parts. That much was clear as day. Her type came from NOLA or Charleston or Richmond or maybe even Hilton Head. A practicing siren, tall and lithe and beautiful in a hypnotic way. As shiny as a brand-new penny, she was, in her flowered summer dress that fluttered in the wind like gossamer angel wings, as if she might take flight. Jericho coulda swore he whiffed her fruity aroma from 'cross the street, full of lemon and berry and orange blossom. Her scent was captivatin'. Later, he learned it was chewin' gum, shampoo, and dime-store lotion, but that didn't wear the magic off.

Jericho was naturally horny. Everybody knew it too, as Jericho Junior often saluted in public without bein' asked, eager to jump to attention at the slightest provocation. So the minute he glimpsed the seductress, he immediately got hard as an ironwood tree, makin' two passin' schoolgirls giggle and grin with their hands across their mouths when they seen his whopper bulgin' in them tight black denim pants. Jericho vowed to have the prancin' gal as soon as possible, but even though women flocked to him and generally gave him whatever he wanted, maybe this newbie wouldn't pee on him if his mustache caught on fire.

"Where'd that slice of heaven come from?" Jericho thought as he licked his lips and rubbed his palms together. And where was them had-to-have hips of hers headed?

He followed her.

Let's see…

She glided almost half a mile before flouncin' up to that robin's-egg-blue house with the wraparound veranda Jericho had dreamed of since he was only six years old. He used to pass it on his way to school when he was a hapless kid, and he swore he'd live in a manor some fine day with some fine wife. The object of his affections tiptoed 'cross its steep, majestic lawn, threaded through its maze of weepin' willows, climbed its wide white staircase to its wooden double doors, her head held as high as a Nubian queen's. She stabbed a key into the lock.

Jericho's shiny new Trans Am slowed to a stop and idled across the street as she tossed her suitcase in. He watched the door close when she went inside. He cut the engine, sat and stared, his mouth so wide open a fly flew down his throat and he had to swallow it. He washed it down with cherry pop without blinkin', hopin' she'd come back out. Prayin' she'd somehow notice him. He sat visualizin' him and her in a four-poster bed in the master bedroom, frolickin' under a canopy, wilin' away the afternoon. But hours later, to his chagrin, after the tangerine sun sliced into a blazin' sky-blue-pink horizon, he was still parked aslant in the gloom without her, keepin' a vigil there, heart beatin' as hard as rock candy, mind racin' as fast as an Indy car.

A light flickered on in the kitchen window. Pale yellow glimmers on hot pink curtains gently wafted on the breeze, callin' to him, softly whisperin', temptin' his gullibility, tantalizin' his fantasies, and achin' in his loins. He leaned forward and hugged the steerin' wheel. Crickets started singin', harmonizin' with the frogs, as the dark rolled down and the smell of fryin' chicken and bakin' cornbread greased the humid summer air.

Good only comes to a man in this hard life when he reaches high to catch it, Jericho concluded. He committed to light out toward the girl, and he hopped from the seat of his hot-red ride, his lust afire, his stomach clenched. Rakin' his calloused fingers through the length of his tightly cornrowed hair, he loped to the gate of a place he knew he could never begin to belong.

Jericho's strides were sure and quick, his lean muscles ripplin' like chocolate waves in a sea of unfounded certitude. What was he gonna say to her? How would he explain his presence? Shirt off, body beggin' for touchin', givin' off tinges of wood and musk, his horniness overcame him as he sneaked paint-speckled Nikes through the grass at the side of the house. He was itchin' to catch a glimpse of her, this dream girl in his dream house. The kitchen had a Dutch door that was open at the top. Piano music drifted out, liltin' on the air like a lullaby meant to lull his lust to sleep. Romantic as an opera song. Like tunes that played in elevators at some jobs he worked.

Through the doorway of the kitchen, he caught sight of her in the drawin' room. His heart stopped when he saw her. She was strokin' them black and white keys like they was a phallus, makin' the keyboard purr. Swayin' her head and lithesome torso. Naked as the day she was born.

Jericho's feral instincts flared, and he felt a sense of fight or flight. He knew if he ventured one more step he couldn't be responsible. So he ran like the wind back to his car and drove like a madman through the streets to the highway back to his home. To his bed. Where he spent the night alone. And all that long and tortured, lonely eve, his dreams were ripe with her, with imagined tastes of her luscious lips, and him lickin' her petal-soft, silky skin. But all he could do was pray and wait till daybreak, toss and turn and pine, take a cold shower and then a cold bath, make do with attemptin' to please himself, and bite down on his feather pillow.

The door dinged at the Circle K the next morning just after seven a.m.

"Mornin', Mizz Mooray," Chantress chirped as she plucked up a bag of red-hot chips.

Chantress Webb knew good and well Miss Mooray thought she was trailer trash, and Miss Mooray didn't want nothin' to do with Chantress's reappearance. Especially now that Chantress's aunt had gone to her reward. But Chantress didn't care who dissed her. Those who did were ill-informed. They'd beg for her attention soon. "Mizz Mooray…? I said, Mizz Mooray! Kinda heatin' up 'round here, don't you think? Why don't you crank up the dang AC?"

Miss Mooray owned the Circle K and was perched on a stool at the register, imperious, like she owned the world instead of a little convenience store with a license to sell beer. "I heard ya," snapped Miss Mooray, sneering, peering up from her morning paper, wrinklin' her crinkly, turned-up nose. "What you gonna *buy* to cool yourself? Or better yet, you could go your way."

"And deprive you of my presence? I wouldn't think of doin' such a thing. I need me some supplies. I gotta stay put till the estate is settled. Everybody knows Aunt Donna left me a bundle. You should be nice to me. Heck, I'm'a be rich as pecan pie."

"Tramp," Miss Mooray muttered, snappin' her paper, pursin' her lips. Her calico cat meowed and hissed.

Chantress stuck her tongue out at the cat. "Mizz Mooray, what'd you say?"

"I asked if you wanted to purchase *stamps.* You'll be writin' to NOLA, I expect. You got some poor soul waitin' there? A fella to return to?"

"That's a subject for me to know and for you to find out, as far as I can tell. Besides, who sends out snail mail nowadays? Just ancient relics. And not that it's any of your beeswax, but I'm leavin' that beat-up, broke-down town. Them hoity-toities there is just as stuck-up as y'all here. As nosy and as stingy too… bless their hater hearts. I plan to head up north from here. Or west. I ain't decided yet. You gon' read about me in that paper of yours."

"Ain't got one doubt on that." Miss Mooray snickered, bent, picked up the cat.

"Say, who's that hunka brown delight out front there in the T-bird?" Chantress asked.

"What T-Bird?" asked Miss Mooray, havin' a look-see past the spit-shined storefront out into the parking lot. "That ain't no T-Bird, that's a Firebird. Jericho Jordan's. Leave him alone. That boy got a future in this town. He sure don't need the likes of you." Miss Mooray rolled her paper, held it like a bayonet. "Don't set your sights on Jericho. I mean it. He's a good boy."

"Funny how he's followin' me around then, ain't it? In that pretty car. I guess he don't agree with you."

Miss Mooray left her wooden stool to wave Jericho off her property.

The Pontiac fled in a cloud of dust.

The cat leaped onto the counter, lunged at Chantress, scratched her chest.

"Ouch! You get that mangy thang away from me. I'll wring its neck." The cat leaped down and pawed her ankles, rakin' them like a scratching post and raisin' a track of angry welts.

Miss Mooray pounded the counter, waggled her finger, shouted a warning. "Leave Jericho Jordan alone, y'hear? Don't try to cause no trouble."

Chantress bolted toward the exit, pluckin' more chips and mini donuts off a rack and yellin' back. "Lovely doin' business with ya, Mizz Mooray. A pleasure." She grabbed six packs of Bubble Yum. "And don't you frown your prune face up. That's how it gets so wrinkled."

Thunder rolled down to the Circle K in his rickety old Ford pickup in a puff of noxious gray exhaust, his face as dark as a pastor's robe and as dazzling as black onyx. With his trumpet snuggled in his arm like a baby in a bunting, he hopped from the cab to the gravel with a crunch in Superman-blue boots with silver chains and snakeskin bootstraps, poked out his chin and the chip on his shoulder, and bopped to the store wearing wireless earphones and a killer blue-white smile.

Chantress was exitin', squintin', raisin' one arm to shade her amber eyes and cradlin' her pilfered goodies in the other, teeterin' on platform shoes. "Why, Thunder Preston, is that you? Well, if it ain't the music man. I ain't seen you since the Lord made dirt."

"Dag, I wouldn't'a knowed you. You're a sight for sore eyes, Chantress Webb. Girl, you look finer than strawberry wine. Wassup?" He looked her up and down, took her hand and spun her around. "How's New Orleans treatin' ya, baby doll? You must be married now."

"I *was*," she said and rolled her eyes. "You know lovers don't miss they water till they well run dry. Don't matter much. It's over. I've moved on. Romance is like grabbin' a handful of sand." She gave him a side-eye to see if he'd picked up what she'd just put down. "You still workin' in there for Mizz Mooray? She ain't jetted away on her broomstick yet."

"Aw, she all right. She treats me good. She jus' ain't got no time for *you*. Your aunt kept tellin' her you was trouble, and you know how close they was. Like two yolks in one shell."

"I *am* trouble. And you like it. Don't go actin' like you don't." Chantress's tongue slid over her glossy lips. She bumped him with her hip. "In case you forgot, I can jog your memory. Pick me up later for steak and wine?"

"Why you want to play me, Chantress? You jus' huntin' a good free meal."

Chantress stroked his chin and grinned. "Don't look a gift horse in the mouth."

He bent to rub his nose on hers. "Okay, you got me. Seven sharp. But mean it, gal. Don't tease." Thunder cuddled his trumpet and entered the storefront, turnin' around to blow a kiss.

The day went by as clouds swept in, and the night fell like a Wall Street crash.

After a dinner that set Thunder back a hundred fifty bucks plus tip, he drove off with his date and sky-high expectations for the night ahead. The blue house lit up with the duo's music, Chantress ticklin' the ivories, Thunder on trumpet, playin' the blues, the tap of a warm purple rain on the roof. They played past midnight, rockin' the neighborhood, singin' self-written songs.

But unbeknownst to both of them, out at the curb on the slippery street, Jericho brooded in his sedan, while Thunder clapped and rain poured all night long on his parade.

"Ms. Webb, I'm afraid I have difficult news," Arthur Bradshaw of Bradshaw, Tinker and Dunnan told Chantress as she plunked her jade-green miniskirt onto his pricey leather couch and sized him up. His office reeked of top-shelf vodka, imported cigar smoke, furniture polish, heavy designer men's cologne, fresh paint, and jelly beans. A whining rasp of drills and saws ringing out from a nearby renovation caused the attorney to have to shout. "You see," he hollered and cleared his throat, "in regard to your aunt's bequest to you—"

"Spit it out, Artie, how much do I get?"

"Well, that's just it. You don't," the lawyer announced and cleared his throat again.

"Don't, what?" asked Chantress, sitting forward, pinning him down with narrowed eyes.

"You don't inherit anything. Though she suffered a sudden death, her will is in order. She left her entire estate to the foundling home where she sat on the board, the Orphans of Briarcrest Manor. You have to move out of her house by the first, or they'll charge you a sizable rental fee."

Chantress laughed. "You're joking, right?"

"Not in the least. I don't jest like that," the lawyer declared. "Would you like a drink?"

"No, I don't want no friggin' drink. What the hell do you think this is? Do somethin'. You gotta get on the case. There must be some mistake. I'm her only survivin' relative. Her estate belongs to me. You better not try to rip me off, or I'll tell the whole world you're a thief. Where will I go now? What will I do? I come all this way. I quit my job. I gave up my place and everythin'. You gotta fix it. This ain't right!" As reality hit like a roadside bomb, Chantress had to be helped to the lobby. Well, actually, *escorted* out. Forcibly ejected. By security guards and a barking dog. The hammering got louder, and she covered her ears and balked and screamed while they hustled her to a revolving door. "Get away from me!" Chantress kicked and clawed.

"Go, ma'am. Or we'll have you arrested. Quit. Stop makin' a scene," a guard implored.

"It's okay. I'll take her home," a male voice quickly interjected. Jericho seemed to appear out of nowhere, spinning the heavy revolving door, trapping a wailing Chantress in an enclosure, forcing her into the sun as he exited behind her. He nodded back over his shoulder to the guards, who loped to the elevator, one sucking the tip of his finger, the other one rubbing his lower back.

Chantress, diggin' in her heels, slapped Jericho's face and clasped her purse. "You're the creep who's been trailin' me all over town. Bug off, you perv. I'll call the cops."

"Now why would you do a thing like that?" asked Jericho. "I just saved your skin."

"You wish," she carped. "You have some nerve. How dare you. What if someone sees?" She craned up at the building to scout for the law firm's third-floor suite and saw the lawyer.

Bradshaw was glued to a window, leerin' at them, puttin' eyeglasses on.

Chantress ran under a pergola, signaled Jericho to come away.

"Who's he?" inquired Jericho. "You sure got a lot of testosterone around you."

"Mind your business. I'm gonna sue that old snake in the grass and wipe that smirk right off his face." She smoothed her skirt and tossed her hair, peeked up at the window and bit a nail with a look of onrushing anxiety. "Hey, Daddy, do you have a home of your own?"

"Yes'm," Jericho said. "Three bedrooms. Built it by myself."

"Hmm… You're a builder, are ya? Got a nice paycheck comin' from carpentry?"

Jericho nodded. "Very. Why?" He cut his eyes, looked down at her, and watched the wheels turn in her head.

"You single?" She was pickin' up speed, seizin' the opportunity, hangin' her frilly Victoria's Secrets up in his closet in her mind, movin' her flimsy, yellow suitcase in for the kill while the gettin' was good, before she got evicted. "Got a wife or a girlfriend at your place?"

"I ain't seein' nobody at the moment. Nobody special anyway. How 'bout you?" He held his breath, rememberin' Thunder the night before, wonderin' if Thunder was in the blue house.

"Same. Nobody *special*." She noticed his suspicious glare. "I guess you think you're special, huh?"

"I am. And I'm nobody's fool."

We'll see about that. "Yeah, I can tell… I don't suppose you'd like a guest?"

"I don't suppose I would. What I'd like is a woman I knew I could trust." He started to walk away from her. "But I don't think I found one yet."

"I thought you said you'd take me home." She took a single, panicked step.

"*Your* home, not mine," was his retort. "And why would you need to be my guest and wave that red flag in my face? I ain't sayin' you're unwelcome, but you oughta be more subtle."

She fidgeted, looked at the lawyer still watchin' the convo from his windowsill, drinkin' the drink he'd offered her. "Wait." She hurried to Jericho and pressed her breast against his arm. She put her fingers on his thigh and saw his manhood point directly northward like a compass, concluded she literally had him by the balls and she could squeeze. "Ain't you even curious?"

Jericho scrutinized her stare and, winkin', suddenly bent her backward, makin' her lose her balance, whiskin' a stray hair off her face. "They say," he intoned, "if you give someone a fish, you feed them for a day; teach them to fish and you feed them for a lifetime. Is that what you want?" His voice was deep and sexy. "If a girl is my friend, I will teach her to fish. But my woman, I'll fish *for* her."

That nearly knocked Chantress off her feet, and she swooned, unexpectedly taken aback. A flash of uncharacteristic vulnerability lit her face. "You think you'd catch some fish for me?"

He relented, and she regained her stance. "I'll have to catch *you* first."

She batted her lashes, latched onto his elbow, moved in with him that very day.

Thunder's truck cruised up Miss Mooray's driveway at a stealthy speed, into the space she'd provided him ever since his daddy bit the dust. Thunder cradled his trumpet, snatched his groceries, bopped along Jericho's cedar fence by the brand-new house he saw Jericho build on the empty lot next door. Thunder yearned for a house of his own like that. Nah, not just *like* it. Jericho's. He wanted what Jericho had so he could prove he was really the better man. Why the heck was Jericho so smart? And lucky. And creative. How was he able to get what he wanted all the time from everyone? Particularly the ladies. Thunder treaded into Miss Mooray's yard. And that's when he heard 'em. Laughin' and gigglin'. Gruntin' and moanin'. Pantin' and callin' each other's names. *It couldn't be. No way.* Now Thunder was peerin' into a window. It was his turn to witness a beast with two backs, a sight best left unseen. Chantress and Jericho. Makin' love.

Thunder was strong, but his porcelain heartstrings shattered like a china cup. He was a Taurus, a bull seeing red. He felt a sensation of molten lava coursin' through his veins and makin' his blood boil and his mind explode. *Crash!* He broke through a slider and slashed his forearm, spurtin' blood, strikin' at Jericho in his bed, attackin' the way his father had been attacked by the man he'd cuckolded. Thunder leaped onto the mattress on top of the twosome with an unholy cry, punchin', then bearin' down with a wrestling hold to strangle Jericho.

Thunder staggered around to the Bottle & Cork, swaggerin' and swayin' to its bar and proppin' himself on a vinyl barstool, drinkin' until he was high as a kite.

The bartender told him, "Ease up, bro." The bartender must've been six feet five, with a navy tattoo on his left hand and two different-colored eyes. "You want to put some ice on that?"

Thunder patted the pad of his swollen jaw. "No, leave me alone. I want to die."

The bartender chuckled sardonically. "Don't sweat it. You're an endangered species. Plenty of folks are trying to kill you just for living in your skin. Man, you don't have to self-destruct. You've got a big target on your back. Take a nap. When you wake up, you'll feel like a baller. Amazing what some sleep can do. If I had a dime for every guy talkin' a permanent solution to a temporary problem, I would never pour another shot. I'd fly my ass to Cozumel."

Thunder slurred, "You from up North?"

"New York," said the barkeeper. "Bedford-Stuy."

"It figures. I ain't seen you here." Thunder took another swig. "You don't understand."

"Nobody understands anybody. That includes themselves. Why don't you try to meditate? What you need is peace of mind."

"I need fast cash," drunk Thunder confided, wavering on his barstool. He burped and blinked his watery eyes. "I need me a woman. Fine women are scarce."

"So are unicorns. Do you hunt them too?"

"Nope, but I bet it's cheaper. Say…" Thunder coughed and leaned over the bar, a bandage on his forearm. "You ever done somethin' really bad to get the thing you wanted most?"

"Story of my life, bruh. Join the crowd," the bartender replied as he polished a beer mug with a towel and held the mug up to the light. "Damn near everything I really want requires me to do some wrong. Look around. Equal opportunity don't exactly drop in for a drink. Welcome to being a Black man, partner. Nobody's gonna give you squat. When you do it all right and get treated wrongly over and over and over again, and the rules get changed, and the goal line shifts, you eventually plot your own course and decide for yourself what's right and wrong."

"I shoulda stopped by earlier. It sounds like you got it figured out."

"After four hundred years of our ancestors getting screwed, it's factored in. When you know who you're meant to be and you figure out what you're meant to do, you have to stick to that to be a man. It's all about priorities. I mean, look, you've gotta ask yourself: How is this gonna make things better? Who do you want to see in the mirror? Let that guy take action. Let that fellah think your thoughts. Decisions you make will shift the landscape, whether you want to accept it or not, so you might as well get it right, you dig? One choice you make can change the world. You know, maybe your dream isn't big enough if there's too few people in it."

"Dude, I ain't even got a dream. The way I see it," Thunder reasoned, "when you got a woman who's easy on the eyes, you ain't gotta check no mirror. You jus' keep eyeballin' her."

"That's where you're making your big mistake, bruh. You gotta look *inside* to see. Everyone has to have a dream. The trick is in making your dream come true."

"Thunder, you home? I need some help," Miss Mooray called upstairs.

Thunder popped peppermints into his mouth. "Yes, ma'am," he replied. "I'm occupied."

"Boy, bring me a cup of sweet tea down here. I'm thirsty as a cactus plant."

Yeah, and you prickly as one too. "I ain't no boy, ma'am. I'm a man."

"A drunk man," she shot back. "You ain't slick. I can smell you with my ears. Come on now, boy. My pressure's up." She kicked off her shoes and rubbed her feet, nestled into her sandalwood rockin' chair, pulled her rainbow-colored, hand-knit afghan over her legs and her calico cat. "Clean up in that kitchen, baby. One of these days, it's gonna be yours."

"Jericho, wake up! What's that noise?" Chantress sat up in his bed.

"Huh?" moaned Jericho, fast asleep. He was havin' a wet dream, suckin' her boobies, feelin' her up in his scorchin' sheets, spoonin' her into his manliness.

"Somebody's tryin' to break into the house!" she hissed into his ear.

Jericho sat bolt upright, cracked his eyelids open, yawned, and stretched. He leaned and listened to the dark. "It better not be Thunder, or I'll open a bigger can of whoop ass than the one he ate before. Wait here. I'll see what's goin' on. Lock the door when I'm gone and grab your phone." He rolled out of the bed, and he searched with his feet for his flip-flops, groped for the baseball bat by his nightstand, hesitated, crossed the floor, forged out, and closed the door.

A loud pop shattered the still of the night.

A gunshot? Chantress dove onto a rug, dragged the top sheet over her nudity, crawled on her knees and elbows to the door, reached up to flip the lock. "Jericho? Are you okay?"

The doorknob jiggled, clicked, and rattled. Chantress scooted away from it.

Bam! Something crashed to the hardwood flooring. Chantress muffled a scream. She shivered, broke out in an icy sweat, eyes scanning the length of the bedroom as a shadow flashed on the moonlit pale gray walls and crept along. She balled herself up by a closet, and as its door stood ajar with a gaping mouth, men's clothing draping over it, she thought she saw a monster. A figure spread fright on a window shade.

"Help!" screamed Chantress. "Jericho!"

The doorknob rattled. The whole wall shook.

"It's me," said Jericho. "Let me in," he implored as he banged on the bedroom door. "Ain't nothin' to be scared of. Some old car backfired outside, is all."

Chantress opened the door and flew into his arms. "I thought you—"

"Don't be afraid," he said. "Hey, look, it's only Mooray's cat. Ain't nobody here but you and me." He scooped up the calico cat to deposit it onto the edge of a windowsill, and it made its escape to the patio. "Hush. I got you. It's okay. You jus' feel like a fish outta water now. You're safe here. Come on back to bed. I know how to relax you."

Chantress gathered the sheet around her, frowned. "But how'd it get out so late at night? That cat is an omen. It's bad luck." She marched to the window, snapped open the shade, stared darts at Miss Mooray's Victorian. It's somethin' unnatural happenin' in that house. I bet—"

"Girl, move away. Go splash cold water on your face and put you on a nightie."

When Chantress returned from the bathroom in her lingerie and cherry scent, Jericho had a candle lit, and a breeze blew down from a ceiling fan. The man looked good enough to eat a second helping of. His body resembled Olorun's, the African King of the Heavens.

"Where'd you get them underthings, girl? You got a price tag on your butt."

"Oh these? Why, Thunder give 'em to me." Chantress fanned around and smiled in a pink lace push-up bra and scanty string bikini panties trimmed with tiny satin bows. "Like 'em?"

"Take 'em off right now! What is he givin' you dainties for?"

"He's a friend. I told you, we worked together. He's just tryin' to be nice, is all."

"I bet. I'm'a throw 'em right back in his face. After what he did this afternoon? Don't look like no damn friend to me. He tried to take me out. Now I gotta replace that slidin' door. That deadbeat ain't gon' pay for it. Whose side are you on, gal? His or mine? I'll buy you all the frills you want. You don't have to get nothin' from no other man, far less wacky Thunder. He's nuts. I think he lost his mind. Don't play us against each other or you may regret the outcome."

Chantress guffawed, threw the curtain aside. "So you want me to strip 'em off, is that it? Thunder might even get a peek. Is that what you're after, a pissin' contest? Fine. I can put on a show if you like." She started by droppin' her bra straps, twirlin' and prancin' in front of the open window. A light flickered on across the street as she whipped off her 34 double D bralette and spun it above her head.

"Gimme! Act like a lady," he shouted, tugging the curtains closed and draping a bathrobe over her shoulders. He lifted her off her feet and into the bed and pinned her down. "Whaddaya want, all the neighbors to see?" He yanked off her undies, plunged Jericho Junior deep inside her, bucked his hips.

"Ooh…" She moaned and met his thrusts. "Oh more," she begged. "It feels so good."

After they both were satiated, Jericho went on the march, tromping his bare feet through the dewy grass of his front yard, clumping a path to Thunder's truck and slingshotting Chantress's sheer sleepwear to the back of its muddy flatbed. It landed on a thick blue tarp on the rear of the ancient 4x4. He paused to reconnoiter underneath and saw big sacks of lye, a shovel, a box of garbage bags, and a stained, imported, antique rug.

What's Thunder doin' with all that lye? he wondered as he turned toward home. Was he fixin' to make hair straightener? Candles? Lotion? Clean Miss Mooray's drains? "Who cares?" he concluded with a shrug. "I got what I want waitin' for me in my bedroom with no panties on. It ain't none of my business what Thunder does. As long as it ain't with my wife-to-be."

Jericho strode back to his house to make love all night long to the spoils of war.

That Friday, when the eagle flew and Jericho cashed a massive check, he brought a dozen roses home to Chantress from a construction site, but when he arrived he got shocking news.

"Yippee, you're back. Mizz Mooray took poison!" Chantress greeted breathlessly.

But Miss Mooray did not *take* the poison; someone *poisoned* Miss Mooray. That was splashed on the crawl of the evening news. The next-door neighbor was dead, and reports said her killer was still at large. The murderer tried to get rid of her body, but did so unsuccessfully. What little remained of her corpse was found by a sheriff's deputy after a call from a tipster at the city dump, where residents were free to dispose of garbage as large as their pickup trucks to fill the local landfill. The cadaver was bundled up into a rug, and now cops were crawling all over the dump to mine for latent clues. Like the serial number they found on her pacemaker linkin' to the barcode on the label in her medical files, immediately allowin' the cops to identify both implant and patient.

Jericho pondered the sum of the items he'd seen in Thunder's truck. Had Thunder done the dirty deed? That's what they added up to. The shovel, the rug, the bags, the lye. They all held Jericho's fingerprints. Did Thunder know he'd scoped it all? If so, then what would he do now?

Chantress, her hair up in pink foam rollers, was pacing the length of the family room, fannin' herself while observin' what was takin' place outside the house, narratin' blow-by-blow details to Jericho, who sat deep in thought. "That family from the mid-century house is outside lickin' Kool-Aid pops. Can you imagine? Slurpin' treats. I couldn't eat a bite," said Chantress. "Not with all this fuss. And what's with that couple snappin' cell phone pics? To post on Instagram? They'll wind up goin' viral. And some pregnant teen is out there too, bouncin' her baby right out in the middle of the road with cop cars racin' up and swarmin' this entire block."

"The police are gonna question people. What you gonna tell 'em, girl?"

Chantress, later in Jericho's kitchen, a shaky hand holdin' a cigarette, said, "Yeah, I went to the Circle K, but only once. My first day here. Since I been stayin' with Jericho, like I said, I don't shop at Mizz Mooray's. I go to the supermarket out on Lattimore and Watley Street. They got much better prices there and a nicer selection, if you ask me. It's a lot of rich white folks out that way. That's why they got fresher veggies, more whole foods, and leaner meats. I don't shop at the Circle K no more. They only carry junk food."

"But nevertheless, you just moved in next door to the Circle K's owner, miss," said a Black cop wearing a deadpan expression, his elbows on the table. "Thunder Preston informed us you hated the deceased and the feeling was mutual. That true?"

"No, officer, that's a lie," said Chantress, tryin' her best to look aghast, aggrieved, and innocent. "It's a shame he would say such a terrible thing. Why, it's not a shred of truth. In fact, Mizz Mooray and my Aunt Donna—she passed so I came to bury her—them two was as close as a pair of tits. Mizz Mooray was family. More or less. And anyhoo, Thunder's a villainous liar. He's envious, that's all. He's mad that I'm being with Jericho 'cause he wants me for hisself."

"Interesting," the cop said, jerking his head toward the barn-style basement door. "But the evidence speaks for itself, and you haven't explained—"

"I don't know how her blood got down there," Chantress wailed. "It wasn't me."

"Hey, barkeep!" Thunder triumphantly shouted. "Gimme another round."

"Be cool," the bartender told him. "I'm obliged to cut you off. And this is the second time this week."

"A martini this time," said Thunder. "Bottoms up." He polished off his drink.

"Slow down. A martini costs more than a beer."

"No worries. I got piles of cash. I'm celebratin'. Life is good."

"Don't advertise. It don't look right. The 411's all over town about you getting the Circle K, gas station, car wash, and the house. Not to mention all Miss Mooray's dough."

"So? What about it?" Thunder asked. "Just what are you implyin'?"

"That Jericho Jordan is rottin' in jail for a crime he didn't really do," said a man on a stool at the end of the bar who was white, red-haired, and drinking

Irish whiskey straight, no chaser. "No one's buyin' that Jericho bumped her off. The killer just made it look that way. Jericho is a stand-up guy. He ain't got no motive and ain't the type. Plus, *you* got his ladylove."

"Real sweet, ain't it?" Thunder chuckled. "Loverboy's headed to death row, and I'm headed to the bank." He laughed. "Where's that martini? Put two olives. No, let's make it three."

"You might as well tell us how you did it," the bartender said as he shook the martini.

"Yeah, you're in the clear now you got Jericho fitted up for it," said the man at the end of the bar.

"I don't know what you're talkin' about," said Thunder, chewin' a mouthful of olives. Y'all are trippin'. Yo, I'm out."

Thunder drunkenly drove his new black Jeep from the Bottle & Cork past the muddy FOR SALE sign tilting askew on Jericho's lawn. Jericho's grass was dried and brown, his colorful flowers withered. The home seemed to shrink with a grief all its own. Thunder stumbled into Miss Mooray's and ran right into Chantress Webb. "Get over here. Do me," he insisted. "You ain't stayin' here for free."

Chantress attempted to push him away, but he shoved her to her knees. "I don't wanna."

"Really? That's too bad. You gotta do what I say or I'll toss you back out on the street."

Chantress, her face pressed into his crotch, yelled, "No!" She wriggled. "Let me be!"

"Damnit, you gave it to Jericho Jordan when and however he asked you to."

"That's because Jericho—"

"Jericho what?" He jerked her to her feet and punched her, twisted her bony arm around. "Jericho what!"

"I didn't say nothin.'" Chantress cowered, her red lips pressed together.

"I didn't think so, glamour girl. You ain't so high-and-mighty now. Go fry a catfish, cook some grits, and bring me a cerveza." He smacked her face and, glaring, taunted. "Now that we're married, I get it whenever I want. Your soul belongs to me. Fix me my dinner before I get mad."

Chantress, blood trickling from her nose, her flawless complexion as bruised as her ego, mumbled as she slipped away. "I'll fix you, all right. You wait and see."

Three days later, Thunder died.

"We did it, handsome," Chantress said as a Jeep crossed the border to Mexico, huggin' the shore as it sailed down the coast and a tropical breeze blew through her hair.

"I told you we could jump it off," said the Bottle & Cork's bartender as he steered around a curve, his right hand roaming beneath her dress.

"Won't be long before they come lookin' for us, and that could cause a problem."

"You mean looking for *you*," the bartender declared. "I didn't poison anyone."

She laughed. "Okay, but we're in it together. I couldn't'a done it without your help. And anyway, we'll be long gone by the time they learn how Thunder died. I shoulda killed him twice. You're gonna make sure they don't catch us, right?"

"No one ever catches *me*. You'll have to look out for yourself."

"I don't think I like the way that sounds." She pouted, pushed his hand away. "It was you who planned to kill Aunt Donna. And then when her money was fallin' through, you told me I had to get Thunder all pumped up to murder Miss Mooray, so when Thunder inherited, you and I could—"

"Right. As long as the money lasts, we're good. We're both adults."

"Wait. I thought you wanted *me*. You said this cash is for our future." Frowning, she picked up the messenger bag she'd stuffed with thousand-dollar bills and held it to her chest.

"Don't worry, baby. It's all good. You got me wrapped around your pinky finger like those other guys." He smiled and snatched the bag and over-the-shouldered it to the backseat. "You got trumpet boy so into you he got down and proposed to you off the bat. The sucker didn't have a clue you were already married to me. I've got to hand it to you; you sure led him down the primrose path. I knew you were more than a pretty face when I met you in New Orleans. You worked your mojo, that's for sure. You put that poor sap Jericho in jail, and he still loves you."

"Somebody had to take the rap," said Chantress. "Might as well be him. Let's hope he gets convicted. After that, they won't come look for us. It was easy to plant that blood down in his basement. What a chump. He does have a certain somethin', but he ain't as good as you… Once we get settled on the beach, I'm'a get me a grand piano. If it's the last thing I do, I'll—"

Bang! A shot plowed into the woman sunning herself in the passenger seat, her bare feet on the dashboard. A yellow straw hat flew out of the Jeep as Chantress sang her swan song.

Jericho's house sold superquick. So fast he had nowhere to go when the jury acquitted him and turned him loose. New evidence pointed to Chantress Webb. And when Chantress's body washed up in the Gulf of Mexico in Thunder's Jeep, identified only by her teeth, what remained was a mystery involving the solid gold wedding band stuck on the bloated third finger of her small left hand. It wasn't the ring Thunder gave her from Miss Mooray's full safe deposit box, or the diamond Jericho bought her before she landed him in jail. No, this was a handcrafted, one-of-a-kind piece made and sold in New Orleans. It was purchased by an unknown man. Or a man who was not pinpointed *yet*.

Now that Jericho's free—well, except from his rage—he is wendin' his way down the Mexican coast, stayin' hot on the murderer's cold-hearted trail.

WEB
OF
GUYS

SHE THOUGHT JUSTICE WAS BLIND AND TRUE LOVE WOULD BE TOO. But she realized the hard way that neither was true.

When Love Dies was the title of the romance movie flickering on the old-school TV. The grainy film's syrupy sex scenes featured an innocent heroine living in happily-ever-after mode. The script held no hint that her love or her life could be snuffed out in an instant. But Arrow knew better. Her love was gone. And all that was left was her bitter regret, a pale glimmer of passion that might have been, and the aftershock of brutality streaming concurrently in her mind.

Her fingers were numb from the rough rope binding her wrists and making her skin grow raw and her palms turn red and swollen. Her throat was so dry she could barely swallow water, if some ever came. Her stomach growled from lack of food, but she didn't feel hungry or thirsty now, she just longed to take a breath. Clinging to life was her only goal. That and breaking free.

The volume of the music grew louder, rocking the television on its stand, and the thuds of crazy dancing feet kicked into high gear overhead. *What was going on up there?*

How soon would the dancing stop and the cycle of torture begin anew?

The space was freezing, dank, and musty. Like a cellar, Arrow thought. She whiffed the sweet and sour aroma of foods like dill pickles and homemade preserves mingled into the stench of old black mold. She heard *tap, tap, tap* from leaky pipes and imagined a colorful image of her weightless body flying over trees on soaring mountaintops. These expanded the breadth of her consciousness as she pondered the billions of galaxies expanding to eternity, propelling herself from her confines into empty, open airspace, drifting out of the atmosphere into the stratosphere, traveling through the universe. Free. As free as a glittering starburst floating in the Milky Way.

Her head throbbed like a rotten tooth, and her prone position strapped against the cold stone ceiling rendered her suspended and as still as in the confines of a grave. Blood cascaded in steady drips from her temple into her eyes, leaving a netherworld-ish pall of red that blurred her vision. Dangling in a foggy haze, she felt just one step on this side of the veil, and she wondered how long she'd hung like this, how long she'd been knocked out. An hour, a day, a week, a month? She had no way of telling. The sense of her being a new-age, female Rip van Winkle crowded in, as if she had time-traveled into a futuristic, Brothers Grimm fable. The atoms of her body came awake in stiff discomfort as the gravity of her situation sank into her cognizance. She was out of her element, out of answers, running out of time.

"Arrow," she heard her faint voice croak. "Arrow, what are you waiting for?" Inches away, she saw her face. It stared at her with sunken eyes, beckoning to her, insistent, weary, wearing its usual full-lipped smile, radiating angelic energy, encouraging her to fight for her survival while she still could try. "Think fast. It's now or never. Move!"

Gathering her resolve and renewing remembered efforts to escape before she was hoisted off her feet, she struggled against the ties that bound her to the creaky rafters. The raw earthen floor seemed miles away. Cords tightened around her neck increasingly with every achy move, her writhing motions shaving splinters from the wood beams through the arch of her spine. Her jaw was pried open by a burlap gag that served to muffle screams, and the crunching noise the fibrous fabric made between her clenching teeth sent shivers up her spine. Adhesive from duct tape stuck to the delicate skin around her eyes. There appeared to be no way out while the grim reaper stalked the shadows curled about her, shrouding the quickening breath of her captor's yearning for her demise. A malevolent presence worked to creep inside her restless, dwindling soul. Trying to break her spirit. Longing to watch it leave her body. *Go away!* she bade it, yet it loomed.

"Mind over matter," Pop would say. "The mind controls the body." The gist of her dead father's ethos jammed the corners of her mindfulness, setting her willful fantasies adrift to safer times—ice cream and cake, balloons and gifts, family and friends at a birthday party. Picnics at the beach. Her first morning attending Sunday school. Graduation from strict Our Lady of Grace high school, then Stanford, then through Yale. These were the memory movies that projected on the big screen of her disconcerted mind, none of them real in the present save the terror threatening life and limb.

It seemed such a good idea back then, yet now it seemed so stupid. Even hindsight wasn't twenty-twenty as her thoughts fell back, back, back to the day the adventure first began…

"Dave Blaylock?" Tiffany suggested, swiping through her legions of cell contacts.

"Too rigid." Arrow waved him off.

"Rigidity on a man is great," quipped Tiffany. "How about Tony Cloud?"

Arrow judged, "He's too controlling."

"This from the woman who wants to pick her dream man's occupation, hobbies, height, religion, diet, car, and color and style of underwear… Well, fine, there's always Clayton Dunn."

"Are you kidding?" Arrow flicked a hand. "He arranges the books on his office shelves in alphabetical order. If Clayton were any more anal retentive, he'd have to go see a proctologist."

"Choosy sisters choose Clay, Row. I hear his—"

"I'm not interested. We're looking for Mr. Right, not Mr. Left Because He's So Uptight."

"Hmm. Okay, let's deep dive, then…" Tiffany bit her lower lip, kept scrolling through her contacts app. "Sloan Fortuneau."

"He's really sweet. But face it, he has a bubblehead."

"That means he has a bigger brain. And what has his head got to do with it?"

"Ratings, that's what it has to do. You saw Sloan at the beach in Sag Harbor this summer. His Speedos were slowed to a crawl. We have to pick someone superfine. The guy must be telegenic. Consider the demographic, Tiff. Women eighteen to thirty-four aren't trying to watch Pumpkinhead get wed. They're into Black Panther or 007. The Rock, not the Michelin Man."

"Good point," said Tiffany. "Let's press on." Her fingers alit on an entry in her phone that made her eyes light up. "Okay, perfect. Here he is. I've got it. What about Bruce Head?"

Arrow slow-burned, turned, and smirked. "My name would then be Arrow Head?"

"Oh. I didn't think of that… Now look, this is getting ridiculous. You're my bestie, but I have to say you're being way too picky."

"Picky? Well, you have some nerve. You didn't exactly settle. I notice your husband is not only gorgeous but nice, big-hearted, supersmart, and totally over the moon for you. He's generous, sensitive, sober, straight, Ivy League-frigging-educated, funny, and oh, did I mention rich? Excuse me, I almost forgot that part."

"Okay, okay, I see your point. Relax. We're going to find someone. Trust me, this is my forte. But whatever happened to rocking that spiritual, meta-physical, new-age thing you were into before we started this? That old dating objective you used to spout about how you must work through your personal issues, transform into someone you'd want to date, and indulge in self-care on a regular basis so karma will gift you your perfect mate at the abso-perfect time?"

"It went out with rotary phones, real hair, MySpace, and eight-track tapes. Are you down to work this out or not?"

"I'm trying. I'm not hunks dot com."

"Oh no? Well, you sure used to be. Since we're strolling down memory lane and all, I remember the days when you had two dates each night and four on weekends."

"That's different. See? You made my point. I wasn't all that picky. Single women should be like butterflies, happily flitting from flower to flower, gaining strength and sustenance as they go… Hey, let's update your dating profile. Ditch the 'long walks at the beach,' for one."

"Ix-nay on the internet dating sites. That guy with the purple car and suit and hat and pointy wing-tip shoes who took me to In-N-Out Burger for dinner demolished that dream in one fell swoop. Those dating profiles lie like dogs." Arrow plunked down onto Tiffany's sectional, buried her head in a furry pillow. "Look, I don't mean to roll you up, but I feel like my life is on the line. We built companies for successful men, and what do we have to show for it? Now that we're out on our own, we have to get every detail right. Our first production has to smoke."

"I know, and it's freaking me out. I've been running and starving and joined a gym—despite the equipment here at home—and I even signed on with Jenny Craig."

"I scheduled liposuction."

"Don't think for a minute that being a wifey stifles insecurities. Hollywood isn't exactly opening its arms, awaiting our next premiere. They think we're the walking dead at forty. Reality shows are a dime a dozen. If we don't drum up some major buzz, this show is our last shot."

"We have to come up with a catchy name. Show title is a make or break."

"For real. We've been narrowing it down for weeks," said Tiffany, opening her laptop. "We need to decide on a working title, something to pitch that really zings."

"Let's go over the names we like the most and pick the one that sounds the bomb." Arrow tapped into her Notable app. "How do you feel about *Double Trouble*?"

"Meh. That one's been done to death."

"*Married or Harried* is kinda cute. Or what about this one, *Give Me a Ring*? The double entendre might catch on."

"Hold on, let's see if it's been done," said Tiffany, tapping her laptop keys. "Nope, no movies, shows, or books. Okay, it's cool. I like it best. I'm thinking it's our fave."

"Agreed. We'll go with it for now. It could bag a big jewelry advertiser too, and that'd be really dope. Our sponsor appeal is everything."

"And speaking of that, let's nail our hook and edit our elevator pitch."

"We already have the logline set. We said our tagline could be this." Arrow tapped her tablet. "What if a happily wedded woman vows to marry her best friend off and film the whole thing as a TV show without her girlfriend's knowledge?"

"It's tight. It sums up our idea. If we flesh it out into a two-minute max—"

"Whoa, Tiff, let's not get ahead of ourselves. Before we take another step, we have to be sure there's a guy out there who's willing to go all in with us. Without that, there's no premise. He'll have to pretend I'm unaware and be willing to marry me on cam. That's a pretty tall order for any man, so we thought we could work with a guy we know, but—"

"No one seems to fit the bill," said Tiffany, biting her lip again. "I feel you. And beyond the show, Row, he could be a lifetime. I get it. I've been tripping too. I've been trying to come up with a gimmick that can hike our platform up a notch, a way to hack into huge audience share before we shoot the pilot. Bottom line, we have to monetize."

"You're right. We lack two giant things. The man and the way to go viral," Arrow said. "Without those, nothing works. We need to be able to answer those questions, or no one will get behind us, and our marketing plan will be a bust… unless we can combine the two."

"But how in the world could we jump that off?"

The two women sat silently, churning their thoughts, Tiffany rocking from side to side and Arrow staring at the ceiling, sucking on a fingernail.

In a flash, Arrow bounded to her feet. "I have a fanrific idea!" she yelled. "To kill the two birds with one stone."

"I'm almost scared to ask," said Tiffany, leaning forward, eyes ablaze.

"One word."

"And that is…"

"Crowdsource."

Tiffany tilted her beautiful head and wrinkled her nose in puzzlement. "Yeah, I know we said we would. But later, after we shoot some footage. Then we can post a trailer too."

"We said we'd crowdfund up the line to supplement the budget, but we didn't discuss crowd*sourcing* yet."

"I don't get it. That's for money, right? What else are we going to crowdsource for?"

"The man."

"What man?"

"The marriage man."

"Oh, I get it. They're for different things."

"We do a crowdfunding campaign to raise money to reach production budget goals, but before that we can problem-solve with a really exciting crowdsource that could gather a team to help with stuff—like finding the perfect mate for me. Hey, what about starting a crowd contest to get people to hunt for the marriage man in order to win some prizes? We could also trawl for men ourselves by setting up a spot where eligible bachelors could apply."

"Awesome. Sexy. Interactive. Lots of possibilities."

"Folks can submit a guy they know," said Arrow.

"That'll increase the odds."

"A woman could set up a man as a way of gently breaking up with him."

"A groom can nominate groomsmen or a widower—"

"Or coworker. Divorcées can submit their ex."

"The pool will expand exponentially. The show will blow up like crazy even before we film a single frame."

"It's hipper than casting an actor or rummaging through your black book day and night."

"We're sure to find your perfect match," said Tiffany. "Let's get on it."

"Imagine the hits we'll generate, all the social network posts we'll prompt."

Tiffany squealed and clapped her hands. "And think about the overflow. We can give away men as prizes when the crowd campaign is over if we have them sign permission forms."

"The Marriage Man Giveaway. It'll be huge," said Arrow with a toothy grin.

"Most people give crappy key chains or some lame product they're out to sell. A real live man trumps any bait. And the men will find true love for free. Win-win. I love it. Plus the cash."

"It's a bunch of seed money in the bag. And when we narrow the men to ten, we simply select the marriage man by taking a vote on the website, driving tons of traffic to our page."

"And scoring awesome SEO. That's when we do our crowdfund."

"Where the dollars will come pouring in. We'll feature the ideal marriage man when the guy who gets the most votes wins. Fan favorite. He'll have real star power. The viewers will love to watch a show they're casting from day one. You're the couple they'll matchmake from the start," said Arrow, slapping her knee. "Audience participation no one's ever seen before."

"We'll probably crash the internet."

"Show budget, audience survey, marriage man, and ratings all in one. This bad boy's bound to win awards. It rocks. It's revolutionary," Tiffany declared.

"Think of the buzz by the time we air."

"By the time we hunt for sponsors."

"By the time we pitch the networks, Tiff. There's bound to be a bidding war."

"Let's start by shooting a promo with our phones to get things rolling, 'kay?"

"Uh-huh. And hit up cell phone sponsors once we get the trailer done."

"Guys will be itching to get on board."

"We'll turn them into superstars."

"Celebrities will want in too—and bachelors tired of dating sites," Tiffany concluded.

"And I'm loving your phrase for the title, Row. Let's call the show *The Marriage Man*."

"Sweeet! That's what it's all about."

"A dream girl searching for her dreamboat. It'll be like a fairy tale."

"I'll shoot Prince Charming through the heart." Arrow hopped into her archer stance and pretended to aim and release a bow.

They slapped high fives.

They had their show. They envisioned awards, renewals, and good times rolling.

What they didn't see was the trouble—spelled with a capital T—awaiting them online.

The Marriage Man crowdsource went live in two weeks, up on RaiseIt. com, the hottest crowdsourcing website you could find anywhere on the internet.

Arrow designed the stunning site from a trip on the road with Arrow and Tiffany's former boss, Sebastian Bronco Blazer. Bronco was loath to let his girls go to pursue other projects of their own, and he made no bones about it. That made for a sticky situation, but they felt they owed him one, and they thought they might need him at some point, so Arrow consented to work on a movie Bronco was filming outside LA on location down in New Orleans—a biopic featuring Sweet Daddy Raines, the one-armed jazz musician. It was scheduled to shoot for just a week, but the shoot got delayed due to thunderstorms that threatened the Gulf of Mexico.

While Arrow placated their erstwhile boss, Tiffany held it

down in the industrial loft in Marina del Rey that housed GirlPower Entertainment on the upper floor. The office was small but überhip, a new level of independence for the crack-shot TV team. The besties had helmed it for six short months. Tiffany found it déclassé because she was used to finer digs, but only for the past few years. She'd grown up poor in Houston, Texas, made it to college at USC, and after post-gradding at UCLA, scored architect Byrdley Benchmark, who was in demand around the globe. Byrd was finishing renos on their massive Malibu Beach enclave, a four-story seaside showplace sporting panoramic shoreline views—twenty thousand square feet of hardwood floors, sleek ultramodern furnishings, and outdoor space ten times the size of the shack young Tiffany grew up in. These days, her sunny, airy bedroom opened to a white-sand beach.

Tiffany's house seemed a distant dream to Arrow, who was on her own and longing for a hearth and home, who wondered if and when her slice of heaven would appear. Despite the upcoming reality show, she feared true love was fiction and her love light might not ever shine. Arrow thought Tiffany's man was great and her lifestyle was incredible, and Tiff herself was beautiful. She towered as straight and lithesome as a tree, with a shock of light brown kinks, doe eyes that were brown and hazel-flecked, and skin like golden honey.

Arrow thought Tiffany had it all and never imagined she did too, so oblivious was she to her gifts and beauty and pure energy. Arrow was wrapped in ebony on a tiny, fragile, flawless frame. An original creative, she was ingenious; multitalented; fluently spoke five languages; wrote screenplays; coded; cooked; woodworked; could sing like a lark, though she seldom did; designed jewelry, clothing, and home goods; and edited film and audio so well she won awards. As a former freelance journalist, she interviewed famous people who were fascinated by her wit, and yet as a writer-producer, she was quite the mystery woman. Single, lonely, insecure, devoid of social life and skills, she was rarely seen in company or with a male plus-one. At five feet and ninety-eight lean pounds, she was barely a cup of brown sugar, but her presence was a stunning blend of lengthy braids, a jaded smirk, and the courage of a lioness. Arrow planned to take the world by storm, or she'd die trying.

By contrast, Tiff was self-assured. Prancing around like she always did, she was squeezed into skintight denim shorts, a shimmery gold lamé tank top, Byrd's dazzling diamond earrings gift, and a necklace of gold sea-shells. She looked like a sea goddess washed onto shore from a fanciful, exotic realm. A barely human Nubian princess striding among far lesser mortals, comfy in her astonishing incarnation of feminine pulchritude and ready to take the world by storm.

The day after the wrap of the Bronco shoot, after Bronco forcefully hit on her for the nine gazillion jillionth time, Arrow flew home to Hollywood Hills and out of Bronco's clutches. Tingling with the coming thrill of viewing *The Marriage Man* crowdsource site without Bronco hovering over her shoulder, Arrow was keen to dislodge recollections of Bronco's final desperate gropes. The harassment she suffered at Bronco's hands was fading like sepia photographs until a florist truck showed up with a giant bouquet of chocolate-scented *Cosmos atrosanguineus*, fire lilies, Queen of the Night Kadupul blossoms, and Indonesian corpse flower buds that smelled like rotting flesh. From Bronco, of course, a small card read, "Please. You need me. Let me in."

Bronco, considered a major catch, was really just exhausting. He had a good heart and all that stuff, but he had a tempestuous temper too and was bullying and invasive. And to boot, he was needy for everything—attention, ego gratification, food, wine, drugs, sex, everything. His weirdo fixation with Arrow gave her a pain in the butt that never stopped.

Once safely ensconced in the coolness of her Afrofuturistic tiny house at the edge of a cliff in the Hollywood Hills, Arrow warmed a quick bowl of her veggie soup and a veggie burger topped with peppers, eggplant, grilled zucchini steaks, and a generous slab of manchego cheese. She made an identical sandwich for Tiffany—adding sriracha sauce to it—and she peered out the window to look for her bud, who was due to arrive any minute.

Today the campaign was going live, and they wanted to share the big event, but Tiff was late as usual, so while waiting, Arrow climbed up in her loft bed, booted her laptop, tapped on the web, and googled several articles: "How to Tame the Crowdsource Beast," "Crowdsourcing Like a Real Boss Babe," "Crowdsourcing Men Crazy with Cool Clickbait," and "Love Bytes: Let the Crowd Source You." She skimmed sad stories of crowdsourcing mishaps—slowdowns to slackers to hidden costs to rip-offs of lucrative ideas—but none of the pitfalls scared her off, and she leaped to the door when Tiffany rang the bell and gave her friend a hug.

"How many?" Tiffany gushed, face flushed, rushing in as if she were being chased.

"I didn't look. I waited for you," Arrow said. "C'mon, let's go log in."

They hurried to Arrow's minisofa, Arrow cradling her laptop on one arm and setting it on the couch, crossing her legs in a yoga position and logging into the RaiseIt site. "I'm glad we chose this platform. It has such amazing features. It was a snap to submit our idea. Community support is off the charts, there's a panel to review and score, we can pick out winners as we go, and the app can announce who they are and distribute rewards. Your tip about it worked."

"Well, Byrdley recommended it. I'm just happy it panned out. I'm jazzed about the way it looks, and I'm really glad you're back in town. I sent the giant email blast to my address list, your list, and Byrd's—so I'm hoping we get some folks we know."

"It's happening. Cross your fingers."

Tiffany reached for Arrow's hand as they focused on the laptop screen, and Arrow swirled around her mouse pad, bringing up a landing page.

A list of usernames appeared, their numbers mounting on a scoreboard.

"Whoa. Check those submissions, Tiff."

"We almost have two thousand votes, and we've only been up for half an hour."

"It looks like RaiseIt's rating them according to our specs."

"It's working, Row. We're getting nibbles."

"Nibbles? These are shark bites." Arrow pointed at the screen. "Those are the votes for the show idea. Ninety-nine percent five-star."

"Wait'll we post on social. We'll be going through the roof."

"I guess we wrote the challenge right," Arrow decided. "They're responding."

"Sending us some good ideas. I can't wait to scroll through here and see what we can implement."

"Over three hundred men submitted. I feel like a kid in a candy store."

"I'll say. Let's click on that one there. He's called Eighth Wonder of the World."

Arrow tapped a subject line. A message pop-up box appeared, and Arrow read its contents: "'Tall. Athletic. Kind. A pro. Commitment no problem.

Marriage material. Project manager if you need one. Production experience 12+ yrs. Honest. Potential family man. Hit me up. I'll help you guys.' Okay, this dude goes on the list. I don't care if he's a vampire. I'm adding him to our favorites box." Arrow clicked a heart, and it turned red and started dancing.

"Next?" said Tiffany, fanning herself. "Crowdsourcing turns me on."

Arrow scrolled down to the next icon. "West Indian Master Dominator."

"Bump you. Dominate yourself," said Tiffany.

"Yup, amen to that," said Arrow. "Who does he think he is? I have people oppressing me all day long because of my complexion, and he thinks I want him on my back? Delete. He goes in the round file. Hey, this dude looks interesting. Wounded Warrior. Fought in Afghanistan. He says he needs to turn the page. Legally blind but a graphic artist. Look at the artwork he attached. Got hit by an IED in Kabul. Check out his amazing eyes. Hold on, I want to message him."

"Okay, but do it when we're done. There are too many fish in the sea right now, and we have to get them vetted. We said we'd hire a private eye for background checks and all like that, so we don't hook you up with who-knows-who. Byrd says there are world-class liars running around out there in cyberspace, and a lot of men prefer to tell a lie to women than the truth. A walk on the wild side does sound fun, but we'd better know who we're dealing with. The marriage man has to be squeaky clean and… ooh la la, check that one there."

"But you just said—"

"We're window shopping. Looking. We don't have to buy. Trust me, I'm a dating wiz."

"And I'm a dating *was*, I guess."

"No, Arrow, you're the prize. You're everything a man could want, and you deserve your perfect match. We're not selling you one iota short, you hear me? You're a queen."

"Hold on while I sit on the throne, okay?" Arrow hurried to the bathroom.

Tiffany shouted after her. "I'll set the match filter for best to least to weed out some of the cornballs, stiffs, and wackos off the bat. I watched a YouTube video on several ways to sort."

When Arrow returned, the sort was done. "Let's set up another challenge too, a call for an unpaid intern. Somebody has to go through this. It's bound to take up time. We need to be free for other things," Arrow said and rubbed her temple. "Let's mentor a smart young girl in exchange for doing minor grunt work. If she's good, we can hire her later on."

"You betcha. We're a rising tide. We can lift all boats." Tiffany browsed the database. "But this is a lot of machismo, sis. Are you confident we're up for this?"

"We're fine. We're learning as we go. Don't punk out on me now. We're just feeling a little overwhelmed. It's called impostor syndrome. Women get it all the time. No matter what we accomplish, we can sense success is only luck. We're scared we might be frauds. We think we'll get exposed as not the experts we purport to be. But we've been putting in our time. We're smart and brave. We know our stuff. We have what it takes. We got this."

"Inspire, sister. Break it down. We're boss babes. We are in control."

Arrow gasped, began to swoon. "Far out!"

"Oh no. What now?"

"The one," Arrow said leaning into the screen so close that her nose nearly touched it. "I don't need to look any further, Tiff. A guy named Adonis just signed in, and man, is he a killer."

In the crazy days that followed, Arrow fell madly head-over-heels in love. Not with a smile or a sensuous kiss or a kindly attentive tilt of a head or the sparkle in a young man's eye. Not with the allure of workmen's hands or the humor of lightning wit or other criteria she once held, but with lustful words on her monitor screen deep into her sleepless, cold-sheet nights. When she woke to the beats of her bleeding heart and the ticks of her biological clock, Arrow fell in love with love itself, the hardest kind to shake. To attain it, she worked out tirelessly, charged a new wardrobe, threaded her eyebrows, got facials and a brand-new weave, and bought bras and pricey panties. All her waking hours, save those spent on work or glamming up, she invested in hope for the next email.

After two weeks of cyber-canoodling, she gave the stranger her address. Tiffany insisted she rent a private mailbox for the purpose, but Arrow cast caution to the wind as his flowers and gifts arrived daily, dozens of roses, diamonds, and balloons. Fancy boxes of African chocolates came, imported perfumes, silk lingerie. Adonis met Arrow in sexy chat rooms, urged her to set a rendezvous at a Greet-Me mixer or Dateable fest, and then he proposed the inevitable—a one-on-one meeting, face-to-face. On a fantasy, odyssey mystery date.

"I don't like it," Tiffany blurted out when Arrow shared the red-hot news.

"I don't care," countered Arrow, tossing her hair. "What, you expected I'd be content hooking up in some distant cyberlife with a cyberdude in cyberspace and two-and-a-half avatar cyberkids? Wake up. I need to meet the man."

"Slow down. You're moving way too fast. Stay focused. What about the show?"

"The show is all you care about?"

"No, Row, I'm concerned about you. Who goes on a destination date on a plane to an undisclosed location for a first date? It's not reasonable."

"No one does, and that's the point. I have a chance for my dream come true. A world other girls can't imagine. Don't you see? The guy wants to fly off with me. That's something not one of our friends has done. For a change, they'll finally envy me."

Tiffany fell back on her heels and stared at her friend, eyes bugged out, lips agape. "Do your ears hear what your mouth just said? Why are you making comparisons?"

"Well, aren't you the hypocrite. We've pitted these guys against each other for almost a month, and you didn't beef that. You sure didn't care about how they felt or how they might take losing out if their I-Married-Barbie fantasy fell flat for the sake of our stupid TV show."

"Stupid?" Tiffany's jaw went slack as if she were struck with a pie in the face. "Wait. I thought you were into it. I thought we were partners and this was our goal. I know it's not the ultimate—we want to make movies and fight for inclusion and be a creative force and all—but this is our first step. We're in production. We're building something."

"What if I need to build something for *me*? It's easy for you; you have everything."

"No one has everything, Arrow. Nothing's perfect. Yeah, I'm blessed. I am. But I don't have kids because I can't. And you know Byrd has sickle cell. I'm not complaining; I'm stating the facts. Nothing is perfect, but everything's good if you're grateful for what you have. You have nothing to prove to anyone. Who cares if some bougies we knew back in school couldn't deal with the way we dressed or behaved? We weren't obsessed with fitting in. We were born to stand out, not live their life. And where are they now? What's up with them? What are they doing to change the world so you'd stretch yourself out to impress them, huh? Where is this coming from? Why are you tripping? Does one date mean that much to you?"

Arrow's eyes reduced to slits. "How trippingly all those platitudes come rolling off your winning tongue. Why not? You're beautiful, wealthy, brainy. Everyone wants to be you."

"Oh, don't start singing that old tune," Tiffany protested. "I want to be me most of all, and I'm struggling to be the best I can. I married and worked for accomplished men, but I know I can do much more than that. I compromised my own career to walk in the shadow of others' aspirations, and that needs to change. You're looking for something outside you that's within you. Realize that. No man is going to fulfill you, Row. You can only do that yourself."

"Look around you." Arrow scoffed and stretched her arms out toward the sea. "Look at this house, your clothes, your lifestyle, how your man adores you. Nothing I ever create can take the place of one true love. Love is all, and family's everything. Nothing else comes close to it."

Tiffany took a long, deep breath, looked down at the marble floor. "You're right. I was insensitive. I'm sorry. I apologize." Tiffany rushed to squeeze her pal. "I know. It's true. Love's everything. And I want you to have every blessing. You know that. You deserve it, Row. I don't mean to be a spoiler." Tears trickled down Tiffany's cheeks to Arrow's shoulder, puddling on her tee. "I'm here for you. I love you, Row," she relented. "I'm on your side. I'm in. I just feel it's unwise to take the risk of rendezvousing with a stranger in some far-off port."

"I know you're just being my bestie, Tiff. Don't worry. I won't fly off with him. I'll meet him somewhere here in town. Feel better? That should be safer, right?"

"If that's what your instincts tell you, count on me to back you up."

Midnight at the edge of the Hollywood Hills.

Lake Hollywood looked as inky as a leaky fountain pen. The winding road up the steep hill toward its entrance loomed like the incline Sisyphus had to push the rock up in the arduous Greek myth. The gates to the lake were long since closed, and the rocky dirt turf, devoid of the trail of bicycles that circled the water in daylight hours like a necklace around the lake's watery neck, seemed too daunting in the blackness. Gone were the joggers, the power walkers, the teen sports teams on training jaunts, the cycling clubs and marathoners, the brightly colored Rollerbladers, top-shelf baby jogging strollers, glaring neon running bras, and sprayed-on spandex yoga pants. These were replaced by hooting owls, the chirps of crickets in teeming thickets, and leaves crackling under snake bellies that hid in the thick, dry underbrush. Even the smog-shrouded moon drew its blinds to lie down on night's cool pillow.

"Maybe you were right," said Arrow, her fists curling tight on the steering wheel. "It'd be better to meet at a restaurant."

"Duh. But it's not too late," said Tiffany. "Put on the brakes and rethink this thing. You can still turn around and re-sched with him… When Byrd finds out I came up here to meet another man with you—"

"Relax, you said he's out of town."

"Right, and unable to rescue us in case we get in trouble."

"At least I didn't go out of town like Adonis first suggested. We're only a few miles from my crib."

"Uh-huh, but how did he find out? You didn't give out your home address. Or did you?"

"Nope, he doesn't know," lied Arrow, checking her rearview mirror. "I'm meeting him at the solstice celebration. It's romantic."

"He said that and you fell for it?" asked Tiffany. "I don't see a crowd." She ducked back down in the rear seat, pulling her hood up over her head.

"He's the one, Row. I just know he is. He's sweet and smart and sensitive."

"You don't know this guy from Adam, Row. His pic could be a mug shot. Or a Russian bot. Or Chinese troll. It's crazy. Let's just go back home."

"The idea to meet here was in the webzine *Love Link-ups*. I saw it there. It's Dating Destination 4."

"And what is Destination 5, you both jump off a bridge?"

"C'mon, admit it, it's exciting."

"Nothing like taking your life in your hands to really turn you on."

"Look, I see his green Jaguar!" Arrow swerved her silver Porsche Carrera to the curb and parked. She fumbled for eyewash, splashed two drops, slid on a slash of crimson lipstick, fluffed up her hairdo, hitched up her bra, and fingered the car door handle.

"Forget it, we're not getting out," said Tiffany, popping up out of the rear well, struggling to climb to the passenger seat.

"No, *we're* not. *I'm* getting out. I'm doing this alone. I have to trust someone, somehow, sometime, somewhere. This is it."

"This ain't it, sweetie. Use your head. You wouldn't let me do it." Tiffany reached for Arrow's collar, one leg in the back and the other in front. "Arrow, stop! Let's talk this out."

"No way. I'm going now!" They struggled, tugging each other's clothes and hair and limbs like little kids, with Arrow getting the best of it and Tiff astride the seat backs. Before Tiff knew it, Arrow split, the car door clicking locked behind her, Tiffany yelling through the glass.

Tiffany watched as Arrow swished her hips to the Jaguar's tinted windows, smoothing her tight black miniskirt, and turning on a smile. Arrow licked her luscious lips, tossed her new unbraided weave, and moved in what appeared to be slow motion, stepping toward the car, the red soles of her shoes flashing up and down until she reached the driver's door. She hesitated, touched the glass, hurried around to the passenger side... and hollered bloody murder.

Their hearts were still thumping when they arrived at Tiffany's place and locked the doors. When they checked all the windows and closed the blinds, when they set the alarm, when they checked every room, when they peered into each of the seventeen closets and looked under every couch and bed.

"How do we know that corpse was him?" Tiffany shuddered, bit her lip.

"I tried to tell you in the car," said Arrow, head in hands. "We Zoomed and Facetimed all the time. I saw his face, and he saw mine. I'm telling you, that was Adonis!"

"Were you guys sexting pictures too? Other than your profiles? Like nudes or anything like that? They'd be proof you were in a relationship. Did you text that you were meeting there tonight when he was murdered? What if somebody watched us run around that Jaguar, trying to wake him up, like chickens with our heads cut off?" asked Tiffany. "What if video surveillance cameras filmed us by the lake? Depending on what they caught, it could be evidence that we're involved. The cops could think we killed the guy."

"Let's not panic. We'll be fine. It was black as the hole of Calcutta. The place was deserted. Nobody saw us. Nobody followed us… I don't think."

Tiffany ran to peek outside. The ocean roiled with bubbling whitecaps surging to the shore. "Are you serious? They could be watching now. A killer. Out there on the sand. Just because we saw no one doesn't mean no one saw us. Whoever blew his brains out could've tracked us here, you think of that? And they might think we know too much. We're lucky we're alive."

"Oh crap, you're right, I'm in his phone. I'm logged in there a jillion times."

"When did you last communicate?"

"Before I picked you up." Arrow rolled her eyes and groaned.

"You're right at the top of his recents list, and who knows where his phone is now."

"Ugh, I think I'm feeling sick." Arrow, pacing, stutter stepped. "No one can prove we did it. We didn't hurt him. We didn't touch a thing."

"I saw you touch his window! I bet we left a bunch of clues—tire tracks, footprints, fibers, even photographs at traffic lights—"

"Screw it. It's crazy. Let's call the cops," said Arrow, digging out her phone.

"Police? Are you kidding? They'll eat us up. Forget the show and our careers. They'll trash our whole damn lives. He was white. They'll slap the cuffs on us and throw away the keys. We'll be lucky if we get to jail and don't get killed along the way. Don't you watch the news? The guy was already DOA, but they'll say it was us who knocked him off. That's why we didn't report it when we *found* him dead; we didn't. They'll say it was premedi-ated. Who could believe you went up there this time of night for a dumb blind date? No way. We're keeping this a secret, dropping this entire mess. Acting as if it never happened. What possible good could calling the cops do now? They won't protect us. And who do you think he was dealing with that iced him, Mickey Mouse? Why do you think they killed the guy? Do you want to get tangled up in that?"

"You're scaring me," cried Arrow. "I'm so sorry. This is all my fault."

"That doesn't matter anymore. It's water under the bridge. We've en-tered the survival mode. Let's keep our mouths shut. Pinky swear." Tiffany held her pinky out.

Arrow reluctantly stuck out hers. Their slender fingers formed a knot. "What about the RaiseIt?"

"What about it?" Tiffany shrugged. "We're going on as usual. We'll focus like we always did. We got off track. We'll get back on."

"But that was how I met Adonis. What if his killer tracks me down?"

"What reason would they have for it if you go about your business? They'll figure you're staying out of it, that you're letting a sleeping dog lie."

"But if they saw us, I'm a witness. They would think you're one as well."

A cell phone chimed. They jumped and yelped.

Arrow shook, stared at her phone, her fingers trembling, eyes held wide.

"Don't answer it," Tiffany mumbled.

"But a call could establish an alibi. Cell towers track locations, Tiff."

"Oh shoot, that's right. I thought of something. Was GPS enabled in your car when we were at the lake?"

"It's busted."

"Whew."

"It doesn't track. I need to get it fixed."

"Location is turned on in my cell, but I turned it off to charge it fast."

"I turned mine off so it wouldn't ring while I was with Adonis. I just turned it back on when we came inside."

"Cool, we're clear on GPS pinpointing where we went tonight." Tiffany heaved a sigh.

The ringtone started up again. The voice mail app picked up. For a moment the phone was inanimate. But soon it made an eerie bleep, a voice mail notification blinked, and the phone vibrated across the couch as though it were trying to crawl to them.

"See who it is," said Tiffany. "Maybe you can call them back to establish your alibi like you said. I'll call the gate and engage a guard so I can do the same."

Arrow tapped her voice mail app. The message played, a warning. A deep male tone, a dirty rasp. Menacing, rumbling, icy, slashing the silence like a sword. "Pick up the phone, or I'll come for you. I see you, bitch. I know you're there."

Arrow dropped her smartphone, pedaled backward, hands up to her throat.

"Who the heck is *that*?" asked Tiffany, eyelashes fluttering like butterflies.

"Trouble," Arrow stuttered. "I don't recognize the voice."

The phone lit up with the vibrator buzz and sang its little tune again.

"Oh no." Arrow fell to her knees and wept. She lunged for the phone and answered it.

"Forget what you saw. Forget who you saw there. Forget where you live and forget this call." The threatening voice morphed into laughter. Arrow hit the End Call tab.

"That does it, we'll get you a bodyguard," said Tiffany.

"Nope, I'm out of here. I'll book a bargain flight to Rio. I can lie low till the worst of it blows over and just work remote. I thought I might go to Brazil if Bronco didn't let up and slow his roll. Since the movie wrapped in NOLA, he's all over me like chicken pox. I haven't chilled in who knows when. No better time than now." She twirled three-sixty, making a circle, unable to figure which way to turn. "Can I borrow a suitcase and some clothes?"

"What, you're leaving just like that?" Tiffany's face looked frantic.

Arrow snapped her fingers. "Just like that. You heard the man. I can't go back to the tiny house. My cyberlover just got killed. I'm not hanging around to see who's next."

Ding-dong! Tiffany's doorbell rang. The women froze like statues.

Tiffany closed her eyes and moaned. "No, no, no, this can't be real. Quick," said Tiffany. "Follow me." She reached for Arrow's trembling hand, and they rushed upstairs to the master bedroom, hurrying down a long, dark hall to enter the mansion's western wing. They peeked through decorator shades but couldn't see who rang the bell at the double doors under the portico. The knocking grew louder. They picked up their pace. "Whoever is out there got over the fence," said Tiffany, speeding from trot to run. "I don't think it's the FedEx guy."

They shimmied through a plate glass slider, tiptoed onto a balcony. It was three flights down to the sand and five hundred feet from the pool to Arrow's ride in Byrd's six-car garage. The salty air and ocean spray felt dizzying to Arrow. Confident, Tiffany led the way, her high heels wobbling, hairdo bobbing. Arrow clenched her teeth and followed, zipping around one corner of the wraparound porch to where it ended hovering over the swimming pool, an infinity pool in an ultramodern outdoor space with waterfalls. The two hitched up their miniskirts, climbed over a balcony railing, and perched themselves on a narrow concrete ledge beside a waterslide.

"We have to jump," said Tiffany. "My car is in the garage with Byrd's. It's

way too hard to get to yours. And maybe he knows what yours looks like."
She pulled a lever. Water flowed.

"You know I can't swim. I'll drown down there. You go. I'll hide up here."

"No, we do this all the time. Byrd set it up to land on floats. You'll splash in the pool and I'll be waiting. I'll go first. You watch, okay? Just keep your arms down at your sides."

Arrow nodded vigorously as she checked back over her shoulder.

Tiffany kicked her shoes off, hopped in the waterslide, keeping her arms at her sides, and disappeared into a steep drop-off and a rush of gushing water.

As Arrow approached the slide, she heard loud footsteps thud across the porch.

A squadron of men filed past a guest room, wearing matching dark-green wet suits, sending an icicle up her spine. Fanning out like a Navy SEAL squad, heavily armed and tactical, they moved with precision like a SWAT team closing in on criminals. Arrow could see them through the glass wall that ringed the opulent master bath, but none of their heads were turned her way.

Arrow kicked into hyperdrive, hurling her slim frame onto the waterslide, plunging, trying not to scream. But midway down the waterslide, she faltered, listing to the left, off-balance, catching a heel in the guardrail, slamming her head on the side of the slide, shredding her blouse and scraping her back. Her skirt was gouged, then skin and flesh, exposing bone and tissue. The more she tried to free her shoe, the tighter grew the guardrail's grip. Twisting and turning, she tore herself free and plummeted past the family room into the pool, just left of a simulated grotto and a stand of brightly striped cabanas, darting straight into the pool's deep end. Submerged, she kicked and flailed her arms as water jetted up her nose, a pink float several feet away. Weak, light-headed, overcome, she held her breath and tried to surface, but the pool was fathomless. The more she thrashed, the less she floated up through the warm chlorine morass.

Dazed and close to passing out, she felt herself begin to drown and start hallucinating. Arrow thought she saw a mermaid's dazzling face and floating hair strands undulating close to her, its mesmerizing deep-blue eyes and copper skin pulsating. She felt a clamp around her ankle, kicked to resist it but could not. "Caught," she thought, but she couldn't shake the strong hands' frantic yanking as they pulled her through a hatch.

"You okay?" said Tiffany, calling to Arrow, readying her for CPR. "Speak to me! Are you all right?"

Arrow coughed and looked around, choking, spitting H_2O. "Where are we?"

"In the safe room Byrd constructed under the swimming pool. For a minute I thought… Thank heaven, Row. I wanted to tell you this was here, but Byrd kept it a secret. No one will find us. See those steps?" Tiffany's arm swung to the left. "They lead to a tunnel to the garage. There's a trapdoor hidden beneath Byrd's Bentley. I know how to open it."

Arrow marveled, gazed around, coughed up a splash of water.

The walls appeared to be solid rock aglow with changing colored lights. A rainbow of neon lighting undulated in the floor. Contemporary furnishings were sparse and appeared to grow out of the ground. Midair, directly in front of her, Arrow saw a large fluorescent panel flashing images of various rooms about the house. "This is unbelievable," said Arrow, her eyes as big as cookies.

"Byrd designs these safety nets for superrich people around the world. He figured we should have one, too… Can you walk?"

"I have to," Arrow said.

Tiffany bent, helped Arrow stand, and whipped her girlfriend's thin, bruised arm around her stately shoulders. The sickening smell of Arrow's blood nauseated Tiffany and caused her to survey the wounds. "Let's grab the first aid kit and breeze. I'll patch you up, and then we'll go."

"I'm good. We need to hurry. There's an army prowling around your house. We have to leave here yesterday."

"You need a doctor. Let's get out." Tiffany bolstered Arrow as they hustled up a narrow staircase, through the trapdoor under the Bentley, and into the garage. Tiffany settled Arrow into the passenger seat, jumped into hers, and fished around the glove compartment, tossing a remote for the garage door into Arrow's lap. "Quick, you press this button, Row. I'll gun it as soon as the door slides up… Hit it!"

Arrow engaged the door.

The Bentley sped backward, tires spinning, engine revving in overdrive.

A horrid sight awaited it.

A hulk in a wet suit, wielding an AK-47, blocked the driveway, blasting a volley of deadly rounds. Tiffany plowed right over him, the Bentley's windshield spider-webbing, obscuring the driver's field of vision. The car popped over the shooter's body as if it'd hit a speed bump. It plopped back into the concrete driveway, fishtailing out toward the PCH, where vehicles whizzed by, honking horns. More high-powered gunshots blasted, bullets pinging off the trunk, roof, doors, and screeching hubcapped tires. The Bentley roared up the driveway in reverse until it neared a curb, and Tiffany slammed it into D, careening the car into oncoming traffic, lurching, dinging a fire hydrant, side-swiping parked cars and a line of dirt bikes, and kicking up a cloud of sand. Three wet-suited goons were firing now. The ladies yelled and sucked in smoke as they raced into the center lane and melted into the starry night.

Hard knocks on a window woke Arrow and Tiffany, wresting them from restless sleep.

A gentleman begging to wash their shattered windshield spit on the passenger window, assiduously wiping his spittle with a dirty rag and toothless grin. Squinting as daylight danced in palm fronds hovering above his indigence, Arrow lowered her window an inch or so and slipped the man a fiver from her bra as he looked on. He planted a wet kiss on the window, flattening his lips against the glass while rubbernecking Arrow as the window rolled back up again.

"Where do we go from here?" asked Tiffany. "How can I explain to Byrd? When he gets home, we're supposed to throw a client party in the house, and chances are it's torn apart."

"I'm sorry," said Arrow. "Maybe there's not much damage there. I'll pay for the repairs… for the rest of my life, apparently. Your place is such a castle."

"Maybe insurance will handle it. It's technically under construction. According to Byrd, our insurance covers vandals. This should qualify."

"I'll tell Byrd it's all my fault. If I hadn't acted like such a jerk—"

"You were chasing a dream, and it had a dead end. Who knew? It's all a crap shoot… I'm starving. Let's find breakfast, Row. My stomach is growling like a bear."

They wandered on foot up PCH, tooled into a convenience store, got morning snacks and juice, and grabbed a morning paper off a rack. The front-page headline read in bold print: RaiseIt Megamogul Adonis Duke Gunned Down at Lake Hollywood.

"Oh no!" said Tiffany, stopping in midchew, hand stuffed into a trail mix bag. "And we figured it couldn't get worse."

"It can't be him. You think it's… No, it must be someone else." Arrow attempted to shoo a fly that buzzed around her gaping mouth.

"I thought that was a username. His *real* name was Adonis?"

"Yeah, but who knew he was *the* Adonis," Arrow replied. "He never said. He didn't let on he owned the site and pretty much everything else on earth."

"He was the founder, the CEO. Everyone and his brother is probably out to hunt his killer now," said Tiffany, scouting the store for cameras, shoppers, or hidden workers who might see them stressing out. "Let's pay for this stuff and get back to the car."

In the Bentley, Arrow read aloud while nibbling cheese and crackers. "An unidentified woman is sought in connection with the brutal murder of business behemoth Adonis Duke. The woman is said to have been in communication with the victim, and as his schedule reportedly cites, he arranged an ill-fated tryst with her last night at the spot where his body was found. A press conference by local authorities is scheduled for three p.m. today, at which a sketch will be revealed to the public in hopes of locating the female, a party of interest in the case. Anyone with information about the crime is urged to report it to the anonymous tip line shown below."

"His schedule. We didn't think of that. Your name is in there. Oh my gosh." Tiffany closed the trail mix bag as Arrow continued to skim the page. "What else does it say?"

"A bunch of stuff. RaiseIt.com has a parent company. The site is a wholly owned subsidiary of Orbit Communications Inc., the largest privately held conglomerate anywhere in the world. Adonis privately owned it. He was the fourth richest guy in the universe. He was worth—wait for it—seventy billion bucks."

Tiffany whistled. "Whew! That much? The dude was overloaded. That sucks. Your ship was coming in, and you didn't get a chance to board it. You could've been a gazillionaire."

"Yeah, in a parallel universe." She snapped the paper, folded it. "Though even that's a stretch… Hey, here's another tasty tidbit. As of next week, Orbit's stock goes public."

"Really? Can that happen now?"

"I guess. If it's still viable. With Adonis dead, the stock could tank. I wonder if it will."

"I wonder who killed the golden goose before it laid that platinum egg."

"A murder before a big cash influx seems awfully synchronistic, right?"

"Fishy, is more like it. I wonder how much that IPO is worth."

"I wonder who gains from it?" Arrow retorted, deep in thought.

"Or who stood to lose," said Tiffany. "Fear of loss weighs more than hope for gain."

"It's a mystery which the killer had… but I think I know how to find out."

"You're advanced in IT?" a stone-faced, redheaded woman queried Tiffany, who sat opposite a brass desk plate that labeled the woman Polly Prizz, executive personnel manager.

"I have a masters," Tiffany lied, disguised in a short, cheap, platinum wig.

"You'll have to take a drug test. Did you realize that?"

"I know it now."

"It's standard Orbit policy. Any objections disqualify."

"No worries. I'm clean as the Board of Health," said Tiffany with a nervous laugh that elicited only a stolid stare from Prizz, whose face was hard as stone.

"A lie detector test as well." The woman donned bifocals. "To ascertain your truthfulness vis-à-vis your résumé. It's a privilege, being hired here. Employees have to earn it. I've only worked here several months, but I could see that off the bat. Your cousin's recommendation only goes so far. Fifteen percent. And that's because we value her and this is an emergency."

"I'm aware it's for only a couple of days. To fill in for her while she's gone."

"Ordinarily, hiring processes take several months to implement. But today our staff is grieving, and we need all hands on deck… Too bad your cousin broke her arm."

"It's really a shame. But she's healing now. I promise I'll bring seamlessness."

"You'd better deliver," the woman snipped. "I'll show you what the job entails." Prizz ran Tiffany through a trial, but in the end gave her the job. Phase Two was locked and loaded.

Phase One wasn't easy to implement. It'd been tough for Arrow and Tiffany to negotiate the Orbit staff to find a girl to call in sick and recommend Tiffany as a temp. It cost a pretty penny. It might be fraught with peril too, but being on Orbit's inside could be worth its weight in gold.

Arrow entered the Orbit building via the back-door service entrance, rolling in baskets of croissant sandwiches, soup, chilled salads, and fresh-baked goods, and taking the elevator to the executive fortieth floor. It required a ruse to obtain a security clearance from the security chief, a lecherous middle-aged Black man sporting a paunch, a cauliflower ear, and a barrel-chested uniform. Arrow plied him with samples of her food, bending over with her butt up to ostensibly reach for a pumpkin scone from the low rack of her shiny cart. She saw him admire her alluring attire—a blood-red hairpiece, snug red blouse, and the Salvation Army pencil skirt she'd bought near the convenience store. Arrow turned on the charm, flashed the fake ID that bore her new fictitious name, and got waved through the company turnstile for the price of a bogus cell phone deet. It was lunchtime when Arrow rolled into Adonis's offices to get the scoop.

"Light yogurt?" asked Adonis's mushroom-colored assistant, Liza. Young and pretty, she was fashionable, wearing a floral dress, small stylish pearls, and ankle boots with leather bows. A tattoo peeked out from the edge of her cuff, though its shape was indiscernible, and she smelled like fruity Bubble Yum. She dug in a purse for a wallet, and while waiting, Arrow eyed her desk and Hello Kitty ornaments. She gave the girl a yogurt and received a mousy giggle.

"Chicken salad and three peanut butter cookies," the worker at the next desk ordered, her pleasant Latina accent lilting on heavy, celebrity-brand perfume. The girl was petite, had a warm, ready smile, an olive complexion, impeccable posture, a curly black mane piled on her head and a ring on every finger. Her hair was held up with a Spanish comb that looked to be a real antique, and she wore a broach choker around her neck and dangling turquoise earrings.

Arrow pretended to rearrange food as Liza leaned in to her coworker, prying her yogurt lid up with long blue fingernails. "Psst. Can you keep a secret, Boca?"

"No. But tell me anyway." Boca tittered, typing.

"I hear it was the wife who did it," Liza whispered. "Shot him dead."

Adonis was married? Arrow dropped a cup of Jell-O on the floor.

"Why, because of the divorce? She was squeezing him for lots of dough."

"Who wouldn't under the circumstances? Only, there was a prenup, so when she took him to the cleaners she'd be lucky to get a small percent. This way she's liable to get it all."

"*Dios mio.* Billions, right?" Boca cast a furtive glance around the confines of her cubicle, standing to scan adjacent booths and sitting back down to chew the fat. "With the stock going public in just a few days and the profit-sharing deal with us employees, she just cut her losses."

"Right. Consolidated power."

"Consolidated funds, you mean. That sister is cold-blooded… Yoo-hoo!" Boca snapped her fingers, signaling Arrow, jerking her head. "Where's my peanut butter cookies?"

Arrow dug in a basket, got three cookies plus an extra one, and sustaining a volley of ocular darts, set off for the lunchroom chitchat to make sense of what she'd heard.

"This will be your cubicle," the personnel manager instructed Tiffany, pointing into an alcove the size of a soup can next to a water cooler abutting the elevator shaft.

Tiffany managed to crack a smile. "So far away from you, Ms. Prizz?"

Prizz answered, "Neither here nor there. Focus on your first assignment—answering all condolence cards, signing for flowers, gifts, and such, and databasing every mourner sending their well-wishes. Any questions, I'm right down the second hall on the right, then left, then right again. The gift room is there by the copier." She crooked her index finger.

"Pay dirt," Tiffany whispered to herself as Prizz proceeded off. Tiffany watched Prizz round the corner, crashing the vibe of the staff she passed, and she rushed to the gift room to form a list she hoped would hold a treasure trove of suspects she could mine.

"I'm bummed about Adonis, man. Bet Prudence Boggs is pleased as punch," said a stunning young man with blue-black skin as smooth as his buttery leather coat. Tall, early twenties, a phone in hand, he extracted a frozen meal from a microwave with a plastic fork.

A white-haired gentleman sat in the seat beside him, coughing, reading a tablet, slurping from a noodle bowl, his dentures emitting a clacking noise. He was Asian with glasses hung low on his nose, and he wore a three-piece flannel suit and polished, spit-shined, soft-soled shoes. "Don't worry, she'll get hers someday, kid. Trust me, her kind always does."

Arrow sold the millennial guy a cupcake and the elder man a bowl of melon slices.

"Boggs was undermining him. Now she's dancing in the streets. It pisses me off," said the young guy, eating his cupcake, letting his meal grow cold while ogling Tiffany's ample butt.

"It's gross, the way she celebrates. She ought to show respect." The older man stabbed a chunk of melon, savored it with both eyes closed, then folded his napkin in four equal parts and wiped juice from his mouth. "She's a company founder like Duke was. With Duke out the way and the ball of confusion bouncing around here, she's on top. She's stepping up plans to snatch the majority share when Orbit's stock goes on the market. She could do it too."

"I heard the IPO is off," the younger man exhorted. "It might be just a rumor, but it stands to reason, doesn't it?"

"With the company's brand in the grave with Duke, it doesn't make a lick of sense to offer to investors now. Of course, that doesn't mean they won't. If they don't go public, we'll be stable. We'll maintain the status quo. On the other hand, if they profit share, retirement funds will get a boost. No telling what Prudence Boggs will do, and either way the boss is gone."

"What all went down between them, Mr. Sage? Ms. Boggs and Mr. Duke?"

"That's an ugly story, kid. Their struggle raged for years. Adonis won the business, but that caused him other problems. Ask me, she had the hots for him. That's why she was always stirring the pot, to try to get attention.

And when he ran off and married her daughter instead of her, it sealed his fate. A woman scorned, is what she is. She lost it. Vowed to get him good."

"So you figure she offed Mr. Duke for that?" the younger man inquired.

"Son, at my age, you know anything's possible. I'm not betting either way."

"You think we might still profit share?" the younger man said with a wrinkled brow as he launched a swift kick at the soda machine. "I'm sure looking forward to getting my piece of the pie, if you know what I mean. Or else my girl won't marry me."

"You better not count on it, youngblood. I'll be surprised if we keep our jobs."

Tiffany summoned the personnel manager, stepping lively toward her desk. "Ms. Prizz!"

"Yes, Tiffany, what do you want?" Ms. Prizz said, clipping the sentence short, irritation evident in her tone. She stiffened and clicked her wireless mouse in a hurry to clear her monitor.

"I finished the list. Can you help me out? I need to know something about these people since I'm sending thank-you notes. I can't tell his close friends from his colleagues now, and I don't want to risk offending folks. I need to be appropriate."

Prizz snatched and scanned the printed list. "The nerve of that hussy."

"Who?"

"Who else? That Prudence Boggs has all the gall. She likely pulled the trigger." Prizz tore the top name off the paper and tossed the scrap into her shredder bin. "She nearly destroys this company and its owner and sends condolences? Her gift could not be less sincere. Just send a generic thank-you and no badge for the memorial." Her large-knuckled finger trailed the list and landed on another name. "Flint Fleischman sent a giant wreath of Roman Gladioli. How sweet and so befitting too. Flint was Adonis's golf buddy and a crony of his… wife. And isn't this a lovely gift? Army Bolinger named a star after Adonis. What a thoughtful gesture. He's an attorney and personal friend… The next is Cookie Freeman. She's the eldest sister. Tragic soul. She was his trusted assistant before she married that boxer, who knows why."

Tiffany, legal pad in hand, took copious notes. "Who else, Ms. Prizz?"

"You'd better not breathe a word of this." Prizz arose and closed the door.

Tiffany licked her finger, crossed her heart. "Of course. My lips are sealed."

"Be careful with the next name down. Dianza Boggs Duke. The first young wife. She's the daughter of Prudence Boggs. She's a model and tone-deaf singer who finagled her way to a rap career. The only thing worse than her music is her dancing on that reality show with those other washed-up, has-been types. Her social networking is off the charts, so we have to kiss up to her nonetheless, but that marriage created a corporate rift that nearly imploded Orbit." Prizz looked down at the list again. "Now, Raquel Zolar, she's a doll. Adonis's baby sister. Too bad they had that disastrous row. They fell out while skiing in Aspen last Thanksgiving. It was tragic… The next two were best men at all his weddings—Legs Duran and Skipper Lomax. What value Adonis saw in those social climbers, I will never know. I find them rather déclassé… And dear, you'll need a correction here. It's not *Miss* Petra Djackov. Call her Mrs. She's the widow. Didn't you read about that debacle? What a bad error he made with her. A gold-digging, bulimic space case Adonis bumped into online. I mean, seriously, what did he expect?"

Adonis met Arrow online as well, thought Tiffany. *Très intéressant.*

Miss Prizz breathed in and pursed thin lips. "It was scandal-ridden, their divorce. But at least that threat is over now," she said with shades of triumph. "I mean it, that Petra is as dumb as a brick. She paraded a tawdry succession of men as long as the Macy's Thanksgiving Parade in his face and in the tabloids. Adonis wasn't an angel, but cuckolding he did not deserve." She trundled down the list again. "Oh, here's a good pal who deserves to be thanked. Send Hartford Wundermint a text. Adonis's personal trainer. A specimen. You won't believe your eyes."

"I'll google him. Is that all, Miss Prizz?"

Prizz cut a wide swath through the rest of the list, slinging mud and hurling invectives at every name she hit upon. *No wonder he was murdered,* Tiffany mused as Prizz kept gossiping.

"The rest are neighbors, hangers-on, acquaintances, business associates, Orbit employees who worshiped the ground he walked on. He was a wonderful boss. He treated all his staff so well. It's unthinkable someone would take his life." Prizz's voice cracked, her translucent white skin instantaneously mottling to veiny blue. "A prince of a man," she warbled, rubbing a circle of mascara. She sniffed, plucked tissues from a box, and quaked as she dabbed her runny nose.

Tiffany couldn't help but determine Ms. Prizz had a thing for Adonis too. "He certainly commanded a ton of respect," Tiffany ventured, lowering her pen, sensing rare vulnerability and wanting to strike while the iron was hot. "Why do you think it happened then?"

"I'd bet a year's pay it had something to do with Orbit posting to the Big Board," Prizz divulged and blew her nose. "And then again, someone on that list might have a secret in their past. Adonis knew how to find things out, and he didn't let anyone get in his way. He had vision, purpose, drive, a clear direction for his company. And that breakthrough he was about to drop—"

"Breakthrough?" Tiffany interrupted, causing Ms. Prizz to slit her eyes.

"The man was a giant walking among Lilliputians. He'll make history soon."

"Is it anything you can talk about? You make me wish I'd met the guy."

"No, I'm the one who watched his back, and I won't stop now because he's dead. Just let it suffice to say it's big, and the principals of a company have more power when it's closely held. Most of them have their daggers out to stab the leader when they can, and they don't all agree about casting their fate to the whims of the New York Stock Exchange with its greedy investors, tricky brokers, cagey Wall Street market makers and media hacks whose fortunes rise and fall, manipulating stocks with shady recommendations. None on the board of directors wanted Orbit to go public, but they felt they were obliged to back Adonis or be ostracized."

"Who are the other principles?" Tiffany tried to ask offhandedly.

"Adonis's sisters," Prizz apprised. "And siblings can be murder." She tilted her head with a wink and a nod. "It's a risky proposition, going public in these days and times. Stock prices can be volatile. Particularly for a company with such huge potential as we have. Ambitious corporate raiders set their sights on taking over, and they stop at nothing when you're weak… You're new here. How do you think we'd do?"

Tiffany shook her head a bit. "I don't do corporate politics."

Prizz did an incredulous double take. "You'd better start. And quick."

It was quarter past six when they met at the Bentley. "What've we got?" asked Arrow when they jumped in the car, snatched off their shoes, and jettisoned their fake hairdos.

Tiffany launched in, speaking fast. "I got in Adonis's offices after everyone went home. His computers are password protected, so his files weren't so accessible. They were already raided by the cops in the early-morning hours today. They imaged the hard drives and left them there, but according to his assistant, files were missing even before they came. She tried to get in to enter data when she arrived at six a.m., but many files were tampered with. She can't imagine where they went or how a hacker got to them. She thinks the wife had someone wipe his laptop and then murder him. She can't locate it anywhere, and she's frightened the killer might come back. But that's not half of what I learned. His work is fascinating, Row. The lab above the office. I snuck up the stairs when the janitor left the door ajar to take a leak. The place has wall-to-wall monitors, sensors, VR hookups, AR headsets, telekinetics and headphones built in the ceiling that answer to voice commands. The floor looks like blue fiberglass with copper tracks aligned inside. It's like a gigantic motherboard with interconnected components and a mass of awesome housing chips. I'm not sure exactly what it does, but I'm telling you it looks insane."

"He said he was into new forms of humanotronic communication. Whatever that is."

"He didn't explain?"

"No, but it might be what you saw. I'd never heard the term before, and I'm guessing no one has. He said he would show me as soon as he could and what he did would blow my mind."

"The personnel manager mentioned a big breakthrough was coming any day."

"Adonis hinted at that too. He told me it would change the world. He wanted to tell me, but it was confidential. He said dangerous. I thought he was pulling my leg or trying to impress me with his accomplishments, but I didn't realize who he was. Oh, Tiff, he was special and now he's gone. We were star-crossed from the start. We seemed so right but went so wrong."

"It wasn't meant to be. How could you know about all that stuff? You couldn't foresee what happened. You kissed another frog, so what? The right guy's going to come along. You have to keep believing that and not give in to fear. You know everything's working together for good. It might not seem that way right now, but we need faith when things go wrong… Hey, this'll cheer you up a bit. Look what I snuck out. A list." She pulled a flash drive from her waistband. "Everyone who sent him flowers, sympathy cards, emails, or voice mails. This is just his office stuff, and there are fifty thousand. Just counting ones that came so far. More pour in every minute. And that doesn't include his DM hits." She handed off the thumb drive. "I tried to highlight his closest contacts, but there's still a ton of them. The killer is a needle in the haystack, but we're after them, and once we expose them, you'll be safe and the nightmare will be over… And get this. There's this real weird dude. Flint Fleischman. They played golf last week. Adonis did eighteen holes up in Carmel. I found receipts. After that, Flint Fleischman disappeared."

"Shut the front door! Are you serious, Tiff?"

"Right? It's creepy, isn't it?"

"Maybe he killed him and escaped."

"Or maybe they'll find his body too."

"Whatever went on, they can't blame me. I never met Flint Fleischman."

"And wait, I called the attorney too. Adonis's personal lawyer, Army Bolinger. He was so tight-lipped. I said I was a reporter, and he wouldn't divulge one hint of who might win big in the will. But he's a good friend of Adonis's wife so… oops. My bad. I blurted that."

"It's fine. I knew he was married," Arrow admitted in a monotone.

"Oh my. You knew that all along?"

"Of course not. Who do you think I am? He lied. I just found out. I don't hang out with married men. Not knowingly at least. What a crummy thing to do to me. Why the heck was he on our RaiseIt page, pretending he was a bachelor when he was married from square one?"

"Men lie all the time about status, you know that. And so do women."

"But he couldn't become the marriage man. Didn't he know we'd find him out?"

"I guess he didn't care. He might've just wanted to date someone who'd love him for who he really was and not his fame and fortune. He might've been a lonely guy. He met his current wife online."

"My point. And how's that working out? I feel like I got trolled. I'm starting to wonder if I was just one in a million and got singled out."

"You mean, if the murderer picked you for a scapegoat? You, specifically?"

"All this can't just be happenstance."

"You're right. It could be jealousy, revenge, or for the money… Let's talk to the older sister, Cookie Freeman. She's gone off the grid. Her phone goes straight to voice mail, and the same goes for his ex. Dianza Boggs is ghosting too."

"The one on the *Prance with Celebrities* show? The press called them Adanza."

"Girlfriend's a YouTube superstar with a super-crazy following. Her channel is really blowing up. I don't blame her for keeping a low profile, or her sister-in-law for bugging off… But I did get ahold of the baby sister, Raquel. She's inconsolable. Raquel was estranged from Adonis for almost a year, and boy is she distraught."

"We can scratch her off the short list then?" Arrow concluded.

"Not so fast. She and Cookie are now the principals. It's a two-way split instead of three. Which gives each of them half the blame and twice the motive as far as I can tell."

"My sleuthing paid off big time too." Arrow held up the red flash drive. "Adonis accrued arch enemies. Let's visit the worst I heard of then investigate your list."

They caught up with the overweight Prudence Boggs at her chic boutique for equestrians, the Clotheshorse, in a fashion square by the beach in Santa Barbara. They recognized Boggs from the Orbit website as they moved inside the store, so Arrow flashed an old press ID card for credibility.

"Ms. Boggs," said Arrow. "I'm Paige Turner. This is my partner, Kamara Lenz. We're here for the *Malibu Sentinel*. We're new there. May we have a word?" Arrow pumped Boggs's fleshy hand.

"Sorry, girls, no interviews. This a difficult time," said Prudence.

Arrow probed her nonetheless. "Sorry for your loss, Ms. Boggs. If you'll only hear us out a sec for a profile of your former partner, Adonis Duke. It's a gigantic spread. We're honoring his accomplishments and presenting a sensitive portrait of the man nobody really knew. Not the Adonis victim angle—frankly, that's being done to death—but a titan his business colleagues encountered and how he conducted megadeals. We're working on an in-depth piece on his life and times as he fought his way up before he became a household name and built the Orbit empire. No whitewash but the nitty-gritty facts of his iconic rise and how he came to make his mark. We understand you were instrumental in his success, and we'd like to quote a few words from you to counteract the rumors."

"Rumors?" Prudence Boggs drew back. "What sort of rumors? Not about me. Not about Orbit going public. Rumors lead to scandals. More scandal could cause the price to plunge." Tall and plus-sized with pale pink skin, Boggs wore a muumuu of African kente cloth and a pair of beaded flats with curled-up toes on pudgy feet. Acne pocked her pitted cheeks, and her stringy blond hair was cornrowed. Her breath so reeked of Irish whiskey Arrow was fighting a contact high. Boggs's eyes were round and gray. The gentleness in her face looked real. Nothing about her comported with her rancorous reputation.

"I meant any rumors that might crop up. You know, what with the way he died and all," said Arrow, sticking her cell phone out. "You don't mind if we record you, right?"

"Good heavens, put that down. I told you I can't contribute much," said Boggs. "I know what you people think. But trust me, you are ill-informed… Babs!" she called to an employee. "Take over. I have urgent biz. I'll be heading to LA afterward. Stock the new jodhpurs and velvet show jackets and see the front windows are dressed for success." Boggs turned, pressed a section of mirror behind the counter that had an electric eye. A hidden doorway opened into a narrow hallway lined with quartz. Arrow and Tiffany followed Boggs to an eye-popping, three-story, vaulted rotunda replete with African objets d'art. Red marble covered the walls and floor.

"You want a drink?" their hostess slurred, her gray eyes trailing a silver-framed photo of Duke dressed up in riding gear, lit up in a niche in a marble wall.

"No, thank you. I don't drink," said Arrow.

"I'd love a Smartwater if you have it," said Tiffany, scanning the hidden room. Arrow regarded Tiffany with a barely perceptible headshake. "Or not. I'm good. I won't impose."

"You must be aware of the talk, Ms. Boggs," said Arrow with a churlish smirk. "About how you formed Orbit with Mr. Duke but there was a split some time ago when he married your daughter rather than you. You withdrew, swore revenge, and now he's dead."

"That's par for the course," Boggs slurred and swayed. "They're all against me. I'm the fall girl. Everyone blames this villainess. They think I'm celebrating." Boggs swaggered to a marble wall and tapped a wall switch. Shelves appeared with a bucket of ice, three glasses, and a crystal decanter engraved with Orbit's logo on the side. "This may come as a surprise to you, but Adonis was neither the love of my life nor the cause of my undoing. Before him, I thought I could take on the world, but I gave up my power along the way. Losing him was an amputation not because of a romance. Adonis was a tour de force that caused me to start to doubt myself. But Orbit is worth zippo now. It's a brand without its brain. I'm on my way in to resign my post. I want to be happy for a change." She poured three drinks and drained them dry. "Now run along, girls, you've got your scoop… and kill the preposterous pen names. They're not fooling anyone."

"I thought we had pretty good pen names," Tiffany said as they fled to the car.

"Never mind that. What about her place? What else is Petra hiding there? That red room freaked me out. When it opened, I thought Jordan Peele would appear and tell us to get out."

"If customers saw that creepy space behind the expensive riding clothes—"

"I wonder if Adonis saw," said Arrow. "She had a major crush on him."

"You felt it too? She was drunk and she was hurting bad no matter what she said to us."

"She looked like she'd been crying, not engineering a vicious corporate raid."

"Either way, she could be the killer though. Appearances can be deceptive."

"Yeah, but I don't think she did it," Arrow ventured. "Just an instinct. Not unless she paid someone. I don't see her getting the drop on a guy like Adonis at that time of night. Sneaking up on him in the dark like that. She's slow and scared and out of shape. And not only that, if she set me up, she'd have recognized me off the bat, but I didn't get that sense from her."

"I almost wish she did it now. If a takeover got Adonis killed by a player who's even more powerful, we're David fighting Goliath. If she isn't staging a takeover—not that we can take her word for it—it doesn't mean another faction isn't making moves right now."

"Any entity planning a takeover had to position itself for quite some time. That's why I got lured to the scene of the crime. I was part of a master plan. Someone or something had more to gain from Adonis's death than they had to lose. I'm not certain that describes Ms. Boggs."

"A secret that big is hard to keep. Someone must see who's poised to strike." Tiffany snapped her fingers. "I know. I'll call our broker. He's connected. I'll see what he knows. I'll bet he's got the scuttlebutt on Wall Street. He gets all the scoops." Tiffany called but barely spoke before her cell switched off. "Well, that was a really weird encounter."

"Why?"

"The guy hung up on me and didn't even say goodbye. I've never heard him act so rude. He's usually sucking up to me. He denied a maneuver to scoop up blocks of Orbit shares but it's a lie. He sounded way too nervous. He was stumbling on his words."

"A broker lying? What a shock. He might be cashing in. Or he might have his own lttle dastardly plot. But to give him the benefit of the doubt, he wouldn't divulge insider information even if he could. It'd probably be unethical. Plus, Orbit's CEO is dead and not of natural causes. That would give him pause if nothing else. Nice try, but even if he'd said a takeover bid was in the offing, that wouldn't prove who shot Adonis. Several people stood to gain."

"That points to the two ex-wives and Adonis's sisters. They're in the driver's seat."

"And Adonis's widow, Petra Djackov. She went at it tooth and nail in a very contentious divorce. But that's no issue for her now, because she could inherit the whole shebang."

"And let's not forget his life insurance," Arrow said. "She might get that."

"She'll have to scratch and claw for it. Adonis charmed the Spanx off every woman everywhere. If you want to feel sorry Adonis crossed your path, take a number and wait in line. Prizz, the personnel manager? They had a thing, I'll tell you that. She did more for Adonis than hire and fire employees, that's for sure. She only knew him several months—though we only have her word for that—but I'll wager a bunch of Orbit stock that they knocked the boots on lonely nights. He could've bequeathed a chunk to her if she'd threatened to expose him. And there's also business interests he might share with his golf buddies." Tiffany opened her Orbit notepad. "Legs Duran and Skipper Lomax."

"Skipper and Legs were Adonis's friends?"

"Evidently. What, you know those guys?"

"I met them in college. Wow, that's wild. Legs was a BMOC—a big man on campus. He ran track. The brother took off at the speed of light. That's how he got the nickname Legs. He trained for the Olympics. Skipper was the editor of the school newspaper in those days. We worked on the *Gazette* together and dated throughout my sophomore year. He's now a reporter on Capitol Hill. We all still text from time to time. What possible motive could they have?"

"Beats me. I guess we'll have to see."

La Dolce Vita restaurant was off the main drag by the shore in Santa Monica's trendy seaside sands in Malibu, close to where Tiffany lived. Its opera-singing servers Rollerbladed trays of pasta to a chichi clientele of locals, tourists, birthday boys and girls, and Hollywood hopefuls doing deals. They threaded through elegant Roman columns by ocean-view tables adorned with checkered cloths, astronomically priced red wines, buckets of fresh-baked rolls and breadsticks, salad bowls big enough to swim in, and couples that needed to get a room.

A maître d' seated Arrow and Tiffany in a semicircular booth by a trompe l'oeil painting of the Amalfi Coast in a candlelit corner of the room. "Skipper's in town for the funeral," Arrow noted. "This is so deceptive, meeting to pump him for information like we're on a dinner date."

"Remember the reason we're here is so *our* funerals won't be next."

"Good point. Drink up. I'm hungry now. When you put it like that—"

"Hey, is that him?" asked Tiffany, signaling toward the door.

Skipper arrived looking finer than ever—to Arrow's chagrin and her friend's delight.

"Why didn't you tell me he was fine?" asked Tiffany as he approached the booth.

"Yeah, superfine. And single too," said Arrow.

"Jackpot!" Tiffany said. "I should've sent you here alone."

Skipper descended like Superman, with walnut skin, a dark blue suit, and a devastating swagger. He was tall, lean, muscular, self-assured, and well-groomed, with a Fu Manchu mustache and roving midnight bedroom eyes. He leaned over and kissed Arrow hungrily.

To her utter surprise, she smooched him back. "Down, bowser," she commanded.

"Grr," he growled. "Don't look so fine if you want me to act like a gentleman. There's only so much a man can take before his primal instincts flare." He breathed heat in her ear. "It's hard to tame a feral beast, and you know I can't control myself when you're looking good enough to eat. Can I order you off the menu, babe?"

Tiffany started to fan herself. "Well, don't mind me. I'm just the wing-girl. Carry on like I'm not here. I need to record this dialogue to script into the show. Let me snap a picture, y'all," she cajoled them, reaching for her phone. "I think we've found the marriage man."

"Don't be ridiculous," Arrow protested. "You couldn't rope Skipper into a marriage if you were a cowgirl's lasso and he was a bull in a rodeo."

"That's the old Skipper. I'm the update," Skipper crooned and kissed her hand.

"There's Legs," said Arrow. "By the door." She waved at Legs and smiled.

"Saved by the bell," said Skipper. "You can't dart and dodge forever, girl."

Legs limped to them on rubbery knees, having abandoned the rigors of track for an order of fried mozzarella sticks, chicken parmesan, penne Alfredo, and a mountain of spumoni. His sense of humor seemed intact despite the ill health he claimed to have, and Arrow valued his Rolex at over three times the cost of her tiny house. "We didn't off Adonis," Legs declared when the server cleared the plates and lavished them with rich desserts.

Arrow responded, "How did you—?"

"Know why you came? I'm not a fool. I've been trying to date you again since college, and all of a sudden, you respond," said Skipper. "It didn't take a wiz to figure what was up."

"Adonis told us all about you," Legs chimed in. "Skip nearly freaked."

"Let's put all our cards on the table, Row. We know why you reached out to us because we planned to contact you." Skipper cleared his throat. "We know you had nothing to do with the murder. We want you to know we're not involved. We were the only real friends he had."

"Word," said Legs.

"I believe you guys. I wasn't aware you knew Adonis. Tiffany got that 411," said Arrow. I never met him in person. It was only our first date."

"And last," said Tiffany. "One-shot deal."

"He told us he met this cool chick on the web and was dying to meet her," Legs revealed.

"Apparently it was a fatal attraction," said Tiffany under her breath.

"I didn't know how to handle it," said Skipper, "when he said your name. At first I thought it was a joke. But the joke was on me this time, I guess. I didn't let on we used to date or how I feel about you, Row. I swear. I didn't have the heart. I thought I'd blown my chance."

"This is the movie we need to produce," said Tiffany, chomping cannoli crumbs with a glob of cream stuck on her nose. "Mayhem. Murder. Mystery. Romance. It would be a giant hit."

Skipper had to chuckle. "I'm assigned to the story for CBC. I've been working to follow the money trail," he said, his energy picking up. "Here's what I found out so far—Petra collects it soup to nuts as the sole beneficiary. But the glitch is a new will was scheduled for signing the day after someone killed her hubby. Papers were drawn up and ready to go, leaving Petra out in the cold with a tiny fraction of his huge estate. Their prenup was tight as a drum from what Adonis told us weeks ago, and he was dead set on divorcing her as quickly as he could. See, they had to be married at least three years for her to collect a settlement, but he caught her sleeping around on him before she hit the two-year mark. She was destined to leave the marriage down and out. She wouldn't stand for that. She was determined to try to be kept in the manner she was accustomed to. In two words—filthy rich. With him gone, she'll inherit a mint as his widow with nothing anyone can do. She did it, Row. We're sure of it, but we don't have the proof."

Legs dropped his fork on his empty plate with a clink. "She's getting away with it. We think she set you up. She probably found out he was meeting you and saw it as her chance. We think she had him trailed again. And just when his work was about to pay off."

"What work? Were you guys in on it?" asked Arrow.

"Adonis stayed mum about business," Legs confided, "but it was something deep. He was worried and distracted. It was tech he invented, that's all we know."

Skipper reached for Arrow's hand. "He told us he needed a fast infusion of cash so he could change the world. That's why he was going public. We told him he could count on us to help him fight takeover bids, and that's when he clammed up on us. Row, maybe I shouldn't tell you this, but we think it had something to do with you."

"Well, that was a heavy convo." Tiffany drove toward the marina in Ventura, heading to Petra's geodesic dome. "We should've dialed 911 when you said to. I was wrong. We might've been able to head this off. As it is, they're pinning the death on you and his wife is collecting billions she's not owed and no one knows. And now that Adonis is out of the way, control is in his sisters' hands. We could go to the cops and tell them that and see what they can do with it."

"But if Skipper and Legs say I'm involved, that solves an unsolved crime. And they've already plastered my face all over the news like I'm a felon. Do you think they'll look for other suspects once I'm in their custody? No way. You know they won't. They'll take his wife's word as the gospel truth. The sisters' too. They're loaded. They'll be acting like butter won't melt in their mouths. And I'll have no one on my side. I'll be lucky to get some freeway-billboard legal hack to take the case of the loser producer who once had a shot at a star on the Hollywood Walk of Fame and wound up doing the walk of shame. Uh-uh. I plan to solve this thing, not be their sacrificial lamb."

"Okay, but we need unassailable proof. We need some solid evidence. I'm afraid if they catch you on the run, your life won't matter. They'll just shoot."

"Your destination is on your right," said the GPS in Byrdley's car as they rounded a tree-lined bend in a beachy section of Ventura.

A team of screaming first responder vehicle sirens wailed ahead.

"Twenty-six eighty-four Winchester Lane." Arrow gulped. "Oh no, that's it down there."

Tiffany gasped and mashed the brakes then pulled over under a cocoa palm to watch the sight at Petra's house, a compendium of giant domes connected by angling concrete paths.

A half dozen police cars and other emergency vehicles huddled with flashing lights at the end of the shadowed cul-de-sac as another speeding ambulance whizzed through the intersection to their left. It skidded and mowed down a tricycle in the yard at twenty-six eighty-eight. Bright lights popped on at the porch of the neighboring house as the ambulance screeched to the end of the roadway, spilling two harried attendants dragging a crooked gurney with a clattering wheel onto the street.

"No, it can't be!" Arrow whined. But less than ten minutes later, as they soon learned over the radio, the bullet-ridden body of Petra Djackov was whisked to the hospital, and for a second night in a row, to the growing concern of all involved, a Duke arrived at Emergency and was labeled DOA.

News of another Orbit Communications-related murder set off bombshells in the media. By seven the following morning, Adonis's ex, Dianza Boggs Duke, and his sisters, Cookie and Raquel, had reportedly fled the country separately. Or maybe all three were disposed of too, depending on which pundit spun the tale and through which outlet.

Regardless of what she'd said before, the ensuing hubbub convinced Arrow she had to give up and turn herself in. But confinement went as Arrow feared. The cops didn't buy her story about her relationship with Adonis or its lack of any one-on-one. The police weren't inclined to be gentle with her, neither physically nor verbally. In less than half an hour, Arrow felt she'd made her last poor choice.

With Arrow unsafely in custody, Tiffany sent out a mayday to Skipper, and Skipper contacted Legs. They couldn't provide Arrow an alibi for when Adonis died, but they sure could corroborate Arrow's account of her whereabouts when Petra's killer broke into Petra's house. Owing to statements by Skipper and Legs, the string of texts in Arrow's phone, the gas station footage from Sold-and-Rolled across from La Dolce Vita, and the waiter and maître d's confirmation, Arrow got released. But the caveat "pending further investigation" loomed as Arrow left the cell, and back on the street there was no relief. The pressure on her doubled. Predators seemed to come out of the woodwork—tabloid recruiters, attorneys, publishers, bloggers, conspiracy theorists, cable newsmen, inmates on the prowl. Not to mention more scary messages from the creep who blew up Arrow's voice mail back at Tiffany's home. With killers loose, the crowdsource trolled, death threats, and bodies in the morgue, Arrow was target number one.

"Come and stay with us a while," Byrd offered upon his return to LA. "Till the fuss dies down and the killer gets caught. Forget the damage to the house. It's you who we're concerned about. Repairs are simple enough to do, but Tiff will never find a friend like you again in life."

"Thank you, Byrd. That means a lot. But you guys need some time alone," said Arrow. "I know a hideaway. No one will ever find me there. I'll call you tomorrow. I'll be fine."

Over Byrdley and Tiffany's protests, Arrow waved and drove away. But not to any small hotel. She drove home to her lonely tiny house to get some things and plot next steps.

The tiny house was cold and gray, and clouds of dread loomed over it. Arrow boohooed when her cell phone rang. *Oh no, it's him again*, she thought. She let the caller go to voice mail.

"Where are you, baby?" Skipper asked when she dared to check her messages. "What's up? Did you go to Tiffany's? I'm worried sick about you. Call me when you get this, Row. I'm here for you, you know I am."

Arrow called back immediately. "I'm home alone. I'm frightened, Skip."

"Stay where you are. I'm on the way," said Skipper. "It'll be all right. Lock all the doors. I got you, babe. I know I let you down before, but we're not kiddos anymore. I'm grown and I'll take care of you. I'll be there before you know it."

The welcome sight of Skipper's Aston Martin zooming to the rescue flooded Arrow's eyes with tears. "My place is a fortress. Stay with me. I'm not taking no for an answer."

Skipper spirited her into Beverly Hills for a night of rediscovery, of laughter and loving companionship Arrow feared she could no longer feel. They shared a closeness and a bond she once deemed him incapable of giving or receiving. And that magical night, for the very first time, Arrow, while locked in his loving arms, overflowed with the sense she was where she belonged.

The next day, when the COO of BT&T rang the bell to open the stock exchange, most of the major brokerage houses reduced Orbit's rating from "superstrong buy" to "don't do it to yourself." Active investors pooh-poohed the stock. Many decided to short it so they could profit when it tanked. The price plunged like an astronaut into a cosmic void in space. Not one major taker was buying in. In a matter of minutes, Adonis's dream submersed into a nightmare. An hour after the opening bell, the Duke sisters, apparently acting by proxy, made a big buy on the internet, as did their erstwhile sister-in-law Dianza Boggs Duke, their nemesis. By then Orbit's stock had ravaged the market for over sixty minutes, selling for pennies on the dollar of what it was actually worth.

To top off the worst-case scenario, the rumor got out that a shrewd, or perhaps foolhardy, mystery investor managed to cop a majority share. Fifty-one percent of the corporation now was owned by who-knows-who.

After that came another astonishing new announcement at high noon.

A press release was delivered over all the wire services—orchestrated and timed by Adonis himself as profoundly as though he were still alive. The startling dispatch came across in part: "Orbit Communications Inc. announces the introduction of a revolutionary technology that enables human beings, as well as other animal species, plants, and various targeted minerals—for the very first time in history and without the use of audio, video, text, computer, or any device that operates externally—to communicate via thought transference using a breakthrough implant. Orbit is proud to unveil Adonis Arrow to a whole new world. This super-affordable ultranano equipment, a visionary aid, digitizes alpha brain waves, converts them to a language transmitted directly and osmotically, and allows the average user to communicate around the globe—by the power of simply thinking thoughts."

The next press release bore another shock. "Majority stockholder Polly Prizz, of Orbit Communications Inc., is available for interviews."

Arrow watched Skipper deliver the news on CBC from where she sat on his patio next to the firepit, grateful that he'd tipped her off before she saw him on TV. She muted his flat screen, took a swig of berry probiotic water, grabbed her phone to buzz her bestie, and was quick to clue her in. "Girl,

you won't believe it. Polly Prizz bought up the stock. The personnel manager. She's the one. She's the majority stockholder. Polly Prizz is in control."

Tiffany gasped. "I knew she was trouble. Being the boss's biggest fan."

"Or pretending to be for a very short time. It seems like she only got
with him to find out what his secret was. To check out what the offering
held and what it might be worth. Maybe she only took that job as head of
the personnel department in order to wangle her way inside. We did that,
and it worked for us. She could've done it too."

"If so, then she's the killer, Row. She waylaid him and set you up. She
sent those hit men to my house to find out what you knew. Or to get you
out of her way for good. But what can we do about it now? How can we try
to clear your name?"

"I'll take it from here. You hang back, Tiff. You've done too much
already."

Prizz picked up the phone on the first ring, cleared her throat, and chirped,
"Hell-o!"

Arrow matched her cheery tone. "Polly Prizz? Congratulations! Orbit
stock is through the roof. This is Paige Turner, *Malibu Sentinel*. Let's arrange
an interview. You made the buy of the century, making an absolute killing,
right? Everyone thinks you're awesome. Tell us about it. Share your trading
tips. Are you able to meet today at four?"

"No. I have major interviews, and then I have to leave by three."

"Maybe another time then?" Arrow offered. But the signal dropped.

Tiffany's silver Mercedes idled by a curb as Arrow left at promptly two fifteen.

"Tiffany, what are you doing here?" asked Arrow.

"Whaddaya think, Miss Marple? Keeping an eye on you while I still
can. You're going kamikaze. I figured you'd be traipsing off to Prizz and into
danger."

"I have to get her to—"

"Confess? Oh sure, she'll spill the beans right off."

"That isn't what I'm after. I'm going to hunt for evidence. She had to leave a clue somewhere. Some trace of what she did to him. If I can just get close to her—"

"You might end up the way he did. I'm not letting you go alone."

"But what about Byrd? He'll hit the roof when he finds out how you tagged along."

"He's pitching a new project. He has no idea I'm not at home. Playing Ethel to your Lucy isn't easy, but I'm used to it... Well, don't just stand there, girl. Hop in."

Polly Prizz's log cabin was tucked away in an isolated pass in a rustic canyon of Sun Valley, on a hill by a bone-dry riverbed. The land was horse country right inside the city, where neighbors lived over an acre away and realtors warned people of color not to ignore Confederate flags. Arrow and Tiffany trailed Prizz there from the parking garage at Orbit, where Prizz exited at 3:05. They cut the engine by her mailbox nearly a quarter mile away from the cabin and surveyed the lot.

"If you aren't back in an hour, I'll be sending out an SOS," said Tiffany. "This is crazy. There must be another way, okay? You can't confront her by yourself."

"If you come, she'll spot your face right off, and that'll blow the deal."

"I'm begging you, get a plan B, Row. This is a horror movie set."

"Just cover me. I'll be right back," hissed Arrow. "I brought Mace."

"And I brought a water pistol, but I doubt that's going to cover you... You sure your Facebook Live is up?"

"I'll arm it at the door."

Arrow sneaked to the cabin door by a gravel driveway edged with tall bamboo.

It might have been the dumb pen name that Prudence Boggs had warned her of, or the eighties bouffant brunette wig slapped crookedly on Arrow's head, or maybe Prizz spotted the car on her trail, but whatever it was that tipped her off, Polly Prizz was prepared for her visitor. Arrow got no chance to speak or attempt to defend her presence there, for as soon as the door creaked open, Prizz hauled off and whacked her on the head and dragged her to the basement.

Arrow awakened drowsy, hearing clomping footsteps overhead. Pounding. Pacing.

Plodding. Prancing. Lying in wait till she came around. Suspended from the ceiling of an underground substructure, she was gagged and bound and oozing blood. Pangs of regret and a pall of confusion played on a loop inside her mind, showing all the roads not taken, ways she could've avoided the hurt to come. Like never having the TV show idea or the crowdsource hunt for men. Like not being stupid enough to meet a stranger in a wilderness at night before she checked him out. Like failing to call the police when she saw Adonis was a bloody corpse and like not letting hubris make her swear to track his killer down. That's what led to this disaster.

What about Tiffany? Where was she? How was she? Did she get away?

Arrow sized up her situation, saw no method of escape. All she had was prayer but she knew prayer was all she needed. She prayed that she'd survive her fate. Prayed Tiffany somehow got away. Prayed Tiffany sounded the alarm. Prayed God forgave stupidity. But her prayer was short-lived and it ended in shoes tap-tapping on the wood-grained laminate stairs down to the cellar floor, her captor's hate of everything preceding her by many feet. Old hot sauce reeked on Prizz's breath and raised the hairs on Arrow's neck as Prizz stood underneath her and cut off the burlap gag.

"Quiet, girl. Obey me now. No one can hear you if you scream." A quiver crisscrossed Prizz's chest. She raised a bow and arrow. "Appropriate gizmo, don't you think? Tsk, tsk, if he could see you now. If he could see me do you in. I let him have anything he wanted, do any kinky thing to me. And after all I did for him, he named his precious product Arrow. How do you feel about that, prisoner? Proud of that, his pretty girl? Because you're going to die!" Prizz shot a sharp shaft into Arrow's arm.

Arrow felt her arm explode as if an atom bomb had hit. She cried out, but it didn't last. She didn't squirm or moan. She let a peace wash over her. She bade her eyes affix on Prizz's stare and held her gaze. "I didn't know about you and him."

"Should that be an excuse?"

"I'm sorry."

"Oh? You're going to be. How dare you feel sorry for me, you airhead. You're not fit to shine my shoes. You think I'm past it, plain and dull. A crusty old spinster that nobody wants, with no hope and no plans for a future. That's what everybody thinks—I'd never stand a chance with him. Adonis didn't think that though. I'm younger than I look. I was only a year his senior. I had him years before you came. And okay, I admit it was just the once, but I pleased him. Yeah, he liked my looks. He didn't mind a plain girl then."

An arrow pierced Arrow's other arm.

Help! Arrow thought but didn't say, refusing to give Prizz either the satisfaction or more zeal to shoot. "We had a connection that's hard to find."

"Really? Tell me about it," Prizz said. "All but impossible these days, right? Except that I'm a rich girl now. I'll *buy* connections when I want. Get plastic surgery, hair weaves, fancy clothes, and people too. I give the orders from now on. I'm the gal who outsmarted Adonis and that makes me very popular. I'll get me a hunk and be loved and adored the way he fell for you. He wanted more than sex from you. He wanted to live in your head and your heart, and he wanted you to thrive in his. He barely even met you and preferred you over me. He said it was love at first byte. Get that. First byte. Do you know how that tortured me? But you won't be so cutesy now, with your beautiful face and smooth brown skin. I'll fix you till I'm prettier. No one else will fall in love with you and leave me in the lurch. Adonis could never ride into the sunset with his Princess Barbie doll. Humanotronics belongs to me!" Prizz shot another arrow.

"It belongs to the world and the people in it," Arrow yelled her pained retort. "Ideas are a dime a dozen till someone endeavors to make them materialize for a purpose larger than themselves," she said. "You'll never steal that, Prizz. You can't. You're not that generous. You may benefit. You may collect some coins, but the money won't bring you happiness. Your karma will come around and bite you in the butt. It always does. If you killed everybody on Earth, you still wouldn't own what Adonis created. You can't ever steal another's dream. You can try to pretend but, in the end, you'll still be the afterthought you are. A cheat. A phony. An impostor. Nothing you buy can make you not feel sorry for yourself. You're powerless if you think it can."

"Oh, you think so, smarty pants? Well, why are you at my mercy then? Arrow, have you considered that? Maybe you should, in your dying hour. His sisters did. His foul wives too. And even Adonis, in the end. They've all been at my mercy. I've had big fun these past few hours. Now I'm famous. I'll be rich." Prizz's eyes drifted to Arrow's blood as it ran along the floor and pooled. "His money was all they wanted, all the pretty young girls who flocked to him and kept him from me all these years. Have *you* felt unrequited love? No, certainly not. Why would you?"

"You're going to get caught. Why go through this?"

"Because I know rejection. Adonis didn't remember me from high school when he hired me. He didn't recall my face or name or anything about me. I was a virgin from his past. He was my first, and I never forgot him. Not for a second of my life. But I didn't mean a thing to him. So I took away what did. You. His power. And his money. I have the company he adored. I have his new invention. If I want, I can have your little TV show and even star in it. I didn't need the Adonis Arrow implant thing to read his thoughts of living a perfect life with you instead of loving me." Prizz fired another shaft at Arrow, this time in her lower leg.

Arrow cried out in agony.

Tiffany heard her dear friend scream. She ran to the back of the cabin, sneaked to a basement window, looked for Arrow hidden in its dreary depths. Panicking, crouching, peeping through a pane of dingy frosted glass, she heard her holler, saw her hanging in a filthy fishing net suspended from the ceiling. Tiffany saw Prizz stretch a bow and arrow, pointing at Arrow's face. The scene was so surreal it blurred and faded from her sight.

Without a moment's hesitation, Tiffany picked up a jagged rock and hurled it through the windowpane.

Alarmed by the sudden sound of shattering glass and Tiffany's piercing screams, Prizz reeled around, took aim, and fired. The arrow whizzed through broken glass where only shards remained. All Prizz could see was Tiffany's feet on the grass outside the basement, but the shoes and slender ankles were enough to drive her wild. She bounded forward, loaded the bow, and fired another projectile through the window, hitting a slim brown calf.

Tiffany hollered, bent, limped off.

"What does she think she's doing?" Prizz demanded.

"Run! Get out of here! Go away!" Arrow shouted. "She's insane!"

"Wait till I catch you!" Prizz exclaimed.

Tiffany hid behind a tree and dialed 911. "Hurry. Please. She's killing us!" With the arrow protruding from her leg, she scrabbled to a bush beside the house and dialed her cell again.

Skipper and Byrd ran four red lights. A growing line of cop cars followed.

"Faster. Faster," Skipper shouted, riding shotgun in Byrd's speeding car.

"I knew when they saw two Black men run red lights in a new expensive car, we'd have no problem getting help. They'll chase us to the grave. How far away are we from the girls now, Skip?" Byrd asked as he rounded a hairpin curve.

Skipper consulted the GPS. "Two miles if the address Tiff gave us works and we can beat the cops."

"Let's hope it's not too late."

"So you didn't come up here alone," Prizz grumbled, squatting by the window. "Perfect. Then I'll make you watch. Who is that girl, a friend of yours?" A soft thud hit the floor above. "I'm going to carve that crazy broad to pieces right in front of you."

Prizz whipped out a long, curved hunting knife and hustled up the stairs.

Tiffany breached a main floor window, attempting to hoist herself inside, but the arrow stuck in her calf at an angle made her tumble to the floor. When she hit, she scrambled to her right. Shuffling her booty across the floor, she saw three other bodies. Cookie, Raquel, and Dianza Boggs were laid out in a row on rubber mats, like in a yoga class. Tiffany muffled a scream, got up on one foot, tripped over Dianza's head, and scrabbled toward the door, the shriek of sirens in the distance causing her head to snap around.

She reached for the doorknob… but it turned.

Skipper and Byrd two-wheeled onto the driveway, racing to Prizz's digs, police cars on their tail and bleating helicopters overhead.

Skipper was yanked from the car as soon as it stopped and thrust to the ground. "Inside!" he pleaded. "Please, or wives!" He was handcuffed, cops assaulting him, shouting orders. Tasers crackled. They wrenched his neck, knees in his back.

Byrd, upright with his hands above his head, was taking punches. "Look in the house before they're killed!" Batons rained down like winter hail.

"Check it out," a cop said, and he holstered his gun. "Take a look. There's no harm if they're lying, guys. There may be other perps in there."

"Help!" Arrow screamed. "We're here! Quick! Help! She's out to kill us both!"

The cops heard her and scattered in every direction, leaving Skipper and Byrd facedown.

"We'll break in the front while you head around back," said a cop to his walkie-talkie. "Careful. Suspects may be armed. It sounds like there's a hostage."

"In the bedroom! Hurry!" Tiffany screamed. Fighting in a ground floor bedroom, fending off Prizz's hunting knife with a wireless speaker in her hands, she kicked Prizz in the knee. Prizz buckled, slashing the air with her knife, nicking Tiffany's wrist and drawing blood. The speaker fell out and hit the floor.

Attempting to slit her opponent again, Prizz tripped on the speaker and lost her balance, leading with her head. Tiffany socked Prizz on the jaw so hard it sent Prizz reeling. She bounced off a wall and disgorged the knife. The blade flew through the air. It hit the ceiling, spun around, and landed in Prizz's shoulder. Seizing the moment, Tiffany knocked Prizz down with a series of lefts and rights she'd practiced in kickboxing class. Prizz pulled a lamp cord. Tiffany snatched it. Yanking the lamp off a tabletop, she swung it like a baseball bat, hitting a homer on Prizz's chin. Two teeth flew out of Prizz's mouth as cops burst in the door and trained their guns on Tiffany.

"Wait!" said Tiffany. "Look downstairs. She's got my friend tied up!"

It took some explaining on everyone's part—Tiffany, Arrow, Skipper and Byrd—to get the police to determine what to make of what they'd stumbled on. But what with three bodies on Prizz's floor and Arrow hanging in the cellar, shot with Prizz's bow and arrow, things looked pretty cut and dried. The evidence was overwhelming once it was gathered, and it prevailed.

Polly Prizz was remanded to custody and charged with five murders in the case—Petra and Dianza Boggs, Adonis, and his sisters. She also got nabbed for stock manipulation, tax evasion, felony wire fraud and, of course, insider trading. The Orbit debacle was front-page news for weeks, and Polly Prizz was right. She got her claim to fame. As it turned out, she wasn't alone. Adonis's so-called friend, Flint Fleischman, who had made the threatening calls and sicced the scary thugs on Arrow, had them kill his erstwhile friend, Adonis, just to make a buck. Prizz had promised him Orbit stock worth millions, and he went for it.

Prosecutors decried "rampaging greed," the papers wrote "unrequited lust," and Arrow's forthcoming bestselling book, entitled What I Did for Love, cast the lurid affair as a sign of the times and indictment of the dating scene, where tech replaces interaction, sex can devalue human life, intoxicating romance is the most addictive form of drug, and truth doesn't matter anymore. "All's not fair in love and war," wrote Arrow in her tell-all tome.

The Adonis Arrow never flew. The prototype vanished. The plans disappeared. Adonis's notes got shredded. Adonis's laptop never saw the light of day again. Adonis's legacy didn't arise from the ashes buried in his crypt. The secrecy he instituted killed it in its infancy.

The profit-sharing plan went through. No Orbit employee lost a job. In fact, lots more were hired. They eventually came to own the place. With no individual heir to Adonis's fortune alive to stake a claim, Orbit employees took over according to clauses in their boss's trust.

Arrow and Tiffany healed with the aid of cocoa butter and their show. Its premiere was a record-setting hit. The Marriage Man stayed at the top of the charts with ratings remaining to this day as some of the highest in history. They birthed a long line of hits that aired and streamed around the globe, produced by the showrunner team that survived the adventure that began it all and almost ended both their lives. They reminisce about Arrow looking for love in the cloak of cyberspace, where anything goes, many miracles happen, and more than one grave danger lurks.

Arrow shot for true love and she scored a bull's-eye—when Skipper Lomax pierced her heart.

COOKING WITH GLASS

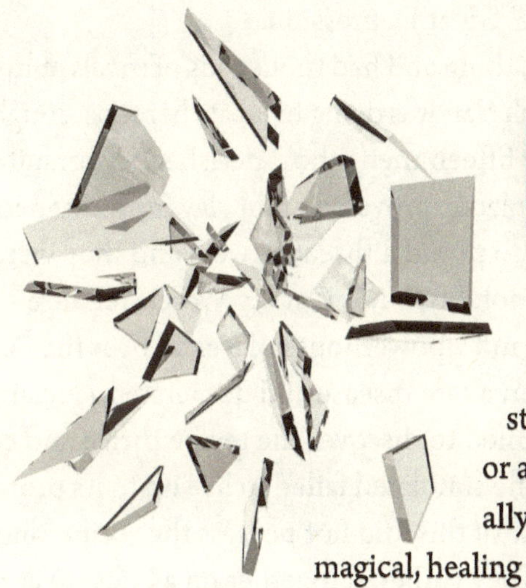

IT ALL BOILED DOWN TO AN old family recipe no one had cooked in two centuries.

Folks were uncertain if it was a baked good, meat dish, veggie concoction, appetizer, stew, soup, casserole, main dish, or a dessert. None of the family really cared. They just heard it had magical, healing powers, took twenty years off a person's looks, and had even brought some people back from the dead, though that was folklore. It thus had more monetary worth than any food, cream, surgical procedure, mask, religious rite, or Western medicine vaccine, according to those who were heir to it: Paprika, Saffron, Basil, Thyme, Rosemary, Mace, and Ginger Dash, the ten-times-great-grandchildren of the gourmet of Primogeniture Plantation in Louisiana.

Primogeniture's culinary wiz was famous throughout the antebellum South as Marjie Cook—a slave and would-have-been master chef if given her rightful due in life. She really was Marjoram Brightweather Dash, a servant who was greatly prized for not only her huge potential income but her bonanza resale value, like a rare painting or plot of land on which any kind of crop could grow. Only Marjoram was human. She endeavored to be low maintenance though, which drove her sale price off the charts. She was stunning and still in her childbearing years, captivating to Black and white men alike, and her reputation spread like wildfire after the owner of Sweetbriar Hill was said to have died of cholera and rebirthed after eating her specialty.

Her prized dish was believed to be corn pone pie, or "potlikker" greens and nasturtium leaves, pear salad, spiced quail with chocolate gravy, Cajun coush-coush, pine bark stew, honeysuckle sorbet, okra soup and fufu, lady pea salad, Jezebel sauce, or low-country chicken bog. In truth, it was likely none of those, as Marjoram served up haute cuisine, painstakingly prepared.

Whatever it was, it was priceless now, more than two hundred years since she cooked it up in the first US Great Depression.

Marjie could whip up anything and had thousands of meals at her fingertips, and as much as the Dash clan was dying to locate her most sought-after recipe, so were apparently fifteen men who'd perished in pursuit of it, plundering for it in dangerous places, provoking foul play from competitors. There were living pursuers who posed a threat as well, and they were numerous, including, and most notably, a Mr. Garvey Worcestershire—current owner of Sweetbriar Hill and a powerhouse player all over the Pelican state—who was perishing from a rare disease and desperate to reclaim his health. It was he who had claimed to discover the recipe thrice and called it his "formula," but whatever he simulated failed to live up to its promise.

Marjoram's progeny knew of this, did not possess the recipe, and had no clue as to where it was, so they gathered together on a quest to at minimum identify the nature of their heirloom.

"She had to hide a cookbook somewhere," Ginger declared over Thanksgiving dinner.

"She was a slave. She couldn't write," said cousin Mace, chomping a turkey leg.

"Who says? I heard she found a way," said Rosemary. "Marjie was hired out. And it wasn't illegal to teach slaves how to read and write until Nat Turner led the successful uprising back in 1831. Grandma Juniper told me when I was a kid how Marjie eventually freed herself. She said Marjie learned to read and write, as egregious as conditions were. In the weeks she got leased for outside work, she arranged a bit of independence, earning room and board and clothes and medical attention. Marjie could travel and self-determine, own her own time to some extent. Just think of it. What would you do in her shoes? I'd fight to the death for that recipe. I'd be like Kunta Kinte in *Roots* when they beat him and cut off his foot. He kept living on purpose no matter what. I bet that's what Marjoram did as a chef and a healer. She was a warrior. She'd use every weapon she could find, and her knowledge would be the most potent, right? If she risked her life for education, surely she'd use it to help other people and make the world a better place."

"Amen to that. I'd kill for it," Paprika interjected. "If I knew I could actually change the world with something I had come up with, anyone trying to shackle me best know I'd do them in. Particularly if I cooked their food and controlled what they ingested. If they treated me less than human and they let me breathe for half a sec, they'd never see my butt again and be lucky to survive. Marjie was either self-taught or got her lessons in a big house. She was light-skinned, so they'd put her there. If she were as dark as I am, they'd have never known how well she cooked. They'd have worked her to death in the fields before she could pick up a single pot or pan."

"I agree with Paprika and Rosie, y'all. She wouldn't create that recipe and not bestow its legacy," said Basil. "We know that. She invented a cure that could save people's lives. She'd never let that go to waste. Heck, look at us. We all succeed and we're her flesh and blood. Her DNA, for heaven's sake. If she didn't write down that recipe, she relayed it through oral history."

"And how are we supposed to get to that?" asked Saffron. "Through osmosis?"

"No, we have to hunt it up. We know about Marjie. That's a start. That tells us our ancestors passed our birthright down to us by hook or crook. Which means we'll uncover it now as long as we work together as a team. How many Black families can trace ten generations back past slavery with their histories purposefully broken, huh? That leaves us all a step ahead. If Marjie did leave us a bread crumb trail, the least we can do is follow it. *We're* her legacy. It's on us. We have to decipher her code, that's all. Imagine what that recipe could do for folks today," Thyme said and let the thought hang in the air. "Besides, I want to taste it."

That night, they began a family search. Siblings and cousins joined together to hunt their genealogy throughout their holiday vacation. It was superfun. Never had they been so close or spent so much time under one of their roofs, up at Rosemary's house in Virginia Beach. They researched all day and cogitated at night over awesome dinner fare which was mostly inspired by Marjoram but also by their daily catch of seafood off of Rosie's dock.

They traced ten generations on their paternal side in just two weeks, taking time off from their various jobs and nuclear family ties back home for a period of acute confab, discovering leaves from their family tree on a list in an old red Bible that was falling apart to nearly dust. And seeing birth and marriage certificates, military service forms, divorce decrees, homeowner deeds, and other vital stats online was more heartwarming than they'd hoped. It engendered a sense of belonging to something bigger than themselves. What it didn't provide was any hint to where the recipe might be, which heightened their frustration as they split in mid-December.

By Christmas, one of them was dead, and the others feared they might be soon.

Rosemary was buried the afternoon of a truly dismal New Year's Eve.

"How did it happen?" Basil asked. "She was fine when I called on Christmas Eve."

"She was found by a fisherman, under her dock. That's all the cops would tell me, guys. But her hands were tied behind her back, and her body was floating in seaweed," Ginger said and shivered at the thought. "They have to do DNA and all, 'cause a gator apparently got to her."

"Are you serious?" Paprika groaned. "Nobody told us that over the phone."

"It's gruesome," Saffron said and coughed.

"For real," said Mace.

"It's murder," Thyme concluded.

"Not necessarily," said Paprika.

"What other explanation is there?" Basil said and clenched his fists. "She didn't tie her hands behind her back and jump in the water herself. Somebody killed her."

"Who?" asked Mace.

"How should I know? I'm not Sherlock Holmes. I just know when I catch him, his ass is mine," barked Basil, and he kicked a rock. The stone catapulted off the grass and landed on the casket down in the grave with a sickening hollow sound.

"Get it together," Saffron chided. "This is defiling Rosie's memory. We're in a cemetery, y'all. What are you trying to do, raise the dead?"

"That's exactly what we're doing. Think about it," Ginger posed.

"Yeah, Gin's right." Mace doubled down. "We're digging up old secrets. How can it be a coincidence that Rosie gets murdered right at the time we're hunting for the recipe? That recipe could change the world. Who knows who's in its history? Look how many died while searching for it… that we know of. There could be several folks we don't. I'm wondering who'll be next."

"You're seriously starting to creep me out," said Saffron, tossing her braided hair. "You think we're all in danger too?" She hiccupped, backed up, looked around. "Let's get in the limo and out of the cold. We'll hash it out in private."

Rosemary's house was filled with mourners up until midnight and beyond. Many brought trays of comfort food—macaroni and cheese, greens, candied yams, sliced turkey, barbecued ribs, fried shrimp, baked fish, and sweet potato pie. There were buckets of Caesar salad, sautéed spinach, squash, and gumbo too. And black-eyed peas and rice, fresh corn on the cob, and cornbread stuffing. Someone baked two hundred buttery rolls that were hot and melted in your mouth. None of the Dash descendants had much of an appetite except for Mace. He was six feet six and three hundred pounds, and nothing could quench his desire for greasing grub at any hour.

After the crowd had cleared and the paper plates and cups were tossed in plastic bags, Basil and Mace lugged the garbage out to containers by the curb.

"Garvey Worcestershire's son had the nerve to come, did you notice?" asked Basil.

"How could I not?" said Mace, breathing in, looking up at the stars. "Them people don't peck for the heck of it. Chester was nosing around the funeral, listening in on conversations, trying to learn what we might know. He only wants one thing in this world. The recipe. Period."

"He's a snake. He wants to mass produce it. He hit on Rosie all the time to try to ferret out a clue, but the dude didn't care if she lived or died. If he horns in, dissing her one more time, he'll get what he deserves."

"Don't get yourself in trouble, Basil. We have better things to do. Forgive and forget for your own sake. He's not worth it. You'll be off to jail, and he'll be off to Sweetbriar Hill to squander his daddy's inheritance. Let's just keep him away from the fam, okay? Especially the girls." Mace pointed aloft to a constellation. "Yo, man, that's Orion there. Those three bright stars make up his belt, and the stars in the arc are his shield."

"I see it. Yeah," said Basil. "There's the North Star over there. What's it called?"

"Polaris."

"Right. It shows you how to head due north. That's comforting when you think you're lost… Rosemary was our Polaris, man. I miss my sister like the moon would miss the sun if it went out."

"I know that's right. I loved her like a sister too, even though she was my cousin. She was closer to me than Paprika, and Paprika *is* my sister. I could tell Rosie anything. I almost can't believe she's gone."

"Yeah, I feel you. Rose was magic. Sometimes it isn't your siblings who are your brothers and sisters when it counts. You always have someone to bless you though."

"And Rosie was there for more than most."

"You think she slept with Chester, Mace?"

"I don't know, cuz. I'm not touching that. If she lay with him, it was her business. Rosie had excellent judgment, so if she—"

"What are y'all doing out here in the dark?" asked Ginger. "The séance is starting."

Rosemary's eat-in kitchen table was round and made of cypress wood. It had knots and lots of character and was shaped like the tree from which it came, as its top had been cut by bisecting a trunk that was two yards in diameter and had climbed to over fifty feet, irregularly formed. Seven cups of hot cider sat on top, the seventh cup for Rosie. A Christmas tree blinked in a far corner of the kitchen, by the pantry. The kitchen was appointed with the latest appliances, finishes, and an open concept, adjoining, through French doors, a vaulted great room that had been culled, when Rosie renovated, from footage of the original kitchen plus a study next to it and what once was butler's quarters.

Basil, Saffron, Mace, Paprika, Thyme, and a nervous Ginger Dash sat at the table, joining hands, lit only by a violet candle and the flashing colored lights and star on top of the Christmas tree. The bulbs on the tree were lit up too, with letters of the alphabet and little Black angels with glowing wings that flapped to the tune of Christmas songs.

"This is silly," said Paprika. "No one comes back from the grave, you guys."

"Tell that to Mary Magdalene," said Mace.

"But spirits aren't real," said Saffron.

"Why are you nervous then?" said Ginger, chafing. "Humor us."

"I'm not nervous. It's just chilly. That's why I'm shaking," Saffron pleaded. She pulled a shawl up on her back but shiver harder. "I'm okay. I'm fine. I'm as calm as a yoga instructor."

Paprika cackled. "That's a laugh. We can see you're a bundle of nerves."

Thyme bristled. "Paprika, check yourself. For once, it's not about you. You don't have to believe to cooperate. Be kind and show respect."

"For what? This hocus-pocus? Ghosts, ghouls, goblins, and fake spirits?"

"Fake? Our spirits are all that's real. They're who we are and who we'll be—eternally spiritual beings inhabiting a physical body on this plane. When you realize that, you'll—"

"Be as airy fairy as you sound right now." Paprika whooped another howl.

"Or maybe you'll start to behave like what you say and do has an effect," said Thyme. He took a swig of cider. "Maybe one day you'll catch that drift."

"Stop bickering. We're on the same side, right?" said Ginger. "We need a family bond. I learned that when my husband drove off with a blonde and never returned. I'd still be a ranger if not for that marijuana she planted in my car. C'mon, you guys, let's show some love. Or else we'll have a funky vibe. The séance won't work if we don't believe."

"Might as well call it a day then," said Paprika, and she rose and turned.

"You got any better ideas, Paprika?" Basil asked and got no answer. "Thought so."

"I rest Basil's case," said Mace. "Sit your butt down."

Paprika wilted, took her seat. Withering under her brothers' glare, she plucked a vial of sage spray off the table, spritzed it in the air, and caught hold of Saffron's hand.

"Okay," said Ginger. "Here we go." She lifted a basket off the floor and spread items out in front of them. "Here's Rosemary's Thanksgiving picture. It's supposed to help us contact her. In this box are three of Marjie's teeth that got knocked out in a slave rebellion. She saved them to remind her what she sacrificed for freedom. Careful, y'all, they're precious. They've been passed down to us all these years." Ginger settled the box beside a shell incense holder and lit an incense stick, and frankincense wafted through the air. "Everyone turn your phones off, 'kay?"

They did, except for Saffron. "We should record this, don't you think?"

"Good thinking," said Basil, taking the phone and pressing Record in the camera app as he stood her cell up by its red kickstand.

"I'll act as a medium," Ginger announced. "I'm the one who believes it's going to work. I meditated all night long, and I'm totally in the Zen zone even after all that's happened… Close your eyes, everybody. We're ready to start. Relax. Concentrate on why we're here—to find out who killed Rosemary and where Marjoram hid the recipe. Let everything else fall away from your thoughts, and focus on those two questions."

The room got quiet. No one budged. Three silent minutes passed.

"We're here to contact the spirit world," said Ginger. "Calling for family. Specifically, Marjoram Brightweather Dash and Rosemary Dash, our relatives. They love us, and we adore them both. We're here to seek their guidance. We pray for protection from ill intent on the part of any errant soul, and we ask that only the blessed come into our midst, now and forever. Only goodness may enter and love prevail within and about us. Keep us safe… Rosemary, please make your presence known, and Marjoram, kindly watch over us and lead us to your special gift of healing and enlightenment. Knock once for yes and twice for no when you're ready to answer our questions."

Several more minutes passed as the family sat breathing in and out as one.

"Please help us," Ginger entreated. "We beseech you to give us some kind of a sign."

A pot on a burner on the stove made a barely perceptible rattle.

"Did you hear that?" asked Saffron. "Someone's here."

Paprika said, "There it goes again." She opened her eyes, peered toward the stove.

"I bet you believe in spirits now," Thyme whispered.

"I sure do," said Mace. "Ask questions. See what they reply."

"Sh!" said Ginger. "Quiet down. Don't break up the vibration."

"Rosemary? Sister, is that you?" asked Basil with his face lit up.

Two knocks indicated the answer was no.

"It isn't Rosie," Saffron said. "I think I'm going to faint."

"Who are you? Are you an ancestor?" Ginger implored. "Please let us know your name."

"Who killed Rosie?" Basil asked. "Please find a way to let us know."

A burner lit under the empty pot, its gas flame shooting toward the vent. The pot flew through the air. It spun and whizzed past Saffron's head, cracking a decorative tile on the wall.

The oven door cantilevered.

Cabinet doors slammed open and closed, and dishes crashed onto the floor.

A bottle of bubbly that'd been delivered popped its cork, and champagne spewed.

Sharp nails burst out of the rafters, and large copper ceiling tiles rained down.

The family, scattering, fled the kitchen, hauling past the great room, through the French doors, into amassing fog.

Chester Worcestershire and two hired thugs hung around at the corner of the block and watched as the Dashes dashed out of the house as rain began to fall.

"What's got into them?" asked Morton Corn behind the wheel of a tricked-out Silverado truck with a trailer hitch, mag wheels, and a wiring harness.

"Dunno," said Bull Montgomery. "They look scared as a frog in hot Brunswick stew, and we ain't even started to spook 'em yet."

"Should be easy to run them out for good," said Morton. "Ain't that what you want?"

"Never mind," said Chester from the back seat. "Follow them like a shadow, wherever they go, whatever they happen to do, for as long as they're in the county. Report it all right back to me. Here." He held out burner phones. "Use these. Don't talk on nothin' else. If they look like they're diggin' or pickin' up something or headin' to, say, a PO box or a locker where they have a key or a safe deposit box somewhere, or they head into, heaven forbid, Emporia, Franklin, Petersburg, or Hampton, stay on their tail and shoot video of whoever they contact in the hood."

"They don't look much like hood types, boss," Bull ventured to evaluate.

"Oh, look who became a hood expert," said Morton.

"I got a sidepiece there," Bull crowed. "You oughta try it."

"Don't let these people get away. The minute they try to leave for home, their packing will signal they got what they came for. When they bolt, be sure you see."

"What are we lookin' for though, boss?" asked Bull.

"A paycheck, dufus balls. Cold cash for keepin' your damn mouth shut," warned Chester.

"Got it," Morton agreed and shot a castigating look at Bull, whose head hung low.

"My daddy can be very generous or as ornery as a Georgia mule. Stay on his good side, boys, or else… you might wind up like those folks will when everything gets settled."

The following morning, Ginger awoke with a strange idea stuck in her head.

On reentering the house the night before, when her traumatized family was still shaken up, she noticed the letters on the Christmas bulbs seemed different than they'd been, like they were rearranged. She hadn't noticed this at first, what with the cleanup of the disarray the poltergeist had caused, but the colors began to seem tampered with while they drank hot cocoa afterward, and during the night she pondered what it was that made the tree seem off. She ran down in her nightie at three a.m. but couldn't make heads or tails of it. Then, as sunshine streamed in through her window, she recalled what she had read online while prepping for the séance, and she felt she had a clue. She donned her fleece robe and zipped into the hall, bellowing as she pounded doors along the upper floor. "Hey, everybody, quick, wake up!"

"Did somebody sound the breakfast call?" asked Basil with a yawn. He stretched as he opened his door and stumbled out with just one slipper on.

"I don't smell coffee or bacon. This better be good," said Mace. "I'm starved."

"What's wrong?" said Saffron, racing at them, sliding her negligee up on her shoulders. "It's nothing about the ghost, I hope. I don't think I can stand another fright."

"I'm up," said Thyme in boxer briefs, his privates as hard as a candy cane.

"You sure are, bro. Put something on," Paprika said. "Zip up."

"Come on. I'll bake a batch of sweet rolls," Ginger proffered. "I've got news."

When all were gathered in the kitchen, Thyme said, "I need a pitcher or something. We didn't water the Christmas tree."

"Here, Mr. Sensitive," said Paprika. "Use this empty cider bottle."

"That's what I wanted to talk about," said Ginger, starting to make the rolls.

"What, this jar?" Paprika laughed. "Have at it. Knock yourself out."

"No, the tree," said Ginger. "Look."

"It's dying." Saffron shuddered. "That could be a real bad omen."

"Get ahold of yourself," said Basil. "I won't let anything happen to you, Saff."

"I wouldn't be so sure," said Mace. "Someone's out there watching us. I spotted a truck on the street last night. I think whoever murdered Rosie might be after the recipe."

"You're imagining things," Paprika carped. "I don't know why you're all so terrified. We know where Rosie kept her gun. We'll arm ourselves. If someone comes—"

"Will you listen to me for a second? I think I figured something out. Remember the summers when we were kids, Grandma Juniper had that Ouija board?" asked Ginger.

"Yeah," said Thyme. "It worked."

"You were deluded to *think* it worked," Paprika droned. "She made that thing."

"Doesn't matter," said Ginger. "People do. It's a way to communicate with the dead."

"Is everyone in this family totally bonkers?" asked Paprika.

"It's a portal," Ginger explained. "A means for the dead to connect and tell us stuff. To keep us on our path and help reveal our destinies. Letters and numbers is all it takes, and we have some right there." She swiveled, pointed at the tree.

"What do you mean?" said Mace.

"The decorations," Ginger said.

"Yeah. Check it out," said Thyme. "We had the tree lit up last night. It's like a giant Ouija board." He knelt, poured water in the stand, stood up, and examined a lighted bulb.

"I think the letters spell out words they didn't spell out yesterday," said Ginger.

Basil scratched his head. "Oh yeah? Well, what do you think they say?"

Ginger hesitated. "I'm not sure, but I think the spirits answered us."

"It could be a clue to the mysteries we're not solving by ourselves," said Mace.

"Let's take a look right now," Thyme advocated, whipping out his Android phone and tapping into Notes. "Call off the letters. I'll type them in. That way, we can make sense of them."

"Let's count the bulbs first," Saffron said. "To see how long the message is." She did, and so did Mace and Thyme. "Okay, there are thirty-six. Makes sense. If they're packed a dozen bulbs per box. Twenty-six alphabet letters and ten numbers, one through zero."

"Start at the top," said Ginger. "By the star. The star was Rosie's fave."

"Yeah, Papa would lift her in his arms to put the tree topper on every year," said Basil. "Starting when she was one. By the time she was two, she'd kiss it first, kiss each of us, and place it there." His eyes welled up and he wiped tears away with a striped pajama sleeve.

"What's the top letter?" Paprika asked. "I can't see it, I'm too short."

Mace used his height to turn the bulb. "It's... *R*," he announced. "How interesting."

Saffron gasped. "For Rosemary."

"Or recipe," said Basil.

"Not necessarily," said Paprika, crossing her arms and pursing her lips in a manner conveying dissent. "If the letters wind up in a sentence, who's to say they'll be in order? Plus, Rosemary has two *R*s, but there's only one each of every letter here."

"So maybe the letters repeat somehow," Mace reasoned. "There might be a code."

"Right," said Ginger. "Got that, Thyme?"

"I'm entering them into a word processor app so we can move the text," Thyme offered.

"Next one's *E*," said Mace, his mitt on a sunshine-yellow bulb.

"How will we know how many *E*s? Probably vowels repeat the most," Paprika said.

"That's logical. There are only five vowels, but twenty-one consonants. Let's jot them all down and go from there," said Basil. "Get an overview before we draw conclusions."

"Okay," said Mace. "The next one's I. Then O. Then T. Then H. The number two. Then A. Then C. Then N. Then D. Then S." He reached and groaned. "And this red one at the back—"

A floorboard creaked above their heads.

"What was that?" asked Saffron, clutching Basil.

"Something that has no business here," said Ginger, snatching a kitchen knife.

The Dash crew headed for the stairs.

"Hold on, y'all. Let me head up first," said Mace, and he seized a big cast-iron pan.

The crew lined up behind him as they crept upstairs to trace the noise.

"Look, it's a kitten," Saffron cooed and rushed to scoop the small cat up.

"Duh. But how'd it get inside?" Paprika shooed the cat away. "We closed the doors and windows when we came in out of the rain last night."

"Who cares, guys? Look how cute it is." Saffron stroked the kitty cat. "Let's keep it, y'all. It's soft and sweet."

The kitten lashed out, scratched Saffron's cheek.

"It's sweet, huh?" Basil grabbed it by the scruff and started down the steps.

"I'm bleeding." Saffron faltered, cupping her cheek like it might fall off her face.

Out in the driveway, a truck engine cranked up, revved its engine, sped away.

"Someone was here!" Thyme shouted, jetting toward the dormer up the hall.

Basil dropped the kitten, ran with Mace down toward the kitchen door.

"The tree's on fire!" Basil shouted.

Ginger rushed out to the porch, returned with a hose, and began to spray. Paprika filled a pot with water, hurled it at the Christmas tree, ran back, and filled the pot again, while Saffron cried and cringed and clung to the cat, which scratched her neck and squirmed. Thyme rifled through the linen closet, found a king-size patchwork quilt, and returned to battle the blaze with it. The quilt caught fire, singeing the hairy skin on Thyme's long arms and searing his flesh. Hot sparks ignited in Thyme's thick beard, and Ginger turned the hose on them.

By the time the fire was out and there was ointment on Thyme's chin and arms, the tree was a mound of ash, and the phantom message was destroyed for good.

Meanwhile, up on Sweetbriar Hill, another loss was taking place.

"He passed," said Dr. Baxter Simms in the vast foyer of Sweetbriar Manor. "Where's that no-good son of his?" he asked housekeeper Lola Marsh.

"Why, Mister Chester's… out of town," said Lola.

"In somebody else," said Chester's drunk wife, Anabelle. "Betraying me. As usual. I'm sure he'll be distraught when he hears Daddy dear has bit the dust while he was out philandering."

The physician asked with clear disdain, "Will you notify Chester, or shall I?"

"Whatever. It'll go to voice mail either way. He won't pick up. Chester can't hear a sound or see a sight or even breathe a breath unless his father tells him how… Well, don't look so surprised I said it. Everybody knows it's true. Chess never even tried to love nobody but hisself." She gulped another swig of brandy, breathed it into Simms's gaunt face. "He'll go to pieces over this, but Lola here will clean them up. I'll let him know you dropped by, Doc, but didn't do no good."

Word of the death of Garvey Worcestershire spread like flu in wintertime. Via the news, the internet, and the grapevine's lightning word of mouth.

When it hit Chester, he flew home and was avidly grieving at the deathbed, planning a funeral "like no other ever happened in the South."

Anabelle—simulating sadness in the west wing of the manse, her stylist showing her chic black frocks and shoes for the memorial—was plotting what it meant for her, this passing of the patriarch. What might she gain in the estate? Nothing from that recipe that Chess and Garvey never found. What a bunch of hooey, that was. An elixir Fountain of Youth. A resurrection for the dead. Whoever heard of such a thing as zombies in real life? Besides, it'd be a tragedy if Chester were to stick around an instant past this New Year's Eve, far less in some eternal life. He wasn't in her plans.

Mace regarded the ashes and shook his head. "Well, that's the end of that."

"I told you it would never work," Paprika moaned. "Those gaudy bulbs."

"You jinxed it," Mace accused her. "You malign and poo-poo everything."

"Guys, let's not fret for what we *don't* have," Ginger said. "Let's use what's left."

"There's nothing left. It's all destroyed," whined Saffron, bursting into tears.

"No, we have a lot to work with," Thyme said. "Nearly half. We know twelve of twenty-six letters, and I formed some words already, see?"

They sat on the floor in the great room, gathered to home in on his cell phone screen.

"It's fun, like any word game, guys," said Thyme. "Right off of the top of my head are *coin, threat, hot, can, car, note, dire, thin.* There are plenty more that we can try."

"And I see *dither* too," said Saffron, sniffling. "*Cart* and *stretch* as well, if we can count the *T* two times."

"Maybe that's what the two means, get it? Double the letters," Mace chimed in.

Ginger suggested, "Let's make lists. We'll put them together and see what we get."

They did, for an hour, and when they were through, they decided the word *Search* should come first if the letters formed a sentence. That word popped up on all their lists.

"Okay, *search* then. So what comes next?" asked Ginger.

"Search *in,*" Basil said. "It's a two-letter word, but it's on all lists and it's logical."

"Yeah, *inside* is too." Mace ruminated. "Search inside?"

"But inside what?" asked Saffron. "This whole process gives me chills. I mean, where could it be? A bag? A bin? A basement? Maybe a closet?"

"Down in a grave?" Thyme mused. "It's gross, but people hide stuff there."

"You could be onto something," Basil said. "Whose grave though, Rosie's?"

"Probably more like Marjoram's," said Mace. "The recipe was hers."

"We all agreed she'd die for it," Ginger muttered. "And she did. She took her *secret* to the grave. Maybe she took the proof there too."

The brothers and sisters exchanged a look.

"Well, don't look at me. I'm not down with it. If you think I'm grave-robbing, you must be smoking some herb from Marjie's recipe," Paprika protested. "You're on your own. As much as I want to find it too, I'm drawing the line at exhumation. Looting a corpse is against the law. You freaks could go to jail. You can't really be thinking of digging Marjie up. She's spinning in her grave."

"I wonder what she'd have to say." A bulb rolled out of the ashes, across the hardwood, straight into Ginger's lap, where she sat on the floor in a lotus pose. "Okay, I'll pretend I don't see that."

"I see it," said Saffron, crabbing away from it, running shoes squeaking on old oak planks.

"What letter is on it?" Thyme inquired.

"Beats me. I ain't reading it. Do it yourself," Paprika declared. "Don't touch it, Ginger."

Ginger tapped it with her toes, and the ball rolled over and over and over, ping-ponging a foot of each family member, finally resting against a table leg with a forceful knock.

"One knock. That means *yes*," Ginger said. She gulped.

"That's it! I'm leaving! Let's get out! I'm not spending another minute here." Paprika popped up, bumped into a wall, and braced herself against it.

"It's a *T*," said Thyme. "I saw a *T*."

Basil concurred. "I clocked it too. Only, what kind of *T* are we supposed to search?"

"I don't know," said Saffron, hiccupping. "*Grave* begins with *G* last time I looked."

"The table?" Ginger guessed. "*Table* begins with a *T*, and that dining table is antique. Grandma Juniper had it at her house."

"I'm'a take it apart," said Mace. He rose.

"You can't. It's an heirloom," Saffron protested.

"Bump that. You're just scared to check," said Mace. "I'm taking the bull by the horns."

The table came up empty.

"Sorry," said Mace with one leg in his hand, the unassembled table wrecked, and a hang-dog look on his chubby face, arms dangling at his sides. "I really don't know what got into me."

"No sweet rolls," Ginger purred. "You're hungry. I never fixed our breakfast."

"Okay, you win," Paprika griped. "You're obviously not going to be deterred no matter what crazy scheme it takes… Where's Marjoram buried?"

"Louisiana. Up on Sweetbriar Hill," said Ginger. "In a segregated cemetery, in a shallow grave without a proper headstone. They buried her there after she broke free from Primogeniture Plantation. Slave patrols caught her and sold her all over again, and she wound up on Sweetbriar Hill. Sweetbriar wanted her magic cure and the lure of her celebrity, so loath to diminish her value, they bartered her kids away to break her spirit. When that didn't happen, on they went. They cut off her breasts and lashed her to a twelve-foot cross for several days, torturing her with red-hot chips from the wood-burning stove where she cooked their food. After that, she became a martyr more beloved than she had ever been, and the legend of Marjoram Cook spread past the South into the North. And when the plantation owners died and their land got bequeathed to their wicked son, rather than live in his tyranny, she led a slave rebellion and she liberated forty slaves but didn't get away herself. Grandma Juniper said they boiled her hands and ate them in a pot of stew, so she couldn't cook her recipe in this life or beyond the veil. She survived but had to cook with stumps."

"Ain't that a blip," said Basil as he deflated like a squashed balloon.

"We know where Chester gets it from. Depravity is the only thing he's actually come by honestly," said Mace. "He's mean and inhumane, and his business is corrupt."

"Is there really no end to their cruelty?" Saffron gagged and took off for the bathroom.

"Apparently not," Paprika declared as a pall fell over the living room.

"It's reason enough to exhume her, you ask me, to a decent resting place," said Thyme.

With that, they headed south.

"They're driving your way, but we don't know why," Morton Corn reported via text. "In a red SUV with Georgia plates."

Chester replied, "You just keep on their trail and let me know when they arrive. I need you to track their every move. I'll pay you on delivery… And Morton, if they get wise to you, call the cops and tell them they ripped me off. They'll roust them so they can't escape."

Those texts were retrieved by Chester's wife while he lay with a red-headed prostitute in a five-star hotel in Destrehan. Anabelle, who had put her nephew, Cyrus, up to cloning Chester's cell last week, had not yet learned to whom the "they" referred, or why Chester was after them. That left her with unsettling thoughts, the most prominent of which was how this "they" might sway her fortunes. Bereaved daughters-in-law weren't having any rip-offs up on Sweetbriar Hill. One thing Anabelle learned as the daughter-in-law of the richest old coot in Louisiana was money ruled most everything, and a girl without money of her own broke rules or got ruled out.

The cemetery security guard was hired in 1982, after decades of desecration of the Worcestershire marble mausoleums by intruders seeking treasure, information, or revenge. Centuries of folklore touting Marjie's homeopathic cure caused six of fifteen men who'd cruelly perished in pursuit of it to meet their end on Sweetbriar Hill—e.g. one Herbert Ironwerks, who croaked in 1981, supposedly from a self-inflicted gunshot wound that pierced his heart.

Ironwerks was a fortune hunter, snubbed and obscure on Louisiana's banks but far more celebrated off the Moorish coast of Spain. There, he retrieved a sunken galleon loaded with a cache of gold coins worth a billion bucks. After the Ironwerks fiasco, back when Garvey Worcestershire was dubiously in his prime, Cane Shelfling came on as an evening guard, patrolling the plots on the graveyard shift from Monday through Saturday every week between nine p.m. and dawn. That duty passed down to Cane's son, Doug, after Cane succumbed to liver damage in the wake of thirty years of boozing on the job. Doug appeared to resent the graveyard gig, but as he was rudderless and broke, he reveled in its many perks. The upside was, he surfed all day, chased tourist girls until past eight, and smoked weed in the dark of the Worcestershire necropolis with impunity. And nor did he need to sentinel the entirety of the property, because part of the sacred sepulcher held Black slaves from the old-school days, so nobody cared what happened there. Except, of course, the Blacks in town who were struggling to bring it up to code and enforce desegregation.

Doug, with his pants down around his ankles, laying the wood to Melanie Pringle, whose name he had carved, along with his own, in the trunk of the tree they were pressed against, was not even faintly interested in his mission when the fam arrived. They climbed over the wall at the south end dressed in black and bearing shovels.

Paprika, Saffron, Basil, Thyme, Mace, Ginger, and six new flashlights invaded a cemetery demarcated by a separate entrance and a half-mile chain-link fence that cordoned Black corpses off from white. This caused an uproar in the town, for ensconced in 1869, a mile from the manor house, the scene was the final resting place of hundreds of people of color, including Union soldiers, World War II vets, Hall of Famers, singers, film stars, TV hosts, gold medalists, Catholic bishops, and even a billionaire CEO who had himself buried there to illustrate its preposterousness. And though it was once a private spot, Garvey's father, in 1950, before the Civil Rights Movement hit its stride, began selling graves to make a buck, mainly to local residents whose forebears might be buried there, so they could join their families in death if not in life—adults and often children too.

Slave gravesites on the property were identified by coded markers. Largely due to the white population's fear of funeral gatherings where slaves might join to plot escapes, mourners banned from burying loved ones with a shred of dignity were forced to be clever about the task, using the deceased's belongings, stones, or wooden stakes to mark the graves, and adhering to African burial customs when and where they could. But at least these plots were not paved over, supplanted by grocery chains and banks and bars like public segregated cemeteries elsewhere were. Whole cemeteries had been known to disappear with time as well, overcome by flooding, overgrowth, land shifts, and other natural causes, serving to dissemble the unnatural separation of the skin-toned dear departed. These facts made finding a predecessor's grave all but impossible.

The Dash clan searched the eerie nightfall into the early-morning hours, having located so few graves. Some tired and nearly turned their backs on ever finding Marjie.

But a sighting allayed their discouragement when Ginger stopped and said, "Oh no."

"What is it?" Basil crossed to her as she put her hand up to her mouth.

Ginger bent over and picked something up. "This button. It was Rosie's. It's from her Christmas blouse, remember?"

Saffron prodded. "Are you sure?"

"Of course," said Ginger, taking out her phone to swipe through her gallery app. "There it is, see? She's wearing it. I complimented her on it." She showed a family photo. "It's shaped like a star with a rhinestone center. On the red blouse, it really popped. I'd never seen one like it."

"Word. It's distinctive," Mace agreed.

Basil shined his flashlight on the button, then the digipic. "They look the same," he evaluated, lifting the button from Ginger's palm.

Thyme, with two fingers, enlarged the photo, gawking and putting his glasses on to compare the picture with the real-time button Basil passed to him. "But if it came off Rosie's blouse, what's it doing here?"

"Freaking me out at the moment," Paprika complained. "We need to amscray. Now."

"She's right. Something happened to Rosie here, and whatever it was, it wasn't good," said Saffron, pulling a hood up over her head. "Let's give it to the cops."

"They'll think we had something to do with it," Thyme said. "We may be suspects now. And where will we say we found the thing, out here? That could lead to a trespassing rap. If any of us gets busted, how will we ever find Marjie's grave?"

"We're looking for a needle in a haystack," said Paprika. "It's too dangerous. It's freezing, and we might get caught. It's over. Let's give up."

"Dashes never give up!" snapped Ginger with a stern voice, finger wagging. "What if Marjoram gave up, where'd we be? We didn't come from quitters. Stop naysaying and start digging in. The quicker we find it, the quicker we'll leave."

"We've come this far," said Saffron. "Let's just change our methodology." She snapped her fingers. "Hey, I know. I'll Google-map the overhead and look down from the aerial."

"Another hour. Then we'll stop," said Basil, laying down the law. "Fan out. We need to cover ground." With that, they dispersed in a wider pattern, everyone but Saffron, who was all but Basil's shadow as she consulted with the bird's-eye view on her Google Pixel screen.

Ginger set off to the chain-link fence, sweeping her flashlight side to side, illuminating pampas grass and thigh-high brush in open field, eventually peeking through towering trees to the multimillion-dollar mansion on the distant hill. Struck by the stark, unholy differentiation on the grounds, dividing the well-kept lawns and burial chambers situated north from the blight the Black interment spaces signified, she got resolved. More determined than ever, inverting her shovel to use as a sort of divining rod, she entered a forested area, noting that twenty minutes had elapsed in the clock app on her cell. Picking up her pace and drenched with sweat despite the damp and cloying cold, she noticed a clump of climbing weeds advancing to the whites-only sector, migrating through the chain-link fence in a clearing to her left. No ground cover grew in a softer spot, and gravitating to it, she could see a shiny object. Ginger squatted to free it of fallen leaves.

It was a large, smooth cabochon that was carved from Louisiana palm in the shape of an eye, like a pointed ellipse a careful hand had honed. It was tricolored—orange, light amber, and pink—and the length of it measured about three feet. The sight of it was incongruous with the small, sharp stones in irregular shapes that appeared to mark surrounding graves, the few the crew had found so far.

Ginger dug with blue-polished fingernails until she had uncovered it. "Hey, look what I found," she called as she rushed to the south through tall and dewy grass, hustling her relatives back to her find. They passed an old water well with a rusty crank to check the headstone out.

"What is it?" asked Saffron, eyeing the stone.

"It's cool." Thyme knelt to scrape it clean and burnish the top of it with his sleeve.

"Sedimentary rock," Ginger speculated. "Probably a slab of Palmoxylon, a fragment of fossilized palm trunk people sometimes polish into gems."

"Dag," said Mace. "It sure does bling to just be a chunk of polished wood."

"Cross-sectioned from a tree, looks like," said Basil. "Must be really old."

"It's huge to be a mineral. I wonder what it's worth," Paprika puzzled, perking up.

"Whatever," said Mace. "It isn't ours. Do you ever stop thinking of cold, hard cash?"

"Not really. Why, do you?" Paprika leaned over, touched the edge. "It's as smooth as a baby's booty. Makes me wonder who would leave it here."

"Yo, check it out." Thyme waved them close. "There's a drawing carved into the face of it." They pointed their flashlights at the stone, and its chalcedony sparkled.

On the petrified wood was the shape of an herb whittled skillfully into the silica.

The intent was unmistakable.

"It's a Marjoram leaf," Mace blurted. "Marjie's grave. We found it, y'all!"

The Dash crew hugged and happy danced.

"Hold on there," Ginger warned. "We can't be sure until we dig her up."

"But that could take hours," Saffron protested. "It's too creepy. Let's come back. We'll be pressing our luck if we stay too long."

"We're pressing our luck if we punk out now," Paprika said. "It could be gone."

"It looks like it's been here a jillion years," said Saffron. "Who would take it now?"

"Who'd kill Rosie?" Mace contended. "No one should've, but they did."

"It's way too spooky in these woods," said Saffron.

"Wait, let's get this done," said Basil, plunging the head of his shovel into the earth by the cabochon. "The Christmas decorations spelled out 'Look in the *T*.' That might mean trees."

"I hear you," Mace said, breaching topsoil. "Marjoram doesn't belong out here."

"Neither do you, so don't get cute." A voice and a crackle of twigs and dry leaves behind them caused their ears to perk. "Stop digging and put your hands up in the air," Doug threatened. "Do it now."

The family slowly turned and stared.

Emerging into the clearing like a prowler, puffing on a joint, Doug tossed his long blond hair and waved a Glock, knees bent and lumbering, skinny Melanie glowering at his side, a beer can in her hand. "Well, well, look who we have here."

"I should say the same," said Morton, seeming to come out of nowhere, pointing a semiautomatic.

"What the…? Who the heck are you?" Doug asked, his gun hand

quivering, his slit eyes darting back and forth, confused as to where to train the Glock.

"We're your tomorrows, stoner. We're about to slip away," Bull quipped from the dark on the other side of the clearing. "Drop it and get your ass into the well."

"The water well?" Doug stammered.

"No, the wishing well," Bull barked. "Go now, or I'll ice that bony broad."

"What for?" said Melanie, sucking her thumbnail. "I didn't do nothing. Did I, babe?"

Bull shot her in the head.

"Oh no!" cried Ginger. "Oh my Lord."

Saffron swooned and fainted.

Thyme raised his palms, stepped back, implored, "Look, man, chill out. Let's talk."

"Let's not," Bull shouted. "I won't tell you twice. I thought I made that clear with her."

He shot Doug's date again.

Melanie's scrawny body spasmed. Blood seeped out into the ground.

Doug ran and hopped into the well. He yelled, but no one heard a splash.

"No water's in that well, man," Basil realized with a clenching fist.

"Yup. Congratulations, dude. You won. You get the booby prize. There happens to be a ladder though. You can either climb in or get pushed, you dig? It don't matter to me which one you choose. Either way, you're goin' down."

"Please, handsome, let's be reasonable. We're lost," Paprika cajoled. "Let us go, and we won't breathe a word of this."

"Shut up or you won't breathe at all," Bull blustered.

"True dat. He likes chokin' girls," said Morton. "And you're just his type."

Paprika retreated, her eyes bugged out, clutching the neck of her short wool coat.

"Come over here by me," a voice intoned in the shade of a willow tree.

"Who, me?" Paprika asked. "Who's there?"

Garvey Worcestershire's daughter-in-law appeared in a misty shaft of moonlight, baring her teeth, skin pale as chalk. She was dressed all in white, from her cashmere coat to her suede Ugg boots to her fur-trimmed hat and gold-chained purse.

"I should've known," said Ginger, surging forward in sheer disbelief. "*You* were behind this all along?" She raised her flashlight and her voice.

"You know her?" Mace inquired, grabbing hold of Ginger by her wrist.

"Goldilocks Ironwerks. Riding her broom. What rock did you crawl out from under? Followed us down from Virginia, did you? What are you trying to steal this time? I thought I saw the last of you in Richmond, when you stole my man." She wrenched from Mace's grip.

"It's Anabelle Worcestershire nowadays." The woman in white betrayed herself. "And I didn't run off with your hubby, I shot him. I actually thought you knew. I thought you'd figured it out by now, that he wouldn't kick up where the recipe was."

"He didn't know," said Ginger. "Are you serious? You *murdered* Jax?"

"I did what my daddy told me to," Anabelle admitted. "I seduced Jax, but he wouldn't cave. So I had to find another way. Where is the recipe, down in there?" Her chin jerked toward the cabochon.

"What are you talking about?" Thyme uttered, lifting Saffron in his arms and preparing to make a quick getaway. "We're not—"

"Look, don't play dumb with me. Put her down. She won't be leaving here."

Saffron moaned and came around, her eyes uncomprehending.

"Only we know the secret ingredient," Ginger bluffed. "You'll need us."

"Get in the well, bitch," Anabelle shrieked, and she brandished a pearl-handled gun from her purse, directing it at Ginger. "I didn't get hitched to a psychopath, play nursemaid to his cranky father, take all that crap off those ne'er-do-wells, and hole up in that haunted house for years to come up empty, understand? I want that cure."

"And I want Obama, but he ain't mine," yelled Ginger, stepping to Anabelle.

"Back off, Ginger," Mace advised. "She's crazy. Don't engage her." He tugged on the back of Ginger's coat, his steely eyes on Anabelle. "Take it. Whatever you want. It's yours," Mace tendered, shielding Ginger. "Go for it, Snow Queen. Be our guest."

"What are you, nuts?" Paprika objected. "There's a fortune down in there."

"Seize it," Anabelle ordered Morton.

"No way. That's our endowment, fool," Paprika yelled and broke for it, throwing herself on the cabochon.

Bull pounced and grabbed her kicking legs. He dragged her screaming by her ankles, raking her torso and head across the rocky terrain like a rubbish bin.

"Let me go!" she wailed.

But in a flash, their images vanished through the trees as if the deep woods swallowed them.

"Paprika!" Ginger hollered. "Bring her back. You're gonna pay for this."

Saffron rallied. "I'm okay," she whispered. "Please go after them."

Thyme set her down and bolted.

Morton volleyed lightning rounds, peppering branches and leaves surrounding Thyme and making him dart and dodge.

"Unh," Thyme grunted, staggering, dragging his right leg as he ran, squeezing his thigh to staunch the heavy bleeding from a bullet wound.

Basil burst forth like a linebacker, butting his head into Morton's abdomen, and Mace charged Morton like a bull, landing a haymaker on his jaw. Morton, doubling over from the blows and losing his balance, tipped forward, and his gun went off, pocking the ground and stripping bushes, firing from his jerking arm. Basil clocked him with an uppercut, a left, and then a right, and Mace delivered a roundhouse kick that flung his weapon to the turf.

Anabelle fired. *Bang, bang, bang!*

Ginger lunged for Morton's rifle, aimed, and squeezed the trigger, and gunshots pinged off tree trunks, ricocheting rapid-fire.

A red rose bloomed on the right lapel of Anabelle's snow-white winter coat, and eyes agape, she bumbled forward, mouthing silent threats and reaching toward the glinty cabochon, stumbling onto Marjie's grave, face-planting on a shovel.

Morton reached for his ankle holster, writhing and wriggling in the dirt. He came up with a revolver, and with Mace's and Basil's back to him, he cocked it and regrouped to shoot.

Ginger, detecting Morton's gun, volleyed another round of shots, and Morton collapsed in a quavering heap, large holes in his orange field jacket.

"Help me, please!" Paprika called.

Basil and Mace took off, and Ginger and Saffron followed on their heels, Ginger—shocked and breathing in jagged rasps—weighed down by Morton's weapon, and Saffron wielding a shovel and towing Ginger by the hand.

Minutes later, they spied Paprika's plight. She hung suspended from a tree limb, thick rope tight around her neck, her toes barely touching the forest floor, a rivulet of blood trailing down her slender thighs and dainty calves, her panties dangling from Bull's right hand, the taut rope wound around his left, Paprika's glistening, pleading eyes a light just about to go out.

A look of surprise and consternation painted the crags in Bull's flat face, and without hesitation, Ginger ran forward, howling like an army vet attacking a terrorist enemy camp, and shot Bull as he turned to run. He crabbed to the side to effect an escape, lurched through a thicket zombie-like, fell sideways into a bear spring trap, and literally lost his head.

In the frenzy that followed, Basil and Mace tossed Bull's limp body in the well, and they followed with Morton and Anabelle, obscuring three stiffs with branches, covering their tracks with mad dispatch.

Meanwhile, inside Mace's red Escalade, Paprika—attended by Ginger and Saffron and stoic about Bull's brutal assault—eschewed being taken for medical care until Marjie got exhumed. Even then, she thought but didn't say, she'd never seek a doctor's help, as turning up in the ER as a visible victim of recent violence could raise many unanswerable questions and betray the evening's felonies. But Thyme had a through-and-through bullet wound, so Saffron, once a navy nurse, got busy taking care of it, employing the first aid kit that Mace had purchased along with his Cadillac.

It didn't take long for the exhumation. It couldn't, at a crime scene where four corpses were still warm. The defensible killings of Morton, Bull, and Anabelle by Ginger, and the ghastly deaths of the guard and his girlfriend certainly would fall on Basil, Mace, and Thyme if they got caught. And maybe the Dash females as well. The victims, after all, were white in a hamlet of bodies of color, and it was predictable Basil, Mace, and Thyme would not be appraised for their human value any more than Marjie was and the hundreds of other bodies quarantined in the run-down boneyard. If a cop car arrived, all bets were off.

Digging in turns in quick order, Basil and Mace disentombed a rotted mummy wrapped in tattered burlap bags and enshrined in a crude black-walnut box. They loaded those into the SUV and with care drove back to Rosie's place so as not to disturb their cargo or get rousted by police. The stress in the car was palpable, as was the withering stench of the carcass, and the sixteen-hour ride seemed more like years, with only five pit stops—for gas and meals and potty breaks and refills for the cooler.

They managed to endure the trip. Only, when they arrived and unloaded the carrion, laying it out on a workbench under a tool wall in the neat garage, their inspection of it dealt another blow—there was no body.

"Nothing's inside here," Saffron confirmed as she shed her bright blue nitrile gloves. "It's nothing but burlap all the way through."

"Why would they bury an empty coffin," Paprika asked rhetorically.

"To cover up some dirt, I'd say," said Basil. "Pun intended."

"She was obviously there at some point," Ginger surmised and wiped her beaded brow. "Somebody beat us to the punch."

"But if Marjoram's not where she's supposed to be, where is she?" asked Paprika.

"No telling where," said Mace. "Or what they found about the recipe."

"Let's go inside," Thyme cautioned. "Staying here could draw attention. We need to keep a low profile. Let's turn the garage lights out so the neighbors don't wonder what's going on."

They trudged to the kitchen, lit the candle, put a kettle on.

"Well, there we go, coming up empty again," Paprika recapitulated in a bitter-sounding tone. "And we almost all got killed this time. What *is* it with that recipe?"

"It isn't a keepsake. It's a curse," said Basil.

"You can say that again. That monster did horrible things to me. When I close my eyes, I see his face." Paprika wailed, burying her face in her hands. "I've never been so humiliated. Never felt so violated. If that Bull guy wasn't dead already, I'd—"

"Guys, they're going to come for me. I know it. What are we going to do? I don't think I can live with myself as it is," groaned Ginger as she wrung her hands. "I never thought I'd kill someone," she burbled, "far less three at once. I'm so ashamed. I feel so guilty." Ginger paced the kitchen floor, ran fingers through her tousled hair. "I'd do it again for you, Paprika, but I wish we'd never gone."

"You did what you had to," Basil consoled her. "No one set out to hurt someone. We'll tell them it was self-defense. If they come, we'll all be witnesses. Forensics will bear us out."

"If forensics don't, then *I'll* confess," Paprika volunteered. "We took pictures of me, didn't we? And look at what he did to me," she cried. "I'm living proof. I'm evidence. You see? I brought my panties. They can't argue these." Paprika pulled undies out of her pocket. "Voilà!" she declared like a Vegas magician pulling a scarf from an old top hat. "They'll find his semen. DNA. No one can call us liars then." Paprika screamed and banged the counter, flinging its contents to the floor, her visage wet with sweat and tears, her body caked with blood and mud. "Don't you see, Ginger? You saved my life. If it weren't for you guys, I'd be dead!"

The family fell silent.

No one moved.

The facts marinated.

Paprika wept.

After awkward minutes, Ginger murmured, "Want some cocoa?"

Everyone nodded in reply.

Nobody wanted to speak, but they needed to break the crippling tension.

Thyme limped into a great room chair and propped his injured leg up on an ottoman with weighty sighs. "Y'all, we need to keep it Zen. Nervous people make mistakes. I'm thinking nobody will ever find out. The bodies are hidden way down in the well, and that graveyard is deserted… Paprika, come sit here by me." She did, and he cuddled her close to him, drawing a Sherpa throw up on her shoulders, kissing the top of her frazzled head.

"Well, I'm willing to stand guard here tonight. I'm not as tired as I look," said Basil. "Y'all can go upstairs. I'll stay here and keep watch."

Saffron objected, "Sleep alone? What if I'm needed and dozing off? What about Paprika? What if Thyme's leg starts to bleed again? I'm going to stay downstairs as well."

"Well, I guess we can sleep on the sectional then," said Mace. "There's plenty of room on it. I'll turn on the TV, get out the Xbox, hang with Basil while you nap. Basil can stand to lose some games. How's that?" He turned the kettle off.

"Fine, I'll make some cocoa," Ginger said. "And we'll relax."

The doorbell jangled.

Ginger jumped.

Saffron let out a squeaky yelp. "Who the heck can that be at this time of night?"

"Stay calm," said Basil. "I'll go see." He crossed to the door, winked into the fish-eye lens, and said, "Who is it?"

"My name is Detective Dent. And this is my partner, Detective Forbes. We need to come in and ask some questions."

"Crap," said Paprika. "They found out already."

Ginger, trembling, crossed herself. "Oh please, God. Help us."

"Open up!" a voice on the porch demanded.

Basil shooed the others out, and they ran to the kitchen, hid in the pantry, quieted, flipped the light switch off. Basil grabbed his coat, stepped onto the porch, and closed the door behind him. "How can I help you?" Basil asked. "I'm Basil Dash, Rosemary's brother. She's the owner of this house. She's recently deceased," he offered, extending his hand to Detective Dent, who was tall and beefy, ruddy, olive-skinned, and wearing a fleece-lined coat and a hefty pair of fur-lined gloves. He huffed, and Basil saw his breath.

Dent shook Basil's hand, said, "Yes, we know. We're assigned to your sister's case. I remember you played for the Rams and the Seahawks, then got traded to the Jets."

"Yeah," said Basil, feeling queasy, bobbing his head, blowing into his hands. "Is there news about Rosie?"

"Yes, there's progress," Forbes replied.

"The rest of my family are asleep," Basil misrepresented. "But if you come back in the morning—"

"We need something you can tell us now," said Dent with an unsettling glare cast toward a curtained window. "You see, we've come up with a possible suspect, but we can't be sure until we find out who the father is."

Basil moved farther away from the door and closer to the front porch steps, relieved the interrogation had to do with Rosie, not the crime spree he and his family just pulled off. "A suspect? Who? Is he arrested?"

"We aren't at liberty to divulge, but any facts about the dad will allow us to follow up our lead and possibly tie him to Rosemary's death," said Dent. "You understand?"

"But what could our dad have to do with her murder? Dad passed on when she was six."

"Not hers. The father of the child," said Forbes, his forehead wrinkled.

"She doesn't... didn't have a kid," said Basil. "She was single."

"She was pregnant nonetheless," Dent stated. "Who's the baby's father?"

Basil felt like he'd been tackled. "I don't have no clue. We didn't talk about her dates. I'm a big brother. I'm overprotective… Wait. Are you certain she was pregnant?"

"Absolutely. There's no doubt," said Dent.

"And depending on what went down," said Forbes, "that could be motive."

"I don't believe it. That's insane. If Rosie got pregnant, she'd tell us. Not you guys, but all us girls," said Ginger.

"Sure," Saffron confirmed. "She confided in us about everything."

"Maybe not everything," Mace shot back.

The family huddled together on the sectional, dumbfounded.

"If she had a baby on the way, she'd need us for support," Paprika said. "She wouldn't hide from us."

"But what if she just found out or didn't even know herself," said Thyme.

"That's possible," Paprika said. "Did they say how far along she was?"

"They were looking for info, not doling it out," said Basil. "They're tight-lipped."

"Well, if you say she told you stuff," Mace reasoned, "who did she hang out with in the weeks and months before she died?"

"Nobody I know," Ginger admitted, tugging her bra strap, lip poked out. "We can't let them smear her now she's dead. They're victim-shaming her. We can't have lost her baby too."

"It's a bald-faced lie. Rosie was keeping to herself," Paprika said. "Ironically."

"The truth is, she was celibate," said Saffron. "All year long. Last March, she joined a group at church and a Facebook group called Single Souls: A Woman's Path to Abstinence. It was all about self-sacrifice and repurposing sexual energy."

"Sounds like a drag," Mace commented. "No wonder a man can't get no dates."

"*You* can't," Thyme repudiated. "I ain't in no No-Date Club. My equipment's working fine. I'm pulling more than I can stand."

"Why am I hearing this?" Saffron asked. "It's too much information."

"This is deteriorating," Ginger avowed. "Let's all adjourn till eight."

They settled in and went to sleep, the six of them prone on the sectional, a wreath by the stairwell blinking lights, flames waning in the fireplace, and the recipe closer than they thought.

Two hours later, a rendezvous went down by the shed in the big backyard.

"Did you find it?" the man said.

"No," said the woman. "I'm going to need more time."

"How much? You have to get it now. I can't wait any longer. What's the holdup?"

"Same as always. Just be patient. Chill out. It'll be worth the wait. I told you, don't come around anymore or you'll blow the whole thing up. We're close. I'll text you when it's done."

Less than an hour after that, Mace woke up feeling hungry. He arose and stirred Paprika, who was anxious and afraid to sleep lest someone attack her while she dreamed.

"I left the kitchen in a mess," Paprika said. "Come on, let's go. I'll make you pancakes while I clean."

"You'll turn me into pancakes?" Mace laughed and followed down the stairs. He gobbled flapjacks while she tidied up the items she'd knocked off the counter in her angry rant.

While she was sweeping, something clanked. She squatted to see what it was. "Oh no, it's Marjie's tooth box. Guess it opened when it fell. I hope I didn't break her teeth." She looked into the open box. "They aren't here. I've lost them, Mace."

"Hold on, I think I see them." Mace leaned down and plucked them off the floor. "They ricocheted under the toe kick. Here they are. They're wrapped in cotton. No harm done."

"That's a relief." Paprika unwrapped the wisdom teeth and noticed they were hollowed out. "What's this?" she asked, her heartbeat spurred. "They're stuffed with a tea-colored blob." She used her long pink fingernails to try to pry the objects loose but found the task required tweezers. "Looks like paper."

"Yeah, it does."

Employing tweezers and a pen knife, Paprika finally teased the small wads out into a saucer. Working to unravel them, she strained to make out something else. "There's writing, Mace. I think it's script. It's teeny, but it's legible."

He eyed the scraps and, squinting, said, "It's Marjie's recipe!"

Several trips through a total of thirteen stores—some of them alchemy vendor shops—secured most items they would need. Other ingredients sent them on a scavenger hunt for days.

Some of the herbs grew in Rosemary's garden. Others they found on Amazon. Still others took perseverance and all their resolve and ingenuity to locate and procure. In the end, they amassed the entire list: Angelica, skullcap, jellyfish venom, hemlock, wolfsbane, pennyroyal, absinthe, alum, ectoplasm, mandrake, figwort, belladonna, horehound, thieves oil, bayberry, chicken blood, honey, a calf's hoof, vervain, sumac, silphium seed, a butterfly wing, *Xylopia aethiopica*, meadowsweet, pippali, spikenard oil, a pink votive candle, Dead Sea salt, jujube thorns, grains of paradise, a cup and a half of graveyard dirt, black sand, *Boswellia frereana*, a lock of hair, an owl eyelash, a fingernail clipping, a four-leaf clover, hummingbird feathers, fresh Solomon's seal, holy water, and two wishbones.

In addition, they had to use healing crystals—malachite, hematite, turquoise, amethyst, moonstone, bloodstone, and clear quartz. And the recipe said to take care where they got the ingredients, so they did. The vibration these held was at least as important as adding them, straining the brewed results, and believing the remedy would work.

The recipe wasn't a food at all. It was actually a powerful potion. Marjoram placed it in different foods depending on whom she was cooking for, demanding she make each dish alone. This to ensure its purity and the sanctity of her secret sauce.

Adhering to this policy, the crew burned sage in the kitchen before they began, and they cleared it with sage smudge spray infused with a rose-quartz crystal gem pod charged in Northern Africa in a vortex in an Algerian mega-lith monument set in Mechra Sfa in the Mina River valley.

"Let's get some Wakanda up in here," said Thyme as they started to mix the brew.

"Uh-huh, I feel like Sister Night in an episode of *Watchmen* now," Paprika said.

They prayed a prayer and followed the recipe to a *T*.

And then it came time to try it out.

Ginger and Mace made a lobster frittata that Thyme and Paprika ate, because they were the wounded ones who needed most to heal. Lying under the quilt on Rosie's bed in the master on the upper floor, they stilled and began to hallucinate, reporting visitations.

"Who are you? What are you doing?" Paprika screamed to a person who wasn't there.

"Wait," Thyme uttered. "Take me with you."

Paprika and Thyme became agitated, started to seem disoriented, flailing, combative and slurring their speech. Paprika presented confusion. Thyme had a seizure and convulsed.

Frightened by what they were witnessing and about to dial 911, Ginger, Basil, Mace, and Saffron tried to snap them out of it, afraid they had poi-soned them, jinxed them, or worse. They shook them, making desperate pleas and applying cold compresses to their heads.

None of them heard the back door open. Nobody dreamed it'd been left unlocked by a loved one already inside the house.

As Paprika and Thyme lost consciousness, falling still on the bed as though comatose, Rosemary flew down from a trap door in the ceiling under the attic space, descending like a megabat down a wooden attic ladder. "Let them alone. It's happening. Take your hands off them. They're being healed," she yelled with a butcher knife in hand.

"Rosie, is it really you?" said Basil, who blinked in astonishment.

Mace said, "Rosie, what the heck—?"

"Get back. You'll ruin everything," hissed Rosie.

Boots ran up the hall.

"Who's that?" asked Saffron. "What's up now?" She picked up a brass lamp, yanked its cord out, held it high behind the door. "Rosie, we need to get your gun."

Chester burst in, and Saffron crowned him, sending him reeling off-balance onto the Nubian rug with a forehead gash.

Rosemary scurried to Chester. "What have you done?" She whirled around on Saffron, slashing the air with the razor-sharp cutting blade, shouting, "Get away!"

"Rosie, you're protecting *him*?" Mace asked her. "Have you lost your mind? You left us here grieving and all this time you were hiding in the attic?"

"Get out and leave us alone. You don't understand," she said.

"You got that right," said Basil. "I don't get it." He grabbed ahold of Rosie's hand.

"Hands off her," Chester demanded, easing his way to his feet, wiping blood from his head. He reached in his five-thousand-dollar suit and pulled a .45. "You've lost it all. Get over it. Rosemary and the recipe. They both belong to me."

"You don't own diddly up in here," said Ginger. "We're all grown and free. You think because your founding fathers fantasized that they owned ours, you own us? Here's a news flash, pal, the jig is up. White privilege died outside our door. You're not the master of our fate. You're about as extinct as a dodo egg if you don't understand we're equals. And furthermore, you're cowardly. You own Rosemary over my dead body, get it? Shoot me. I'm not afraid of you."

"Okay," said Chester crooking his gun arm. "Matter of fact, that's fine by me. I could kill you at noon on Virginia Beach Boardwalk and slide without getting a slap on the wrist."

"But you can't shoot us all at once," said Mace. "Shoot her, and I'll tear you apart before you can fire a second round."

"You think you can take out one of us and the rest of us will just look on?" said Basil. "You must not watch sports. Have at it. See how far you get. I'm betting on that door."

"What'll it be?" said Ginger. "You can leave alone or not at all."

"And don't think you can steal the recipe either. Y'all ripped off too much as it is. You'll look over your shoulder the rest of your life," said Mace. "Which won't be long."

Chester's eyes darted back and forth. "Why? We're relatives, you and me." He cracked a sly, sardonic smile. "My forebears rented one of you people back in the day, in Louisiana. In fact, your precious Marjoram had twins my ancestor bartered away because they looked so much like him his poor wife poked her eyes out. She blinded herself so as not to see their faces and then killed herself."

"No, Sparky, that's not how it went," said Saffron. "He sold Marjie's kids to punish her for being brave. See, it's Margie, resourceful as she was, who mixed glass shards in with their grits. They never knew what hit them. They didn't even suspect it when she served it to that blinded wife, till she poured hot grits on the master's privates as the glass sliced through his gut. You ought to get your story straight. We heard that tale, but ours is true. We won out in the end."

Chester's gun struck Saffron's cheek. "Pack that stuff in the kitchen, and get to the yard."

"Don't hurt them, baby," Rosie pleaded. "We got what we need from them."

"Rosie, what is wrong with you?" asked Basil. "Why are you helping him?"

"Because. He's going to mass produce," said Rosie. "He's putting the money up so we can help people all over the world." Her green eyes shone like emeralds.

"He's played you. You can't see that?" Saffron said. "He'll do a snatch and grab."

"He loves me. We're all family," said Rosie. "Like he said."

"Whose body was found beneath your dock?" Mace asked. "He'll dump you next."

"Some stripper got killed in a cheap motel, and they brought her to my graveyard," Chester said. "I own this town. Cops. Politicians. Judges. Bankers. I got dirt on all of them."

"You're nuts," said Basil, lunging out to grab for Rosie's knife.

Chester fired shots into the ceiling. Plaster dust rained down onto the bed and fouled the air. "My chopper will be here in ten," said Chester, checking his Rolex watch. "You—"

Suddenly everyone heard a moan.

"What happened? Did I fall asleep?" Thyme sputtered. "I'm so thirsty."

"You're awake!" said Saffron. "We're right here." She ran to the bed and cradled Thyme. "You had us worried half to death. Thank heaven. Here's water. Take a sip." She lifted a cup to Thyme's dry lips and stroked his impossibly handsome face. "You feel all right?"

"I'm great," Thyme said, but his voice was low and thick and hoarse. "Hey, what did you do to my leg? It isn't hurting anymore."

"Let's take a look," said Saffron, peeling off his gauzy bandages. She gasped. "The wound is… whoa, it's gone. My goodness, it's completely healed. Come look."

"Don't anyone move a muscle," Chester snarled. "We knew it'd work. Didn't we, precious?" he said to Rosie. Then he turned and said to Basil, "Now we don't need y'all at all."

It was windy. The chopper ride was rough. In ten minutes, it got rougher. The Bell 525 Relentless dipped and banked and finally leveled, lending a view of the roiling James River curving its flow toward Newport News. The interior of the helicopter, though it was luxurious, failed to belie the danger being at Chester's behest in the clouds imposed.

Ginger asked Chester, "Where's Paprika?"

"Gone," said Chester. "You all killed her. After you drugged her, she never woke up."

A yowl from Saffron turned to screams. "She was breathing. What did you do with her?"

"If it takes me the rest of my life, I'll get you, Chester. You can count on it," Mace said.

"Good thing your life ain't long then," Chester retorted. "You go next." He brandished his gun as he opened the chopper door, and a blast of air howled in. Chester commanded, "Get up and out." He appeared to be talking to Mace at first, but it soon became clear he meant everyone, including complicit Rosemary, who now looked stunned and guilty.

Rosemary said, "But—"

"You jump first," said Chester, yanking her by the arm. "It's been fun, but out you go, my dear."

Rosemary's clothes and hair caught wind as Chester dragged her toward the door.

Without warning, Rosie turned and shot. *Bang! Bang!*

The helicopter banked. Chester almost flew out the door, but he clutched the jamb and held on tight, fighting the tilt of the angling chopper, gripping the doorjamb, begging for help. Basil jumped up and clung to Rosie, grasping the arm of his seat with one hand, Rosie with the other. Rosie bit into the fingers of Chester's right hand, and he had to cling on with his left, but he slipped as the chopper leaned out of control and could barely hang on to the chopper floor. His grip no match for the bumpy ride as the chopper began a steep descent, Chester plummeted over a thousand feet. Then a parachute opened and off he went.

The chopper careened and listed port.

"Get to the pilot. We're going down," said Saffron. "Check out the bullet hole going into the left cabin door. We can still land if you get me in."

"What?" asked Mace.

"The navy," Thyme said. "Saffron's trained to fly this thing." He pointed to the cockpit. "Quick. We have to bust in there." Basil drew back and kicked one door. Mace heaved the other with a shoulder, breaking the hinges and cracking the jamb. The others joined in as the chopper zoomed downward, wildly spinning to the river, whirling and pitching them this way and that.

When they finally entered the cockpit, the pilot was shot and slumped on a large display, his right arm slung over a black control panel, an empty copilot seat next to him. Saffron took over and stuck an impossible landing, skirting a lake by a large state park, brushing tall treetops, and setting them down in a parking lot close to the riverbed. Twenty feet more to the right or left, they'd have suffered a catastrophic crash.

As they piled out wondering where they were, a boy with a fisherman casting for bass asked, "How'd y'all fly that big bird down?"

The young father and his three-year-old bobbed in a replica bateau boat like the kind in the 1700s. Made of hardwood, long and flat, it had oars and a covered midsection.

"Is that your boat?" Rosemary asked.

The boy nodded. The father said nothing.

"If you let us rent it now and don't ask questions and don't say we came," said Thyme, "we'll pay you a thousand bucks and tell you where to pick it up."

"I'll bill you on PayPal," the father consented, quick to whip his smartphone out.

Ginger admonished, "If anyone comes for us—"

"Don't want to hear it," the fisherman said. "Your struggle's yours, and mine is mine."

"Hey, Dad, I caught a big one. Yay!" the boy said.

"So did I," the dad said. "We'll eat more than fish tonight."

Five minutes later, Rosie, Ginger, Basil, Saffron, Mace, and Thyme rowed west to find Paprika.

Six hours later, on Sweetbriar Hill, its new owner returned looking worse for the wear.

"Where's Anabelle? Tell her we need to talk."

"Mr. Worcestershire, she ain't got back yet." Lola the housekeeper swept the floor. "She didn't come home last night at all, and I'll tell ya, I'm kinda concerned. I called to ask Doug if he seen where she went, but I can't get ahold of him neither… Mr. Worcestershire, don't you want a drink? You're lookin' like something the cat drug in, if you don't mind me sayin'. I'll draw you a bath and set out your clean clothes. Mr. Fortesque left the cremation house when you didn't show up to meet him."

"Well, what about Daddy?" Chester asked. "Oh heck, I'll do it myself."

Garvey Worcestershire's body was ashes when the crew pulled up to Sweetbriar Hill to rescue Paprika if they could, if their prayers had kept her alive.

"I can't stand this place," said Ginger. "If I'd never found that cabochon—"

"Sh," said Saffron. "Over there."

"What is it?" asked Mace as they hid in the woods on the melanin side of the chain-link fence and peered at what looked like a mausoleum sporting vermiculite doors with stained glass windows that had flame designs. A light emanated from inside. One door stood ajar. It creaked.

"Crematorium," Rosie said, wincing.

"Dag," Mace whispered. "Must be nice. Kill folks and burn them in your own backyard. Convenient, huh? The Worcestershires are some sho'nuff ghouls."

"The dad just died," said Rosie. "And he didn't go out by accident."

"Aren't you the Mata Hari," Ginger remarked. "Ms. Espionage. You might've divulged that sooner, don't you think? Oh yeah, that's right. Your ass was too busy betraying us."

"What else are you keeping from us?" Basil asked. "You better spill it now."

"Save it," said Saffron. "We'll deal with her later. Rosie, is that where Paprika could be?"

"Likely as not," said Rosie. "They dispose of all their dirt in there."

Before anyone knew it, Mace had scaled the fence and touched down on the other side. "This is on me. I'm heading in."

"Wait." Rosemary extended her hand. But Mace, like a phantom, was sneaking over the plush, green-carpeted, white-side lawn, wide-stepping up the hill.

Saffron ascended the fence in a wink.

Ginger, who was a plus-size girl, was unable to make the climb. "I'll run to the front," said Ginger. "Thyme and I can try the other side."

Basil boosted Rosie over and clumsily clambered over next.

As Rosie, Basil, Mace, and Ginger mounted the hill, two pit bulls charged, one gold, one gunmetal gray and white, both baring their teeth and bearing down, unleashed and unleashing barks and growls. The gold one chomped on Basil's arm and dragged him to the ground. Basil socked it so hard with his other fist it retreated and had to regroup. Bold floodlights lit the area outside the crematorium, first flashing on, then flashing off, and the dogs, reacting like Pavlov's, heeled and sat still, frothing, panting.

"I knew you'd come," said Chester when the Dash crew breached two inner doors. The entrance slammed shut electronically and they found themselves locked in.

Behind bulletproof glass lay a helpless Paprika with Chester looming at her side. Trapped in a cardboard cremation container printed with an outdoor scene, she was face up by an oven door, eyes closed and dressed in fiery red, flames licking at her heels.

"Welcome. You're on my turf now," said Chester. "How do you like the view?"

"Let her go. You won't get away with this," said Rosie. "This is murder."

"Isn't it fun? You guys can watch. No one's going to stop me. She's alive, but sadly not for long," said Chester. "She won't feel a thing. Until she gets fried by the eighteen hundred degrees inside the chamber. That heat is enough to wake the dead, if you'll pardon my expression. It's computer-pro-grammed. Easy-breezy. Sip on that Spirytus vodka behind you." He upended his bottle and took a chug. "Tastes great. It's 192-proof."

A conveyor belt started. Paprika stirred. The Dash crew battered the wall.

"Wait'll you see what happens next," said Chester, mounting Paprika's body, unzipping his fly and looking around. He caught Rosemary's eye and winked his own. "Even the dead ones are livelier than Anabelle. Rosemary knows. Right, Rose? And it's thrilling to beat the conveyor belt. Rosie gave it a whirl here more than once. Tell them, Rosie. Don't be shy. You did it to get that investment." Chester guzzled another swig, and the alcohol drib-bled down his chin. Groggy and buzzed, he bowed his head to brush the vodka off his chest.

Paprika—apparently more alert and conscious than she appeared to be—sat up and got the best of Chester, pinning him down, headbutting him, kneeing his pelvis, breaking the rum bottle over his head, and leverag-ing all her weight to press down on his windpipe. Caught off guard, he bat-tled back, but with rum in his eyes, his privates throbbing, and the sudden lack of air, his defenses proved no match for Paprika's thrust of the broken bottle's jagged edges into his jugular. She leapt off the conveyor belt and kicked him into the raging pyre, the alcohol soaked in his shirt beginning to act as an accelerant.

Chester went up like a bottle rocket, quick as a wick in a Molotov cock-tail, caterwauling, scrambling, kicking, burning—due to his own program-ming—head to toe for two whole hours. Then his bones got crushed to dust and scattered near the segregated graves he'd desecrated.

The weeks after the battle with Chester were fraught with fear and laden with inquiries about his mysterious disappearance, his wife's, and Doug's and Melanie's. Two Sweetbriar thugs were missing too, and none of the bodies had turned up yet, for the segregated graveyard wasn't on the radar of the cops, who regarded it as an abominable space and were loath to step foot there. But with Chester literally pushing up daisies all around the cab-ochon, only Lola remained on Sweetbriar Hill—flitting her liberated curves around the estate like she owned the place. The public relations nightmare she brought on was something fierce, and soon Lola became the prime suspect in lieu of other leads.

The Dash crew fled from Rosie's house back to their separate residences, hoping the sordid debacle would stay buried in the past. They'd forfeited the recipe in the violence up on Sweetbriar Hill, and they wanted to kick themselves for failing to type it into someone's phone or take a picture of it while at last they had it in their hands. But they were alive; that was all that mattered—and they had receipts for what they'd bought to replicate the brew, so there was a chance they could reconstruct it, deciding to try in February on a return to Rosie's house, where police were a constant presence that did not make pleasant company. It seemed word had leaked out that Rosie and Chester had fornicated from time to time, but neither had left a shred of proof.

It was calm, and a measure of peace returned when the Dash crew gathered at Rosie's house, though most were still struggling to try to forgive her tryst with Chester Worcestershire. Even among the tumult, still the family reached a truce of sorts, with the nemesis of Sweetbriar Hill unable to do them further harm and the miracle cure uncertain, what with the side effects plaguing Paprika and Thyme, which seemed to worsen by the day like a whammy borne of destiny. They had blackouts, vivid hallucinations, and other maladies pestering them.

It felt as if Marjoram's mystery was a force to forever inhabit their lives… that is, until midnight on Valentine's Day, when the fragile veneer of the family's tranquility vanished because of a visitation.

The crew was assembled to try to remake the concoction in Rosemary's kitchen when the lights flickered out and they heard a creepy-sounding voice emanating somewhere about Ginger.

She seemed to lapse into a trance and said, "Garvey Worcestershire. Chester's father," Ginger mumbled in the scary gloam. "He's the one polished the cabochon."

"Ginger, snap out of it," Basil said.

"I think she's channeling Marjoram. Wait," said Rosie. "Listen up."

"Marjie?" asked Paprika. "Are you with us? Is that you?"

"I ain't in no grave. He pulled me out to use me for his experiments." Ginger's body began to vibrate. "He figured the antigen in my cells would help him make a magic cure to save his unrepentant life. He violated my body, but he couldn't control my soul. I came to him night after night in that house until Anabelle finally killed him."

"*She* killed Garvey?" Saffron asked. "You haunted him while he was still alive?"

"I couldn't let that man forget. I ain't never let none of them fools forget. But y'all… You can forget my trials and go on with your lives. Y'all can make a mark in this here world for those who came before and the babies who'll walk in your footsteps way beyond the bounds of time. Y'all are the hope for the future. Live. Don't waste a single day."

"But what about the recipe?"

"It's a secret. And it's yours."

Those were ostensibly Marjie's last words on the subject of her magic cure and the last the Dash crew mentioned of their adventurous quest for her recipe. They resolved to not bring it up again, even to spouses, shrinks, or each other, no matter how much it occupied their thoughts and they felt it mattered—especially after an image of Marjie emerged in the background of the séance video in Saffron's phone. Seeing that, they kept their powder dry.

During family reunions on Zoom each month, they catch up on sundry births and deaths, promotions, firings, moves and renos, dreams and goals, awards and trophies, healings, illnesses, loves and breakups, triumphs, tragedies, victories and vicissitudes, but not the cure.

Only, next month's video chat will change, and trouble will surface all over again, in the form of a hot new patent owned by all but developed by only two, in secret and undying faith.

The name of the curative treat is apt—it's MarjiesMeal, Your Food for Life.

Coming to a store near you.

OPTION

TO DIE

WAS WASHING THE BLOOD FROM MY NAKED BODY, FRANTIC, TRYING TO undo the deed.

All this blood could bring serious trouble my way—particularly since it wasn't mine.

What was left of poor Harry was gooey red paste that stuck to every inch of me, even the bottoms of my feet and my soft brown inner thighs. My partner was dead, and I couldn't deny it. I could deny I killed him, though, because it was the truth. Only, no one was going to believe me if they caught me with his body. As hard as it was to conceptualize that I was the likeliest person to be accused, it wasn't my sole concern. I knew the real murderer lurked in shadows, slicing and dicing whomever they chose, and I figured I'd be next.

If the cops found me nude, bloody, bruised, and disheveled—the victim's sole heir and only friend—I'd be guilty as sin in their jaundiced eyes. I was coated with Harry's DNA, my fingerprints were ubiquitous on the corpse and all over the murder scene, and my alibi was nonexistent. I had tremendous motive too. I glared at the crimson coating on my chestnut-colored hands, arms, legs, and torso, pondering what they'd see and start to draw conclusions from. Like Elmo, Red the Angry Bird, or Clifford on a real bad day, I appeared to blush from head to toe.

If I were a cop, I'd arrest myself. If I were a juror, I'd convict.

The blood odor alone could make a girl hurl, but Harry was kicking out noxious fumes and fouling the air like sulfur gas. The stench was overwhelming. I worried somebody would smell the stink and catch me in the act. If I could feel anything, it would be terror, but I was past terror, past horror, past grief— the emotions I'd fought twenty minutes ago. Now I was sober and trying to be sensible, starting to think about where I stood and the reasons I shouldn't stand there.

That's why I made a quick decision.

Caught in the lunacy of the moment, lost in sensory overload, I chose to do something that made things worse. The goal was good, but the plan was dumb.

I planned be nowhere to be found when Harry's corpse turned up.

I would ditch my plasma-soaked white sundress, chuck my Marvel bra and panties, purge the whole scene of my fingerprints, and get in the wind before Harry's cadaver caught the attention of someone else. I was less than four miles from arriving and departing rolling carts at Burbank airport where I could dump my clothes and hop the next plane to anywhere. If law enforcement rang my bell, I'd be thoroughly prepared. I'd be ready for interrogation, typing, sipping herbal tea, and sporting a suitably shocked veneer when they broke the news about Harry. I was innocent. I would act that way. I would tap the emotions I'd be feeling now if I hadn't gone numb. I'd be genuinely traumatized, grieving the loss of my biggest fan, work husband, confidant, and bud. Big Harry was my champion. I would never forget, but I had to go.

Launching my harebrained scheme into action, I tiptoed across the creaky top floor of the dilapidated building housing the funky company loft space Harry and I had come to love. I had to be superquiet about it as old lady Crampton's crib was just below us, and her walls had ears.

Crampy was a world-class busybody, nosy and obsessed. Lacking a social life of their own, the prying eyes of suite 6C were always, always on the case. And that was before her husband croaked and she sadly became a widow. After that, her inquisitive instincts revved in a constant state of overdrive. A police squad topped her Christmas list and was often called to her neat-freak digs because persons of color dared come near and invade her comfort zone.

You could rarely traverse the building without Crampy getting in your face—chatting you up about restless legs or how, when you get old, you get dissed so much. I would have to refrain from comparing her level of diss to my own as a woman of color as she either extolled about somebody else's life or disclosed every act she saw and heard me do in my abode. The last thing I needed to draw at this point was the snoopy retiree's prurient interest, equal to placing an ad on the front of the Sunday LA Times. Tell Crampy, tell the entire planet. Let her find out on her own, and she'd notify billions of galaxies out in space.

Against this backdrop, I set forth. I started the delicate operation holding my breath as I made my escape, bloody clothing in hand in a garbage bag. I opened the squeaky back door and slid out to the rickety metal fire escape. It had broken stairs on floors below, so I had to watch my step. Scrambling toward the alley, I watched windows in the tall skyscraper west and the gray brick structure opposite, skirting past glass in the balcony doors of apartments in our building. I saw no one but couldn't be sure that meant no one was seeing me. When I got to underground parking, I hopped into my vintage green Volkswagen Bug, Pea Pod, with its maximum speed of forty-five miles per hour if it got tuned up, and chugged into the moonless night. A cool mist tickled the backs of my ears as I coasted down Olive Avenue, heart flopping when I spotted my gas gauge registering on E. Oh great, the ultimate getaway car. Bald tires and out of gas.

I swung a wide right onto Forest Lawn Drive, the desolate, unlit boulevard on the boundary between Los Angeles and beautiful downtown Burbank, home of movie studios, TV stations, tourist attractions, and pricey cheap motels that catered to actors and other wannabes looking to land some kind of job. The glitzy Glendale foothills loomed in peaks and valleys up ahead, dotted with lights like sparkling stars from houses far above my pay grade.

The Grunge, a notorious serial killer, dropped off victims' bodies on this road in the dark on several nights, a fact that slashed into my mind as I drove along naked and shivering from cold, repeatedly checking my rearview mirror, coasting on fumes by the sprawling cemetery hovering to my right, putt-putting past burial grounds of iconic Hollywood celebrities— Bette Davis, Lucille Ball, Isabel Sanford who'd moved on up, Lou Rawls, and even the Gloved One, Michael Jackson, who was memorialized in this park and interred at its Glendale site. The mountainside boneyard loomed on my path as if I were steering straight into a grave.

Fuel or no fuel, I floored it past.

A plume of blue-gray smoke billowed out of the tailpipe due to leaky valves, the worst my mechanic had ever seen. He said it'd cost thirty-five hundred bucks to fix, which was more than the car was worth. I'd be better off buying another ride, but I didn't have that kind of cash. I couldn't afford a go-kart. I sank every cent into our business, StarShine, my priority. So I typically rode around spewing exhaust, which was über humiliating. Now I was risking a stop by police out cruising for last-minute, end-of-the-month citations. If they spotted me, they'd lick their chops and pull me over. Here, where they wouldn't be seen doing any frigging thing they wanted to. Getting caught at this stage would be it for me. Game over. Jumpy, I drove on.

I swung to the eastbound 134, veered onto the Golden State Freeway south, and trundled on it for just two exits, hearing my brakes let out a squeal as I veered to Los Feliz Boulevard. After passing the road to the kiddy train and the pony ride ring, I climbed the hill, my engine straining as I sloped past bus stops, heading to Griffith Park, entering it via a lesser-known route as, even at this spectral hour, eager visitors came to check it out. The park was a popular tourist spot, especially after the stars came out. Pea Pod eased under a canopy of trees as I crept through greenery, steadily climbing thick terrain and encountering several crossing deer as I angled toward landmark Griffith Observatory perching at the hilltop. Its domes were an astronomical site for tourists, boasting a panoramic view from curving terraces. From there, you could see the whole valley below, south to downtown Los Angeles and west clear to the ocean.

Steeper and steeper up I went, with Pea Pod stressing, puffing smoke. I traversed a short tunnel as dark as a coal mine, dipped, then climbed another winding hill, lurching into a parking space by a hiking trail I'd jogged before but only in bright daylight. I grabbed my plastic water bottle, jeans, a T-shirt from the trunk, and the bag of discarded bloody clothes, and snuck from the car to a side path, treading awkwardly on wobbly knees as I parted dense hedges and ventured several yards to a rotted wooden stump.

In the murk, I tripped on a sharp black rock. My shoe burst like a piñata, and I heard my toe crack, felt a pang, a sting, and a gush of tepid blood. I strained to not cry out in pain, and as I reflexively grabbed my foot, a quick imbalance made me lose my purchase, causing a backward pitch. I tried to recover but started to fall. I slipped, and as I was edging a cliff, the ground gave way beneath me. Before I could right myself again, I found my legs plummeting out of control, skidding downward on a precipitous slope, tumbling through stones and bramble, twigs and thorns, traversing a sliding pond of gravel, plants, loose dirt, and thick ground cover filled with rats and mice. Just as I thought I might come to a stop, I pitched forward, spinning out head-over-heels and landing in a hollow. I'd gotten sprawled at the foot of a dried-up waterfall, my mouth agape.

Panicked, I peered at the wilderness around me, hearing an animal keen and spotting two glinting eyes that glared and went darting off into a thicket. I backpedaled into crunching leaves and bumped into a bramble bush on my butt and scraped my thigh. Panting, I hopped onto my feet and attempted to gauge my surroundings, get my bearings, find a route back to my car.

The nightlife of wildlife teemed around me, raucous, starving, on the prowl. If a pack of coyotes smelled the blood on me, I'd be their dinner. Or what if a bear whiffed the bloody clothes in the bag that served to pad my fall, or a mountain lion growled downwind? I realized if I chucked the bag I could maybe throw animals off the scent, so I tossed it as far as I could into the woodland, hearing it land in the distance, the stench of a startled skunk's eau de cologne spraying heavily into the ether. My itchy eyes darted between tall oaks. My heart beat like a hammer strike.

I located my plastic water bottle nesting in mariposa lilies. Retrieving it, I calmed myself enough to perform what I came to do. Setting aside my painful fall, it seemed a convenient spot to bathe. Bare, agitated, freezing cold, I washed myself as best I could with the water in the bottle. Forensics would never find Harry's spilled blood here like they would if I'd bathed in the loft. No one was watching. Nobody cared. There was no nexus between him and here.

When an owl hooted, I wet myself but, thank goodness, before I donned my jeans. The owl above me hooted again, blinking, accusingly tilting his head, staring me down as I swiftly dressed. Its glare made me eager to shift other blame I was sure would inevitably come my way.

If Pennington Davis had any good sense, this horror would never have happened.

"We're shutting down," said Mr. Davis, mocking us with his crooked smile. He was our former employer, Harry's and mine, a selfish little prick whose pill-popping, rude, shopaholic wife was always clinging to his side, waiting for any crumb to fall, mouth open, carping orders. Commands like, Harry should shuttle her daughters around when they left their private school. Like I should babysit the dog, a snooty Pomeranian who pooped more than a herd of goats. Like couldn't I drop by the cleaners on my way to a client meeting Pennington dumped on me while he was drunk? Like I needed to write our social posts while she was in service to Pennington's errant libido. "He has the biggest schlong," she overshared one morning.

Harry, a four-hundred pounder, shifted in his seat across the board room, farting, scratching his dirty-blond hair and rubbing his nose with his index finger. "What? We're shutting down? But why?"

"Why do you think? We can't meet payroll… Harry, take some probiotics," Pennington blustered, flapping his hands, waving the stinky poot away.

"It's the day before Christmas. Christmas Eve," Harry moaned, folding into a conference chair like a circus elephant on a stool. "Don't do it. We can make this work. Your father made a go of it. We're fine. If you let me trim some fat, we—"

"Harry, it's done. Pack up and leave," ordered Pennington, smug and self-absorbed. He was talentless and callous. Dissing others made him feel important. He was a balding miniman with a Napoleon complex bigger than his bank account would ever be, and that was saying something. The guy wasn't broke; he was mean and stingy. Spoiled, slow, dissatisfied, and slinking past the dumpy side of forty on his stomach. As I watched the drama unfold, I could only conclude the three-piece suit he wore—which probably cost more than the weekly salaries combined of the workers he'd just let go—looked better on the mannequin in the window than it did on him. The creep was loving this ghastly moment, lording it over his employees, some of whom were crying.

LaShonda stormed out and slammed the door. Ming began chewing a fingernail. Roger turned green, began to gag, and vomited into the shredder bin.

Rodrigo gave his boss the finger under the edge of the conference table, puffing a vape with his other hand. "Yo, Penn, do we get to the end of the year?"

Pennington shot him a dirty look.

"Guess not," Rodrigo said under his breath, then muttered, "Muthafucka."

Harry discharged an angry belch. "Mentag agreed to close the doors?"

"He doesn't run the business now. I do. It's over. Get your things."

Mentag was the family patriarch who, for over three decades, had run a respectable marketing agency boasting a roster of top-shelf clients tapping his genius for advertising. Pennington… well, not so much. He knew nothing and wanted to learn even less. The world-renowned, sought-after brand the dad built tanked in the hands of his nitwit son, who was born with a mouthful of silver spoons. In the days when Mentag helmed StarShine, Fortune 500 staples counted on him to build their brands—TV networks, tech behemoths, internet bigwigs, fashion houses, athletic shoe manufacturers, restaurant chains, cosmetic companies, and everyone else who was anyone or became somebody in Mentag's hands. Up until several months ago, we created campaigns for sports stars, Oscar-winning actors, rock groups, rappers, entrepreneurs, and overseas governments looking for status and stature in the world.

Mentag was a man of great character. You could take him at his word. Pennington didn't have a word. Whichever lie served him at the moment was the mantra of the hour. Penn was capricious, disloyal, and vain. Mentag was aware of that, but he held out hope for his offspring even in the face of sagging sales. When Mentag had fallen ill and was forced to retire, he handed the business to Pennington only because he had no choice.

Pennington, in just half a year, ran StarShine into the ground, siphoning company funds to other enterprises on the sly and pocketing every dime he could. Pennington was lax and lazy, lacking direction and leadership skills. His father had the Midas touch, but Penn had the opposite Sadim touch. His ruinous gambling addiction became the means to our collective end. Add to that a wanton wife's outrageous whims and purchases, four spoiled toddlers, nannies, chauffeurs, personal assistants, pool boys, chefs, and more vacation days than workdays, and you get what we had now.

"I won't be treated this way," Harry bellowed, poking the air with a laser pointer.

That's when they brought the big guns out. The spouse. The shrew. The closer. Mandy Davis—bony, brittle, chewing a giant wad of gum, red hairdo as hard as a biker helmet, flat-chested as a garden snake—stood up and started shrieking. "Suck it up, Harry. It's over. We're thrilled. We can finally go out and enjoy our lives." Mouth flapping like a Venus flytrap, Mandy took another jab. "Mentag was your meal ticket twenty years. Go mooch off someone else."

My fists spontaneously balled as I gazed out the window, numbed, removed. I watched myself from a corner of the ceiling, focusing on the good. Attempting to reinterpret what was happening into a positive change, instinctively sensing something more suitable had to be on the horizon. In my mind, I conjured up a gig that was new, exciting, fresh, upbeat. Getting fired had to be making space for a far better energy to unfold. A world where Mandys and Penningtons didn't exist or at least were neutralized and couldn't do the harm they did. But I knew my dream was a crock of crap in the withered job market facing us, and a feeling like anger surged in me so potent that, as I often did at meetings in those waning days, I rope-a-doped like a flyweight boxer waiting to seize an opening, looking to land a knockout punch.

A bee buzzed over the windowsill and tried to get in. I warned it off.

"Wanda," Pennington barked at me. "Wake up, girl. What do you have to say?"

"Nothing," I colorlessly declared.

"I doubt that. You're too clever."

Okay, jerkwad, you asked for it. I spoke up in a cool, calm, crisp, clipped tone that came straight from the depths my diaphragm. "When will paychecks be issued for salary?"

"Wanda," Mandy snarled my name. "Haven't we treated you people fairly, kindly, with utmost respect?" Before I could proffer the peppery reply impulsively forming on my lips, she hit us with the coup de grâce. "We haven't drawn a profit from you people all year long. Ending paychecks are out of the question. You're the reason StarShine failed."

"This is outrageous!" Harry yelled, his cheeks billowing like an angel fish. "That's nuts. We've kept this place afloat. You've done less than nothing all year long." He leaped up, shaking the hardwood floor. Red-faced, Harry advanced on Mandy, hands as puffy as boxing gloves, lurching like Frankenstein's monster feeling wronged and seeking revenge. "After two decades, you think you can dump me like toxic waste and slip-slide off? You think, while I made you a mountain of money, I didn't watch the goings on? 'You people,' is that what you call us? Well, *you* people need to process something—I know where the bodies are buried. I know how the books are cooked. Why? Because I cooked them. I know what evil lurks in the hearts of *you* people. Don't forget it." Harry was all up in Pennington's face so close as to bend him backward like a willow in a gathering storm.

"You're threatening us?" Pennington gulped, wide-eyed.

"You bet. More like previewing coming attractions," Harry blustered, spittle flying. "I have plenty more to say. You can read all about it in my blog."

"Why, you big oaf. You wouldn't dare." Mandy banged the table. "You don't have the balls," she said as she tugged on the sleeve of her blue Armani dress with a nod to Pennington, who recoiled. "Come on, let's go. The Dough Boy's trash."

She shouldn't have uttered those last remarks.

The conference table overturned.

Our coworkers scattered like roaches in a kitchen when the lights come on. Harry began to quake like Mount Kilauea about to erupt—first his feet and ankles, then his calves and knees, his hunky thighs. Then his whole body began to shake, and the walls of the half-glass conference room. I pressed myself against the whiteboard, a feeble attempt to get out of his way. The bee, which was somehow inside the room, buzzed loud and flew into my ear. I ducked and scampered toward the door.

Harry had Mandy jammed into a corner. King Kong about to grab Fay Wray. "What do you think you're doing?" she taunted. "Hit me. I dare you. I'll call the cops."

"You'll get your money," Pennington promised.

"Go away, you gorilla," Mandy spat out. "You're nothing but a brute."

"Stop! We'll pay," said Pennington. "Back off. All right, I'll write your check."

Harry stopped in his tracks, disoriented, his huge arms melting to his sides. He shrank like a condom after sex, deflated, useless, spent.

"All of us?" I quickly asked, making the most of the mortifying moment for the greater good. I ran to retrieve my laptop, clicked on a file, began to read. Dispassionate and cold as ice, I ticked off a list of payments owed—unpaid commissions past and future, customary two weeks' notice, severance pay, health benefits, tallied accrued unused sick days, unemployment insurance eligibility, glowing letters of recommendation, accounts we brought from prior jobs, our iPhones, laptops, office supplies, T-shirts, software, the works.

I proposed this hefty settlement in lieu of a sexual harassment lawsuit filed by my Harvard law professor cousin, Victor Scales. Pennington "the Octopus" dared grope my five-star booty a total of two hundred eighty-three documented times—ten of which were caught on tape—landing himself in an awkward position now as he dared to place me then. He accosted me in closets, doorjambs, several times in the copy room, three times at last year's Christmas bash, and once in my car when I drove him home when someone slashed his left rear tire. I saw this debacle coming and an ignominious exit wasn't in the cards when it arrived, not if I could help it.

My detailed accounting drew mass applause. LaShonda even reappeared. The terms were nonnegotiable. I didn't give Pennington any choice, so we landed the whole enchilada.

Those last two weeks were tough for us. Rarely did anyone come to work. Harry and I comprised the skeleton staff, and during the holiday drawdown, little remained for us to do but try to fend off creditors. The Davis Duo went AWOL. Off to the Andes, so we heard. And the worst part was, they owed back rent and didn't even bother to break the lease, which extended three more years. Mr. Crum, the anxious landlord, was a constant presence at my desk, but I had no way to allay his fears. All I could do was tie up loose ends that didn't involve some manner of debt, put out feelers to find another gig, and call upon stores of strength my father the boxing trainer instilled in me.

My daddy taught me courage, heart, and discipline were skills one learned, and mastering them took practice and desire to reach for excellence. He said nothing surprising was ever bad because all things had a good upside, and you only had to look for it. His wisdom resonated as I steeled myself to take next steps and prayed to envision a better life. Guided by my inner voice, I bought a new file cabinet to take the client folders out. One couldn't call it stealing now.

New Year's was coming. The rent was due. I didn't have cash for a Christmas tree.

Harry was drinking himself into stupors, arriving late and leaving early, spending his working hours poring over dog-eared papers, hacking away at a calculator, hunting through my metal file, inhaling Hostess Twinkies. Harry was the corporate accountant, as was Harry's dad. His father was Mentag's dearest friend, so the company going down the tubes was more than just downsizing. It was a personal loss for Harry and he took it very hard, inundating his desk with outdated tax forms, ledgers, pay sheets, old invoices, any and every clue he could find to help explain the failure and to grapple with the turnaround.

I felt for Harry. He was kind. When I arrived three years ago, he took me under his wing. He was strong, and I learned he protected me from enemies in the company I didn't even know I had. I integrated StarShine. The firm was all white until I was hired. Not everyone was down with that. But Harry stuck up for me right from the start. He was sensitive and smart. He had drive, work ethic, loyalty, mind-numbing mathematic skills. He had major career goals and ambitions. They all dissolved when Mentag left. Now Harry was lost in a problem he didn't create but felt he had to solve.

I could almost reach out and touch his palpable loneliness during the holidays. He had no friends or family, and he overate to soothe his soul. He told me he had a twin brother who was estranged and held ill will toward him or maybe just sibling rivalry. Harry apparently beat the brother out for the father's accountant gig, and the twin was filled with fury. Not only because of the job but also as Harry had their father's trust and was their parents' favorite son. After they passed, there was no one left. Harry was alone. I observed his nonstop eating, nonstop drinking, nonstop pain and anger, noting his instability and emotional distress. Harry was headed for a fall.

At least that's what I'd thought until New Year's Eve, when I saw a change. A few days before the doors were due to shut down, Harry suddenly turned up sober, ready to let the good times roll and plying me with cheap champagne. "Let's take over the business," he proposed. "We can make a go of it, if you have a little faith in me. C'mon, work with me. Be my partner."

"What?" I asked, though I heard him fine.

"Let's run it ourselves. We can buy them out."

"With what, our good looks or our A-1 credit? Wait. Our colossal collateral. Oh right, that's just your lumpy couch and my dilapidated car."

"I wrote a dyno business plan. We know the industry backward and forward."

"I guess. But I want to do something else. I'm not feeling I'm really cut out for this."

"Don't sell yourself short. You're a mastermind. Your leadership skills are amazing. Your worst is head and shoulders over every other employee's best. You have more creativity in your pinky finger than the Davis clan, and look what they accomplished. Do this, cupcake. Think about it. It'll be easy as one two three. The infrastructure's all in place. We'll call the employees and give them jobs, and offer the clients tip-top service." Harry bit into a king-size Baby Ruth. He had a point.

"What would we use for capital?" I asked.

"I got it figured. Trust me, cupcake. Run the show."

"I don't know, Harry, it sounds shaky. I'm not up for shady deals. It would have to be straight-up legit. You think we can buy it fair and square?"

Harry chuckled, belly wiggling, mouth circled by a chocolate ring. "Anyone who would buy this business fair must be a square. The sellers are very motivated, if you get my drift. Leave it to me to negotiate with the Penningtons, and we'll make a fortune doing what we love to do. It's gonna work, I promise."

That night, I went home tingling. *Could we do it? Could we make it happen?*

Harry's idea was very sexy. Opportunity knocks but once. I couldn't pass it up.

As new as the partnership concept was, and as much as it had to be based on trust—which was not my stock-in-trade after being cheated on too many times—I suddenly felt I might do anything to make the dream come true. And sure enough, I almost did.

After all I did after Harry died and I happened to stumble upon his body, I reconsidered running off when the sun rose over the mountaintops. Maybe I was still in shock, but little could make me look guiltier, even during the holiday season, I thought, than absconding to a time-share or some distant cheap motel. Nothing I did last night made sense. I slept in my car in the park, but I couldn't recall why I made that particular perilous choice, and driving on empty, naked, seemed absolutely irrational. Who does that? It was totally nuts. I could have worn my bloody clothes to the park but was scared to be caught in them, and yet I still took them along in a bag. I wasn't on my game. I had to pull myself together, get my behavior in check, and think about my safety too.

Whoever killed Harry might off me. Of that I was certain, if nothing else. If StarShine was the motive. I wasn't sure that was the case, but our business was Harry's everything. What other motive could there be? Everyone adored him.

Traveling sounded scarier the more I thought about a trip. How could I protect myself secluded at some hideaway? In LA, at least I had some peeps. Not many, but a few. I had coworkers who'd mourn Harry too, who'd also be addled by his death. Staying put was a better option the more I considered my alternatives. I'd do better to stand my ground. I'd uncover the body, alert the police, and preserve the only chance I had to maintain the business, save my life, and possibly keep my freedom.

The trickiest part would be going to StarShine, putting on a show, pretending I was unaware of Harry's death until today. But in part, it was easier than I thought when it actually came right down to it. I snuck in without any hassle and prepared myself to call the cops. The sooner, the better, I deduced. I couldn't be perceived as having waited to report the crime. It'd make me look responsible. I needed to avoid any possible hint of impropriety.

Last night, I'd returned to the loft to bring Harry a tuna-and-noodle casserole, his fave and my way of apologizing for the argument we'd had. It was only a budgetary tiff, but everyone who'd heard the fight could misconstrue a motive. The truth wouldn't sound like the truth to anyone else any more than it did to me.

You see, when I'd returned to work, the office was dank, blinds drawn, the AC off, the door ajar. I was nervous that Harry fell off the wagon, worried about what he might do. When I entered, Brownian motion was filtering through dense, fetid, putrid air. So I opened a window near the door. Harry was ripening odorously, and the reek of it took me by surprise. I'd never smelled that stench before. I couldn't discern if it was death or Crampy cooking chitterlings. That is, until I took a look.

The bed in the private space behind the office partition was in shambles, a bloodstained mattress topped by a tangle of bedsheets knotted at its foot. The mattress sagged from Harry's weight, a crater dipping in its middle, its belabored box spring tilted at an angle to the floor. It looked like the violent after-effects of a kinky encounter or torture spree. Blood dyed the carpet dookie brown, and what might appear to the untrained eye as a throw rug near the bedside proved to be a giant shirt, an extralong pair of holey, white tube socks, a polyester necktie, and the khakis Harry wore to work.

In one corner, a broken cardboard box sat brimming with a sordid mélange of aging porno DVDs. One titled *Debbie Does Donald Duck* sat open on the top. Fettuccini Alfredo, salami, smashed potato chips, and doughnut crumbs were sprinkled on the blanket, giving the overall impression of a night of debauchery gone dead wrong. The murderer needn't have bothered, Harry was already digging his grave with his fork.

Then there it was in all its glory—Harry's bloated cadaver. It looked like the site of a beached white whale or the crashed remains of a Goodyear Blimp. Harry was hacked up butcher-style, like hundreds of cuts of pork loin that a grocer reassembled. I crouched by his face to discern his expression and try to assess his gaping wounds. His head bent at an impossible angle, his expression that of complete surprise. His paper-thin lips were cracked and parted. Tears flowed. I began to gag. I was sure I heard him call my name. Was I hallucinating? I had to hurry, call the cops. No, wait. This wouldn't look good to them. Would they ever believe I was innocent? What was I doing there? Why was this happening? How was I going to get out of it?

That's when I heard somebody call. "Honey!" It was a female voice. And just when I needed to call the cops. Well, maybe I shouldn't call the cops. Maybe this woman could take the heat. Maybe she'd stumble upon the body. Perhaps she might be found in here if I hurried away and dropped a dime. Whoever it was, better her than me.

I heard more knocking, calling out. "Sweetheart, open up, it's me. Darling, I have fantastic news."

Before I could give it further thought, my fight-or-flight response kicked in, and I frantically searched for a hiding place.

"Enough of this, I'm coming in." From out in the hall, the voice was muffled but familiar in its tone. The front door closed. Stilettos clicked.

I dove under the bed with labored breath, wedging my achy, slender frame beside a lipstick videocam and a brand-new DVR. *What are these doing under here?*

"Harry?" a voice said, tentative. "Oh, Harry, don't tease, we don't have time. We've got urgent matters to discuss. We're in too deep to back out now. You're with me, right?" she said.

From my scary perspective on the floor, expensive high heels emerged from the other side of the glass partition. Red snakeskin pumps came sauntering in. Thin ankles in satiny stockings. "Harry!" The voice was anxious now. I knew the next sounds would be loud screams, and I thought to race out while I had the chance but knew I would be seen.

A gasp, and then the shoes stopped short just inches from my awestruck face.

I braced for yelling, sobs, loud cries. None of which occurred.

Instead, what emitted was laughter, giggling. *Was somebody playing a joke on me?*

A beat. Then a strange thought came to me, an instinct for survival.

I silently reached for the lipstick cam, examined it, armed it to record.

The scarlet shoes pivoted on their heels, sashaying to the cardboard box. Their inhabitant guffawed. "Blackmail, huh? Well, think again," whooped Mandy Davis. "Really? You were a loser, Harry. Bright, but not enough to stay the course. You actually thought you mattered." Ten manicured fingernails painted peach reached in and fished around inside the box to rifle through the pornos, working the cardboard like it was a sale bin after Labor Day. They plucked out an unlabeled Blu-ray disc. "This better be it, buster. Somebody did a number on you, but you got what you deserve. And if this isn't what I think it is or you already showed it to someone else, I swear I'll kill your ass again."

As confused as I was when the high heels left, as soon as they did, I called 911. Right after, I scooted to Crampy's and asked her to come upstairs to witness things, but she got so troubled by the sight she had a minor stroke. A temporary ischemic attack, an ER doctor later said. LAPD rolled down five minutes later, first the beat cops, then detectives, then a forensic team. A Groutman and a Stix began detecting almost instantly, proceeding just as I'd feared they would to try to pin the crime on me.

Groutman was early fifties, medium height, straight out of central casting for a protein powder ad or a steroid infomercial. He kept scratching at scaly psoriasis along his arms and dry pink hands, and he had a textured New York accent, waves of thick, coarse, dark-brown hair, and a humorless demeanor. "You co-owned this business with the deceased. Correct?" he asked.

"That's right," I answered, trying to think one step ahead.

"Were you and him friends?"

"We were partners. We didn't ever hang out or anything."

"You and him didn't…"

"We did not."

"You never had sexual intercourse?" he asked me even though I'd answered.

"Partners was all the relationship was?" he inquired, implying that wasn't the case, raising an eyebrow in dispute, and scratching at his scales again. "Did you and him get along okay?"

"For sure. We were an efficient team."

"When was the last you seen him?"

"Yesterday evening."

"Yeah? What time was that?"

"Well, I'm usually here until eight or so, but I happened to have a dinner meeting, so I took off earlier. I probably left around quarter to six."

"You got anyone who can attest to that?"

"Yes, I met with Ringold Kanz, the owner of Ringold Studios."

Groutman made a note of it in a tablet in a worn black case. "Was the victim alive when you saw him last?"

"Oh yeah. He was fine. He was hard at work."

"And you never saw him after that? Until today, I mean."

"Correct." Real tears sprang forth from me. "Detective, I don't get it. I really don't see how this could happen. People loved Harry. He was so gentle."

To Groutman's left, Detective Stix whipped out a stark white handkerchief and looked at my legs as though they were life-size sausages and he was starved. The color of barbecued chicken and licking one juicy pair of lover's lips, he handed me the handkerchief and smiled a blue-white smile. His exotic features, mighty stance, and bod to die for made the man the finest cop I'd ever seen, not to mention his yummy pheromones. "Well, I guess that's it," he mumbled. Eyes on my thighs, he bit his lip. "You can get back to your *husband* now," he fished.

"I'm single," I demurred.

"Awesome… I mean, interesting." He glanced at Groutman, dropped his gaze.

Groutman loudly cleared his throat. He grabbed my arm and pulled me from the sofa I was sitting on. "Ma'am, you'll have to come with us."

Once Harry and I had set our sights on acquiring the company, every angle of providence worked to help us meet our goal. Harry talked Pennington into selling, which was a miracle in itself. He managed to get a loan and convince the bank to issue a credit line contingent on our business plan, bank statements showing severance payments Pennington kicked up by that time, and fundamentals of the firm. We found a new office immediately. Every employee we invited aboard came skipping back to us. New client satisfaction soared. For the first time since my college graduation, I could see success, unlimited potential, and a world of possibilities.

I embarked on a big makeover too. First I cut and dyed my hair and let it go natural for once in my life. I shopped for a discount wardrobe at the Camarillo outlet mall and spruced up my apartment with the help of the local dollar store. Our handsome client, Hooper Manley, asked me out and courted me, despite the long hours I spent at work. He wined and dined me royally, but the whirlwind romance soon went kaput when I found out he was married.

Harry did Weight Watchers, lost a hundred fifty pounds, and then took up with a mystery woman whom he never introduced, buying a ramshackle property he remodeled in twelve weeks. He said he planned to marry her, but he flipped a house for me as well, which didn't quite jibe with his romance, but I didn't look the gift horse in the mouth. The reno kept apace. The world was opening like a summer rose. We were starting to live the dream.

One Monday morning, all that changed.

As I later heard from Harry, his assistant had buzzed his intercom, stammering, "M-Mr. Rutherford, I don't know exactly how to say this… there's a man out here to see you and he's saying he's your twin. It's wild; he looks exactly like you."

Harry had fallen silent for a moment, sneezed, chomped into a carrot, and droned into the intercom. "Send him in, Tasha. It's okay… No, wait. First ask him what he wants."

There was a pause. The assistant came back. "He answered 'what he always wants.' But it's not true he looks like you. There's something different in his face… You sure I ought to send him in?"

"No, but you can't stop him."

Harry's mirror image entered an office full of hand-me-downs, swaggering like he owned the place and looking mean and menacing, grizzled, haunted, rough, and ready. Wearing fatigues, black boots, a shoulder holster, and a green beret, he crossed to Harry, wordless, rumbling at him like a commuter train speeding into Grand Central station. "Impressive digs here, baby bro. I got a good look at your partner too. Not bad. She'll do just fine. Hot as a pistol. How'd you pull that? Hope you got a pen here 'cause you're handing her over to me as well."

Harry stood up and curled his lip. "I'm wonderful, Larry. How are you? So nice of you to ask. The past eight years were heavenly without you… What are you doing here?"

"Don't even try to play me, boy. Give me my due, or I'll take you out."

"Don't you think I know that, Larry? You're why Mom and Dad are dead. That's why I wouldn't piss on you if your hot head caught on fire. Get out before I throw you out."

"I'm not playing with you. Cough it up," said Larry, pulling a loaded Glock.

At that moment, I burst in, my new white pantsuit tattooed on. "Incoming!" I shouted, stopping short to stare at double Harrys. "Wanda, meet the netherworld," said Harry.

Late that day, he died.

I never saw a police precinct before they dragged me into one, ostensibly for questioning. I saw Pennington Davis and his wife on a bench with what looked like a lawyer or a mobster, I could not tell which. Pennington waved. I turned my head, pretending not to see. I got ushered toward a tiny room after StarShine workers wandered in while I was playing Solitaire on my phone, attempting not to retch. One of them, Harry's assistant, said the search was on for Larry, who had evidently vaporized. I reflected on what that meant for me and I gauged the extent of the mess I was in as I sized up the ambient crowd I spied in the halls that I was passing.

The station was crawling with reprobates on both sides of the law from what I could see—cops, attorneys, thugs, and cons. In their midst, my person of interest status didn't seem the existential threat it had when I came in. Everything was relative. I reminded myself I did nothing wrong. But then neither did lots of other girls who got locked in jail and left feet first. I called my cousin, Victor Scales, and his lawyerly presence changed the vibe the instant he alighted. He advised me to tell the truth but keep it short and simple as I did, not volunteering anything.

I was honest, omitting few details when Stix and Groutman questioned me. Some of what they asked, I frankly had no answer to: Why didn't I call the cops when I stumbled on Harry's body in the loft? Was I sure he was dead when I arrived? Then why did I run away? Why'd I go back to the office that night? Why did I argue with Harry that day? Was I angry enough to bump him off? Did Harry and I have insurance on each other? For how much? Was StarShine mine with Harry gone? Were we dating as other folks implied? Was Harry dating someone else? Was I certain Mandy Davis was the woman who swiped the CD from the cardboard box of pornos? Did I know what was on that DVD? What did I know about Harry and Larry? On and on it went until my cousin dropped an ultimatum and they had to let me go a jillion hours later.

Victor insisted on eating out. I picked at a salad, lost in thought, my stomach cramping as I chewed, bitter lettuce catching in my throat. Victor graciously offered to stay for a couple of days. I put him off. I didn't want to prevail on him any more than I had already.

When sunset fell, he took me home.

Night seemed to drag on endlessly. I tossed and turned. I meditated. Nothing seemed to ease my mind. In the wee hours, restless, raw, I trudged to the fridge for a bottle of cold water, trying to relieve my aches and pains from my fall in Griffith Park. *How in the world did it come to this?* They were thinking I killed Harry. I turned on the TV. I turned on the light. I turned off the TV. I turned off the light. I turned the light back on. I downloaded a book from the library. I jumped up, doused the lights, peeked out the window and surveyed the street. An unmarked cop car ambled up and parked right in a red zone. How subtle. They were watching me.

My clock-radio said it was three fifteen, its volume turned down very low, conveying smooth jazz to my consciousness. But just as I dozed, I heard a knock. I thought it was a dream. A quiet rapping on my door. Sitting up, I licked dry lips and froze, my every muscle tense and sore, my eyes surveying dark, stark shapes in the stillness of my blackened room. I harkened again. There was someone there. I crept out of bed and tiptoed barefoot, silently stealing up the hall to a closet where I grabbed a hammer. I snatched my cell phone off its wireless charger, padded to the door, and peeked out through the fish-eye peephole.

All I could see was a shoulder at first, but then a face came into view…

Oh my gosh, it's Larry!

It was true, he was coming to bump me off.

"It's Harry, Wanda, let me in."

Oh right, like I'm gonna fall for that. Harry was dead. It had to be Larry trying to get the jump on me, thinking he could trick me. "Wanda, please, it's me. It's Harry. C'mon, cupcake, open up." No one but Harry called me cupcake. How could Larry know?

"Hurry, before they see me here. I spotted cops outside."

I blurted, "If it's really you, then tell me the name of the car I drive."

"Pea Pod. She's a green Volkswagen. Pennington fondled your beautiful butt over two hundred eighty-three times. Ask me anything you want. I adore you. I know everything about you, even your fingernail polish, cupcake. It's Lamumba Blue. I noticed you cut your hair on the seventh day we had our partnership. A bee flew into your ear when we got fired, and I envied it. I longed to be that close to you. Let me in, cupcake. Trust me. I'm your friend. Unlock the door."

I was torn, but it had to be Harry. No one else could know that much. But was it Harry, really? There was only one way to find out. I had to bet my life on it. I took a chance and let him.

Harry blew in like a hurricane wind and threw his arms around me. "Oh, thank heaven you're all right."

"Harry, good grief, I thought you died."

"I may as well have," Harry groaned. His stubbly chin dipped to smile at me in my moonlit living room. "Wanda, I gotta come clean with you. I never meant to bring you grief." Tears navigated down his cheeks.

"From what? What's going on?"

"I didn't get the business fair and square for us."

"You promised me."

"I know, but it was complicated. There's a lot you didn't know."

"Well, I don't think I want to know. Not now, if it's going to get me killed."

"I blackmailed Mandy, made her sell. That's how I pulled it off."

"Whoa. You blackmailed Mandy? How? Are you kidding me, Harry? That's illegal. We don't really own it then. Is StarShine even ours?"

"Of course it is. We paid for it. The viper had it coming, cupcake, you know that as well as I. They'd never have sold to us unless we had some kind of leverage. I figured out how to get back at her and net us what we wanted too, so I went for it. We needed it. Nobody can contest the deal. I got it all on paper. Mandy played me for a fool. So, yeah, I committed extortion, but that tramp did so much worse. I knew it was wrong, but—"

"This isn't happening. How could you set me up like this? What did you get me into?"

Harry moaned and looked away. "Whitewashing the books so she and Penn could suck out all the cash. I wasn't aware they were doing it. I thought they were trying to stay afloat by fooling the investors, and I figured we'd give their money back when our cash flow evened out. The investors wouldn't suffer then. At least that's what I thought. But she and Penn were greedy. They just wanted to bleed the business dry. They couldn't buy me off at first, while Mentag was still CEO, to keep me from telling what I knew, so she slept with me when he retired to try to seal the deal."

"You've been sleeping with Mandy all this time? Are you kidding me right now? You and Pennington's wife have been having a thing and you kept me in the dark?"

"You know I'm not a ladies' man. She made me think she wanted me."

"You bought that?" I was incredulous.

"Uh-huh. Hook, line, and sinker. The woman I really wanted didn't know that I existed."

"Wait. Hold on a second. What'd you say? Did I hear you right? You juggled the books then bought the firm? Is StarShine not worth what we paid?"

Harry shook his head and looked at me with pleading eyes. "Don't judge until you hear me out. I'm sure of StarShine's value. It's worth a lot *more* than we showed in the books, a ton more than we paid. I promise you, we got a steal. We got a bargain, cupcake. Mandy valued StarShine at much *less* than what it's really worth, not more, so they could claim a loss. That's why they had to get out quick. They were guilty of tax evasion. When they got an audit letter from the IRS, they went berserk. They'd used the phony books to file. They had to cover up. If they didn't sell out really fast, they knew the ax would fall."

"You bought us into all of that?"

"To help Mentag. To make it right. Mandy said he'd go to jail, that Penn would blame it all on him. She said she was trying to save StarShine or Mentag would be ruined. That's why I agreed to cook the books. I didn't know the half of it. She only cares about herself. She told me Penn made purchases and didn't track expenditures, so I would have to set things straight. That wasn't true at all. But at least I kept us in the clear. I had the real books stashed away. I'd say she cooked them on her own if anything went wrong. I did the hanky-panky on her desktop, not on mine. I only used her passwords too, though she was way ahead of me. I wasn't aware she was scamming for herself until I dug in deep and found shell corporations linked to her and no one else. I'd broken the law for *her* and even covered for the audit. I'd helped her rip investors off. Unknowingly, but still… and then I found out something else." He coughed and looked away.

"Well, go on, Harry, spit it out."

He cracked his knuckles, glanced around. "You know, Mentag didn't just get sick. She's poisoned him for months. She's probably doing it as we speak."

"What? She's killing Mentag?"

"Yup, I just caught on to it. And then she plans on killing me."

"Why, because you know too much?"

"Uh-huh, and even more. Because I made a tape of me and Mandy. We were doing it. She calls it *Beauty and the Beast*. She told me if folks saw it, she could never show her face again. She wants to run for office, and she said that tape would ruin her. She admitted she only married Penn because of his connections. He thinks she's on his side, but she's just tricking him like she tricked me. I couldn't take it anymore."

I felt the blood drain from my face. "Well, why not give her what she wants?"

"She wants more than the video. She wants to shut me up. I told her I would turn her in. I guess she's thinking if I am dead, I'll can't tell what I know. I think she plans to kill Penn too."

"Back up. I still don't understand. I saw you dead already. No breath. No heartbeat. Cut to pieces. I got covered with your blood."

"That was Larry, cupcake. Don't you get it? Larry blew it. He's always had it in for me. He wanted to tear me down. He was mean and vengeful. He blamed all his faults on me. He raged about our father getting me the stupid StarShine job way back before the Ice Age. It was always someone else's fault whenever he screwed up. I bet Dad's spinning in his grave. My brother was insane." Harry sniffled, wiped his nose. "It took me years to realize how much he hated who I was. He wanted to *be* me, Mother said. He copied everything I did and had me tracked for several years while he was overseas. When he caught me banging Mandy, he swooped in to make his move. I loved him, but his jealousy condemned him in the end."

"What do you mean? If Larry's dead—"

"He came over last night to hand me to the IRS. Imagine that. He threatened to tell the attorney general too if he didn't get his way. I would have let the business go to be free of him forever, but not at your expense, cupcake. I couldn't let him wreck your life. After fighting for years in the Middle East, Ukraine, Sudan and Myanmar, he still resented me enough to want to do me in at home. He didn't care who else he harmed." Harry held my trembling hands. "He couldn't ruin it, cupcake. Not for me and not for you… Larry pulled his gun, and I attacked. And this time, I prevailed."

"Police. Step away from the door!" we heard.

The order came in from the outer hall, and my pounding heart began to gong.

"Harry, say you didn't kill him. Tell me you didn't stab your twin."

"It was Pennington who did it, when he learned about his wife and me. Mandy must have told him. I think she provoked him to knock me off and pin my death on you. But it was Larry who got killed. I was in the bathroom. I'd hit Larry so hard that he fell on the bed and broke it. I'd split my knuckles too, so I went to wash them off. Evidently, that's when Penn snuck in and thought he caught me sleeping. He didn't know Larry had come to town and couldn't tell the difference. He had knifed poor Larry in a rage when I came back into the room. It blew him away when I reappeared and he fled, but I couldn't catch up with him. Now he's nowhere to be found. I don't know what he might do next."

"Forget Penn. Pennington's filthy rich. Rich folks don't go to jail. If he stole any money from Mentag, he can live on it eternally. Especially overseas. He's probably out of the country now. Long gone. It's her we need to find."

"You'd better stay away from her. And me. I'll take the blame. I left him there. You're not involved." Harry lumbered toward the door. "You don't deserve to be implicated."

"What are you going to do?" I asked. "Don't go."

"It's over. Bye-bye, cupcake. I'll be thinking of you."

"No, Harry, there's another way. Be Larry. Harry's dead. Unless you tell, no one will know. No one can prove otherwise. You two have identical DNA. As long as they don't take fingerprints, you'll get a brand-new start. You don't have to be someone who cooked the books or murdered anyone. They'll think you're Larry Rutherford, a decorated veteran. You arrived here only yesterday. You came to see your brother, whom you loved and wanted to protect. He called to say he needed you, so you came running to his aid. He said he was in danger, and it turns out he was right." I reached into my yoga pants, pulled out a tube and held it up. The tiny lipstick cam. "The killer's words are on this tape. They'll give you all the proof you need."

"Gee, thank you, cupcake. You're the best."

Nobody asked, and we never told. Well, not until I'm telling you.

When Harry turned over the lipstick cam, it was Mandy's admission heard on tape. Under the stress of questioning when they thought I was the murderer, I didn't tell the cops about the little hidden camera. I forgot I'd slipped it in my purse when I climbed from under the broken bed. I forgot what Mandy said that day until Harry was on the hot seat: "And if this isn't what I think it is or you already showed it to someone else, I swear I'll kill your ass again."

Well, in order to murder a man *again*, you have to have killed him previously.

That's what the prosecution argued, sending Mandy off to jail and convicting Penn for murder, clearing my and Larry's names. It didn't help their cause at all that Mentag recovered as soon as the couple got caught and was arrested. It's interesting, how a poison can lose its effect when it's no longer being administered. Mentag almost bit the dust, but he was sharp enough to point the finger at his daughter-in-law and cast suspicion on his son. He didn't sue medical personnel for missing the lethal doses of the toxin in his blood. He was too happy to be alive.

He and Harry—Larry, technically—and I have a thriving business now, a generous conglomerate that donates half its profits to the causes closest to our hearts. It's headquartered in downtown LA in a compound with a tower stretching seventy luxury floors above our pasts and employing three hundred souls.

Our company is branded The Phoenix, but that isn't all that's rising now.

I just got a call a few minutes ago, in the penthouse where I'm hard at work. A buddy of Larry's arrived today, on a flight from overseas. A soldier of fortune. A hired gun. A mercenary with a "score to settle" with Larry Rutherford, related, he told me, to war crimes.

I dare not imagine what he wants or what horrors his threat is referring to.

Will he recognize Harry as Larry, or out him?

Either way, it isn't good.

Something will have to be done about this.

Not much time to think of what.

He's in the elevator and he'll be here any second.

SHOOTING

OKAY, SO THEY SAY IT was jealousy— the green-eyed monster's evil force, a version of *I want what you've got*—and I guess you could make a case for that.

But that wasn't how it was with me, why I started to trail her like I did, what led to all the trouble. It was supposed to be just an experiment. A lark. A sort of adventurous thrill. Who'd have dreamed it would take a disastrous turn? That someone would wind up stone-cold dead. It's not like that was planned. But one thing I learned from all this mess is, once you set something in motion, well, you have to accept what happens next as your responsibility. When you roll a snowball down a hill, it's bound to gain size and momentum that could mow somebody down.

Life can be full of twists and turns, especially here in Hollywood, where careers result in precarious states of being, if you catch my drift. One minute you're hot, the next you're not, and it might take a moment to realize a transition has already taken place and suddenly you're the last to know. Like maybe your parking space changes names, or your calls no longer get put through. You're cooking with gas by gradations here—ice cold, lukewarm, hot, simmer, sauté—and then *poof!* If you're blessed and possessed of great timing, you might even blaze to a raging broil, start sizzling, and boil over.

Like Aphrodite Valentine.

She was the flavor of the month.

I guess I was sort of a staple then. A cash cow, one of my agents said. That actress who booked job after job, consistently working but not moving up. Recognizable, not a household word. Dependable, versatile, popular, had the look, delivered the goods. But I was essentially frozen in place. Not landing that juicy breakthrough role. Now, don't get me wrong, I was happy there. I was hopeful I'd make it too someday. I had privacy and self-respect, and yet I was able to pay my bills. A neat trick for any actress, far less one of any color.

However, my shelf life wasn't long. I looked young but was cresting forty. I didn't have time to fool around.

Maybe that's why it didn't seem fair. Not that life comes with a fairness clause, but I wondered how she managed it. Aphrodite, I mean, how she hit the heights. She wasn't trained or talented, or attractive, or magnetic. Not generous, charming, sexy, kind, hard-working, or even fun. Yet and still, she was a superstar. Self-centered, boastful, tardy, mean. It wasn't so much I was envious as I wanted to figure it out. I binged on videos, books, motivational speakers and gurus who seemed to suggest it'd be helpful to model my own career after someone who'd reached a lofty goal. Aphrodite was a case study, and through the filter of my naivete, I actually thought I could take a page out of her book, how she clawed her way up to the top. After all, she was a nemesis. I could scarcely count the distressing times she landed plum roles I auditioned for.

Then too, I'd heard the rumors. Aphrodite was sleeping around. Strategically leveraging sex like a crowbar to pry into studio offices. Languishing on casting couches, blow-jobbing her way to expensive gifts. And maybe I wanted to prove the gossip true, ascertain that I steered the more earnest course if not the more successful. I think that's where I might have erred. Right now, I just wish I could turn back time, evaluate my choices, and decide to mind my business.

But alas, that isn't possible. It's all about consequences now, not returning to my wrong turn on that gorgeous autumn day on Sunset Strip when I should have gone off to the gym or had a massage or bikini wax, or taken that Groupon offer for a Brazilian hair straightener and manicure. It was early evening with clear blue skies, a rarity here in the City of Angels, where smog is a veritable fait accompli, the pollution beneath the angel's wings. The air was as hot as a cup of tea. Warm Santa Ana winds the day before blew in from the east and morphed the skies into gunmetal grays that warned of the torrent of El Niño rain, another LA rarity, that washed the celestial canopy and painted it sparkling azure shades air-brushed with cotton candy clouds.

I bulleted past the Burbank airport, south in the traffic on Hollywood Way, crept through the crush in Toluca Lake alongside the Burbank Studios with their colorful billboards of cartoon characters, movie heroes, TV stars, and gates and high walls that kept fans at bay. I climbed up the Barham Boulevard hill, passed Universal's famed back lot, the 101, Cahuenga Pass. I zipped across Franklin, wound over to Fairfax, and jetted down to Sunset.

My heart sort of sank as I breezed up the Strip, bejeweled with billboards, trendy shops, comedy clubs, and restaurants. There were days when great film posters graced the Strip, bedazzling it into a Milky Way that fed the ambitions of Hollywood hopefuls turned crestfallen waiters with dreams deferred. I longed to see my face on it as I ferried my goals to my agent's office deep in the glitter of Beverly Hills to peek my head in for a meet and greet. Now the Strip was a caricature of itself, in the form of a cheesy video arcade featuring cookie-cutter cable movies, rappers, and overpriced, understyled clothing lines repped by anorexic teens sporting outfits more scant than the emperor's clothes. It was beer and perfume ads, embellished jeans, and album covers artists hardly made a cent on once their hard work went online.

As I crossed Doheny, I heaved a sigh. A shield-shaped sign announced to me the privilege of entering Beverly Hills and the peril of overparking there. One second over your meter time and you said goodbye to a mortgage payment, ticketed to a fare-thee-well. But traffic let up, eye pollution abated, face-lifted old manses took center stage on sloping green carpets that served as lawns, and pricey prams pushed by imported au pairs airlifted up the side streets.

I swung left by the Beverly Hills Hotel and got blinded by glints of refracted sun reflected off a sheet of glass—the windshield of a gold Lamborghini so new it still boasted the dealer's plates. It revved to declare it was bling on wheels in case you didn't notice. Aphrodite slouched, posing chin up at the wheel in a matching gold-leather bustier hugging her famous mahogany skin. It was leather studded with rhinestones almost hurtful to my eyes. I wasn't the only gawker though, as La Diva was decked out in ten grand at least, not counting her softball-sized diamond stud earrings or ruby-and-platinum Cartier watch or Oscar de la Renta shades.

And to top it all off, she honked at me. Laid on her horn like a trumpeter. She waved with a mixture of *Leave my streets* and *Oh it's you, check out my ride. I hope you never get one.*

Raw heat rose up behind my ears. I waved back, managed a smile, turned left, and refused to indulge my temper. Although had I known what was coming next, merely chilling would not have been possible. But in good faith, I sped to Wilshire, bogarted a newly vacated spot, swiped on my pink lipstick, primped my hair, and parked my leased red Audi.

As I zoomed from my agent's office after meeting the newest agent there, my ears tuned in to idle chatter whispered in the copy room beside the elevator shaft. I peeked around a corner.

"Yeah, it's a coupe. She came in today. Bailed IZN to sign with us. After all those agents did for her." Faith, an assistant, chewed the fat with a bud down at the scanner, popping her gum and taking names, her pudgy toes lopped over blue suede mules. "We have to let some clients go. The witch demanded we drop every actress remotely her type when we take her on."

"Diabolical. What a dragon. I heard she was actually naming names to cut."

"It's true. She brought a list. Girlfriend is a bitch on wheels."

Faith's colleague sported a seam-strained chartreuse sheath and orange fingernails. "Guess that axes Nova Keene."

My stomach did a flip-flop. What, my name was gossip now?

"Oh wow." Faith gasped. "Poor Nova. Right. She'll probably be the first to go." She shuffled her paperwork, stapled it, groaned. "A Black leading lady, great résumé—"

"I wonder if they dumped her yet."

"Are you kidding? They'll wait till she calls in next and make a receptionist break the news." Faith sucked her teeth and waved a hand.

"Nah, they won't. They wouldn't dare… They'll fire off an email."

"A shame, if you ask my opinion."

"They won't. No one here cares what we have to say." Chartreuse tacked on a surly smirk. "One wind shift, *bam!* You're outta here."

"Although Nova is so beautiful. Bet they'll scramble to sign her somewhere else."

"Don't be so sure. It's rough out there. Top agencies are dropping clients faster than a bungee cord." Chartreuse beat a path to the copier and snatched a yellow sticky note. "You remember when they fired Dan, that agent? He couldn't relocate. He's out there on his own. New house, car payments, wife, the twins—"

"Loyalty. Good luck finding that."

"Particularly in this zip code. Nova's a thousand times the actress you-know-who is."

"Yeah, you're right. She's prettier, sweeter, smarter—"

"But not younger. That's the cardinal sin."

"Right? Amen."

"That chick's a star. Remember her in *Party Girl?*"

"*Insider* was my favorite. And that break-up scene in *Heart of Gold*. What a bummer."

"Yeah. Oh well. It's done."

A beat as they nailed my coffin shut. A moment of silence for Nova Keene, once near, now dear departed.

Faith kicked and slapped the copier. "When are they gonna fix this thing?"

"Never… Don't bring the new client up. You don't want to wind up on her enemies list."

Who was it? Who were they yacking about?

"For sure. She flew in on her broomstick. Aphrodite's reign of terror. Huh!"

I froze. Cold vapor hissed out of my lungs. A prickle of sweat beaded up on my brow. The black hardwood telescoped up from the floor as if to meet my fall. I steeled myself and sucked in air, abandoned my wait for the elevator, raced up the hall on the balls of my feet so as not to be detected, and tore down the stairs, a dizzy wreck. I was signed to my agents my whole career, and now they were set to abandon me, to blow me off for you-know-who. The rats. The snakes. The traitors. *Yikes!* Well, bump those turncoats. I'd show them. But that night whirled by in a blurry haze, with my mind too undone to snap out of it or to formulate any kind of plan.

I awoke, ran lines, got all dolled up, dashed over to Fantasy Studios. I'd have to audition my heart out now. I needed the gig more than ever before—to attract new representation. With the pilot season months away and a union strike threatened a week down the road, there were scads of expenses nipping at my heels and I had to make a move.

And who did I see when I walked in the door?

The shrike called Aphrodite.

My oatmeal leaped into my throat. I thought I would hurl it then and there.

The audition took every ounce of grace. The producers' domain was standing-room only, with wannabe, would-be, and once-were stars in the stench of Aphrodite's overconfidence and ill intent as strong as the odor of garlic cloves.

Aphrodite went first. A horrendous sign. Casting directors tended to go with their front-runners, where? In front, of course. And no sooner did

Aphrodite waltz off with the smirk of a thousand eat-my-dusts than the rumor mill spun its cutting blades and ground her into powder.

"You hear about her and Princeton Karnes, in casting over at Exohits?" Ashley Billingsly jerked her world of curls, her figure profiled in a zebra-striped dress in the seat Aphrodite vacated. She lowered her volume, scanned the bans, and winked conspiratorially. "They caught them on his glass chair runner. Somebody said it's on YouTube now."

"Grrrl. But the scoop is Bret Daszlo at Lookz," Kiki Cole chirped with a flip of her braids, her honey-colored features animating like a Disney flick. "She dumped him like a bag of trash the minute Her Highness got Sloppy Z to strong-arm her a record deal. Z swears he's her man, but he ain't got a clue; he's too used to enthralling his groupies. He thinks every woman is his, I guess, but he's bumping sloppy seconds there. Wouldn't want to be her when he figures it out. The dude has an arsenal at his crib." She scratched blond cornrows, scrunched her nose, licked a finger, and made an air tick mark.

From there, it streaked on like a runaway train, with multiple ingenues chiming in.

"That brute hung with me till she elbowed me out. If I never see Sloppy Z again…"

"I know for a fact who she slept with to get that role in the new Blake Halsey flick."

"Awesome Martin climbed up on his roof and threatened to jump because of her."

"What? Her butt ain't even real. My sister-in-law screws her surgeon."

"You know about Rooster Bizonette? He's no longer directing since she signed on."

"Ooh, but her stunt with poor Suarez Ozul, the producer of *Harder Way to Go*—"

"Y'all, that ain't even the latest. Girlfriend's sinking her hooks into someone else. Let's chat about the mystery man who's really behind her whole career, some powerful honcho by all accounts, reportedly superconnected. And he's into a bunch of shady stuff. Gunrunning. Dirty politics. Drug smuggling. Human trafficking."

"Whoa."

"Oh snap."

My lips went dry. I inquired about the ladies' room and escaped into the stuffy hall. I buried my concentration in the script, and I was glad I did.

The casting director's assistant came out and beckoned me to the producers' lair in the wake of Aphrodite.

"Like I said, no one follows an act like that," declared a male voice as I entered the room. It was crass and disrespectful, and it got my dander up. My training kicked into overdrive and I gave a great read, if I say so myself, despite all the stress and the funky impression that somehow the fix was indelibly in. The producers applauded and laid on praise, but you never could tell what such kudos might net. Their cheers could mean thanks, no thanks, we hate your guts, or congrats, you got the job. One never knew which till a paycheck arrived. And one cashed it. And it didn't bounce. So I strode out both demoralized and hopeful, if they could coexist, and I hiked in high heels to the parking lot—where I spotted Aphrodite's car.

It was all too irresistible.

I imagined somebody might key it.

Aphrodite was flapping her gums on her gold cell phone, distracted, tossing her weave. She was licking full lips, rubbing cream on her hands, and stuffing her face with plump green grapes some sex slave probably peeled for her, plucking them out of a baggie. All the gossip about her buzzed in my head like a bee trapped in a mayonnaise jar. Who was she talking to, Mystery Man? Or was she undermining *me* with my agents or who knew who else? She threw back her head in a throaty guffaw. Delighted. Triumphant. *Sinister.*

That did it. I set out to follow the tart. To see what she did, who she met, when and where, just how she was getting her program across. It was easier than I suspected too. I got my cell cam ready. Electrical static sent shocks through my veins as I tailed her from the parking lot and eyeballed her rushing about her day, too self-absorbed and single-purposed to notice me glued to her bumper. It seemed all she could see was what stood in her way as she plowed her ambition over it. I felt silly, but much more intensely than that, I was gripped by fascination. Free to observe her in the act as if I were tuned to *A Day in the Life* on the E! network or OWN.

First she sped out to a nail salon called Talon-ted, off Melrose. Then she flitted a path to the Polo Lounge for lunch with—ain't that a kick in the pants!—none other than Comet Bidwell, the male lead we just auditioned with. She worked him like a full-time job, cracking her lobster, jiggling her boobs, batting her lashes like window shades as I watched from a table across the joint, nursing a bowl of vichyssoise that set me back both arms and legs.

When she kissed him goodbye, she took off for the gym and spent two hours working out while I zonked in my car near a tree at the curb and sipped a Lean Green smoothie. She shopped the boutiques in Century City, hunted for groceries at Bristol Farms, gave a squat man a privilege of pumping her gas, and cut across Sunset to Brentwood into a Spanish-style home I presumed to be hers, as she knew the numerical code to its gates and entered its door with two keys.

It was then I should've gone my way, mortified by what I'd done, recommitted to leading a decent life, controlling curiosity. But instead I let it kill the cat, and therein lies my prime regret.

I waited until she changed her clothes and exited dressed in a red silk gown with a gold sequined purse and real mink shawl, her hairdo piled architecturally high and her feet jammed in towering gold-strapped pumps that induced a decidedly awkward gait but accented her world-class booty. By now I was übercurious, so I whipped out the opera glasses I kept in my glove compartment just in case, a gift from the folks at GBC the first time I'd worked on a series there. Aphrodite flashed a nefarious grin as she slid in her golden Aventador, ambling the Lamborghini south. I hung back as she tooled over Sunset again and wended her way through the gates of Bel-Air to a mansion with a guarded fence. I followed, mouth open, hanging back. Now this was really interesting. Getting closer to Mr. X perhaps? Was she here to meet the mystery man all the fuss was about at the casting call?

My pulse danced a rumba in my chest and roared inside my perking ears. I bit my lip and gripped the wheel. A gaggle of goose bumps pecked my arms and skittered about my craning neck. I was into the thick of the action now, too scared to push forward, too jazzed to turn back as I reached the point of no return and the air got heavier and more humid. It was twilight, the crest of the children's hour. Vivid lavender brushed the aging sunset, segued into a chic hot pink, and morphed into a blood-red evening sky around a skinny moon.

I whiffed eucalyptus and bougainvillea, freesia, pink roses, and cold hard cash as I stalled before the forbidding gates and scoped Aphrodite working her wiles on an undiscerning rent-a-cop. She gazed up at him, revved her motor. He looked at her like she was ice cream and cake.

She drove in. I couldn't stop myself. I dug in the ten-cent recyclable bag in my back seat, whipped on the running shoes I stashed there for emergencies, pulled on a hoodie, and yanked up the hood. I picked up the pizza I ordered while casing my clueless quarry earlier, covering my hairdo with a cap. I crossed the street to a gate with two guards, averted my gaze from the one with the clipboard who'd let Aphrodite in easily, hid my face with a hand and loudly coughed, then barked the word "Delivery!" To my massive relief, he let me in, chuckling, mumbling, "Where's your hooptie, loser? What'd you ride, a bike?" He closed the guard booth, grabbed a tablet, popped a Cheeto in his mouth, wedged his cell between his chin and shoulder, sat down, kicked up both his feet, and resumed a conversation.

The place looked like a swank hotel. With a rotunda, marble stairs, a circular entry, a portico, a driveway that was light-years long, a fountain, and hedges that waved like rolling seas out to a sprawling view. And that was just the guesthouse. It bordered a contemporary-style estate made of glass, cement, and a shady past, that boasted tall walls at surprising angles, set like a pearl on a corner lot. It had to be a quarter of a billion bucks of real estate at least. Four stories. Chopper on the roof. Infinity pool with dozens of loungers. So private its front was completely exposed. Decks jutted everywhere you looked. There were massive outdoor movie screens. A putting green. A bowling alley. Multiple fireplaces lit. Battalions of flowering trees and bushes and plants and a twenty-car garage you could see through from the lower yard.

Some lights were quenched, but a gate gaped open.

I saw Aphrodite forge inside. She looked a little different now. Not wearing a disguise like me but profiled in a wide-brimmed hat and carrying a red gift bag or tote.

I waited, deciding which way to go as I scouted my surroundings.

It was pitch-black on the humongous grounds. Even the glow of the sliver of moon was choked by tall king palms. The growl of a barbarous hound emanated close to me, with clanking chains. But undaunted, bereft of my common sense, I crept around the rotunda in front of the mansion where Aphrodite's Lamborghini idled near a Testarossa and spit-shined Rolls-Royce. The scent of jasmine cloyed the darkness. Crickets chirped. The bushes rustled, making me nearly jump out of my skin. Something, or someone, whizzed past in the duskiness, trampling through the underbrush. A scared rabbit darted across my path, to a hedge of yellow oleanders arced like a sunburst around granite pavers that skirted a sculptured fountain.

A lizard zigzagged around my toes and, startled, I dropped the pizza box, undone by the rapid movements. I thought I heard footsteps in the trees.

Minutes passed that seemed like hours.

I debated whether to stay or leave.

Why was I lingering in this space?

Wouldn't the guards come looking for me?

A man's angry shouts muffled out to the lawn and enticed me to check out the side of the house. I sneaked around, chewing a fingernail, and I hid by a jacaranda tree, craning my ears to attempt to the decipher the words spewing out from a library where two-story shelving rimmed black walls, adorned with gilded leather tomes. A rolling ladder leaned on one tier, anchored to a long brass rail, and multiple Oscars inside a glass case on a mantel above a fireplace reflected dazzling gas-lit flames. Leather and metal sex toys dangled from hooks stuck into wooden rods, and a built-in desk—Lucite and chrome—had iron spikes around the edge. It looked like a set from an S&M flick. *Sixty Shades of Prey.*

Then suddenly I spied a man.

A blond with a tall and spindly build. Raking his hands through tousled hair, blinking sunken, red-rimmed eyes, flailing his arms and ranting, raving, waggling a finger, stomping a foot. I thought I recognized him.

I struggled up onto my tippy toes… and I spotted Aphrodite. Naked. Crying. On her knees. Her left hand cuffed to a table leg. Her red dress flung against the door.

The man reeled right and stormed from sight.

Nearby, the dog barked, yelped, and growled.

I scrambled away, toward the rear of the house on a walk by a stand of cabanas. The back of the home was completely uncurtained, with sheets of uninterrupted glass—the proverbial Hollywood fishbowl. A Jacuzzi bubbled by a bar. From there I could hear every word they said.

"You think you can play me for a fool?" He hit her back-handed with thunderous force, the man Aphrodite was toying with. "I know everyone on the planet."

Her cheek split apart like a rotten peach, blood squirting out like fresh-squeezed juice. "I didn't. No, baby, you don't understand. He's lying. I never gave him squat." The tears from her blackened eyes dissolved her mascara, staining her face like ink.

My palms starting sweating. My stomach lurched. I panicked. I didn't know what to do. I'd left my cell phone in the car when I picked up the pizza box. If I bolted to try to retrieve it now, to call the police and report the abuse, by the time they came, it'd be too late. She might not be alive. And how would I explain my presence? What if they clipped me for trespassing? What if they charged me with stalking? It was too risky. I had to stay out of it. Yet she needed help.

He hit her again, with his fists this time. He took off his belt and whipped her. He picked up a silver water bottle and clubbed her on the head. "I made you. I freaking created your life. You think you can sneak around on me? You whore, don't you know who you're dealing with? I'll crush you like a bug. I'll break you. You're nothing. You're less than dirt!"

"You've gotta believe me. I'm telling the truth… Okay, so I met him a couple of times." Aphrodite cowered and pled her case, cajoled him, beseeched him in soothing tones as she might a wounded animal. "I listened to what they offered, sure, but I didn't betray or abandon you."

"I worshipped the ground you walked on, tramp. And this is how you repay me!" *Wham!* He kicked her in the ribs.

She screamed and retched and doubled over, lifting her arm to protect her face.

I hiccupped and tried to catch my breath. I had to do something. It wasn't too late. *Should I run to alert the guards?* But they worked for him. They'd cover up. Maybe I could knock next door and beg them to call the cops on him. Only, next door was so far away I couldn't even see it. And what were the odds his neighbors would buy my story anyway? A Black woman alone in Bel-Air accusing a wealthy white neighbor they probably knew, or actually probably thought they knew, and identified with totally. I might as well land in their yard in a flying saucer and ask them to call the pound and rat out on their puppy. It'd be Aphrodite's word and mine against his with neighbors or police. And what made me think I could count on Aphrodite? She could sell me out. She could side with her abuser. Then where would I be? In cellblock D. If the shoe were on the other foot, she would stand at the window and film my disgrace and sell it to TMZ.

I considered cutting and running away, erasing everything I'd seen.

And then I heard the growl again. So near I could smell the doggie breath.

I turned in slow motion and shrank from its teeth, the rottweiler poised to pounce on me.

It stared at me and forced me back until I hit a concrete wall, snarling at me just feet away, as dread as the hound of the Baskervilles. *How did it get loose?* I tried to be still and not catch its eye, to lend no resistance, allay its fears so it wouldn't sink its fangs in me.

That's when I heard the shots ring out.

Three pops in succession. *Bang, bang, bang!*

The dog turned sharply, loped away, galloping toward them, on the alert. More shots fired in succession. Baring its teeth, the hound hurled its bulk to a sliding glass door of the library, clawing at it desperately, standing on its strong hind legs. A bank of security lights snapped on. The dog started whining and turned toward me, barreling like a cattle herd.

I immediately scrambled up a tree. When I got to a branch that could hold my weight, I straddled it, knowing I couldn't climb down or the canine would tear me to pieces. All I could do was continue to climb and proceed to scream for help. But who might appear if I started to yell?

I was able to swing from a higher branch to a Juliet balcony one flight up. Its glass door stood ajar and let the night air blow gray curtains. I saw a bedroom, empty, dark. I mounted the glass partition, climbed over the thick chrome railing, stole inside. The bedroom was out of a magazine. As spacious as a grocery store. A queen or a princess could hole up there and never, ever leave the joint. Under different circumstances, I'd have kicked off my shoes to luxuriate.

Not wanting my footsteps heard below, I glided across the hardwood floor as if it were lined with burning coals. I exited the bedroom door to a sprawling loft cum hangout space, with pool tables, board games, a Ping-Pong setup, a wall of candy dispensers, and a bona fide video-game arcade. Lights blinked, but the space looked unoccupied. Beyond it was a dual staircase. I hurried to take the left flight down, descending into a vaulted foyer under darkened skylights.

I heard music coming from one side of the open floor plan main floor zone, seemingly emanating from some area off a great room. I followed the music, silently checking for signs of life from Aphrodite, plucking a fireplace poker from a stand by the great room chimney as I skulked from one sector to the next, each grander than anything I had seen before or might likely glimpse again.

Turning right at a hallway, I eyeballed a seeming non sequitur down at the end of it. It appeared to be a pile of books, on the floor by a double-door entryway. *The library?*

I moved to it. I never should've gone inside.

The monstrosity I viewed when I made that mistake was one I can't shake from my mind, no matter how hard or long I try—Aphrodite, unrecognizable, awash in a veritable sea of blood.

And the man, her abuser, dead beside her, glass-eyed and castrated.

It was a ghastly out-of-body experience, and I fainted.

The next sound I heard was the clang of steel bars as a cell door shut behind me.

In the aftermath, no one listened to me. No one believed or stood by me. My life went down the tubes. The police said I fired a gun, but there was no paraffin on my hands. Their so-called gun was never found. I had no motive, no record, no beef with the victims, no blood stains on my clothes. They were dead, I was found at the scene, and I proffered no logical explanation.

I was vilified and locked away.

At the trial, I was convicted. I got sentenced to capital punishment.

I have less than an hour to live at the moment. All I have is hope.

Time ticks away on death row like there's no such thing. Perhaps there's not. Considering this inhumane, bleak space, who wouldn't tout their innocence? What hurts is, mine is real.

But even if I'd done the deed, two wrongs could never make this right. My death could never bring them back. The public can't wash my blood off their hands, and many wouldn't try.

I have faith, so I resign myself to give over my soul to the love of God in Heaven rather than here on earth, and I pray my misfortune might do some good in whatever convoluted way. I believe all things do work together for good in my heart of hearts.

And yet the deaths still puzzle me. When the shots rang out, I was sure that man killed Aphrodite and would pay. She was a woman half his height, beaten and brutally shot to death. But then, when I saw him lying there, for an instant I figured she'd freed herself and managed to somehow grab a gun—perhaps from the tote she carried in—and murdered her ex-agent, Quentin Leech, before she killed herself. Yet I knew that plot could never be. It was way too far-fetched for that self-centered girl to extinguish her life in that barbarous way.

When the time came for my final meal, I ordered a soup-to-nuts veggie plate from Charred and Soul, the soul food joint, a local down-home eatery. I wanted to patronize the owner/chefs. I'd seen how hard they worked and how freely they gave back.

To administer my last rites, Reverend Shepherd Fuller came around. Yep, the one of TV fame. I figured he'd showed for publicity, but I soon learned in his Bible was a note that bore a watermark and a logo with a red G clef.

"I promised to pass this on to you," the Reverend said in somber tones as he handed me the envelope. Read it. Then I'll take it back. May its sentiment bring you comfort, Nova. You don't deserve any part of this, but I pray you reach a lasting peace in the light and the love of the Lord." He leaned closer and whispered in my ear. "He's sorry. He never intended your plight. He just wanted to get away with it. He thought the case would go unsolved."

I slit the elegant ivory flap with my finger to peruse the script.

Signed in a careful artistic hand, it read:

Thanks for the favor. Eternally. I'll dedicate every song to you.

I owe you,

Sloppy Z.

WITH A CHERRIE ON TOP

HE DIED FACEDOWN IN HIS BIRTHDAY CAKE.
There was finally no denying that his platinum hair was frosted.

Coleman Denoire, CEO of the multinational conglomerate Denoire MaxamediaMania, was a celebrated publisher,
producer, and philanthropist. He was a brilliant writer, en-
trepreneur, and notorious ladies' man, manipulative and
widely feared. His death sent shock waves coast to
coast. So when the news broke that he'd bitten the
big one, Cherrie Baker's goose was cooked. It
was Cherrie who'd baked the princess cake her
client's head plopped into on that fateful day
near the private marina of the King Palm Yacht
and Country Club on the coast of Boca Raton.

Coleman's posse was gathered in Florida, composed of competitors raring to start the boat race that
could win this year's Black Yachtsman Prize, a gold cup award for which they'd
trained, connived, and spent big bucks to snare. They'd been lusting for it
like stallions seeking dates for mating season while they'd toiled long, hun-
dred-hour weeks in winters spent in colder climes. They played even harder
than they worked, these unscrupulous money magnets. For these titans of
industry, losing was neither an option nor a fleeting thought. Winning meant
props, fine women, great press, and wind in the hair they no longer possessed.
Their egos ran wild, and they got their way ninety-nine percent of the time.

It was Labor Day, time to celebrate, and in keeping with fifty years of
proud tradition, the Denoire Regatta dotted the raging sea beyond the beach,
in a line at the harbor's edge, like Helvetica print on a title page. The morning sky was crisp, a gusty gray, and churning with cumulus clouds that hov-
ered low and ominous. The wind was up, the tide was high, and the deal was
about to go down.

Coleman awoke with a start from a bad dream just as a butter pat of sun
arose to herald a humid dawn. He yawned and then began to sing, "It's

your birthday. It's your birthday. Go Coley, it's your birthday." He wriggled his hips, lying flat on his back, gyrating to the tune of the 50 Cent rap song "In da Club." He loved that cut. He would play it tonight in three clubs he owned: Twerk City in Miami Beach, Left Coast on the shore in Los Angeles, and the C-Note in Chicago. Birthday Boy was in his element, every chiseled muscle rippling in his pressed red silk pajamas. He fondled himself with a loving caress, running his hands over taut, lean flesh as he stretched spread-eagle in slippery satin sheets on his circular waterbed. The bed was imported, of African teak, the jewel of his all-white stateroom on his boat, the *Carpe Seas 'Em.*

Cole's yacht was a floating metropolis. The three-hundred-foot luxury vessel looked like a cross between a Viking ship and *Star Wars's Millennium Falcon.* All the walls were decked out with photos of Cole himself or flawless plate glass mirror, including the ceiling above his bed.

Coleman gazed at himself, moaned deep in his throat, and started to suck his thumb.

At forty years old this very day, he was six feet, five inches of awesomeness. He bore two hundred pounds under supple skin that looked as if it were carved from mahogany—tough, tight, tanned, and a reddish brown as smooth as chocolate Häagen-Dazs. He had legendary coal-black eyes that twinkled like two shooting stars, and he was able to pump up the wattage of his blue-white smile to a blinding glare as bright as any noonday sun, like some earthbound sun god banished beneath to suffer lesser mortals. He radiated charisma, lightning wit, and boatloads of winning charm, and he had a sense of humor when he wasn't terrorizing folks. He intimidated friend and foe, the latter the most likely. No one took Coleman for a fool, even when he was one. He did unto others before they could do unto him, which was his motto. Cole was the most-envied, least-wanted guy on any guest list everywhere—from the Gold Coast to the Ivory Coast—and his body had the scars to prove it.

Cole had fought his way not only to the top but through amazing fistfights. One huge, gnarled hand alone could stop a freight train in its tracks. He had ginormous knuckles that resembled dried-up purple plums, and his mythic online bio said they'd resulted from baby boxing. It revealed how his parents, in drunk and drugged stupors, had tossed him from their moving car at the tender age of two years old and left him on the London Bridge. When a white boxing trainer came along with his wife and kids, he scooped

Cole up and made him fight every day and night for purses Coleman never saw, pitting the boy against older kids in illegal bouts in British slums until Cole ran away at eight with bulbous thumbs he sucked for comfort's sake for the rest of his natural life.

Cole was proud of himself for surviving that and for sailing to America on his own in the hull of a freighter. A stowaway. A throwaway. Coleman was psyched about what he became. A citizen. A businessman. A hero kids could look up to. A man who gave at every turn. A sage and a provider. He stood tall and erect, his shoulders back, his rippling ribs and chest thrust out, his washboard stomach so concave that, along with his long and lanky limbs, he sometimes lent the appearance not of a man but of a stalwart tree from a deep, enchanted forest.

What little remained of Cole's crinkly hair was dyed a shimmery platinum blond in a haircut curved in a horseshoe, faded along the sides and back with a money-green tuft atop the crown, shaped like a tilting elm tree leaf. Cole was a cartoon character wielding socioeconomic power as a sword, entrée, reward, defense, enticement, aphrodisiac, and existential threat.

People feared Cole, as well they should, and they didn't even know the half of it. But soon all his secrets were bound to come out. Cole's rubber was meeting the road.

Things kicked into gear with a phone call from Cole's grim ex-wife DeNeedra, the first of "The Fearsome Four" ex-wives Cole wed and shed in just twelve years.

"Denoire," Cole barked at his iPhone, rolling his eyes at who the call was from.

"We found her, Coley. This is it. Get ready. Talk will not be cheap. She—"

"Needra, don't be dramatic. I should've never picked up this call. Why are you starting with me already? Where are you ringing from, your cell?"

"I'm on my landline… Oops. Forgot. Oh yeah. I'll call you back." A rustle on DeNeedra's end.

"Why bother? You may as well spill it now. You've alerted whomever may tap the line."

"I'd better come over then, hadn't I?" A tickle of cheer in DeNeedra's voice.

"Why not? You blew my birthday high. You might as well ruin the whole damn day."

"I'm on the way. I'll make it up," she crowed. "You won't be sorry."

"I already am. Just hurry up… and keep your big trap shut, you hear?"

DeNeedra tittered. "Yes, Your Heinie."

"Call me that one more time and see what happens to your credit cards. If one word of this drama hits a Walmart checkout stand, I'll wring your neck. If the rag sheets get ahold of it, there's going to be a bloodbath and your stipend is the first to go. I'm tired of your foolishness."

"Okay, okay. I'm sorry. Damn." DeNeedra became a coquette, albeit a disingenuous one. "Hey, perk up. Happy birthday, Cole. I even got you something, boo."

"All you can get me is out of this bind." Cole hit the End Call icon, groaned, stalked over to his balcony, and punched the polished handrail. "I wish I'd never met that broad."

DeNeedra Denoire cut the price tag off her Prada purse with a careless snip. She zipped up her tight leopard Dior dress and wriggled her perfectly pedicured feet into matching Jimmy Choos. "All right, let's see that mover and shaker maneuver his way out of *this* big mess," she snarled. With a toss of her weave and a swish of the junk in her trunk, she swept through the double glass doors at the head of the winding staircase, hovering over her pale-pink living room, calling down toward her foyer. "Benton." There was no answer. "Benton!" she yelled and sucked her teeth. "Where are you now?" she huffed, descending wide steps with a wobble on towering heels. Making her way through the twelve-million-dollar seaside estate she won from Cole in their hotly contested divorce ten years ago, she looked around. "Ben-ton!" She screamed as cold as a Slurpee, sharp as a steak knife, shrewd as a portfolio of long-held blue-chip stocks. And out of nowhere, her man appeared. Her protégé, arm candy, boy toy, burning cross to bear.

Benton was as tantalizing as he was a flake. The rock-hard nude with an attitude stood munching a raw Vidalia onion, swallowing its peel. "What?" he droned. No eye contact.

"Put on some clothes," DeNeedra scoffed with a withering glare of frustration.

"Why?" Benton whined. "Don't you like what you see?" He struck a bodybuilder pose.

"Of course I do. That's not the point. Aren't you supposed to be out on a job interview?"

"They went another way," he said. His tone was as flat as an ironing board. "You need to cough up my allowance, Dee."

"How old did you say you were again?" she asked under her breath as she clutched her purse, so resigned and barely audible that even she failed to hear her words. "I'll make a deposit this afternoon. Get moving; we're going out," she demanded, her nine-hundred-dollar footwear clicking across the marble atrium floor and clattering back to the vestibule with the urgency of an ambulance, the wide brim of her black mesh hat bobbing down in her face as she strode to the door. Her mate was becoming so tiresome. But then, too, he was prone to be violent. She'd have to move out to get rid of him, and that tactic might not help. *How did everything spiral so out of control?* she thought. "One thing at a time," she muttered, weighing a still more grave concern.

The funkiest chore must be handled first—and she had to make Coley do it.

Coleman Denoire had a plan of his own. He showered, shaved, shampooed, and showed up on deck in a flurry of white silk pants and a white shirt open to his waist. He was sockless, wearing his bone Prada loafers, a white captain's cap, a gold belt and his trademark grin.

Two of his former fraternity buddies, sponsors of the regatta, had jetted in the night before, into quarters on the aft deck. Cole was unable to greet them then and he figured they'd be starving now. Ready to meet some party girls. One of his friends was up on deck.

"Hey-ho!" Coleman greeted his waiting guest. "You can always tell a Morehouse Man."

"You just can't tell him much," was the retort from Austin Whitmore. He turned to clap Cole on the back, and the friends launched into a complicated, old-school college handshake. Coleman's onetime Morehouse roommate laughed, rushed into a warm bear hug, bowed with a flourish, tipped his hat, and topped it all off with a fist bump.

Coleman mock-socked him on the jaw and headed to the bow. "Ready?"

"Man, you know I am. I can't wait to sail out on the open seas. The stress is real, my brutha."

"Yeah, same here. I feel you, bro." Cole sized up Whitmore with a frown. "Packed on a few pounds since last year, huh?"

"I'm good. The ladies like it."

"Uh-uh, that's not what I hear, man. Work out twice a day like me," Cole boasted. "Stay in shape. The ladies like to run your stats. They google your gig, your bank account, your weight, blood pressure, former squeezes, even what condoms you deploy. They're liable to test your urine and your stool before they give you some. You can't look like you're about to croak and try to score a hookup, dude. You're supposed to be my wingman."

Whitmore winced, sucked in his gut. Austin was a Horatio Alger. Born on the east side of Houston, Texas, he was now the CEO of the largest advertising specialties company in the world, his revolutionary engraving patents earning a share of every personalized pen, flash drive, tote, cap, key chain, magnetic business card, phone case, and any other swag gift you could use to build goodwill. He was a cattle baron, too, but as wealthy as he was, he hoarded. Name it, and he acquired it. Cash. Food. Women. Homes. Fast cars. Jet planes. He couldn't get enough. And he was a well-known skinflint too, notorious for being a tightwad, a character flaw Cole now observed reflected in his tattered garb—an ill-fitting seersucker leisure suit, cheap plastic watch, taped dime-store shades and run-down Payless deck shoes. His chili bowl haircut looked like it was trimmed with a Weedwacker.

Coleman crinkled his nose and wagged his head.

"What?" Whitmore boomed with protruding lips that claimed he was indignant.

"A thrift store having a blowout sale?"

"Ha-ha, very funny," Whitmore said as the tips of his ears turned ruby red. "I don't happen to think clothes make the man. My grandma says clotheshorses git rode hard and put up wet. Them gold diggers spot 'em a mile away."

"Speaking of gold diggers, Dee's coming over." Coleman adjusted his captain's cap.

"I thought this was supposed to be boys' day out." Austin turned his head toward shore. "But it's cool. I really don't see your problem. You shoulda probably stuck with Dee. Divorce didn't do you no good but to set you up to get robbed by the next one. You shouldn't'a let that filly bolt, cowboy. She's way too fine. Besides, you've saddled up three more mares since her and ain't won no Triple Crown. At least Dee hangs in there with you… You never did know which side your cornbread's buttered on, if you ask me."

"I didn't ask you, Oprah."

Whitmore bristled, glanced around. "You git that other mess cleared up?"

"Nah, not yet. I'm trying, but she's—"

"Stubborn as stink on a cow chip, huh? If you need any help with that—"

"Hey-ho!" Lance Fairgood hit the deck, bee-bopping, doling out high fives. Lance's voice was deep and dulcet, giving off announcer vibes. A suave TV news anchor in from LA, he was West Coast chic in tailored jeans, suede jacket, and sky-blue linen shirt with notches in the collar. "Breaking news, it's vacay time." He reached to grab a fishing pole. "Whatever's got you debutantes' bras twisted, let it go. Shop talk is canned till further notice. A weekend of fun and frolic is officially declared."

"Some of us still have to work for a living," Whitmore protested and slapped his neck. "Ouch! These darn mosquitoes. Dang."

"Like you guys punch a time clock. Huh. You zillionaires. You make me cry. If I had a penny for every grand you make, I'd take a permanent vacation, not just three short days." Lance rubbed his corrugated abs, breathed deep, drank in the ocean. He was a creamy caramel brown with cashmere eyes, full kiss-me lips, and nuclear sexual energy, sporting hip Aviator shades and a package so huge between his legs that the ladies all called him "the Organ." Sun gleamed like floor wax off his flesh and glinted like solar flares off curly hair and mile-long eyelashes. His butt looked like two metal bowling balls. He rubbed his tummy. "Yo, I could eat a dinosaur. Let's call the chef. It's time to grease."

Cherrie Baker was racing as usual. Not like the boaters Coleman raced—that was a dream she hoped came true—but around her small chef's kitchen. *Oh, why can't I ever be on time?* she thought as she scurried to pack one last food tray and snap its cover. It wasn't that she was lazy or disorganized or slow, she figured, just that she had tons to do. And she got a late start from an early run, hot yoga, and meditation that she wouldn't miss for anything. But Mr. Denoire was a promptness freak who wouldn't be pleased with tardiness or hesitate to say so.

Chef Baker's catering business, Cherrie on Top, was serving a yacht today. The *Carpe Seas 'Em*. That was huge—both for the honor of being its chef for the race and the superyacht's staggering size. Four decks of luxurious opulence. Seven decked-out staterooms. Two pools and a Jacuzzi. A workout room that was better equipped than Cherrie's public gym. The indulgent spa had beauty parlors, nail salons, massage booths, mud baths, saunas, facials, waxing stations, braiders, and even a liposuction room with a floating, concierge plastic surgeon. Guests got IV treatments too. The yacht had a chapel, movie theatre, game room, lounge, confessional, and a racquetball court that was lit at night. In the huge master suite, the ceiling rolled back to reveal the sky and stars above a revolving circular waterbed on a Congolese pedestal made of gold. Two dining rooms and a great room served innumerable guests in palatial settings. One had a silver-leaf ceiling, and the other had walls with lighting panels cycling vivid colors. Sofas as long as football fields were elsewhere on the colossal decks, with waterfalls and sculptures.

Cherrie knew she only got the job because of a dire emergency. And of course, because she knew Denoire. Cole's usual chef had a Michelin star rarely given to African American chefs. When the chef got stopped for a broken taillight which, by the way, was a bogus charge, an encounter ensued that landed the chef not only in jail but also into a week-long stay in a hospital room with a broken jaw, three busted ribs, a dislocated clavicle, and grave internal injuries. The doctors said he was lucky to be alive beyond the choke hold.

Cherrie had tried to visit Chef Malveaux inside the ICU, but only family was allowed. That didn't Cole though. He promised to pay the chef's hospital bills and refurbish the children's wing and wards, and that generous gesture opened doors. Cole visited at will.

Cherrie wasn't familiar with Malveaux's crew, which normally consisted of only three but today would be supplemented by more servers for the birthday fest—deckhands as well as bartenders. But the regulars resented Cherrie landing in the head chef spot. They were an all-male, tight-knit clique that chafed at taking orders. Nonetheless, she was whipping them into shape. The galley crew prepared to serve goose liver mousse in duck-skin rolls; shrimp pâté with crudités; a stone crab bisque in warm bread bowls; coconut shrimp and deep-fried oysters; brie macaroni with truffle crumbs; grilled lobster tails with cornbread stuffing; Waldorf salad; collard greens; and a fountain of cold key-lime fondue.

This gig was Cherrie's dream come true. Well, part of her vision anyway. Yacht catering brought adventure, new opportunities, and boatloads of fun. It gave her a cool side hustle too. To supplement her income, she took pictures in far-off locales and did some travel writing. But her weeks on the sea held no romance. She couldn't date on board.

Her friends called her the M&M, male magnet, and she was. But attracting men could bring her trouble. She didn't need any drama now. With loans to pay off to the CIA—the Culinary Institute—and her website needing an overhaul, she was working on a cookbook and was eager to buy equipment to shoot videos of her recipes. More importantly, her nonprofit had to raise a ton of cash. She farmed organic vegetables to feed the homeless on the street and envisioned an international soup kitchen. Cole could help.

Cherrie scurried into the shower and zoomed through her usual facial regimen, donning a winning natural look from the palettes in her Lancôme gift-with-purchase makeup clutch. Her disarming, almond-shaped doe eyes began watering, and she realized she was tearing up from all the stress. It was silly, she knew, but it happened sometimes when she recalled the instances she'd failed, and she suffered a loss of confidence just when she needed spunk the most. She mused on what Nakia would do. And Shuri, from *Black Panther*. They'd brave it, do what they had to do for their own good and Wakanda's. "Wakanda forever!" Cherrie proclaimed, crossing her forearms against her chest. She worked to tame her bushy mane to mitigate a bad hair day by pinning a band of fresh hibiscus around her massive, curled coiffeur. She snuck a quick peek through her rear French doors to the flowers, pots of herbs and spices, fruits, and colorful vegetables in her thriving little garden.

She learned a lot from how plants grew. Persistence. Adaptability. How to go with the flow to survive. Much of her spiritual journey traveled through her bushes and green grass.

Distracted when her cell alarmed, she shuddered and nearly jumped out of her skin, but the loud tune served to speed her up, and she wriggled her mile-long legs into a pair of jean cut-offs. She slid on a pair of pink stilettos, stuffed her girls into a halter top, grabbed a clean chef uniform, and loaded up her car. She slammed the red hatch of her Audi crossover, ran to the driver's seat, hopped inside.

A lightning bolt. A thunderclap. Angry charcoal clouds squalled overhead above a wind-whipped drizzle. South Florida style. A downpour. She backed from her driveway with a screech and glanced at the digital dashboard clock.

It was seven a.m. *Late again,* she thought as she yanked the wheel and gunned the gas.

Coleman's going to kill me.

DeNeedra parked her custom Tesla. "This could take a while," she purred, tossing an iPad in Benton's lap. "I loaded more cash in your iTunes account."

"Cool," he replied, slouching down in his seat and rolling down his window. "Tell Coleman I said not to mess you around or he's going to have to deal with *me.*"

"Yes, Benton. I'm sure he'll be terrified."

Benton blew a bubble with his gum and recoiled as Dee leaned to the passenger seat and popped him on his chops. Wiping his lips on his hoodie sleeve, he reached over and opened the driver's door. "Tell him he should've invited us to his birthday bash to show respect."

Dee pulled the door handle and rolled her eyes as she wrestled her plaid Burberry umbrella into the rain with a yip and shriek, wind whipping her body back and forth while she sidestepped deepening puddles. Holding on for dear life to the flapping crown of the hat she'd just bought on Worth Avenue, she scrambled toward the slippery dock. Sighting a deckhand, she stopped and waved. "Ahoy!" she yelled in a piercing timbre, snagging a heel between wood dock planks. She recovered her balance and climbed the gangplank, licking her lips conspicuously.

Coleman winced. "Oh, Needra, please. Don't embarrass yourself. Don't embarrass *me*."

"What, jealous? You're lucky I bothered to come… considering you didn't invite us."

"Here we go," said Austin, backing away, a couple of cans of beer in hand.

"Hi, Dee," Lance offered, taking her hand and ushering her along a rail.

Dee emitted a girlish giggle. "Hey, Lance, you're looking extra well." She ran her hand down Lance's shirt then steamed toward Coleman with a scowl, the cracks in her face-lifted visage regrettably rearing their ugly heads.

"Excuse us, fellas," Coleman groaned. "We need to go below."

"But I was going to watch the show," drawled Whitmore, baiting his fishing rod. "I was going to pop corn and everything."

"Believe me, this won't take that long." Cole signaled Dee to go below, and the happy couple left.

As Whitmore plopped down in a deck chair, covering his face with his secondhand, ten-gallon hat, he peeked out from the side of it. "I wouldn't mind being a fly on the wall."

Lance cast off his fishing pole. "Not me. I might get swatted."

Dee settled herself in a cushy chair in the soundproof foredeck viewing room and blew her ex an air kiss. "You might want to take a seat for this. It isn't a very nice birthday gift."

"Cut to the chase. Quit playing games." Cole tugged his ex-wife's arm.

"Let me go. You're hurting me. You can edit your employees, but you'll never censor me." Dee snatched her arm back, stuck out her tongue, kicked off her shoes, and jeered. "You'd better go down and shut *her* up!"

"What's that supposed to mean?" Cole asked.

"She was spotted last night in a fifty-foot sloop moored off the coast of the Caymans."

"Is she stashing the cash?"

"Yup, laundering your *ass*-ets. Taking your butt to the cleaners, Coley." DeNeedra threw back her head and howled.

"How dare she!" Coleman ranted, pacing, boat shoes stomping the hardwood floor.

"Really? How dare she? That's your reaction?" DeNeedra's eyes were blazing. "*You* chose to sleep with that Batwoman, Coley. *You* took her into your bed and your empire. *You* gave that hussy your brand and your billions. You can only blame yourself!"

Cole stiffened. "What are we going to do?"

"We? Now it's 'we'? I'll tell you what. I plan to get what's mine, that's what, and leave you to scramble the egg on your face with that size two, so-called chef you hired. Or whatever rando you sleep with next indiscriminately, big boy. We? Well, ain't that a kick in the butt. Wait. Let me crank up my iPhone cam. I feel a livestream coming on. There is no we, not anymore. Now there's just you with your selfish whims and me with the brunt of the consequences. Well, I'll tell you one damn thing—this dire disaster won't happen to me."

Coleman reluctantly tilted his head, hoping a puppy-dog look might work. "Meaning?"

"Meaning, you still can—"

"What?"

DeNeedra raised a plucked eyebrow.

"Can what?" Cole repeated, averting his gaze, freezing so it could be her idea for the dastardly deed he had in mind.

"You can clear up this horrendous mess. You can save everything we've worked so hard for. This is your chance to secure our holdings, our company, our future, our freedom, our lives. We have an empire to protect. I'm not losing your good name!" The skin on her face squinched to a prune. "Go blow that bitch out of the water, Coley. Do it. Get it done right now."

The cabin temperature dipped so far that it actually made Cole shiver. His features took on a strained aspect, a look of great wonder, a hint of surprise, and a newborn admiration. "You never cease to amaze me, Dee. What are you saying?"

"You heard me," she purred. The avenging feline stalked her quarry, circling him with lethal purpose, rubbing her leopard dress on him. A lioness licking cornered prey, she nuzzled her mouth in his hollow cheekbone, parted her liposuctioned thighs, and positioned her knee between his legs. She shoved him off-balance into a chair, sidled her booty astride his lap, and dug her acrylic manicure into the bulge of his awakening crotch. "Let's do it," she bade his receptive ear, working him like a full-time job. "Come on, baby, do it. Do it. You don't need anyone else but me." Chanting that mantra, she fondled his manhood just as she had on the night he proposed. "I want you, baby. Gimme some. Do me, Coley. Do me now."

Despite his commitment to "never again," Cole made love-hate in a torrid blast that rocked the boat more ways than one. And while in a moment of great ex-lust, his passion swelled like ocean whitecaps as the yacht swayed to and fro, he grunted, "She's. As. Good. As. Gone."

The contract went out a half hour later. Twenty grand, cash. Ten large up front. No mistakes. No corpus delicti. No one could know or could ever find out. There'd be plausible deniability for Coleman and DeNeedra. Six degrees of separation. The dirty deed could be done by any means necessary. Fast. And the hit man would have to send shots of the victim's blood and guts to seal the deal and prove that the target was out of Cole's hair for good. Obliterated.

Hours later, when the guests arrived, Cherrie's crew was in shipshape, delivering a scrumptious feast and a theme of birthday-boy decor. Molecular gastronomy produced Kahlúa Krispies cocktails, Coleman's signature birthday drink. Everybody loved it. Oversized zucchinis that were carved like little catamarans floated in foaming dill dip heavily laced with Bajan rum. A black Poseidon sculpture spewed a geyser gushing chilled Cristal as conch shells laden with caviar and other delicious delectables festooned the interior gold salon. Only the top-tier guests dined there, where the main course elicited rousing cheers and a booming round of applause.

Partiers reveled with hot hors d'oeuvres and a cold buffet that stretched along the stern for more than twenty feet. Guests cut through Cherrie's party fare like Sherman through Atlanta. She'd never been so gratified and stressed out all at once. Coleman ordered for ninety, but over thrice that number crammed the dock. Some without invites made it through while others looked on from the shore amid a throng of thirsty paparazzi. The birthday bash was in full swing. Loud music rang out from the upper deck—from rap to pop to R&B, provided by stars who topped the charts. It wasn't a crowd you could disappoint. VIPs. CEOs. MVPs. MBAs. An alphabet soup of dignitaries, from the richest software kings to presidents of fast-food chains to soft-drink moguls, sports team owners, sheiks, emirs, politicos and famous royal couples. There were ballers, rappers, movie stars, directors, writers, diamond dealers, models, designers, architects. Even a serial killer came.

Oh my gosh! thought Cherrie. Think of the business referrals. I'm pulling it off. Potential clients everywhere. A social network hunting ground. Good thing I brought my business cards. Then again, I don't want to come off like I'm desperate or trying to come up or anything. Oblivious to the eyes on her, all the men who were hungry to get to her, who were drooling as they watched her work, she focused on her princess cake dessert—the pièce de résistance.

When a plane swooped down from overhead and circled the boat, all heads looked up at the banner it was towing. It read HAPPY BIRTHDAY, COLE DENOIRE! SMOOTH SAILING IN YOUR REGATTA. The plane bore Austin's birthday gift, and it dropped a school of shark piñatas bearing advertising goods engraved with Coleman's logo. These items would be treasured status symbols bearing bragging rights. Mementos of the most exclusive shindig of the season. They were also the cue to cut the cake, and that had to go off without a hitch. But there wasn't one deckhand to be spared or even located in the crowd. Cherrie had to jump it off alone to do it timely.

She changed into flats and hurried below, her sandals slapping hand-hewn stairs. A warm, moist wind shot through her hair, and she felt her do frizz up. *Keep moving,* she told herself, *almost done.* But a crashing wave attacked the hull. The boat lurched. *What was that?* From a porthole, a spray of salt water shot onto her face and took her breath away. Her stomach griped. A dizzy spell. Swell after swell rocked the superyacht like a kidnapper robbing a cradle. One doozy after another hit, shifting her from side to side. Cherrie broke into a cold sweat, getting a tummy cramp. A wave of nausea. Why didn't she have the sous chef's help? Where on earth was he anyway, up on deck? Last she saw of him, he was dancing. She suddenly longed to get off the boat, to leave with Cole's fat check in hand but, shaking, she reached the galley floor.

The cake the jittery chef cooked up was mounted on a metal cart in a walk-in fridge at the end of the galley. State of the art, this sucker was. More high-end than she'd dared to dream.

When Cherrie opened the cold room, there it was, and it was a work of art more lovely than a wedding cake. She ventured in to look at it and found herself impressed. It was blue, decorated with buttercream frosting, marzipan icing, starfish made of gold meringue, edible African Neptune treats, and a replica of the Denoire Regatta trophy perched on top.

Prinsesstårta, Cole had called it with a grin from ear to ear. He'd tasted one like it in Sweden with a regal Swedish mistress. Cherrie knew little of their affair, but Cole described the cake enough for Cherrie to put her spin on it. She called overseas to bakeries, charmed recipes out of master chefs, replicated them then created one herself that beat them all. Cole sampled it and said so. She wanted the cake to be special for him. He was giving her a break.

Cherrie opened a box of handmade birthday candles she'd commissioned. With the box in one hand, she climbed onto the counter, riding a gently cresting wave, to arrange forty candles on the cake, in the holders she baked inside it. But just as she tried to insert the last candle, the boat tipped with a violent lurch, knocking her onto the floor and slamming her head on a sharp brass grate. *Ow!* A pain shot down her spine.

The refrigerator door began to close. *Oh no, don't lock me in!*

Cherrie swung out her leg in the nick of time and managed to catch the heavy door, one foot between the door and the door frame holding the door ajar. She lifted herself with stabbing pain, gasping, trying to suck in air. Her back hurt like a toothache. She steadied herself, one hand on the doorknob, the other one gripping the cake cart handle, easing it toward the exit.

The boat swayed again, nearly toppling the cart. Cherrie balanced the cart against her hip, lifting a knee to keep it level, doing her best to save the cake by maneuvering the dolly through the door, her back beginning to spasm. Another wave hit, and thrown off-balance, she groped for the handle of a drawer and hobbled through the doorjamb. But the boat lurched just as she grabbed ahold, and the knob broke off in Cherrie's hand, the force of the handle tearing loose, catapulting her from the tipping cart and sending her flying away from the cake it took her four whole days to make. She sailed the full length of the granite counter, scraping her ear on the oven hood, banging her arm on the microwave and bouncing off a pantry door as she slid across the marble floor like James Brown doing the Slide.

The yacht wavered and stilled. She sighed relief. Heart hammering, she turned to check the cake. It was nothing short of miraculous. The princess cake survived. She laughed. *What a ludicrous stroke of luck.* But her body was so racked with pain, she had the sinking feeling that good luck was a fleeting phenomenon she would not soon sense again.

Blade "the Mangler" Murphy flashed his boarding pass at the flight attendant. Seat 6B. First class, of course. That time he got hired and stuck in coach, his client got stuffed in a laundry bag and swan-dived to the ocean floor with the loser he'd paid Blade to ice. That was after Blade smashed his knuckles, erased his face with a whirring Dremel tool, and ran his guts and pancreas through a juicer Blade bought off TV while watching a late-night infomercial. Surprising how good that appliance was. You could drink a guy down like a smoothie after the Master Blaster whipped him up. Blade really enjoyed that part of hits. People's organs didn't taste half-bad when you blended them with Sriracha sauce and salted the rim of your cocktail glass.

Blade couldn't wait to taste this broad. The contract was gonna be superfun. They faxed a foxy photo. *Bam!* The chick was really hot. A Barbie doll. In the Caymans, no less. All expenses paid. A-ticket ride. *The last casket closed is a rotten egg,* Blade mused and entered the jumbo jet.

The Mangler stowed his carry-on, fastened his seat belt, scanned for air marshals, saw no would-be terrorists. You never could tell these friggin' days.

Can't be too careful, the Mangler thought. *There's a lotta sick puppies out here.*

It was Coleman's big moment in the sun. He was the hub of the universe, the master of all he surveyed, a lodestar shedding blinding light. He was every man's ultimate fantasy life in the flesh for all to see. Cole was richer than Snickers Bar Chunk cheesecake, as fine as wine, his mirror said, a bachelor-to-be, and very soon free of his long-suffered wifely headache. Twenty grand was a bargain price to pay. He would gladly have coughed up twice that much. Two hundred guests sang his birthday song, accompanied by a twelve-piece band and a multiplatinum recording artist who flagrantly blew off a leg of her sold-out tour to serenade him.

Denoire made a wish.

He blew out the candles.

He cut a big slice of his princess cake as everyone looked on.

Cherrie fed him a bite with a silver fork from a plate that had his name on it.

He savored the flavor, licked his lips, and burst out in a grin.

"To my health!" Coleman toasted, raising his glass.

Then, two hours later, he keeled over. Dead. In his third slice of Prinsesstårta.

Blade and his Hasselblad camera checked into the swanky Cay Isle Arms Resort on the beach along Camana Bay, under the alias Jean-Claude Saint Clare. Jean-Claude was a real nice touch, *n'est ce pas*? It gave him sort of a Haitian flair that'd hopefully throw the law off his scent and maybe get him laid. Island girls fell for exotic dudes. Blade heard that from a Jamaican legionnaire he met in Syria on a recent mercenary gig.

Suite 337 overlooked crystalline sand and swaying palm trees by a pale turquoise stretch of Caribbean Sea. An unimpeded view. Yeah, it was more like Blade's jam here. The Caymans life. Real sweet. Forget that Pacific Ocean crap. There were too many tourists, too much chatter. People were not to be seen nor heard. Some square might recognize you.

The desk clerk done him right this time. He was gay, and he said he liked Blade's look. He'd pay for that crack later on. The dumbass bellman tried to snatch the case Blade pulled from the limousine, its contents consisting of weapons so sophisticated and cutting edge they were meant for Blade's eyes only. Grabbing it cost the bellman his tip, but at least he stayed alive. He was fortunate that, when he showed Blade his suite, the joint was laid out like Blade liked it.

Man, if Blade's Pops could see him now. Blade's father worked in a coal mine. All those suckers down there got treated bad, but the African American miners, who could hardly cop a job at all as racist as fossil fuel giants could be, got treated so much worse. They comprised just over four percent and many of them died. Blade's Pops was a good man, treated bad. He got black lung at thirty-six. When he croaked, all he left was a hunk of pyrite Pops swore up and down was gold, an impossible stack of unpaid bills, and a woman with a broken heart and five kids she worked three jobs to feed—and that was mostly grits, spuds, Spam, or Lucky Charms "without no milk."

Blade wasn't goin' out like Pops. Nope, not even close. That's why twenty-seven other poor slobs bit before their time. And nine more deaths were yet to come—to total one soul for every year Blade's Pops roamed Earth in misery. That's what brought Blade to these shores of the Cayman Valhalla's sexy surf-side suite, where a bottle of Bombay Sapphire leaned in a bucket on a table next to a dozen yellow roses in a crystal Tiffany vase.

Blade had a thing for yellow roses.

They symbolized broken relationships.

One would be breaking very soon.

Blade was gonna break it.

An iridescent sunset preened like a peacock through the gauze curtains of the deluxe adjacent room. On a breeze, its drapes began to billow as its terrace doors unlocked. Blade's hit lay sprawled out on a floral-print bedspread, dozing in suite 339, her cocoa curves caressed by a white chiffon gossamer negligee. The scent of cassava cake from her breath was mixed with a whiff of jasmine oil that circled the woman's delicate frame like an undulating serpent.

The air became thick with a pungent smell. *Was it garlic? Chives?* She couldn't tell, but the stench was intoxicating.

Blade sniffed her bouquet by the balcony doors… where he lay in wait.

DeNeedra was getting on Cherrie's nerves. In the three long hours since Cole's death, the first Mrs. Denoire acted aggrieved, her blabbermouth spewing epithets at supersonic speed. DeNeedra was neither taking nor making life easy on anyone on the yacht. The boat was quarantined. Dee's wild accusations flew at will, their venom increasingly virulent and aimed at Cherrie most of all. It appeared at first glance to authorities that Coleman had been poisoned. Chef Cherrie baked the princess cake. "The killer dessert," Dee called the treat, also known as the murder weapon. Thanks to DeNeedra's finger-pointing, Cherrie seemed the prime suspect. By feigning being the inconsolable ex, Dee deflected the blame.

The regatta was canceled, naturally, to the clear chagrin of participants. Never mind that their object of envy was killed right in front of their eyes by an unknown assailant, one who at present remained at large, perhaps among them on the boat. The fun was done. That bummed them out. The trophy would not be awarded. Some guests sat in shock, some in abject fear, some in the midst of the first stage of grief, some feeling in the crosshairs. All the guests were effectively suspects, especially considering most were Black, their skin tones weaponizing them, their profiles conferring baseless guilt unsupported by any evidence.

The *Carpe Seas 'Em* yacht was mobbed. The resultant hubbub of first responders was instant, inescapable. Police. Paramedics. Reporters. Onlookers. Media swarmed like honeybees.

The cops forced Cherrie down into the galley and raked her over the coals.

One grilled her like a swordfish steak. "So it was you who baked the cake?" asked a cop in a cheap, tan, wrinkled suit. Detective Diggs was short, thick, brown, pugnacious, and implacable, with a bulldog's glare in the beady eyes of a face like a shar-pei puppy.

"Yes, sir," Cherrie said with widened eyes.

"And you claim you didn't harm Denoire?"

"No. Not on purpose. I never would… Did a bad egg get in the buttercream?"

"Oh, a bad egg is responsible, all right." Diggs wagged a finger.

"Salmonella?" Cherrie exploded in tears, her face a mask of innocence.

"Try cyanide." Diggs moved closer in.

"Cyanide?! That could kill someone."

"You think?" Diggs quipped. "It killed Denoire. And someone deliberately put it there."

Cherrie's eyes registered deepening dread, her grave situation sinking in. "You think I—"

"Where did you bake the cake?"

"At home. In my kitchen."

"How long did it take?"

"Four days, including the decoration."

"When did you bring the cake onto the yacht?" Diggs burrowed in and pursed his lips.

"A lot of guests ate it, and they didn't die. Why would I—?"

"Answer the question, miss."

Cherrie sniffled, wiped her nose. "But I couldn't. I wouldn't—"

"What time was it?" Diggs asked, his timbre harsher still. "Folks kill for lots of reasons."

Cherrie straightened her back and raised her chin. "I didn't deliver the cake. A driver came over to pick it up. I finally finished it yesterday, and Mr. Denoire sent a limousine. I saw it below in the galley fridge this morning when I boarded."

Diggs backed off, stroked his stubbly beard. "So you didn't transport the cake yourself? It was out of your hands overnight last night?" Scratching his head, he advanced to a balcony, turning his face up toward the sun. "This driver you claim picked up the cake, do you know him?" he asked with his back to the chef.

"No, Officer." Cherrie swallowed.

"Detective," Diggs corrected, turning around and stalking back inside.

"Detective. Sorry."

"Think hard now. Are you certain you had never seen the guy before?"

"Of course. I'd never laid eyes on him. He just showed up at my kitchen door, told me Mr. Denoire sent him out for the cake, and loaded it into the limo. I had no reason to doubt his word. How else could he know I'd baked a cake if Mr. Denoire hadn't told him so?"

"You handed that beautiful cake you created for days to a total stranger?"

"Well, yeah, I guess if you put it that way. But he wasn't a stranger; he came from Cole."

"And you didn't find that unusual?"

"Coleman had orders picked up all the time. For lots of occasions."

"By limos?"

"Yes, Detective. That's how Coleman rolls."

"Rolled," said Diggs, reminding the chef that Cole no longer rolled at all.

"Oh yeah, rolled. I can't believe…" She trailed off, shoulders slumping. "Look, you have to understand. Mr. Denoire was a connoisseur with expertise in many fields. He lived large. He liked to eat gourmet foods. On dates, vacations, weekend excursions, at meetings, even for lunch alone. The man was accustomed to luxury. And everybody knew it." Cherrie's lip quivered.

She flushed and said, "His opinions were valued by millions, so many vendors accommodated him. He micromanaged everyone—and yes, including me. Everything had to be perfect and prompt. He never left anything to chance. He got what he wanted. All the time."

"I'll bet," the detective said, sounding snide, his gaze alighting on her boobs.

Cherrie bristled, blinked, and asked, "Just what are you implying?"

"I'm not implying anything. I'm stating it's rumored you two were involved."

"Involved? Who told you *that*?" Cherrie stood up and cleared her throat.

"Ma'am, you need to sit back down," Diggs threatened in a commanding tone.

Cherrie retreated, retook her stool. "But we weren't—"

"This is a serious situation we have here. You'll do better if you cooperate. This doesn't look so good for you."

"I am cooperating," Cherrie responded with alarm.

"Did you have a romantic relationship with the deceased, or did you not?"

Cherrie leaned forward and trained her eyes directly on the detective's own. "Okay, if you call two dates *involved*. Two dates. Two years ago. That's it. We went straight into the friend zone. Only, when I decided to open my business last year, he helped me out."

"Whoa. So, let me get this straight. A gorgeous young girl like you consents to date this power player twice, and then it's completely over with. You two are strictly business. You were happy to let this lifestyle go?" He indicated the opulence by spreading his arms and showcasing the yacht like a salesman trying to close a deal. "You expect me to believe that?"

Cherrie covered her décolleté. "I really don't care what you believe. I'm telling you the truth. Cole might have had a derisive rep as a cruel and ruthless businessman, but he was sweet and kind to me. He was a friend when I needed one. He got me, is all. And I got him. He enjoyed having someone in his life who didn't ask for anything, who didn't make demands. And not that it's any of your concern, but even a girl like me—whatever perverted stereotype you've been imagining in your never-mind—has standards, 'kay? And scruples. And common sense to bring to bear. You may not be able to grasp the fact, but not everyone is cynical. I didn't date Coleman for power or money or anything approaching that. I liked him. It did not work out. His world and values weren't mine. His life was complicated."

"His life was complicated, how?" Diggs slackened his attack.

"By all the women in his world. Not me. I was merely a sounding board. Cole changed insignificant others like he changed his socks and ties."

"A player."

"That's not what I said. He was looking for something he couldn't find, that's all. Like zillions of folks. He dated. He had four ex-wives. Why aren't you looking there?"

"No one enjoys being dumped," Diggs stated, whipping out a pad and pen.

"I wasn't dumped. I ended it." Cherrie's chin jerked toward the upper deck where Dee lay out sunbathing. Cherrie lowered her voice. "Look around," she said. "Don't you see? DeNeedra's one of them. Would you want to get tangled up with her? Would you like to have something DeNeedra wants and fights to get her mitts on? Think. She had the most to gain. She couldn't stand Coleman. They fought all the time. And she…" Cherrie pressed her lips together. "Don't get me wrong, I'm not saying she did it. I don't tell tales or spill the tea."

"Perhaps. But this is different now. A man has been brutally murdered. If you have any information and you try to withhold any facts you know that might be relevant to his death, you have legal exposure, understand? You're on the hot seat, Princess Cake. You'd better spit it out."

"Don't you realize someone set me up? I'm more anxious to see Cole's killer caught than you, Detective. We were buds. I'm not the one with motive."

"If that cake proves to be the murder weapon, we'll discover your motive soon enough." Diggs stared at Cherrie, touched her hand, sat on a stool across from her, his elbows resting on his knees. "That guy you say picked up the cake, can you identify him? That could help. Would you recognize him if you saw him again? He might be the killer. He's the key to this case, for all we know. A sketch artist could render a drawing. Try to remember him. It's important."

"Right," Cherrie answered openmouthed, seemingly almost catatonic, staring at nothing, lost in space. "For sure, I'd know him anywhere. I'll never forget him. He's burned in my memory. I figure I'll always remember him." Cherrie rubbed between her eyes, a fearsome headache taking hold. "Detective, you know what's even worse?"

"What?"

She looked him in the eye. "The killer knows I can identify him. He'll remember me."

Lance was sweating like hot yoga class. Cole's murder was a scoop. A terrible, horrible, major scoop. Film at eleven was in the bag, but the victim was his friend, the best friend Lance had ever had. So, though he was first to report the story, having assembled a local camera crew, he was feeling sad and angry. Numbness was already wearing off, and a crippling loss was setting in. Lance was a murder witness now, part of the story. That was bad. No ethical journalist wanted that. Getting an interview with Dee could be a feather in his cap, but he wasn't sure how much she knew or if she might be guilty. And reporting the story could kill his career. He might have to answer for questionable things he and Cole did in the past.

Lance and Cole were fraternity brothers, playing college basketball. Their team won national championships that made them alumni legends. After that, they went on to Rhodes scholarships, studying at Oxford and traveling in Europe, postgraduate bachelors sowing wild oats. Not all their news was fit to print. Some iffy stuff went down. Lance knew all the wives and girlfriends, all the mistakes and misunderstandings, all the secrets and the lies. Lance knew where Cole's bodies were buried because he helped Cole bury most of them. Cole's tragic death could dig them up.

"Well, whaddaya know, it's Lance Fairgood. I watch you all the time." Diggs grinned. He grabbed ahold of Lance's hand and gripped it like a vise. "Detective Diggs. I'm glad to meet you. I used to live out in LA myself. I'm starstruck. I'm a fan."

"Cool. Can I ask you a couple of questions?" Lance said with an assertive stance.

"Nah, that's not the way this goes. I ask questions. You respond. I know that isn't what you're used to, but that's how it's going to be."

Lance smiled with rows of straight white teeth. "Anything I can do to cooperate. I want you guys to find who did it. Shoot." He choked, began to cough. "Oops, bad choice of words."

"He wasn't shot. Denoire got poisoned. What do you know about that, Fairgood?"

"Nothing," Lance replied. His eyebrows formed a unibrow. "Wait. I'm a suspect?"

"Should you be? How'd you and the victim get along?"

"We were supertight. Ask anyone… Look, I don't like where this seems to be going. You're not suggesting I killed my best friend, are you? Why would I do that?"

"You tell me, and we'll both know. Doesn't have to make sense when somebody's murdered. I just conduct the investigation. Assuming he didn't poison himself, you were here when it went down. When you prove to me you're not involved, I'll let you go your way."

"Oh, I get it. You want drama," Lance said with a charming smile. "You figure a high-profile suspect is just what you need to get on camera. You smell a career maker, right? 'News Anchor Kills Media Mogul Friend,'" Lance taunted, making a gesture indicating bold headlines. "Is that what you're after, Detective Diggs? Well, sorry, I can't help you out."

Diggs refused to take the bait. "What do you know about Vikki Denoire?"

"Cole's second wife? She passed away. Why? What does she have to do with this?"

"I ask the questions, you answer, remember?"

"Sorry, force of habit. She died of breast cancer. Found it too late. Hung on a few months, and then bam, she was gone. In a flash. It devastated Cole. He never got over it. Funny, though. She was the one Cole really loved. The only one he ever loved. The only one who loved him back. Vikki was his angel. When she succumbed, it broke his heart."

"What about his third wife?" Diggs looked down at his notepad, flipped a page. "Flora."

"Tree hugger. Animal lover. Vegan. Flora saved the whales. Cole met her two years after Vikki died. Cole began writing, then publishing, started his company, quickly moved up."

"And Flora?"

"Not so much. She didn't need upward mobility. She wanted to take Cole off the grid. Wanted a tiny house. Craved seclusion. Read some Marcus Garvey books and longed to move to Africa. That wasn't Coleman's dream at all. Cole's idea of roughing it was a five-star hotel with no room service menu after two a.m. Her demands put an end to their torrid romance. I really felt sorry for Flora then. When Cole divorced her, she boozed out. Hit the opioids hard and spiraled down. When she realized she couldn't hang on to him, it seems she couldn't handle it. She found another lover though. Hooked up with some hotshot ecologist. Fled to the rainforest. Moved to Peru. Rumor was, she wanted to marry the guy but the guy was still hitched to someone else, so that fell through as well. The next thing we knew, she was out on the street. That's what the grapevine said at least. I don't know for sure. Cole looked for her for several years but couldn't find her anywhere. She never took a dime from him. You sure can't say that for the other two."

"Which brings us to Mrs. Denoire, number four."

"She's a different story." Lance moved closer, cleared his throat. "That sister's a mean green fighting machine. Loves a dollar. Monstrous too. Sneaky young lady. Hood rat. Bandit. Robin is her name. A vixen. Earthquake. Femme fatale. She wormed her way into Denoire MaxamediaMania headquarters and embezzled millions. When she got caught, she refused to divorce him. Robbed Cole blind and disappeared. She staged a hit-and-run. She hung a dark cloud over Coleman's head that continued to rain on his parade. She's capable of anything."

"Hmm. How long ago was that?"

"This time last year. Regatta time."

"This boat race can bring out the worst in people," Diggs observed.

"Yeah, maybe so. But I tend to see the best in folks. We see what we believe and not the other way around. If you know the world is on your side and everything's working together for your good, positivity manifests. The flipside brings the opposite. You have to make a choice. Either way, you're going to create your life, for better or for worse. I'm a lover, not a hater."

Diggs handed Lance his pad and pen. "Say, bro, can I have your autograph?"

Lance gave Diggs a sidelong glance. "As long as it's just for your personal use and not a signed confession."

Austin Whitmore was packed and ready to go, planning to fly his private jet to anywhere but where he was—on a boat in troubled waters. As of now, as far as he was concerned, this trip was fried, dyed, laid to the side, and he aimed to head back to the ranch.

"Leaving so soon, Mr. Whitmore?" Diggs asked, blocking Austin's cabin doorway, taking a look around the room.

"I ain't gettin' trampled in this stampede," Austin replied. "Man, move aside."

"I'm afraid I can't let you go just yet."

"And who do you think can stop me?" Austin challenged, charging forward.

"A man who can put your butt in jail and throw away the key, that's who." Diggs rose to his full diminutive height, blocked Whitmore, flashed ID. "You partnered at Denoire, correct?"

Austin double-checked Diggs's badge. "I suppose you might'a called it that."

"What would you call it?" Diggs inquired.

"Difficult. I called it quits. On account of that frisky filly of his who tried to bankrupt both of us."

"You incurred a significant loss with him? Did you resent Denoire for that?"

"Let me tell you somethin', pardner." Austin threw his suitcase down. "Yeah, his last wife stole from us, but Cole was a loyal, true-blue friend. The dude was always there for me. Rode tall in the saddle when times were hard and never let me down. If I had to go into the O.K. Corral with anybody in this world, it's Cole I'd choose to back me up. His kind of friend don't grow on trees. Everything that cowboy touched turned into gold before my eyes. No better investment than Cole Denoire, and I'll defend him to the grave."

"Let's hope you don't have to do just that. Got any idea where Robin went? I mean, that's who you referred to, right? That filly who took you for the ride."

"She's down in the islands, I hear tell. She's probably sippin' Planter's Punch, bleedin' some sucker, and swimmin' with sharks… and them sharks had best look out."

Blade was a survivalist. His knife weighed heavy in his palm, its hand-carved ebony wood shaft sure, its edges laser sharp. Blade loved this old imported shank. His Pops had gave it to him. Its steel was shaped like a stegosaurus. Gems were inlaid in the shaft. This baby could cut through kryptonite. One deep thrust was all it took. Blade could almost feel it slicing through that buttery flesh of hers, to tear her stem to sternum.

She was a bad girl, that's for sure. Bad enough to make some guy up near Miami want her dead. Blade was doing the world a favor, ridding it of the stronger sex. She'd regret it, being bad. She'd be sorry soon. He knew she would. They always were. In the last throes of panic, they all repented when it boiled down to it, but he preferred the female hits. No woman ever loved him. Blade was never kissed, not once, nor ever hugged or smiled upon. Not even by his mother. Somehow ladies sensed his menace. Never would a woman lie with him the way they did with other men, and Blade did not know why. He was unwanted. He was a reject. Pretty girls had called him that. Well, fine. Okay for them. They'd get their comeuppance—and it would hurt.

He parted the curtains. Crept inside. He smelled blood strong as ether. His new size-thirteen Jordans crossed the tile floor without a sound. He was the boss man. He was king. *How you like me now*, he thought, mouth watering, shoes advancing. The kill was so near he tasted it.

But something was wrong.

He heard nearby sounds.

Footsteps. Outside on the walkway. Heading his way. A pair of Florsheims. High heels clacking. High-pitched laughter. A couple of squares out on a date or marrieds out without the kids. They hesitated steps away. Panted. Finally stumbled past.

Blade slipped in closer to the girl. He heard his blood rush. Sidled to her. Waited by her pillow. She was a real showstopper. Yeah, she was. A sexy cover girl.

Blade leaned over to hear her heartbeat. Seeing a pulse he would bring to a screeching halt always made him feel alive, yet her body seemed so lax and calm. He decided to switch it up a little, savor the flavor, take his time, fixated by her lithesome frame and her disarranged hair on the pillow. *Look at her, sleeping so soundly. Clueless.* Check out her baby-soft bulging breasts.

Unsheathing his camera, he snapped three shots.

Hold on. What kind of trick was this? No perceptible rise and fall of her chest the way there was with other broads. No heaves to entice him to end it, urge him on and get him hard. No eyelid flutter, sleepy moan, or loll of her head from side to side. What a dud and disappointment. What a let-down. What the heck. What kinda target was this chick? She was spoiling all the fun. That did it. This bitch pissed him off.

The Mangler clamped his gloved hand over her mouth and nose. He mounted her.

But wait. There came no desperate struggling, scratching, and no muf-fled screams. She didn't wake up. She ignored him. Blade growled and placed his knife up to her neck to try to terrorize her, feeling his manhood rise and swell, hitching up her nightie. His lust depended on her fear but there was no resistance. Blade felt his weenie shrink to a worm on her panties.

"Bitch!" he hissed to the dark. "Wake up and look me in the eye."

But it soon became clear that she couldn't feel terror or fret for her im-minent demise.

Robin Denoire was already dead.

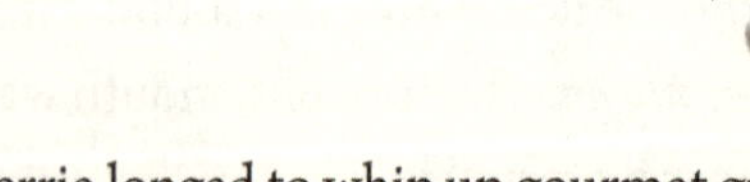

Cherrie longed to whip up gourmet grub, for that was how she beat off stress. Some people cleaned or read or ran or meditated in the dark, worked out, got drunk, took pills, played golf, or hid in their beds with the covers pulled over their heads and cried themselves to sleep. Cooking was Cherrie's way to tune out what she didn't want to deal with. She couldn't process Coleman's death. But finally set free from the swaying boat, she could cook in an effort to cope. The only thing was, she couldn't move. Traumatized and stupefied, she felt she might collapse.

Lance Fairgood stood on the *Carpe Seas 'Em* deck and watched the glow-ing goddess chef who cooked that scrumptious food. Man, she was cute.

But what was she up to? Sitting alone in her cherry-red Audi, gazing out the windshield, dazed. Cherrie got questioned before he did. What clues was she able to give the cops? What details might she share with him? Drawn to Cherrie the moment he'd met her, Lance checked her out throughout the day. He googled her too. She was full of surprises. Girlfriend had a law degree. Passed the bar, quit practicing, and did a one-eighty in her career. He wondered what happened in her life when he found she'd jumped ship from a major firm to study at Le Cordon Bleu and the Culinary Institute.

The girl was hotter than a stove. But it wasn't just her sparkling eyes, the ringlet hair, the awesome bod that drew him, or her sultry voice. There was a freshness about her, a grace, an unjaded sensibility. That quality made her different. Special. Safe. And quite alluring. He loved the floaty way she moved, like the flight of a beautiful butterfly or a hummingbird searching for nectar. He conjured her in his fantasies, and here she was, his live dream girl. She radiated light. He stared at her, longing to see her smile, yearning to have her smile at *him*. Because of him. And him alone. He was shocked to discover that all of a sudden, he wanted to make her happy.

Was love at first sight really possible?

He leaned by the top deck's water ski rack and muttered, "She's the one."

Cherrie spotted the overly handsome Lance and was quick to don her dollar shades. *Oh no, here comes that TV newsman!*

Lance turned on the afterburners, launching into a full-out run.

Cherrie tapped the ignition, switched the gear shift, and backed out with a sudden lurch.

"Wait!" he called to her, catching up. He knocked on her window, smiled that smile.

Cherrie frowned and kept the window closed. *Is he nuts?* "It's been a long day," she yelled through the glass and slammed it into D. But he stationed himself right in front of her car.

Lance stood his ground, threw up his hands. "Okay, you can snub me if you want, but you'll have to run me over."

Blade heard the disturbing news on his iPod. Coleman Denoire was poisoned on his yacht. Some chump was pimping Blade. He knew Cole was the dude who hired him, but the wife the dead man paid him to kill was already iced when Blade arrived. This hit was a frame-up, pure and simple. No one was gonna play Blade like that, not for no amount of dough. He had the first half of his honorarium. It would have to do for now. His seaplane to Bimini breezed in an hour. That would be the end of it. No one would find a trace of him or tie him to either murder.

Whoever was pulling the strings would have to buy another patsy.

Cherrie flung butter in a pan. "I hope you like crepes," she chirped at Lance.

"I like you." Lance smiled as he laid on the suave while surveying her gourmet kitchen.

"I guess I'll take that as *yes*. These crepes are ratatouille swiss." Cherrie sprinkled a handful of grated cheese. "But first, have a bite of this salad. Field greens, goat cheese, craisins, pears, glazed almonds and asparagus, with a tangy raspberry vinaigrette. Voilà!" She filled two salad bowls.

"Looks yum. And I don't mind telling you that *you* look good enough to eat. You know, Cherrie, a guy could get used to this." Lance tried to reach out for her hand and she gently tapped him with her spatula.

"We're just thrown together by circumstance. And you throwing yourself on the hood of my car. So don't get carried away, okay?"

"Too late. I already am." He wiped the smile off his face.

"But you don't even know me, Lance."

"I do. I've searched for you for years. I could tell from the minute I saw you."

"Stop!" she snapped. "I'm not that easy." Flustered, she slid a big crepe on his plate.

"I can wait. It's okay if it's hard. But please, just let me try," Lance pleaded. "I'm not going anywhere. I mean it. Give me a chance."

Cherrie angled the pan into the sink, turned on the cold water. The crepe pan hissed. "If Cole hadn't... Well, if this hadn't occurred, you'd be out on his yacht with your buddies and I'd be helping my workers clean up the mess you guys made wilding out."

"Maybe. But what does that matter?"

Cherrie buried her face in both wet hands. "I'm not the girl you think I am."

"Don't sell yourself short. You captivate me. Don't you believe something good can happen? Don't you believe in miracles? Don't you believe something magical can come from something bad? I do."

Cherrie sat at her kitchen island, served the meal. "We're not a fit."

"How do you know we're not a fit? I've never met anyone like you," Lance said, eyeing her, his face lit up.

"You're pretty unique yourself, Lance Fairgood." Cherrie fed Lance a big bite of crepe, enchanted by his soulful eyes. "Well, what do you think?"

"That you're changing the subject. But never mind that, I think I'm in love. Pinch me. I'm amazed you cook. This crepe is the best I've ever had. Let's go find the hen that laid the eggs so I can marry *her*." They broke into laughter, and when it subsided, Lance launched into his pitch again. "The women I meet all have an agenda."

"You have an agenda when you meet them."

"Touché." He took another bite. "This is outstanding. Seriously."

"It's simple."

"Simply delicious. How come I never meet females who cook?"

"Poor guy. Every shrew in the solar system conspires to make you miserable."

"You noticed. Isn't it cataclysmic? Only you can save me now."

"Or you could sign up for a meal kit service. Then you could learn to feed *yourself*."

"Ouch."

"If you didn't lump all of us together, you might stand a chance."

"Oh yeah? No women in LA cook. Correction. None in America."

"You've been making poor choices, that's all that tells me. You've gotten in a trick."

"Nope, it isn't all on me. It's not my imagination. Susie Homemaker ain't exactly running home to sling pots after slaving all week, okay? You have to admit. And before you go pinning a label on me, I'm no slouch. I love to eat. I've been known to throw down on a grill once or twice. My mom could throw down. My dad could too. I'm no undercover misogynist."

"Okay, okay, I take it back."

"You don't get off that easy. You're going to have to let me cook for you sometime now. Check it out. You owe me. You need to come out to my crib and allow me to show you around."

"And when would I go traipsing off? I happen to work, Mr. TV star."

"I work, and I play. You should try it sometime. As a matter of fact, I could teach you how. I get out too much. Occupational hazard. What can I say? I won't lie, I earned my player rep. I did. I'm not denying it. The tabloids have splashed it all over the web, but I'm over it now. That lifestyle's past. I'm ready to settle down. I'm not trying to be the old guy in the club."

"Well, too late now." Cherrie burst out laughing.

"Oh, that's cold. You're ruthless. That's a wound. I lost my appetite," he complained as he shoveled more food in his mouth.

They kept laughing till Cherrie stopped midlaugh. "What happened today really makes you think, makes you focus on what's important. That's probably what you're feeling, Lance."

"Yeah, you're right. But that's not all. You look at where you are and how you're living, what you want to do, what contribution you can make. It reminds you there's no time to waste. I've been thinking that a while. How life can be over in a wink." His smile morphed to a distant stare. "My mom and dad split when I was two. I've seen many relationships go bad. I guess it put me off. Cole was a perfect example of it. He was always getting hurt. He was always hurting others too. Even when he didn't mean it… Cherrie, I know I'm ready now. I want to find love, and I think I know how. I believe I'm a better man, and better men make better lovers."

"Wow," Cherrie said and fanned herself. "It's getting kind of hot in here… Did I turn off the oven?"

"I don't know, but you definitely turned me on." He moved in closer, licked his lips.

"Are you always this aggressive?"

"Just when I see what I really want."

"It's hard to find your soul mate, Lance. But to answer the question you asked before, I do believe true love exists. I've just never been able to find it. I think you need a treasure map."

Lance gazed at Cherrie, chin in hand, gawking at her googly-eyed. "Things will always work out for an angel like you. But you have to believe it. You have to feel it. It may be starting to happen now. Maybe you ought to allow it, baby. Anything is possible."

"True," she conceded.

"Anything. Like meeting a girl at a party and knowing immediately she's the one."

"Oh wow, that's how my parents met," she confided. "Forty years ago."

"Are you serious? That's an anachronism."

"Not really, if you think about it. Marriages have a fifty-fifty chance of being successful. That's better odds than you had of becoming a TV newsman, isn't it? Like you said, you have to believe in each other and hang in there no matter what. Love is a rare and precious gift. God is love. Love's all that counts. If you're blessed to have true love turn up—"

"Like this?" Lance zoomed in, kissed her, hugged her waist, and took her breath away.

Cherrie melted, closed her eyes. She felt like they floated up into the air. "Like that," she whispered helplessly, lunging into him for a longer smooch. His lips were soft and strong on hers, and his arms around her felt like home. "Our food's getting cold," she breathed in his ear.

"And we're just warming up."

DeNeedra Denoire was sedated. Stoned. Despite all she said and did to incriminate everyone other than herself, she knew spouses and exes topped the list when detectives started snooping. And there was the matter of Coley's will. No telling what was in it, but if it went the way Dee hoped it would, it'd give her a reason to bump him off. What might she inherit and how might it be interpreted if she got it all? The cops would have a field day. Though two other women bore Cole's last name and could take the heat for killing him, neither of them was worth her salt, and the minute Robin and Flora heard that Coley finally got his due, they'd swoop like shoppers at Bergdorf on Black Friday, looking for handouts. That would start a free-for-all.

The only thing that would matter then was what Coley bequeathed to DeNeedra on paper after all was said and done. Where did she stand after years of bickering? How did she rate among four wives? Out in the cold, she suspected, with that evil Robin spouse du jour. Of all the dirty rotten luck. Two murders. Lousy timing. Dee just got Coley to send some nut bar south, down into the sun and surf to rectify the Robin thing. Had he? Was the viper dead? If so, there'd be an inquiry into that affair, too, into Robin's death. Or maybe her disappearance. What would become of that mystery?

The hit man was told to get rid of Robin's body. Did he do it right? Was the hit man as good as they said he was? Would cops view it all as coinkydink, or might the mayhem point to Dee? What would happen then? With Coley and his ex-wife found dead almost simultaneously. Police could connect it to Dee with one dot—that Mangler creature Coley hired. If the Mangler got caught, would he implicate Dee? Could he? How could she know for sure? And one never knew what might crop up when detectives followed the money trail, as winding as Coley said it'd be. She couldn't count on that. She'd put it off on someone else. They did it in politics all the time. Dee knew. She helped candidates hide their sins with shady contributions.

Only, who else could she implicate? Coley, but he couldn't take the fall. Not six feet under like he was. Perhaps the other greedy wives, but Vikki was long since in her grave, and Flora was a basket case out there in Timbuktu. Detective Diggs was pretty smart and likely to pin the rap on Dee, so Dee tried to drag Cherrie into it. But Cherrie scarcely seemed the type to be guilty of double murder. She was an innocent. That was clear. But Robin screwed a lot of losers, ruffians, and ne'er-do-wells. Dee could sic the cops on that red herring when they sniffed around. She'd pretend to mourn, call Robin a slut, and deny she knew where Robin was.

Dee tossed and turned throughout the night. *What secrets were hidden in Coley's will?*

The next morning, Benton was naked to the waist and ready to take a dip. He preened out onto the massive deck where Dee's recliner sat in shade beside the giant heart-shaped pool. He yawned, bit into an unpeeled onion. "Napping, Needra?" Benton quizzed.

"Right. Like I could sleep with those two bod… I mean, with Coley's body not yet in the ground. I didn't get a wink last night, and you're no help at all. Why don't you make yourself useful." Dee carped. "Take out the garbage or clean the pool."

"What, are you kidding?" Benton chuckled, tossing the onion up into the air and catching it in his teeth. "That's what the help is for, my precious." Benton set the onion down. "Wouldn't you rather I helped you relax?" he offered, gyrating, groping his crotch, holding one hand behind his head like a stripper at a bridal shower, slowly peeling off his swim briefs.

"Maybe," Dee conceded, closing her eyes and breathing in salt air.

Benton rushed to clumsily fondle the contents of her gold bikini top. Stirring, she slapped his hands away. "Do something about your breath!" Dee snapped, hand waving the air in front of her. "You stink. Quit chomping onions!"

"You never let me do nothing." Benton pouted like a two-year-old.

"Oh really? Nothing, addle brain? For instance, what did you do last evening? I spent it here alone. I'm sure you were doing something then. Care to share with the class where you slept last night and so many others nowadays? With *my* car, in *my* clothes that I put on your suntanned back by maxing *my* credit cards!" Dee began shrieking at that point, flailing her arms and kicking her feet like a toddler throwing a tantrum. "You think I don't know what you're up to, Bent? You think I don't watch my investments, huh? Don't think I don't keep an eye on you."

"What, you're having me followed?" Benton stormed off to the house.

"Shouldn't I?" Dee yelled after him. "You'd better go dump whoever she is. I lost Coley already. I won't lose you. I bought you, Bent. Remember that. I can toss you out onto the street!"

Five minutes after Diggs showed up at the station house, a call came in.

Coleman Denoire's estranged wife, Robin, turned up in the Cayman Islands, murdered in a hotel suite. Now there were two whodunits and it appeared that they were linked.

Benton roared off in his Tesla at ninety miles an hour, thinking fast.

He hadn't done all he'd done for nothing and didn't intend to come up short. He'd sunk a lot of time in his plan of attack and it could still pan out.

Over the course of the past few months, he'd wooed Coleman's lawyer's fat-ass assistant to get her to show him the big guy's will, and he'd seen that it hadn't been changed in a year, so Robin—the newest of Coleman's wives—was due to inherit his fortune. That was, unless Robin predeceased Cole, in which case Dee would cop it all. That provision was the bonanza. It meant that the guy who was banging Dee copped a winning lotto ticket. That would be Benton—if Robin was dead before Coleman met his just reward. That's what gave Benton his big idea. He was working in the mail room at Denoire MaxamediaMania at the time. His only move was up. He schemed on a way to meet Dee and date her, find and kill Robin, ice Coleman next, cash in, and make his exit.

His plan had worked like a Trojan… but it wasn't over yet.

Battle-ax Dee thought he was dumb, huh? Not too dumb to pull it off. He certainly wasn't a genius, but even a broken clock's right twice a day.

He blew through a red light, sped up Worth Avenue, screeched into a red zone, parked, jogged into Harry Winston's jewelry store, and spent a fortune. He charged up a ring the ball and chain could never resist—on her Mastercard. He'd rush home, sink to bended knee, and cajole the old crone into marrying him. Tonight. It had to be tonight. The sooner the better. Seal the deal. "Make it legal while the gettin's good," he resolved as he zoomed through traffic.

Benton had one more rung to climb on his shaky ladder to success.

Community property might be nice, but widowed with wealth was nicer.

Dee told all her buddies he was nuts, and thanks to her theatrics, he got madder all the time. But there was a method to his madness.

Diggs's motto was always follow the money, so he was on that trail big time, and it was paying off. He phoned Coleman Denoire's sleazy lawyer and discovered the legal eagle had retired a week before the birthday bash. That was a little too convenient. Diggs obtained the number of the attorney's successor, Corby Rippin, and Diggs made Rippin fax him a copy of Coleman's will immediately. The motive was there in black and white. It was just as Diggs suspected.

Cherrie and Lance were feeding each other the last few bites of strawberry shortcake, giggling, when her cell phone rang. "Cherrie on Top," she answered, winking at Lance and pressing the Speaker icon.

"Cherrie, this is Benton Foxx, DeNeedra Denoire's new fiancé."

"DeNeedra's *engaged?*" asked Cherrie. "When'd that happen?"

Lance coughed up some cream. "What?" he blurted.

"Hush," warned Cherrie, planting a napkin on Lance's mouth.

Benton continued, "Is this a bad time? I was hoping to catch you alone tonight."

"Was there something I could help you with?"

"I know it's weird to hear from me, but I just asked Dee to be my bride. I figure now Coleman's gone, she's by herself and that ain't right. A woman needs love and security, and I want to provide all that for her."

"Oh brother," Lance whispered and rolled his eyes, mimicking playing a violin.

Cherrie pressed the phone against her chest, wide-eyed, and mouthed, "Chill out."

"Your catering is off the chain," said Benton. "Coleman's party rocked."

"Thanks," said Cherrie. "You were there?"

"I wasn't invited. I just heard."

"Oh," said Cherrie. "I understand. Sooo?"

"I want you to do us a favor. Think you can bake us a wedding cake?"

"Excuse me?"

"We need a wedding cake. You know, like that smoker you whipped up for Cole."

"Wow, I don't know if that's—"

"Yeah, I get it. Coleman ain't buried yet and all. But it would mean a lot to Dee."

"Oh no, I doubt that seriously. I guess in a pinch I suppose I could, but it doesn't seem appropriate. I don't think so. Thanks for the call, Mr. Foxx, but—"

"Call me Benton."

"Benton. Yeah, okay. I'm sorry, it's so strange. I mean, after what happened today and all. And I'm doubting DeNeedra would want me to. Did you discuss this cake with her?"

"Well, that's just it. It's a surprise. See, Dee don't know about it yet. We're gonna tie the knot tonight, and I want it real fancy, you know what I mean? A night to remember. The whole shebang. Tell you what, Cherrie, I'll sweeten the pot. I'll pay you a grand for a princess cake."

"I couldn't possibly do one by tonight. It would have to be baked and then decorated…" Cherrie frowned and bit her lip, began looking to Lance for a kind way out. "Hold on," she said and tapped on Mute. "What should I say?" She consulted Lance.

"Absolutely not," he advised her, drawing a hand across his neck in a frantic kill-it gesture. "It's crazy. I think it's ridiculous… although, ultimately, it's up to you."

"Okay, *two* grand then. Is that cool?" Benton bellowed from the speaker. "Three grand."

Cherrie gasped. She unmuted the phone and quietly offered, "Benton, I have an idea. I just started a cake for someone else. It isn't exactly the kind you want, but a couple postponed their wedding. Their cake is in my refrigerator. What if I tweaked and finished it like a—?"

"Sweet. I'll make it five. I'll pay five grand, no questions asked."

Cherrie let out a loud hiccup. Five grand for her homeless kitchen project would be so magnificent. It'd feed a lot of hungry mouths. "Well, okay, if you insist."

"It's settled. Deliver it to the estate," Benton ordered. "I'll give you cash."

"It's going to take some doing though. What time do I need to get it there?"

"Eight o'clock. Do whatever you have to. It can be small, but make it amazing."

Benton rattled off Dee's Palm Beach address, and then the phone went dead.

"I don't like it," Lance said, and he clenched his fist. "That Benton is up to no good."

Benton's call caught Lance off guard and put him on guard in one fell swoop.

Cherrie was fragile and naïve, and Lance felt protective and threatened. That Lance could be so vulnerable to a woman he met that very day, thrilled him and scared him equally. But he trusted Cherrie. She was real. So what did Benton want with her? To hit on her surely, but was there more? Something more sinister. What could it be? What was he really after? Lance had dealt with creeps like Benton Foxx that lacked a moral compass. It was bizarre for a guy to set out to marry a woman whose first husband died—was murdered, no less—only hours before. It stank. It wasn't right. And Lance knew Cole distrusted Benton. Cole had often told him so.

Cherrie's last princess cake wound up in a lab, to be tested for what killed Cole. So why would Benton replicate it? What was up with that? And how could the cake have poisoned Cole? Cherrie would never do such a thing, and lots of the partiers ate the cake. Heck, Lance scarfed down a slice himself. That bad boy was delicious. But Cherrie was making another one like it. Was she now in danger too?

Lance vowed to not leave Cherrie's side. He'd already filed an updated report with the latest developments in Cole's case. He'd stick by Cherrie, make some calls, dig up more facts while Cherrie worked, shoot additional footage, upload that, and plumb the Benton angle. There might be another story no other outlets had a lead on.

DeNeedra's heart was palpitating. What if she never saw Benton again or, for that matter, her new Tesla? With Coley totally out of the picture, it would be tough to go it alone. Coley was intimidating, frustrating, arrogant, mean, and cold, but face it, he was a prime meal ticket and also a heckuva hunk of man. Beneath that gruff exterior, there beat a heart of gold. And Dee wasn't getting any younger. Dates weren't banging down her door. She had to admit she wasn't a woman with whom it was easy to get along. Could Benton be her last hurrah? His brain was as dumb as a brick, but below the waist he was a genius. Who else did she have? No fam. No friends. She should've kept her mouth shut. If he never returned, it was all her fault.

But he did come home. With amazing news.

And a diamond the size of a beach ball!

He no doubt charged it to her card, but who cared. Dee had him cornered now. She'd chased him till he caught her. She had him right where she wanted him, and she could tell her snooty friends. A call to her crony, Judge Riley, at city hall delivered a quickie marriage license for a modest fee. Doubtless, it would raise eyebrows, but none of that foolishness mattered. She would wed in a lovely ceremony right on her mansion's private beach. *Oh, this was so romantic.*

Dee was happier than she'd ever felt. The future was actually looking bright. From the pits to a paradise in one day. Forget what anybody thought. Or said. Or wrote in the gossip columns. This was colossal. Her dream was arriving, and she was reveling in it.

Dee stuffed herself into the new peach gown her stylist brought her days ago. Dee knew it'd come in handy. Sequins threw gleaming starbursts all over her bedroom, lit by her fireplace. There was a magic to this moment, however impromptu or ill-advised. DeNeedra was aglow.

Even reports of Robin's death were unable to dim her nuptial ardor. The cops had no clues and weren't hovering around. While that sure didn't mean she was in the clear, Blade's trail was cold as snow for now, and so was any path to her. The killer had failed to collect the rest of his money, and that was a real good sign. The Mangler was obviously on the run.

Dee had cause to celebrate. She'd soon be Mrs. Benton Foxx.

❦

Lance drove along the shore in a heavy fog in the inky dark of night. Cherrie and the five-grand princess cake were snuggled at his side. His rented Porsche gripped the road, but Cherrie winced at every bump, as the cake was only wrapped in a Tupperware holder for the ride. She'd barely finished the cake in time, and it was very delicate. This wasn't her usual method, but she'd done her very best. She always did, and this time there was five grand on the line. They sloshed along in blinding rain, hydroplaning, dodging lightning splitting the sky on the A1A.

Cherrie tightened her grip on the princess cake. "We passed Yamato and Atlantic. Those are the exits just before the turnoff Benton said to take. It shouldn't be much farther now."

"Let's get in and get out of there, okay? Chop-chop. I don't like this arrangement. Cop the cash, and then we split. No socializing. It's a drop-off. Special delivery and we breeze."

"Aye, aye, captain." Cherrie saluted.

Lance rounded a curve past a mini-mall with a cleaners and frozen yogurt shop, just as Benton said they would, while rattling off directions. He said not to count on GPS because the location was off the map, secluded in an exclusive islet jutting off the bay. Instead, they should look for landmarks he'd ticked off or they'd get lost. They drove a few miles past a waterside Hilton Hotel lit up like a tiki torch to a private marina with iron gates at a strip of palatial estates on mega lots that straddled the strip of land between the stormy Atlantic Ocean and the Intracoastal Waterway. "What's the address?" Lance asked again.

"It's 42639," said Cherrie. "It should be coming up on the right… That's it!" She pointed to a massive villa, checking the time on her pink smartwatch. "Pull in. Let's hurry up. We're late."

"Late is the least of our concerns. I probably should be packing."

"A gun?" Cherrie asked in a heightened unease.

"No, a toothbrush… Yeah, a gun."

"You think you're overreacting much?"

"Maybe," Lance admitted, "but I'd rather be safe than sorry. We're rolling in here like sitting ducks, and Dee is a killer bridezilla."

"Well, you're not being very nice."

"I'm being very smart." Lance took her hand, gave it a squeeze.

"Be careful of the cake," she said.

"I'm trying to be careful of *you*," he said as he rounded a circular driveway up to a Spanish-style house with an S-tile roof and a broad taupe-stucco facade. No lights emanated from within. The rain poured down in sheets as they stopped in front by a marble fountain.

Cherrie crinkled her nose and took it in. "Doesn't look like anybody's home."

Lance peered around the lush landscape and the daunting pitch surrounding them. "Let's go up and ring the bell. When they answer the door, we'll come back for the cake."

"Okay, that makes a lot of sense." Cherrie regarded him, stars in her eyes. "What would I do without you?"

"I don't know and don't want to find out tonight. Let's bag the cash and hit the bricks."

"Let's try to make the best of it. Five grand can feed a lot of folks."

They ran to the doorbell and rang several times, waited, and looked around the joint. A path of granite pavers ushered them over a wide expanse of lawn, past a water feature, under an arbor, to a redwood gate with carvings resembling ancient Egyptian gods. Finding the latch ajar, they swung it open and hurried along a path that hugged the vast span of the side of the house and led out toward the ocean. They could hear loud crashing waves. The lawn was surrounded by trellises of fragrant climbing jasmine vines that slapped their faces as they went. They high-stepped through a field full of bougainvillea, hibiscus, and oleander and eventually found a narrow walkway, wet, tree-lined, and slippery. It ended in a cove near pounding surf, wind whistling through their hair.

There was no trace of a wedding party. No sound save the rain and the crashing waves at high tide and the hiss of the mounting breakers. There were no signs of life at all except for the chirping of crickets, the hoot of a seemingly lonely great horned owl, and the crackle of lizards through dense morning glory ground cover that grew on both sides of the path.

They turned and gaped up at the back of the house as they ventured across a patio. The house looked even bigger here, with wide, two-story windows. Lance gripped Cherrie tight as he sheltered her under his arm beneath the forbidding roil of the roaring wind and raging storm. They passed expensive lounge chairs and a dining spot under a portico housing an outdoor kitchen, a barbecue, a pizza oven, a dining set, custom cabinets, and a to-die-for granite wet bar with two champagne flutes.

"Looks like they were here," Lance shouted. "Wonder where they went."

An infinity pool in the shape of a heart with a tiled Jacuzzi bubbling by it sat near a spherical firepit rimmed with sunken seating. Beyond a bright, trompe l'oeil-painted cabana that mimicked the beach at Saint-Tropez, the lot sloped down to a white-sand beach. Footprints in the sand led in that direction, accessible through a tangle of broken bramble, battered by deafening rain.

"What's that?" Cherrie hollered.

Lance yelled, "What?"

"Out there. Is that a flag or something?"

"Might be clothes. C'mon, let's see."

They took off their shoes and crossed the sand.

A peach-colored evening dress plaintively floated on seaweed at the water's edge.

And that's when they heard it. Faint, but shrill. The cry of a drowning female.

Diggs was intrigued by what he saw—Lance Fairgood's rented Porsche.

Diggs had watched Fairgood leave the dock and run toward Cherrie Baker's car. Any man on that yacht would've done the same if he'd thought he had any chance with her. Fairgood might've had one. So why was he at the victim's ex's house? To express his condolences?

"Who's that?" Diggs asked when he heard raised voices. A piercing scream. A muffled shout. He bolted from his unmarked car, dropping the hot dog he was munching, whipping his Glock from his shoulder holster, darting through rain and the billowing fog across the A1A. He huffed and puffed to the circular drive, unable to see much through the rain or to run fast with his jiggling gut. He loped through a gate down the side of the house toward what sounded like a struggle. When he reached the beach, wiping rain from his eyes, two women were grappling in whitecaps, one woman dragging the other through surging waves. It looked like Cherrie Baker was trying to drown DeNeedra Denoire. On the shore, at the edge of a jagged boulder standing midway up a cliff, two males were slugging it out on a ridge.

Diggs shot twice into the air.

But before he could take off toward the scene, his skull exploded, the sky turned red, and the violent scene went blank.

In less than two hours, the jury returned a guilty verdict on all counts.

Benton was apprehended and charged with premeditated murder in the deaths of Cole and Robin. His DNA was found on Robin's body, along with a pubic hair belonging to another man who's yet to be identified, but prosecutors thought they had an airtight case regarding Cole. A count of attempted murder for nearly offing Benton's fiancée and some other offenses were added, including two counts of assault for attacking Cherrie Baker and Lance Fairgood.

Benton did it all for nothing. The day before Cole's birthday, Cole clandestinely altered the terms of his will. Cole's new lawyer, Corby Rippin, drafted the new will amending the trust and bestowing Cole's estate upon, according to the dead's man's words, "the purest woman I have known, my sweet friend Cherrie Baker."

As incredulous as Cherrie was to discover she was bequeathed the largesse, she made excellent use of it instantly by setting up food banks coast to coast in underserved urban areas and installing the Cherrie on Top houseboat on the Jackie Onassis Reservoir in New York City's Central Park. The restaurant was flourishing, as was Cherrie's blissful marriage to gorgeous TV newsman Lance Fairgood, the freshly appointed head of a national network's news department.

Lance rocketed to superstardom after his coverage of Benton's murder trial and other headlining events, including three impeachments. His broadcasts covered the shootout, the arrest, and the extradition of one Blade "the Mangler" Murphy, who was hiding in the islands. Blade had been selling photos of Vikki's corpse along with his other victims', hawking nude flicks on the dark web, where he'd garnered a sizeable following and was raking in a bundle from the sickos on his mailing list. Blade managed to escape the Feds in transit, and nobody knows where he went. Well, almost no one anyway.

Benton was the so-called "limo driver" who picked up Coleman's cake from Cherrie and took it to the yacht before the party started. The cake was his ticket to get on board. As the party wore on, he poisoned the plate Austin Whitmore had personalized for Cole, and with it, Cole's last slice of Prinsesstårta, he admitted. Austin was crushed to learn that Cole was killed with one of his birthday gifts. And everyone else was shocked to find that Benton ordered the wedding cake to not only do away with Dee, but to also lure Cherrie to her death so she couldn't identify him. Cherrie had only heard of Benton, had never seen him face-to-face before she delivered the cake for him, but he figured as soon as she saw him again, she'd say he was the killer.

Diggs stayed in a coma for almost a week, imagining vast conspiracies. Dee's cautious elderly neighbor, walking his dog that foggy night, mistook Diggs for a prowler when he heard the commotion by the shore. He crowned Diggs with the baseball bat he carried when he walked the dog, but when Diggs recovered he got promoted for cracking two cases in just one day.

Dee lived aboard the *Carpe Seas 'Em* yacht, which Cherrie leased to her. A persuasive fundraiser, Dee sat on the board of directors of Cherrie's foundation. Dee was grateful to Cherrie for saving her life after Benton attempted to drown Dee in a get-rich scheme that nearly worked. And Dee also was thankful the wedding cake that Benton intended to poison her with arrived late for their shotgun wedding. Benton decided to toss Dee off the cliff, but thanks to Cherrie, Dee survived. Apparently, Benton didn't count on Lance accompanying Cherrie—or on the power of Lance's mean right hook.

Cherrie Fairgood is expecting now, and not just the baby she's having with Lance, but also a summons from Robin Denoire's new lawyer, contesting Coleman's will. It's a problem causing Cherrie sleepless nights and Lance to dig up dirt.

DeNeedra isn't worried though.

She's already wired funds overseas and contracted to hire The Blade.

BARRAGE

ELL, YEAH, SO IT WASN'T A BRILLIANT IDEA TO do it alone. I get that now. But I needed the money and had no friends to do it with, okay? And the way I always figure it, a girl's gotta do what a girl's gotta do, whether she's on her own or not. I had to keep it moving. Independence is not just a day in July, though July is a watershed month for me. The series of events that changed my life and pretty much almost ended it occurred in that blazing-hot summer month when my hubby, Bill, went out of town to crank up the heat on a deal that seemed a make-or-break for us. For real. We had to dig out of the mammoth financial sinkhole we were in.

We weren't used to massive failures piling up the way they had. We had always been able to scramble, grind, and find a way out when times got tough. But this time, after we relocated, we didn't land on easy street the way we were accustomed to. When our previous home burned down to the studs in a wildfire out in Los Angeles, some small print in our insurance coverage plunged us into foreclosure. A few months had gone by and our payments were late. On top of that, several other surprises popped up in the interim. "Big opportunities," Bill concluded, going all out in pursuit of them without consulting me.

First he won a "free recording studio," the offer claimed. It was made by a well-known retail chain. For a contest, he wrote and produced a promo he thought would take the world by storm. It did, but when it rained, it poured.

We're both professional voice-over talents, AKA suckers for mics and other recording equipment we can use, and the prize was a boon for producing audiobooks that came our way. We also perform in commercials, video games, cartoons, and radio ads. In fact, we met on such a job. And we've done really well with it these ten years, so Bill got superexcited.

Well, he won, but we had to pay taxes on the prizes, along with extended warrantees, the shipping and installation, and other add-ons that were only disclosed in the tiny-print clause he'd signed. So "free" cost a fortune in the end and plunged our finances from worse to worst.

The second so-close-and-yet-so-far was a credit card company bonus-point statement proclaiming our eligibility for two overseas airline tickets. We chose freebies to North Africa, the perfect vacation—and boy, did we need one—for African Americans longing to visit the wondrous motherland. When the tickets arrived, we had no place to live as the fires had pretty much wiped us out, so the timing seemed fortuitous. But we had to spend money for hotels, food, transportation, and other expenses that set us back another chunk insurance didn't want to pay.

More importantly and most damaging, Bill had back taxes he didn't disclose to me until it was too late. We filed our taxes separately as when we got married we both had corporations of our own. So when I found out through collection letters that Bill had a thing with the IRS, I was blindsided and it wasn't fun: "But, baby, I thought I could handle it," he proffered as a weak excuse. "Then the fire happened, we lost our shirts, and—"

"You should've been straight up with me when you found out we were in trouble. You should've warned me before we imploded, when we had options. I could've helped. Why did you have to lie to me? Why keep a secret this big from me? I'm your wife. I have a brain."

"I only wanted to spare you, sugar."

"Well, you did a super job. You spared me every dime we had. You let me believe we could dig our way out, and now the wolf is at the door. How am I supposed to trust you, Bill? Know what? I never will again. You led me down a blind alley with a monster lurking at the end," I accused him, bursting into tears. "I feel like you betrayed me."

"I know, and I'm sorry. I blew it. I know."

"I thought we were in it together, and now I find out I'm alone. How can you make unilateral choices and yet I have to pay for them? It's unfair. We're supposed to be equals."

"We are. I got it wrong, okay?" He paced, his hands up to his head. "I didn't realize how strong you are. I wanted to protect you."

"You wanted to protect *yourself.*"

"Okay, that's fair." His shoulders drooped. "I knew how you'd react."

"Oh no. Don't put it off on me. How would you react?"

"I'd be pissed. I'd go off. We both know that… Look, all I can do is apologize and pray that you'll forgive me. I'll make it right, I swear I will. I'll work my fingers to the bone."

"I forgive you already. That's not the point. I can't help it. I don't feel safe with you. Not anymore. Not after this. What else have you been hiding?"

He recoiled as if I'd slapped his face. "Nothing. Why would you ask me that? That's the total extent of it, babe. For real. I didn't mean to hurt you. Give me a second chance, okay? I know I screwed up really bad. But there's no other woman, no more secrets. That's the truth. I promise. I made some stupid choices, but I'll make it up, you wait and see."

I didn't wait and didn't see. All I saw was accounts that were in arrears and a steady stream of blocked phone numbers signaling more collection calls. I saw us working day and night but not gaining any ground. Something had to be done, and once I'd discovered the full extent of our dire straits, I knew I had to act. In Bill's hands, our financial hole was getting deeper every day. With the rental house, utilities, car payments, sky-high student debt, and our credit scores starting with minus signs, a loan was not an option. So I did what I always do when cornered. I got a two-scoop ice-cream cone and headed for the sand and surf to soak up rays, devise a plan, and get my head together.

I whisked my bikini down to our complex's stretch of pristine private beach to the heavenly spot where I got ideas. That is, when I thought before I acted or actually looked before I leaped, which wasn't often, looking back. And sometimes insufficient.

Our house was located in a pricey enclave at the shoreline thanks to a lucky tip from a friend who managed income rental properties. He needed to get it occupied, so he leased it to us for a song. As I walked on the sand, I paused for the cause at a picnic table under a stand of coco palms that swayed on a lively ocean breeze, my ice cream dripping on my hand. A newspaper on the bench blew open, landing on my chest. Now, I tend to take everything as a sign, and the headline flashing in my face was a column entitled *Garage Sale Gold*, an article jammed with selling tips. I perused it and got jazzed.

Bill and I autopaid for a storage space that was filled with loads of junk we'd evacuated in the days before our LA house burned down. We continued to rent the Pod we'd loaded with what we could before the fire, and after we'd moved to Florida where we thought we could better afford the rent, we had the Pod delivered. But our new digs couldn't fit our stuff. It was less than half the size. We were behind on our payments on the Pod storage like everything else we owed, and the contents were due to be confiscated unless we remitted immediately. We had items we no longer needed—never needed, truth be told—and here was a column suggesting we could easily purge a bunch of it. White elephants were in demand, and the back of the periodical had a classified section filled with ads that proved there was a yard sale boom and we could make a ton of cash. Divesting was the new acquiring. Lean and green was in these days. What better time to empty out the Pod, quit having to pay for it, let go, and make a profit? Buyers were everywhere I looked. Our gated community bulged with status fiends and bingeing shoppers. We lived in an upscale neighborhood flush with scads of wealthy transients who were keen to keep up with the Joneses, and they concluded we *were* the Joneses just because we came from Hollywood.

Opportunity knocked, and I opened the door. I got right to work on the plan I'd hatched, rummaging through the cast-offs piled in our Pod from wall to wall. I sorted stuff we both forgot we had. It was ridiculous. Bill owned so much tech he could start a tech store, and I had useless home decor. We might've wound up on that hoarding show, except our home was spick-and-span and lately we were spendthrifts as we were broke and dared not buy a thing. I dusted, priced the items, and figured out how to display them so they'd sell. The only things spared were inherited dishes and our collection of matchbooks, souvenirs from places we'd traveled that we kept in a giant amber jar. I mocked up posters, got them copied, tacked them to grocery store bulletin boards and utility poles all over town. I touted the sale every place I went, and Bill recorded ads to post online in social networking. We were leaving our baggage behind and starting over. We had a clean slate.

We were happy to divest our junk. We kissed and made up. We were on the same page. Things were looking up. The next Saturday was sale day. We were going to make a killing.

Only, on Tuesday of the same week, Murphy's Law went into effect. Bill got a gig, so *we* turned into *I*. That Thursday, he had to go out of town to voice a show in Canada. He said we ought to postpone the sale to the following week when he'd be home. But our ads were plastered everywhere and neighbors were looking forward to coming out Saturday, so the die was cast. It wasn't a matter of one or the other. We could do them both. And furthermore, we needed to.

The garage sale was a big success. It netted a whopping $12,092.48, excluding the profits from Bill's old car and my diamond tennis bracelet. It was fun. There were lots of surprises too. I met a lot of people. I wished we'd set out even more. The Lucite chairs Aunt Freda gave us as a quirky wedding gift elicited a bidding war, as did the costume jewelry I'd created when my ankle broke. Among other things, bargain-hunters also bought our custom sectional, a Murphy bed, two sofas, lamps, file cabinets, paintings, drawings, mirrors, cocktail tables and dining tables, microphones and music stands, bottles of French perfumes I never used due to my allergies, a chaise, Bill's collectible old ham radio, hardcover books and paperbacks, designer purses, a vacuum cleaner, a Capodimonte statuette, a brass saber I used in a Shakespeare play, our upright piano, an electric rice cooker we got for our first anniversary, and a lava lamp bought in Sedona.

It was after the morning crowd had died down and I was rearranging things that the action really heated up. I was lowering the electric garage door when a fire-engine red Ferrari screeched in our driveway, opened its wings, and revved so loudly items shook. It pulled up so close that the sensor on the automatic door kicked in to stop the door from sliding down.

A supertall guy slinked out of the car, wearing wraparound shades and a crooked smile. He was dressed all in greige but for red leather shoes, a red crocodile belt, and an angry red rash on one side of his face that was filled with pus and oozed. He licked a pair of large pink lips.

"Sorry," I said, instinctively backing away and snatching up my cell, my creepometer needle off the scale. "Everything's already sold or stored," I fudged, my radar buzzing and my fight-or-flight impulses peaked. "Thanks for coming. Maybe next time."

He spoke in an accent I started to place as eastern European. "Vait. You moost," he said too loudly, "geeve me just one thing. I go."

"Sorry, but the sale is over. I just closed up shop today."

His fingers twitched as he advanced. "You are beautiful vooman. Here alone?" he inquired, whipping off his glasses, rolling his half-mast eyeballs over my face and bod salaciously, his rodential orbs on neighboring windows then on the door to the laundry room.

Now I had the major willies. Morphing into arrant fear. Before I knew it, my quivering hand had pressed the button to lower the garage door, but the door got stuck, and he stealthily ducked underneath it, his fender preventing it shutting down and sealing us in the dim garage. I shrieked and bolted toward the door that led into the house. But the entry door was locked, and the key was in the pocket of the shorts. Creep-o saw me dig for it.

"Why you so scare?" he cackled, closing the space between us instantly, grasping my arm in a hurtful grip. I yanked it back and tried to turn, but he slid between me and the entryway.

Trapped. I was locked in my own garage with a stranger projecting ill intent.

He seized me, digging long fingernails into my back like an angry, feral cat. "I like your skin. You feel so soft. You face like a chocolate-cream-caramel pie."

Well, this is it, I feebly thought. The moment my daddy dreaded all my life, his primal fear—his baby girl raped, stabbed, murdered, and who knows what after stupid miscalculations having to do with valuing money over the priceless things in life, like my fragile personal safety. I imagined a tragic nightmare, seeing my hubby a widower, my mother aggrieved, with her grandchildren not yet a gleam in her eye, and my friends from LA at my gravesite. How could I be so dumb and desperate? How was I going to get out of this?

"Take the money," I begged as he twisted my arm behind me, bent me backward, licked my neck with a tongue that felt ten miles long. "Please, just take it and leave me alone. Go now, and I won't tell a soul. Believe me, I won't ever." I fished in the pocket of my tee for cash and averted my gaze. "I'll forget this encounter, forget your face, forget you ever came here."

The sinister would-be shopper sneered and leered. He bit me on the ear and pressed my spine to the water heater, breaking into sardonic laughter, dragging me over the concrete floor in a tango, lifting my feet off the floor. "Where the book?" he hissed as he swung me around.

"The book?" I repeated. "Go look. It's fine. You can have whatever book you want. Take all of them. They're there." I jerked my chin toward unsold books in a corner in a cardboard box.

"The. Book." He spoke as if teaching a unicellular organism how to read.

"Oh, the book," I faked, mind racing, keen to agree with whatever he bellowed. What the heck book was he talking about? "Wait a sec. I'll get it for you."

I broke away, scurrying back to the door, the intruder on my heels. He grumbled in a frightening drone. "You bettah or you die, you unnerstan'?"

"Uh-huh." I nodded coyly, sidling to try to put distance between us.

Outside, in the driveway, there came a pop so loud it made me jump. A toddler let out a bloodcurdling cry, and another unleashed a piercing shriek.

The invader pivoted toward the noises, slinking along the west cinder block wall.

A balloon rolled under the cracked garage door. Four little hands reached out for it.

In that instant, I ran like my shoes were on fire, fumbled my keys into the lock, and hauled into the laundry room. Locking the door behind me, I whipped out my cell and tapped in 911. Seconds later, I heard the Ferrari tear up the street and make a squealing turn. Five harrowing minutes after that, the cops were there, and the guy was gone.

I filed a quick police report with a good cop-bad cop team that came in a cruiser with no flashing lights—a white male smelling like stink bombs and a Native American woman with a short haircut and probing eyes, who acted sympathetic. They told me to describe the thug and what happened to me step by step but didn't appear to be listening to my tale with any interest.

When they left, I huddled alone in the bedroom. Trembling. Wondering about *the book*. Wondering if those cops would come back later. Pondering what I'd do. I realized I was more threatened by the police than even Mr. Creeps, and it made my blood boil that I was. I didn't do scary very well. I wasn't into fear. But the whole thing left me traumatized, and there I stayed in the locked bedroom until I dozed off into sleep and didn't wake up until broad daylight.

The morning was sunny and warm, and when I awoke, it took several seconds before I remembered the creep in the garage. The chilling experience of the day before began to envelop me, but the scent of seaweed and bougainvillea soothed me as I opened a patio door and breathed in deep. Terror vaporized in summer rays and left me to my work.

I recorded an audition and uploaded it onto my agent's online portal in our studio. Bill buzzed and left me a sexy message while my phone was muted so its ringtone didn't disturb my recording session and ruin takes. *Oh no, I missed his call*, I thought, bummed out and wishing he were home. I needed to feel his arms around me, place my ear against his chest. But I knew he'd worry if I told. And I figured he'd come rushing home. That wouldn't be good for his career or our ailing finances. I'd just wait.

I clicked on the TV to distract myself while I tossed a green salad to eat for lunch, and the newswoman gave me another jolt.

"We have breaking news from Mizner Park, following a deadly discovery there. Stunning details released this hour by an FBI spokesperson just confirmed my reporting on earlier broadcasts." This from the fast-talking TV newscaster, Storey Turner, on the scene. "Regarding the overnight murder of gangland enforcer, Franco Muerte, sources now tell us his body was found in a dumpster this morning at two a.m. by a startled sanitation crew, behind me here at Mizner Park, a popular dining and shopping plaza located in Boca Raton. The illusive Muerte, also known as Sergio Bass, Lars Vendegaard, and his well-known nickname, FM Dial, is believed to have been on the hunt for something or someone when he was killed."

Muerte's photo splashed across the screen.

It was him. The creep. The man in greige. The Ferrari guy in my garage.

I blinked and looked at the tube again, but there was no denying it.

I grabbed my phone and googled him. His mug was all over the internet, hatching new hashtags trending on Twitter—#muertemurder and #FMDial were blowing up on Instagram, and the one thing all the blogs agreed was that Muerte came to town to kill. But kill whom, was the question on everyone's lips. Everyone's but mine. For I was aware the goon almost killed *me*.

I got so light-headed I started to faint. I grabbed a cold bottle of water, rolled it across my forehead, popped the cap, and guzzled almost all of it.

The attack had to be a random flub. A gaffe. Mistaken identity. A blunder. A dangerous misconception. Muerte must have been confused. But did hit men even get confused? Did I look that much like someone else?

I called Bill in Toronto, but he was in session. I left a brief message to call me back, and when I didn't hear from him by noon, I got freaked out. Undone, I retrieved the good cop's business card and tried to call her. When she didn't pick up, I decided that leaving a message might not be so wise. How could I know who was listening to recordings, who took payoffs, who iced Muerte, or who sought the book.

"Why was a hit man stalking me?" I asked and felt more tired and weak. The very idea was incredible. Did somebody actually want me killed? I had a stack of unpaid bills, but if that were a capital offense, a bazillion people would be dead. What had I done to become a target? Zippo. I hadn't hurt anyone. Had Bill? I'd have to ask. Another thought occurred to me—if Muerte was really after me and got murdered while he was on my tail, then wouldn't whoever dispatched him send another assassin to finish me off? Maybe the one who took Muerte out? The notion blew my mind.

Who on earth would want to murder me?

I sat in my office chair, bit my knuckle, stared at the bookshelves lining the opposite wall and glaring back at me. *The book.* That's what he came for, right? Yeah. Of course, he told me so. But which book was he after? I had zillions. I was an avid reader. Was it a signed one I got at a book party? Maybe a valuable first edition? A vintage book gone out of print? Was it fiction or nonfiction? Did I still have the book or did I sell it? *Oh my goodness.* If I did…

I jumped to my feet and pored over the bookshelves. That didn't seem to do much good. It wasn't like I had an ancient manuscript in hieroglyphics or da Vinci's *Codex Leicester* science diary thieves would steal. Who could guess what Muerte wanted? Bookhunters valued different genres. Some loved romance, mystery, memoir, thriller, or sci-fi. What sort of books did hit men crave? Horror, I supposed.

I whipped out the checkbook-style receipt book I had used for customers and sat at my glass-top desk to examine who had purchased what from me. I was an anal-retentive record keeper, detailed to a fault, so each stub in the receipt book held the customer's name, address, phone number, email, total, and a note. I'd planned to start a database for e-blasts for my next yard sale, but after this fiasco, if I never set up or attended a yard sale again, it'd be too soon.

The ledger logged seventy books that were bought but by only six couples or families—The McShanes, the Kenubongos, the del Valles, the Two Winghorses, the Worthingtons who lived right next door, and the Lassiters over on Nestling Lane. I called each one of them in turn, but none kicked up a clue. I didn't let on what my problem was. I just thanked them for coming and chatted them up. When that came up empty, I searched through the bookcase again and much more carefully. I examined each book by flipping them open this time and thumbing through. Looking for something that only Muerte knew might be inside. Maybe whomever Muerte worked for already found what they wanted. Maybe not. Which book was worth killing for? I scoured our cookbooks, phone books, chapbooks. Nothing. Zilch. A goose egg. Nada.

Stumped, I fled to the ocean, for though that was the spot where my sea of troubles began, I longed to breathe salt air. While I was walking on the beach, dipping my toes in the water, deep in thought, the house alarm went off. Ours wasn't the only alarm nearby, but I knew the particular sound of it, and the security company quickly buzzed to alert me through their app.

When cops arrived a second time, I filed another report and spilled my guts about the Muerte thing, but they didn't believe a word I said. They filed a false alarm. They said they got calls all the time from people who claimed to have spotted criminals. Nuts, attention-seekers, grifters looking to collect rewards, or criminals wanting ten minutes of fame. True crime bred mass hysteria, they said and blew me off. I was in it alone, just like I thought. And as much as I loved our brand-new nest, to stay there would be dangerous. Only, I had no place to go.

It dawned on me—an orphaned child with one parent struck down in a war overseas and the other destroyed in the war on drugs, of opioid addiction—that Bill and I didn't make friends here like we did out in LA. We counted on each other more. The homes in our town were owned by older snowbirds, who flew south in winter months to warmer, posher digs. Not young professionals like us. Our connections were in Miami Beach, where hipper action happened. We lived in the 'burbs, where we were out of sight and out of mind. There was no one here to take me in, like the parents who adopted and protected me until they passed.

I checked my phone for messages, but there wasn't a single word from Bill. I thought of who else I could reach out to, but my email was crammed with useless spam and my networking timelines were riddled with Muerte's rampant dirty deeds: Children burned in Nicaragua. Young girls raped in Cameroon. Mass murders in Angola. Cocaine smuggling. Piracy. Pimping for the Italian mob. Weapons sales in Yemen. Lynchings in the United States with a band of white supremacists. It seemed nothing truly nefarious in the world lacked Muerte's stamp on it. He had ties to a White House aide accused of torturing his wife and kids, and a senator pocketing donors' cash.

Behind the wheel of my Audi, I dialed Bill again at his hotel, but it seemed he fell off of the edge of the earth. I pulled into a park a block from the gate that guarded our community and gazed at the Intracoastal Waterway and the docked yachts harbored there, waiting for Bill to call me back and opening a granola bar.

That's when I heard the fire engines. Faint at first, then loud and shrill. I don't recall why I started the car or why I hurried home right then, but I did, and I saw our house ablaze. It was déjà vu all over again. I couldn't believe my eyes. I pulled close and ran toward roaring flames.

The fire department arrived in a flash, and after the smoke cleared, I took heart. It wasn't as bad as it looked at first, and trust me, it looked totaled. Most of the ruin was concentrated in our garage, a fireman said. The smoke and water damage was the worst of it, he stated, but we'd need remediation. That'd be one more huge expense we'd have to pony up.

"Good thing you weren't trapped inside," said a firewoman with purple hair tied up inside her helmet.

"Trapped inside?" I parroted.

"Sure," said a burly fireman wearing tissue on a shaving cut. "If you were inside there, you'd be fried."

My intestines somersaulted.

"We're not trying to scare you, ma'am," said another first responder who was carrying a fire hose and fiddling with a fireplug. "Civilian fire fatalities are pretty high in Florida and up the whole East Coast. You have to make sure your house is free of hazards with your electrical wires, combustibles, appliances, fireplace mantels, stuff like that. Whatever might arc or spark. I'm not saying that's what happened here. This fire looks suspicious. We'll investigate how it started, but it might take several weeks or months."

"Looks like arson off the bat," said a Black firewoman with long blue dreads. "There's evidence of an accelerant… but you didn't hear that from me, okay?"

My phone rang. It was finally Bill. I excused myself to update him.

"Wait. Our crib is torched. Again?"

"Yeah, but it's not totaled. Is our renter's insurance up to date?"

"I hope. I'll have to check. Are you okay? You aren't hurt?"

"Yeah, I'm fine, no thanks to them. I mean, whoever set the fire." I crept out of earshot, rounding the corner, skirting a crowd of onlookers and speaking in quiet tones to be discreet. "It had to do with Muerte, Bill. Who else would burn us out? It was no wildfire. It was set. That's what a couple of the firemen said."

"Get out of there, sugar. I'm coming home," said Bill. "I need to look after you."

"But what about the job?" I asked.

"Forget it. I'll scrap it. You need me, babe."

"You've worked too hard to chuck it now. It's an animated series. Catch a plane later. I'll work it out. What more could happen now?" As soon as the words came out of my mouth, I was mortified I'd said them.

"Okay, then I'll leave just as soon as we wrap. Check into a hotel, okay? I'll get my hotel concierge to find a reservation somewhere nice. Where you'll be comfortable."

"All right. Blue skies and happy landings. I'll be fine. I love you, bear."

By the time I'd gathered a few essentials into an Estée Lauder gift-with-purchase tote, some Hi-Tek Security personnel had the charred garage door boarded up and several windows battened down until new glass could be installed. I was able to leave by sunset, but the I-95 was gridlocked by a ten-car pileup triggered by an overturned chocolate delivery truck that blocked the road with candy and the kids that came from miles around to try to snatch it up.

As I waited in stop-and-go traffic, I couldn't stop thinking about the book. I inched to the 595 connector just as the Sirius XM What's Up station broadcast new details in the Franco Muerte murder. It announced that prior to his demise, Muerte had fallen into disfavor with the most powerful Russian oligarch in all Ukraine—Dmitri Bagoyev Siempkinov. And as Muerte's hedge against reprisal, Muerte penned a tell-all book, a scathing autobiography naming names and betraying conspirators. Purportedly, it confessed unspeakable crimes, unmasking a nest of spies. But apparently, now the text was gone. No files and no hard copy.

The publishing house's computer system got hacked in the early-morning hours, implanted with wiper viruses that deleted all their manuscripts, including Muerte's tour de force. Plus, they lost cloud storage and their shredders disappeared. The damage was said to top the billions, and that wasn't all of it. The editor who had bought the book was just unearthed in his toddler's toy box, sunk in the waters off Long Island, sans his writing hand and tongue. Interpol was on the case, and the book was considered evidence of felonies around the globe.

"The book," I heard Muerte say again. So that's what he was after. Why would he think I had it though? A collage began painting the once-blank canvas of one corner of my mind where a synapse fired up a clue.

"Okay, okay," I reasoned, "what if Muerte lived inside our house? Before us. When the home was empty. It was a model home at first, but then it stood vacant for several months before our buddy leased to us. Muerte could've rented it and used it as a safe house. Or maybe he broke into it. Who knows, he could've been injured or just desperate to lie low. He might've ducked in through a window if he was running from his enemies. Any port in a storm, as the saying goes. It could've been his hideout. A place that he secretly occupied between his villainies overseas. It was chilling to think, but he might've even crept inside while we were there and hid up in the attic. Or he could've driven by one day and seen us moving in. He could've slipped in with the movers while the doors were open, couldn't he? And tried to hide his tell-all book where no one would think to look for it. In a house up in suburbia. If so, he'd have blown a gasket when he returned from one of his crime sprees and saw me conducting a yard sale. He'd be frantic to retrieve his book before the text changed hands."

What if he'd seen a woman selling books at the very same address he knew his book was hidden in? A tome that exposed international crimes that'd send him to Old Sparky—the electric chair—or worse, provoke the wrath of one of his deadliest former cohorts, one he feared. A man he had fingered in a scathing book exposing an oligarch, or maybe several oligarchs, or someone even higher up, a politico with a longer reach. An autocrat. A dictator. What if they tracked him and killed him and now they were looking for the book? They might well go to any lengths.

Those prospects made me nauseous, but I had to think them through.

Even if any of that were the case, how could anyone have known that Muerte hid the book with me? If they knew, what on earth would they do if they caught me alone *without* the manuscript? Was it a manuscript or a galley? Did the killers know for sure? Either way, they'd never believe I sold it or it burned up in a fire. Torture or death would ensue from it. But what if the book thing was a ruse, a bluff Muerte fashioned to save his hide? The book might not exist at all. They said it was just an insurance policy. If it was, it didn't work. No murderer would rely on that though. They'd tie up loose ends. As long as Muerte was alive, whomever the book exposed would track it down at any cost. But if Muerte was dead—which was the case— presumably all bets were off. The book could turn up anywhere. And cause a major firestorm.

What if I had the book in a form I hadn't thought of yet? Books got published in so many formats—hardcovers, paperbacks, e-books, Braille. Audiobooks were favorites, spiking in sales by as much as twenty-five percent a year from what I read. Could that be what they're looking for? Downloads were extremely popular. Could Muerte have hacked my computer and stored it in there, as a digital file? Where would I hide a book if I had to? There were even mini books and matchbooks. We collected those.

Wait. It hit like a lightning bolt. Matchbooks. What if it's in a matchbook? Sure. Why didn't I see it before? The only books I didn't search, and that no one else would think to either, were our collection of matchbooks that were once in a box beneath our sink but were now on our fireplace mantel. In the family room. In the giant jar. Muerte's book could be in a matchbook on a mini or micro SD card. Even a mini flash drive fits inside a matchbox, doesn't it? It sure was worth a try.

Whether I engaged the cruise control or automatic pilot, I don't remember contemplating anything more than going back. I took off without another thought, the wheels of the car spinning off the highway like four flying metal Frisbees, backing along the shoulder to the exit half a mile behind.

Under the full moon, Paradise Found community felt like Sleepy Hollow as I eased down toward our house. Not even one light lit a solitary window at this hour of night. I boogied past the entry fountains, whizzed by the Aquatic Center, turned at the fountain on Frontage Road, and slammed on my brakes as a duck mommy shepherded nine yellow ducklings around the bend. I ambled past our own address with my headlights off and killed the engine, coasting into the cul-de-sac kitty-corner to our abandoned pad and parking in an easement set behind a gated dumpster. I got out, noiselessly closed the car door, and sneaked up the street to our portico.

A bouquet of saline, orange, oleander buds, and Spanish moss peppered subtropical currents blowing off the Atlantic into our yard, tickling my scalp and making the hairs stand up on the nape of my neck. I opened the door, took a peek inside, and walked into the shadows, drawing the blinds on our ocean view as acrid smoke shot through my lungs, an after-effect of the earlier blaze.

"Quick. Make it snappy," I urged myself as I gripped my tiny key chain flashlight, shining it over the great room walls, wood floor, and modern furniture. I padded across the family room to the fireplace, reached for the matchbook jar, and heard voices out on the patio. Somebody rattled the French door's nickel knob and pounded the glass.

I snapped up the matchbook jar and ran, crossing the great room, dousing the flashlight, ducking into the storage space under the stairs, and closing its door. The smell of smoke was overpowering. I had to stifle a cough with my hand as muted men's voices argued, cursing, rumbling in bass, ill-tempered tones.

"Hurry up, Numb Nuts, this ain't cool. What asshole returns to the scene of the crime?"

"Yeah, bro, it smells like barbecue."

"Well, you ought to know, you torched the place."

"Will you two idiots shut your mouths and jimmy the lock before we're busted? Jeez, you guys are freaking morons. Pull that plywood off the sidelight, fool, and reach your hand inside."

I could almost hear lock tumblers clicking after the wood plank ripped away. The voices grew louder and closer to me, and the words got bold and clearer.

"She's gone, I'm tellin' ya," one voice urged. "Her car ain't here, the place is dark, and the Mickey Mouse sensors got disarmed. Chillax, or your ulcer will flare."

"You better find that freaking book, or it ain't gonna be all caviar and vodka like it's been, you dig? You pricks will end up dog food, get it? I ain't goin' out like that."

"Whaddaya think I been doin' all this time, reviewin' literature? I flipped through every page on every shelf. The book ain't here. I'm tellin' ya, he lied to us. He sent us down a rabbit hole."

A third, more husky voice chimed in. "You better hope that book burned up. When word gets out that Muerte didn't go down and that ain't his body, you'll be readin' your obituary."

What, was Muerte still alive?

Male feet began clomping up the stairs, and footsteps thumped above my head, so I knew one was up on the second floor. I strangled on smoke and suppressed a cough, and when some guy slammed the pantry door, I knew he was in the kitchen. When the toilet flushed in the guest bathroom, that accounted for all three hoodlums' whereabouts, and it told me the guy in the bath, who was also the hooligan nearest me, could be literally caught with his pants down.

I decided to make a break for it before they discovered my hiding place. I flew out of the closet, raced through the door, began hoofing across the lawn.

"It's her!" a man shouted, giving chase, pursuing me in a full-out sprint. "Get her. The broad ran out the front."

Behind me, a shadow broached the doorframe, trailing me like a line-backer making a play on a wiry quarterback. Sprinklers came on as he crossed the grass. "Dammit," he said. "My brand-new suit. This sucker cost three grand." Out of the corner of my eye, I caught him dodging and darting, brushing groundwater off his sleeves. "Bitch, I'm gonna make you pay."

The others gave chase from the back of the house, one dashing out from either side as the first crook hit the walkway. I kicked it into overdrive, every ligament straining in my calves, my smoke-filled trachea heaving. I had nothing to protect myself. My pepper spray was in the car, but even if it weren't, it was no match for the gunshots ringing out when I reached the slippery garden edge. I leaped onto the concrete easement, tripping over an automatic sprinkler, flying forward. I landed scraped, grass-stained, and reeling from the way I hit my head. "Help!" I screamed. "Help, someone, please!" My vision starting blurring.

A light flickered on in the house by my Audi as I clambered to my feet. I hastened to scoop up the matchbook jar, jetted across the pavement, hoofing it down to the end of the cul-de-sac. I clicked the clicker, hopped inside.

Pop, pop, pop! came rapid-fire. A bullet blasted the rear windshield.

I revved the engine, grabbed the door. *Too late!* One gunman seized my elbow, pointing his gun right at my face, jerking my bicep with his claw. I dug my long fingernails into his flesh, bit into his salty, grasping hand, and gunned the engine, zipping off. My left wrist tore from his mighty grip as my car lurched awkwardly into gear while I turned the steering wheel with my right, and the car took off like a bucking bronco, dragging the thug along the road. I powered forward, twisting the wheel, maneuvering the Audi in a circle, ringing the curb of the cul-de-sac, lugging the killer along with me, road rashing him on his legs and butt. He wouldn't let go. He couldn't let go.

Ammo was flying everywhere. Pinging off house numbers, denting a flagpole, clipping a row of hawthorn hedges, taking out a Barbie car, and creaming a row of gold coach lamps. I ran over a skateboard, took out a bird bath, two-wheeled on and off the neighbors' lawns, and blew my left rear tire. Bright sparks flew from the tire rim as a grapefruit tree sapling fell into the road, and I had to veer around it. A blue heron casualty hit the hood, its wings taking out what was left of my view. By now, all the neighbors' lights were shining. One, in an open Hawaiian shirt, flip-flops, and a baggy pair of shorts recorded a smartphone video as I raced away from gunshots, my exterior passenger finally peeling away from the car when we hit a bump. He landed in a twisted heap on the grate of a drainage ditch. I swung left at the corner, hit the main drag, ran a red light at the third street down, and on-ramped to the highway.

The scariest night of my life was over, but the jeopardy was not.

Bill and I called the FBI as soon as he got back in town.

Our matchbook jar was the break they needed.

Inside the cover of dozens of matchbooks, they found sophisticated codes and small samples of various human bloods that catalogued every hit job Muerte undertook in his career. He confessed who he hit, where the bodies were dumped, the dates, how he killed, how much he received, the method of payment—a money trail—and most saliently, who paid him. There were over two thousand hits in all, not counting collateral damages or "acceptable" loss of life.

Newspapers reported months after the fact that, in efforts to thwart his comeuppance from the mobsters he brutally murdered for, it turned out that Muerte had faked his death and hired the hit men himself. According to plan, he escaped the hit when a litter of his capos died. His gambit was successful to a point, but then it fell apart. A cutthroat caught in an existential bind won't tend to stay there long. Vibrations usually meet their match, and Muerte's vibe was deadly. Before the authorities found him out, the famous assassin was killed for real.

Why a cold-blooded hit man chose our home for a hideout could be horrendous luck or macabre exogenous circumstance, but Muerte's blood money bought Hi-Tek Security just one month before we moved to Boca, so we doubt it was. Hi-Tek was Muerte's first foray into owning legitimate businesses. It was also the company we selected to shield ourselves from men like him. The fox was in charge of our henhouse, and we paid him for the privilege. Owning Hi-Tek allowed him to monitor all its clients and to bypass their security systems regularly. Not a bad asset for someone like him but a sizable liability for his partners in organized crime. They needed security more than most and had the most to spy on.

Bill and I earned a reward for providing the information we dug up. It led to arrests of bad guys, here and abroad, involved in grisly crimes. And learning from blunders in our past, we invested it wisely enough to thrive. Neither of us expected to net a fortune from our matchbook jar, from doing our civic duty, or from solving a mystery to stay alive, but we managed to up our game in life. We conquered our financial woes and now help others do the same. We have to look over our shoulders though, and probably always will.

You never know what you can sell or what trouble you'll buy at a garage sale.

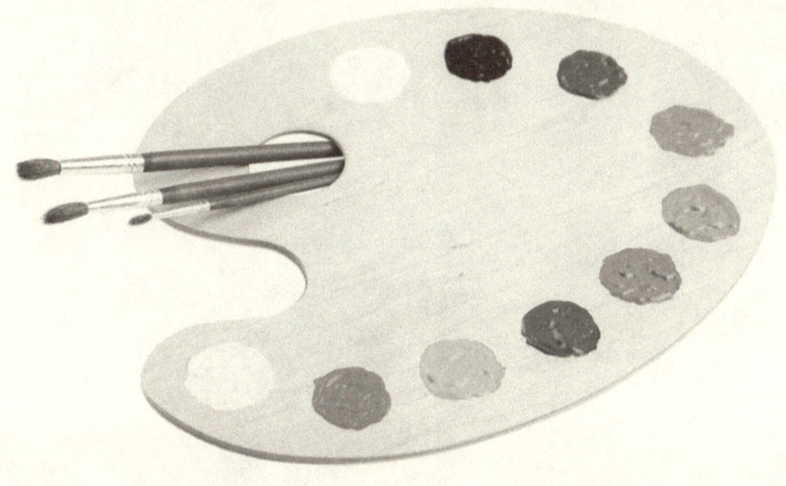

CANVASSING THE NEIGHBORHOOD

S HE FIGURED HER FRIENDS WOULD STAB HER IN THE BACK ONE DAY, and she was right.

Except one of them used a butcher knife.

The Black Beauty Sketchers and Painters Club was giving one member the brush-off. Darlene Masters was their nemesis, and they gave her the boot the day before her nude portrait was found on Starry Lake. They were stressing their Bal Harbor Art Fest entries, anxious to see who'd sell the most, when one of them showed her true colors and literally nailed Darlene to the wall.

Arthur Framingham (a pseudonym) stabbed his Mars-Red key in the dead bolt lock of the Price-Hall Gallery's glass front door, his long, thin fingers trembling. Admiring his rainbow-colored curls and his burnt sienna Armani shirt reflected in the slick facade, he tightened his Rembrandt-inspired tie and licked the tip of his right ring finger, sweeping it over his arched eyebrows and, carrying a large portfolio, glided into the darkened studio.

The first thing he noticed was the smell.

Caustic odors were bad for Art's sinuses, and he instantly began to sneeze.

Why was it so cold inside? The chiller must be on the fritz again. Art—who'd worked at the Louvre, the New York Museum of Modern Art, the Museum of Contemporary Art Africa, and the Fowler Museum at UCLA—knew well that the standard temperature for keeping most paintings' mediums safe was seventy degrees, but it felt like the place was half that now. The humidity seemed to be higher than the fifty percent it should be too.

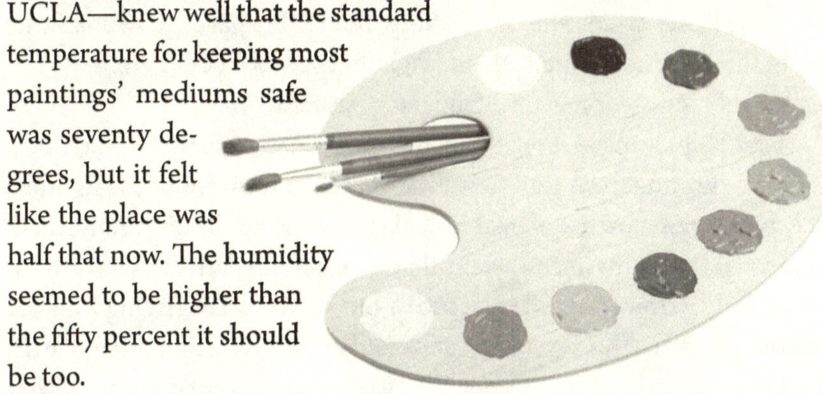

Art was a stickler for proper environment. Barring it, he could not borrow great art. And though there was growing sentiment that a new or refurbished gallery need not strictly adhere to established levels, Art refused to deviate. They were guideposts of integrity, and that was an art dealer's stock-in-trade. Without it, Art had nothing. He refused to lower his standards no matter what other dealers said or did. That's why, in a jiffy, he sensed that all was not right inside his gallery, as he jabbed at the whining alarm pad, poking his code in, dousing its wail. "Always something," he said with a finger snap. "Irresponsible artists, late deliveries, lookie-loos, forgers, crooked workmen. It will be the death of me."

Art ticked his spit-shined loafers across the stone-look laminate floor tile to address the high-tech lighting pad. He groaned, exasperated. "These spend-on-your-lighting-it's-vital bloodsuckers bleed you dry, and what do you get? Mediocrity. If you're lucky." He fiddled with the rheostat that ran the many LEDs, but not a single light came on. "What else can go wrong before the show?" He fussed and shuddered in the cold, the balmy South Florida evening he left outside a distant memory. A shiver skidded up his shaved brown arms and a rivulet of icy sweat began roiling his finely honed mustache when he sensed he wasn't alone. He did a three-sixty in the space, and he jumped as a sort of mirage whizzed by in his failing peripheral vision.

Something fleeting caught his eye, averting his gaze to the vaulted ceiling. *A flashlight beam?* It flickered.

The room was lit only by streetlights other than that, so it was a jarring glare that swept across a tall white wall. A sudden cacophonous clatter of footsteps scrambled through the dusky hall and bolted out the steel back door. *Bam!* A car door slammed in the rear lot. The screech of burning tire rubber peeled to the side street, made a turn, and screamed off to the north.

"Thief!" Art cried reflexively. "Stop, thief!" He gave chase at a futile pace. In the alley, he scouted left and right but saw nobody there.

The intruder—or maybe intruders—escaped.

Heart palpitating, Art retreated, forging back in to survey the artwork, frantically running from wall to wall, from room to room of the lightless space. Nothing seemed stolen at first glance, or vandalized or ransacked. He rearmed the alarm in an eerie stillness, searching dark corners of what was normally Arthur's favorite place to be but now was a terrifying void. He eased on the balls of his feet to his office, slid open its reclaimed-wood barn door, tiptoed in to check things out. This was where he kept cash in a pewter safe in a closet, disguised by an old tea chest. He counted it. All there. He dug in a desk drawer, fished for his Maglite flashlight, turned it on. A cone of intense light spread its glow on towering white-dove-colored walls as he crept back into the gallery proper, sneezing uncontrollably.

The Black Beauty Painters Club pieces, newly displayed in five tasteful art vignettes, hung on free-standing walls that stood in the center of the main hall gallery, awaiting tomorrow's grand debut.

But wait. What's that? How odd, thought Art as he nearly stepped on one of them. It lay flat on the gallery floor with several others. Why were they scattered there? "These can't be what a thief was after," Art mused aloud as he stooped and looked. He had art far more worthy of stealing than the amateur entries he only displayed for the charity auction once a year. Of course, in the art world, one couldn't tell what might command a fortune or attract a collector's eccentric eye. Why, just last week, a travesty sold for a million smackeroos. It was only a rusty pipe dripping plastic feces onto a president's effigy, tinting a part of his hairdo brown. So nothing surprised Art anymore, but that was half the fun. Still, why would someone vandalize Black Beauty art before it sold? They weren't professional artists. They were students in his art class. Purchasers merely bought from them to support a worthy cause—the hospital's children's cancer ward, the minority scholarship artists fund, or practically, for tax write-offs. Except for Darlene. They loved her work.

That was why what Art saw next blew his mind and made him sneeze again.

Suddenly, with sickening lucidity, Art was staring at why the intruder broke in.

Up on a wall at the end of the hall—mounted amid Ruth Yardley's *Man on Fire* abstract portraiture, Crystal Emerson's *Metaphysical Diaspora* landscape art on wood, Satin Cummings's *Stick Figure Erotica,* and Zoey Wright's fanciful illustrations—hung Darlene Masters, in the flesh, enshrined in a life-size gilded frame with a pink-chiffon noose around her neck and the business end of a kitchen knife thrust through her bleeding heart.

Crystal Emerson stood at a standing desk, stringing azure blue Austrian crystals. She was making the necklace she planned to wear to the studio gala tomorrow night. A matching blue bracelet sat in a box beside shimmery bracelets she made for the girls, peace offerings designed to cool them down. The drama among them had to stop. The girls were fighting like cats and dogs, and she couldn't stand it anymore. She felt it was up to her to cleanse the ailing vibe of their group dynamic and balance their karmas and chakra zones. Having managed to break away from *him,* she sure wasn't trying to court more conflict now that she was finally free. All she wanted to do was paint star charts, build her astrology clientele, and live in peace and harmony.

Her necklace was blue to bring freedom and joy.

Crystal was golden-honey brown with shoulder-length, cadmium-yellow hair and a set of arresting violet eyes that sparkled as bright as the gems she wore. Nobody knew where the eyes came from except for her mother, now deceased, who had fallen in love with a handyman who worked in the project where Crystal grew up. His hair wasn't dyed like Crystal's was. Her father was a natural blond. A hardy Norwegian immigrant who was whiter than Casper the Friendly Ghost. He was missing one eye, and the other was violet, a combo so rare it became his brand.

Crystal only found out who her father was at the side of her mother's deathbed. Before that, she believed he was Clifton DeGare, the man her mother was married to until he fell into an empty elevator shaft en route to work. After that, only Crystal's third eye since birth kept her and her grieving mother afloat, a handwritten sign outside their tenement door alerting passersby that the little girl in 13F was a psychic who could see your past and prophesy your future. She predicted the date of her father's death, but unfortunately the only fate she couldn't see was hers.

Crystal's loft, overlooking the lake on the west, was small, but the condo afforded her friendship, fun, and a slew of potential clients. A newcomer to Fort Lauderdale, transplanted from Los Angeles, the astrologer simply adored her space. She didn't regret for an instant leaving the rush or theatrics of Hollywood stars she formerly tendered readings for, and the kaleidoscopic Florida sky and idyllic view of waterfowl worked magic for her daily moods. Crystal loved nature and wanted to keep life Zen. She was working to reinvent and trying to leave her past behind. There was only one thing— one person, really—threatening to ruin her transformation. Darlene Masters was a threat, a rival, and bad energy.

Former cover girl Satin Cummings slid into the cool cerulean sheets of a custom king-size platform waterbed, rubbing argan oil onto one raw-umber breast as her dream man kissed the other. Her husband, Brick Hauser, the wealthy contractor who'd built Dreamland Cove, where their mansion stood, gladly nuzzled her girls and yanked her close. She arched her back and gripped his ears.

"That's right, baby, come to Papa. Bring that sexy fine brown frame to me where you belong."

"Where do you get those corny lines?" She laughed and kissed him on his ear.

"Where else," he said. "I buy online. But don't you worry, trophy wife, what I lack as a poet, I make up in moves." He thrust his pelvis on her.

"I'll vouch for that," she cooed to him, her head disappearing beneath the sheets.

"Uh-oh, what do you want?" he warily droned as she took him in her mouth.

She pumped his erection with one hand and popped out from under the covers. "What do you mean?"

"I mean, what's up? Whenever you act like a porno star, I can bet it's going to cost. What is it this time? A tennis bracelet? Kitchen reno? Vacay, what?"

"That's pretty cynical, don't you think?"

"No, I think it's practical. I'm trying to save us both some time so I can enjoy what you're going to kick up in exchange for whatever's on your mind. We're married, remember? I know the drill. You use what you have to get what you want, and I want what you're going to give for it. So I'm listening. Break it down."

"Okay, I guess that's fair enough."

"Aaand?"

"I want the contest," Satin blurted, rising to her haunches.

"What, you want us to sponsor one?"

"No, I want you to buy me one."

"I'm feeling like Ricky Ricardo now. Can you speak in a language I understand so I don't have to struggle?"

"If you do it, we'll resell. I promise we'll make the money back. And more."

"Well, this sounds interesting." Brick propped himself up on their pillows and laced his fingers behind his head, a hint of amusement in his eyes.

"Don't look at me that way," she said. "I have a good idea this time."

"Okay. I'll bite. Enlighten me. And quick. I'm harder than chromium."

"I wanna sell the most paintings at the exhibit, and I've found a way."

Brick burst out laughing, grabbed his ribs. "*That's* what this is all about? That isn't a contest."

"Yeah, it is. I have to beat the girls."

"You turn everything into a competition. I actually think you're serious. Look, baby girl, your paintings suck. You have plenty of talents, but art ain't one. Darlene has that sewed up. C'mon under the sheets and do your thing." He reached out, came up empty.

Satin jumped out of their bed, put her hands on her hips, threw her pillow at him and sulked, her eyes emitting poison darts and her arms crossed like a statue. "You say I can have anything I want, but whatever I want, you say it's wrong and you never want to kick it up," she whined with her bottom lip poked out. "I don't deny you anything."

"You're denying me what I want right now. I hope lightning doesn't strike us both for that bald-faced whopper you just told. You make me beg for everything from my eggs in the morning to nookie at night. I want to be making love, and instead I wind up in your tantrum."

"So what if my paintings aren't as good as Darlene's? At least I'm trying, and I need you to respect my work. You do what you're good at every day, and what do I have? This house to clean. No babies like Ruth or visions like Crystal or escapades like Zoey has. My life isn't going anywhere. I have to have something of my own."

"Okay, okay, get back in bed. I know you're frustrated, but that isn't how you accomplish things, by scheming. You plan your work and work your plan. You dream, set goals, and grind. I wish you could see what I see in you. You're a leader, not a follower. You just need to set out on a path, that's all."

"Don't you see? That's what I'm trying to do."

Brick breathed an exasperated sigh. "Well, we both know you'll get your way in the end the way you always do, but I really don't know how you think I can get your paintings sold."

"I do," she said. She jiggled and dove on top of him, smothering him with kisses.

"I bet," he said fending her kisses off, chuckling and starting to tickle her. "You might as well spill it, whatever it is. I'll do my best to help you out," he capitulated, cackling.

"Well…" she began, and she ran it down.

The intrigue made Brick's eyes widen.

Ruth Yardley couldn't sleep a wink.

Darlene Masters was bopping Ruth's husband right under her very own aquiline nose. After her years of wedded torture, it didn't matter anymore that Harper Yardley was the most crooked investment broker in all of Florida. It was baked in the cake that Harper got drunk on the weekends and beat Ruth half to death and the fact her whole family disowned her when she consented to be his long-suffering wife. Ruth accepted all of that. Nothing mattered but that she was married to that handsome man and had his kids. Harper was Ruth's sole claim to fame. But his secrets were starting to ruin that as well, which was intolerable.

That's why she had hired a private detective to trail her sorry philanderer when he started to come home late at night. And now, as she checked the nursery, watching their innocent triplet toddlers sleep in their onesies in their custom cribs, her jealous mind was plagued with raunchy images she couldn't shake. The photos the detective sent of Harper and that heifer tied in love knots hit her harder than her husband ever did. It was lucky the kids were asleep when she threw her iPad at the wall. And to think that her painting of Harper would be on display for all to see. The dysfunction her shrink would make of that could get her committed all over again. And Harper would do it. She knew he would.

It wouldn't be the first time she got locked up in a crazy house. She'd spent a year at Hillside Grange, straitjacketed when she first arrived after being gang-raped on her trek to the States from Haiti. Nobody knew about that. Her ordeal could've driven her nuts for good, but she bounced back like a champ. And now she was a rich man's wife, although Harper didn't deserve her love far less her admiration. It sucked. She once believed in Harp. It made her sick to think of it. But she felt she had no alternative with three babies to consider. It sure wouldn't help to confront the man. However, his home-wrecker needed to know exactly who she was messing with. There was more than one way to skin a cat.

She had to fix Darlene.

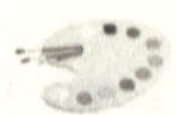

Zoey Wright watched Darlene's patio through her telescope day after day. Some really weird stuff was going on. Darlene had something up. Darlene was embroiled in more than her usual hijinks and sexual escapades. This time she wasn't just sleeping with Ruthie's husband or raking in megabucks for her art and rubbing the other club members' noses in it constantly or dredging up Crystal's sordid past, long gone and best forgotten. Now she was into something weird and wild and Machiavellian. It wasn't just Zoey observing it either. Crystal said she felt it in the air, and what Crystal predicted seemed to always come to pass.

Okay, maybe Zoey, who illustrated African American children's books and wrote sci-fi books and fantasies, had a vivid imagination, but she wasn't imagining how Darlene had gotten nervous lately. Anyone could see that much. She was getting odd visitors at odd hours. Like tonight, after Zoey's live-in boyfriend, Travis, went on a business trip to New York and left Zoey home alone.

Zoey was nibbling a salad when a limo pulled up outside Darlene's. It was green, and a goon in maroon got out with a weaselly guy in a green Fedora out of Central Casting. Zoey would eat her hat if they weren't gangsters. They looked scary. Zoey was a buppie princess, trained to know trouble when she saw it. Inside her gated neighborhood, they stuck out like sore thumbs. And they didn't drop by for a cup of sugar either, that's for sure. They lurked outside Darlene's for hours, messing with her head. Zoey kept munching crispy kale as she watched Darlene run through her house to check the locks when they arrived. She saw her call somebody too. Zoey scoped it from her kitchen sliders where she had a bird's-eye view from her and Travis's rear glass doors directly opposite Darlene's—Darlene's on the north side, Zoey's south.

Witnessing what happened next, Zoey got frightened enough to close her blinds for fear she'd be detected, texting Darlene and getting no answer.

All that happened hours ago.

Now Darlene's place was shuttered.

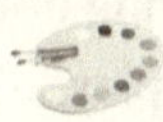

Crystal's phone jangled and jarred her awake. She rolled over and swiped to answer.

"Crystal? Thank goodness. Art Framingham here. Look, I'm at the gallery and I—"

"I'm so excited. Can't wait till tomorrow. Art, what's up? Are we set to go?"

"No, Crystal. I don't know how to say this—"

"Sold. That's all you have to say." She giggled. "Art…?" She heard him sniffle. "Art, are you there? Are you okay? What's wrong? Is the show not ready yet? I can come over. We'll get it done." Her tone was kind and comforting.

"I had to call it off," Art said.

"Oh no! What happened? Why, what's up?"

"Darlene…" Art trailed off, sneezed again.

"Oh, Arthur, what did she do? She flaked? She didn't bring her paintings yet?"

"Darlene…" He struggled to say the words.

"Never a thought of anyone else. Never one shred of consideration. Where is she now?"

"Darlene is… dead."

Satin's crimson Lexus bolted out of Dreamland Cove's front gates, hauling to University Drive in the glow of a fat full moon. The four frightened females inside the car ran a series of stop signs and red lights as they raced to where they feared to go—the site where Darlene's corpse was found. Satin, Crystal, Zoey, and Ruth jabbered and argued at lightning speed, trying to process Darlene's death and how it might redound to them.

"First let's get our story straight," Ruth shrilled in a tone only dogs could hear.

"What story?" Crystal inquired. "Why? We didn't do anything to her."

"Really?" Satin interjected. "After our blowup this afternoon, it sure won't look like that. We told Darlene to get lost, remember? Expelled her from the club. Said after the showing not one of us wanted to see her ever again in life. How will that drama play to the cheap seats, huh?"

"Not very well," said Zoey, wringing her hands and wiggling a foot. "They think she was killed, and they're going to ask why. That fight will make us all look bad."

"Not if they never find out," Ruth chimed in.

Crystal said, "They're bound to though."

"If we keep our mouths shut, it'll stay our secret," Ruth insisted. "Just between us four, okay? Nobody knows but us, am I right? I didn't let on to anyone. Did you?"

Three heads shook briskly.

"Well," said Ruth, "let's make a pact. Nobody ever has to know."

"Not unless someone overheard us," Satin concluded, swallowing hard.

"Or Darlene blabbed her motormouth. She was the biggest grape on the friggin' vine. She probably tweeted it. It's likely on her Instagram. It'd be just like her, wouldn't it? To continue to haunt us from her grave." Zoey turned, gazed out a window. Glum, she chewed fake fingernails.

"Calm down. Don't be so negative. You're talking up bad vibes," said Crystal, "speaking of poor Darlene that way. She was brutally murdered, don't you care? Her body isn't even cold. Doesn't anyone feel the least bit sorry? She was supposed to be our friend."

"We were her friends, but she wasn't ours," said Satin. "Let's not fool ourselves."

"But why assume we're on the hook?" said Crystal. "There'll be tons of suspects, what with how she carried on. Why are we worried it's all on us? Thoughts create, girls. Thoughts are things. You guys are courting trouble… I think we ought to stop and pray."

"Oh, cut it out, Miss Starry Eyes," Ruth snapped with a snarl in her high-pitched voice.

"You think it'll look like coincidence that we have a knock-down-drag-out fight with Darlene the day she turns up dead?"

"Dead," Zoey murmured. "I can't believe it. Satin, pull over. I have to hurl."

"Oh crap, Zo, I just bought this dress. If you ruin it, Harper will throw a fit," Ruth yelled.

"Well, pardon *moi*!" said Zoey. "I have a sensitive stomach, 'kay? When I hear a killer's on the loose, it tends to make me nauseous."

"Oh shoot, I didn't think of that," said Crystal with her pupils fixed. "If none of us killed her, then who did?"

"What do you mean, *if* none of us killed her? Are you suggesting—?"

"They're right, Ruth," said Satin, making a left turn at a red traffic light. "What if he's still out there?"

"Now that you mention it," Crystal added, "Art didn't say they caught the guy."

"Who says it's a guy?" inquired Ruth. "That's only a sexist assumption."

"Get over it. It was a turn of phrase. Do we have to go pick apart every word? Whoever killed our friend is out there somewhere, Ruthie, that's the point. Oh gracious, I need air." Zoey turned and cracked her window. "Her body was found in the gallery with our paintings, did you think of that? And we don't know why she was killed."

"She was killed because she was such a bitch!" Ruth carped. "And I'm not sad she's gone. That witch was a pain in my—"

"Ask yourself. We're neighbors. We're in the same art club with a victim of a homicide. We have no idea who might be next," said Satin.

The car went silent.

"Isn't that a cheery thought," Ruth said after several moments passed.

"It's probably nothing to do with us," Crystal offered with a sickly smile. "It's likely the killer ran away. He's probably gone now. We don't know."

"Well, I bet I do know one damn thing," Ruth said, pitched forward in her seat. "If this awful night teaches me nothing else, it's life is shorter than we think. I'll be damned if I'm punished for one more thing I didn't do, okay? My husband's enough of a judge and jury. Now we're facing cops. We have to get on the same page, y'all. We better be able to explain ourselves by the time we destinate, or else. We have a lot more to worry about from the law than a psycho, get me? We may be the last to have seen Darlene. Except for the killer, of course." Ruth smirked.

Zoey piped up, "No, we're not." She twisted around in the passenger seat to divulge the two strange men she saw, her recap startling her three friends.

"What?" Satin swerved as she turned to Zoey. "What happened after the limo came?" She spun her eyes back to the road ahead, correcting the wheel and braking.

"Darlene got panicky when she saw it. I know because she checked the house and hid in a corner in the dark. Then I saw her run into a closet and close the door."

"Did they break in?" asked Satin.

"I'm not certain," Zoey said, "'cause after that, I closed the blinds. I was petrified they'd see me. But the cops should find them soon enough, and that could let us off the hook."

"Why didn't you say this right away?" asked Ruth in an accusing tone.

"I didn't want to admit I saw them, Ruth. They looked so dangerous."

"If I didn't have the creeps before, I sure do have them now," moaned Crystal, digging in her purse. "I think we'd better burn some sage." She came up with a stick of it.

"Oh yeah, that'll definitely solve our problems," Ruth quipped, ratcheting up her pitch. "I'll kill you myself if you light that thing!"

Crystal breathed in, closed her eyes. "I'm on your side, Ruth. Check yourself."

Ruth continued to taunt and badger. "What are you doing?"

"Meditating. Trying to clear my energy."

"Zip it," said Satin. "This is important. Zoey, is that all you saw?"

"It's all that I remember... Darlene was undressed—"

"What else is new?" Ruth asked with a haughty one-upmanship.

Zoey admonished, "Hush up, Ruth. Crystal is absolutely right. We ought to speak well of the dead, you know. It's the least we can do for Darlene now. No telling what she suffered. If you saw what I saw, you'd have a heart. Those guys were like a goon squad. One was as big as a building, wearing what looked like a burgundy silk zoot suit. It was retro, out of the forties. It was almost like watching a crime cartoon, only scarier and in real life. The other dude was small and wiry. Weaselly. Wearing a green Fedora that had a green feather in the band."

"Zoey, why didn't you call the cops?" asked Satin.

"It didn't cross my mind. I didn't see a crime. It's not like Darlene wasn't into bad boys. How did I know who they were to her? She was grown. It was none of my business. It wasn't the first time kinky stuff was going on at Darlene's place. You know how out-there Darlene was."

"She lived on the ragged edge," said Crystal. "Gotta admit the girl was fierce. Could you tell what they might have wanted, Zo?"

"What they all wanted and what they got. The same thing all men want," Ruth snapped.

"Ruth, will you put a lid on it?" pled Satin. "Lighten up. Besides, when it comes to the men in her life, your Harper is among the suspects, girl. Sit this one out."

Ruth opened and then closed her mouth.

"You bet he is. He tops the list," said Zoey, happy to speculate.

"Go on, finish, Zoey," Crystal urged.

"I did," said Zoey. "I don't want to guess what happened next."

"Hurry up, guys, we're almost there. I can't stay long. Brick's waiting."

"When is he not?" Ruth snapped at Satin. "You have him wrapped around your finger."

"Stop, Ruth," chided Crystal. "You've been lashing out at all of us. Control yourself."

"Oh, she's just jealous," Satin said.

Ruth countered, "You're just spoiled."

"Enough!" said Zoey. "This is wacked. Do you want to come off like maniacs?"

"Focus, sisters. Go within," said Crystal with foreboding. "We have to pull it together now. My third eye sees a horror, girls. Much worse is yet to come."

"I'm telling you, that's all I know." Art sank into his office chair. "Every one of those women is gracious and lovely. How can you think they could do such a thing?"

"She was sleeping with Harper Yardley though," a detective in a blue suit said. He was medium height with straight white teeth, a complexion as white as a stick of chalk and a face full of angry, unchecked zits. His badge read Daniel Harriman, and his face said *I hate guys like you and I would love to bust your ass.* Art didn't see any ink on him, but he bet he had tattoos.

"All right, yes. That's what I heard. I think it was pretty much common knowledge," Art was quick to clarify. "But that doesn't mean—"

"Mrs. Yardley knew? Did she seem to get angry when she found out?"

"I believe that was the scuttlebutt. But I just heard the gossip. Maybe that was how they rolled. The Yardleys, I mean. An open marriage. Ruth could have known and been fine with it. The affair went on for quite a while," Art added as if to mitigate the guilt it might impart to Ruth.

"And the victim was threatening this Crystal Emerson woman with some background dirt, unsavory things about her past?"

"As I said," Art relented with puffy cheeks, "it's gossip, and that's all it is."

"So the one thing of which you have personal knowledge is club members arguing with the victim earlier in the day." Harriman stopped to consult his notes. "When they ousted her from the Black Beauty Sketchers and Painters Club. Correct?"

"That's what I overheard," said Art. "I wish I hadn't."

Ruth fidgeted with her blood-red phone. "I tried to get Harper on his cell, but it's going straight to voice mail."

"Harper Yardley," Harper answered.

"Yardley, it's me. The police are here," Art Framingham whispered on his cell. "They're tearing the place apart right now. So listen, I don't have much time. They know about you and Darlene, man. I think they're headed to your house. You'd better ditch that paperwork. I can't have my silent partner getting mixed up in a murder."

Harper immediately dialed his cell. "Dude, it's Harper. Guess you've heard."

"Unfortunately. But few details," a voice said. "You better keep your cool. Our arrangement is strictly under wraps, you got that? Don't you blow it."

"I'm with you, dude. I'm down. You got it." Harper's leg began to shake.

"Make sure you keep it that way, man. Be a shame if them three tots of yours had a mishap, bro. A cryin' shame."

Zoey's boyfriend, Travis, swerved his Infiniti into a Denny's parking lot in the bowels of Tamarac, hitting a bump as he breached the curb. "Dag, I think I need new shocks," he said as he lowered the jazz music pumping in from the Coral Gables Sirius XM station 109. He sidled his goddess-silver sedan to a space alongside a late-model limo, a boaty, Android-green affair with tinted windows, flashy gold pack, and a set of killer mags.

Travis hopped out with an ear-to-ear smile, his angel face lit like a neon sign the color of Coca Cola, his boxer-like muscles encased in mellow-yellow golf togs hugging him as tightly as a golf glove.

The limo's left rear window whooshed and opened as he crossed the lot.

A Rolex ring with a diamond the size of a soccer ball flashed onto the sill.

"Got it?" asked Travis, shifting his weight.

"Show me the chips," said a tenor voice.

"I got you," Travis assured the void inside the darkened limo.

A metal valise more than two inches thick changed hands, and the limo's trunk popped open. Travis's long arms reached inside and retrieved a flat parcel that measured thirty-six inches by forty-eight. It was wrapped in corrugated cardboard in a slatted wooden crate.

"Done," said Travis to himself as he sped away in triumph.

The limo headed toward the swamp, filled with the odor of marijuana smoke that reeked like age-old cheese.

The goon in the zoot suit took a hit.

The weasel in the Fedora hat began to count the money.

Satin's Lexus hugged a curve and wandered through an amber light at the corner of Sunrise Boulevard and the bustling US 1. Dazed, the driver cut the wheel, skidded, crunched through gritty sand, and ambled into a parking space overlooking the crashing, moonlit waves on the beach in east Fort Lauderdale.

Unease washed over the car's interior as its shocked inhabitants, absently hearing talk radio, tracked the eye of a gathering storm. The moonroof was splashed with raindrops forming tiny puddles on the glass, reminding the girls of painting using their Lucite watercolor trays. Their time at the gallery wasn't fun. The police tape cordoning off the grounds and the crowds and first responder vehicles drew a stark picture of Darlene's death. The burden of grief was settling like the dark clouds hovering overhead.

"I'm going to miss her," Zoey lamented. "Even with everything mean she did, she didn't deserve what happened. Darlene was unique. There was no one like her. She wasn't scared to be herself. She didn't take smack off anyone. I wish I had those qualities."

"Sorry to say I feel relieved," said Crystal with a sigh. "She was one of a kind, and I know it's not an enlightened thought, but I'm not going to miss her blatant threats to ruin me and trash my life. She was holding a sword of Damocles over my head from the instant I arrived."

"I'm glad to get her grubbies off my man," Ruth grumbled and crossed her arms. "I'm not gonna lie or sugarcoat. If that makes me a bad girl, I'll repent, but now I want to celebrate."

"And to think I was jealous of Darlene's talent. She couldn't even stay alive," said Satin.

"Yeah, that resonates. Comparing yourself to others just ensures nobody wins. It's better to wish everybody the best," said Crystal. "Vie with who *you* were. Improve the best you can."

"I'm done with the whole material girl thing. Where does it get you anyway? If I were to die tomorrow, who would notice? Who would care? I mean, look at us, girls. Darlene is gone, and we're analyzing petty things she did to us that left a scar. I'm not going to be someone everyone regrets they knew," said Satin. "I don't know about you, but I want my life to count for something real and good. I want to be a blessing. I have everything a girl could want. But love is all that really lasts. Darlene had only haters."

"The grass ain't always greener, girls," Crystal reflected pensively.

"I don't know why we went to the crime scene. I don't know what we were thinking. The cops weren't going to let us in. We just exposed ourselves," said Zoey.

"We only wanted our paintings back."

"Is that all you can think of, Ruth? Darlene was slaughtered. Butchered. Slain. Wake up and smell the guilt. We said vicious things to hurt Darlene," said Zoey. "We told her to go away, and guess what, kid? She did. We wanted to never be with her again, and now we never will. We wished her away. I feel like dirt." Zoey indicted somberly. "You didn't do it, did you, Ruth?"

"Me?" Ruth squawked and clapped her chest.

"Ruth, don't clutch your pearls," said Satin. "Don't act so surprised. The way you've been spewing gall all night, it's a logical question, isn't it? The cops suspect you."

"What?" asked Ruth.

Crystal agreed, "It's obvious."

"Not to me, it isn't. You were the one with the most to lose. That hussy had it in for you. You said so. You were enemies. Isn't that right, girls?" No one answered. "Oh, I get it, that's your plan. The three of you want to gang up on me and throw me to the wolves. Well, you're not hanging me out to dry," Ruth threatened. "You have secrets too. I dare you, accuse me of that again. I'll point the finger back at you."

"It wasn't me who dissed you, Ruth," said Crystal. "Why are you on *my* case?"

"I wasn't throwing shade, Ruth. I'm stressed out, okay? I'm sorry. Forgive me, but I had to know," said Zoey. "I have a deadline looming. My manuscript's due at the end of the week."

"No biggie. Glad you asked," Ruth lied, her expression hard as marble. "At least now I know where I stand with you. I'm on the outside, looking in. I don't like what I see. I have to get home to the sitter. Let's head back. I think we're done."

A palpable chill swept over the ride, unrelated to the weather.

Satin let loose an awkward chuckle. "I have to get to my sitter too. He smokes cigars and watches sports."

The Lexus rocked with a welcome release of laughter, and the windows fogged.

The short-lived gallows humor fleeted fast from Ruth's tight, glossy lips. "If any of you betray me, I'll return the favor hundredfold." A clap of thunder rumbled, and a silence without a stillness crept in and sucked the air from all their lungs.

"Don't worry, Ruth, you have my word," Zoey proclaimed, her head held high. "I'll stand behind each one of you. And just in case you have your doubts, I give you my word I didn't kill her either. I had no reason to and I'm terribly sorry that she's gone. Cross my heart and hope to… oops." She crossed her heart, held up her hand. "Well, you know what I mean."

"Thanks. That means a lot to me," said Crystal, eyes awash with tears. "I didn't kill her. You know that. I'm a lover, not a hater. Besides, what'd be the point of it? Her murder could put my past on blast. I wouldn't bring that on myself."

"But you believe I would," Ruth snapped.

"Ruthie, give it a rest, okay? We're going to need each other," Zoey said.

"We're at each other's throats," said Satin. "That won't help our cause. I love you guys. I loved Darlene. I'd never try to take her life."

Zoey affirmed, "Let's stick together. Who'll defend us if we don't?"

"She's right," said Satin. "Let's take care. It looks like none of us is safe."

"Danger is close at hand," said Crystal, closing her eyes and lifting her palms. "I can feel it in my bones. The killer is far more treacherous and close than we may think."

At dawn the next morning, a spectrum-yellow sunrise streamed across the lake, lending a sheen of melted butter to the bright, still water's edge.

Detective Daniel Harriman walked the grounds where the victim used to live. Her and her friends were a ritzy crew. He wondered how they could afford to buy in a pricey, posh enclave like this. They were African American women, right? Far down the food chain in his eyes. Were they printing money? Maybe so. Because he and his buddies couldn't begin to pay mortgages on homes like these. Not on his salary. Not these days. No way, José. It'd break the bank. Even with the payoffs.

When he joined the force eight years ago, he was eager and idealistic, but they got to him in just one year, and Dan went on the take. Back then, he never thought he would, but his wife wanted braces—at thirty-three—and his mother had a fiendish stroke. The first kid came and then the next. The pressure mounted more and more. His wife, kids, sergeant, partner, in-laws, siblings, neighbors, friends and foes, and everyone else wanted pieces of him or rather the man they thought he was. They made demands he couldn't meet.

The stress drove Dan to online gambling, betting on football games and hockey, rocketing his mounting debt up to the stratosphere. That was how a fourth-generation homicide detective went from by-the-book to crooked cop. But though he took graft and hung with hoods, he thought his morals were intact. He was better than them, he reasoned. Them minorities stood on the other side of where his ego claimed he stood.

As he combed through Darlene Master's house, with a life-size picture of her in the nude hanging boldly in her master bath, he marveled at her beauty. She was female, single, young, and gorgeous, in a home he coveted. He would've hit that if he could. She was sexier than a movie star. But now all he could do was search and destroy what was left of the dead girl's paradise. That wasn't how it should be. *What happened to the good ole days when men like him came out on top whether or not they deserved to be or cheated every chance they got,* he thought with no small enmity, resentment in his brow. Illegals, that's what happened. Immigrants sopping up the gravy, stealing goodies meant for him. There ought to be a law. There was.

He stepped to the second-floor master bedroom deck to check the view. No sign of forced entry or struggle, but he spotted something on the lake. "Hey, Nuñez, check it out," he shouted.

Harriman's rookie partner, Hector Nuñez, trotted in. Barely five feet eight in height, he appeared as wide as he was tall, owing to his bodybuilding skills, karate black belt, protein shakes, and natural hormone shots. Hector had wide coal-black eyes, swiss-coffee-colored, silky hair, three dogs, two abuelas in his home, and a smile that never, ever quit, no matter what blows he might sustain. The latest setback he suffered came from local immigration hawks who were bent on deporting his mother, his aunt, a sister who had just gone blind, and a young disabled niece. He was first-generation in the States and would never give in to the dirty cops. Going bad would break his mother's heart. He was straight as an arrow and even paid his taxes to the dime. "Yo, what's that?" he asked and stood on tiptoes for a better look.

"Might be anything from this distance," Harriman said. "Could be a clue."

"Gotcha, I'm on it. Let's call a crew. I'll pop down for a closer look." Nuñez descended the stairs two steps at a time and hopped to a landing. He bounded to a sliding door, exited onto a patio filled with towering, flowering potted plants, high-stepped through a muddy grass backyard and, searching as he went along, bloodhounded to the water's edge.

A flat thing floated yards away.

A short time later, a crew arrived in wet suits and took over.

From the water, they fished out a painting, seemingly ruined, by the look of it.

Its subject was barely discernable, but it was wrapped in a flimsy pink nightgown like the one found on the victim's neck. What was odd was the painting disappeared after a preliminary examination by the team's forensics crew. As experts collected and logged other evidence found inside the victim's home, the painting got spirited not to their lab but, instead and surreptitiously, to the trunk of Harriman's unmarked car.

At six p.m. on the night of the gala, signature cocktails were passed around, and everyone who was anyone was decked out in their finest. The art exhibit was DOA because of the killing at Arthur's place, but the other events were sold out, and some scalpers bootlegged tickets. Rather than putting a damper on the festival as some opined, Darlene's death drew the largest crowd in the history of the Art Affaire. Darlene was a local celebrity, and in spite of the tragic loss of life, it was Friday, people were wont to party, and #FridayFeeling ruled. Selfies streamed out over social networks attesting to who was hobnobbing near the mysterious, macabre murder.

In contrast to the prevailing mood, Arthur was having a meltdown. He was ready to call the whole thing off, but the art league wasn't having it. Its board of directors was firm on that. The events were for charity, after all, and though Arthur's gallery was roped off, everything else went on as planned. The gala, art classes, street art sale, panels, symposiums, lectures, signings, sand art exhibit on the mall, youth art scholarship ceremony, and public mural painting.

Tonight was the kickoff, and Murphy's Law was seriously in effect. The gala would be in a ballroom where it was already sweltering hot. The air-conditioning had gone out, and Arthur's lavender Bijan suit was wilting from the heat. The ladies' room toilet was backed up too, and the caterer, Framingham's former fling, arrived a whole two hours late and frantic about the kitchen stoves, which apparently didn't meet his specs. The publicity also took a hit as the local TV station and *Sun-Sentinel* newspaper Theater & Arts reporters were assigned to cover breaking news—a brazen art scam in Miami involving a spate of audacious forgeries.

The guests were beginning to arrive, and the stage was set for disaster.

"You're gonna knock 'em dead tonight," Brick said. "The guys are going to freak. He patted Satin's booty, captivated by the way her sky-high heels accentuated it and her sequined red dress looked airbrushed on. "Your paintings will go like hotcakes once they're released from Arthur's gallery."

"No telling when that'll happen, though. Our paintings are in evidence." Satin attempted to zip her dress, arms straining, locked behind her back. "It's like we're getting punished. Like some sorcerer cast a curse on us. Like sex with no orgasm. After all that work, we have no show. And it doesn't feel right, with Darlene gone, to party like nothing bad went down."

"Life goes on, doll. Let it go. Darlene wouldn't give it a second thought if the shoe were on the other foot and one of you ladies passed away."

"True, she wouldn't bat an eye. But if we only did for others what they'd likely do for us, we wouldn't do squat for anyone."

"You've got a lot invested, doll. You have to make this work. I've been looking for an upside and I see it. So should you. Darlene died so suddenly, she caught the market by surprise, and since her work is in demand and there can't be any more supply, its value will go through the roof. Yours will sell alongside hers. Her rising tide may lift all boats. Bidding could skyrocket."

"Yeah, I think you have a point. Now that you mention it," Satin said, "even my paintings could be in demand." Her eyes lit up as she wriggled in her ball gown, yanking the zipper pull.

"They could with clever marketing. This might just be the break you need. I mean, look at this development. New home sales shot up like a bottle rocket once I changed the name. Lake Homestead wasn't catching on, but the minute I took on Dreamland Cove, every phase of the project picked up steam. With your art, we have to sell the *feeling*, not just paint on canvases. So, what if we coin a new art style and declare you initiated it?" He saw the wheels turning in Satin's head and felt his ardor rise. "Remember that art dealer up in Kissimmee remarking you paint like a two-year-old? Well, let's make a weakness into a strength. I think we could call it Innocentism. Dealers would get on board with that."

"His poison pen blog hurt my feelings. Hurt my valuations too. I'd love to make him eat those words. I see where you're going with it now." Satin turned her back to Brick. "Zip me up. I'm into it. I like it," she agreed. "I'm thinking it's a master stroke."

Brick zipped her dress and kissed her neck. "Wait till I get you home tonight… C'mon, let's go. You got this, babe. Let's wow that crowd. It's showtime."

Ruth couldn't find a thing to wear.

"You knew this was coming," Harper snarled. "You should've gone out and gotten cute. Or don't you know how to anymore? You're finished. You let yourself go."

"With that fortune you spent on Darlene, I wanted to buy a new dress to wear tonight, but I knew we couldn't afford it." Ruth screwed up her face and stomped her foot.

"Know what? You're a broken record, like a pathetic old eight-track tape that just keeps looping over and over again. Why do you push me all the time? You know you're asking for it, right?" Harper's big knuckles curled into a fist that clenched and unclenched like a clam shell. *Cool it*, he tried to convince himself. The last thing he needed was visible bruises tattooing the weak-ass ball and chain, particularly now that cops were likely staring over his shoulder. "I don't give a damn what you wear anymore, and I sure can't afford to look violent. My kids have a ghost for a mother. You're unfit, so I'll let you slide. But you better be dressed in five minutes or less, or you'll wish you never heard my name."

"I already do," Ruth fired back, snatching the first dress on the rack.

"You'll never find another man like me."

"Oh good, you promise?"

"I promise you'll never see the kids again. Try that one on." He exited and slammed the door. Down the hall, the triplets began to wail.

"You've thrown your last punch at me, Harper Yardley." Ruth, with a catatonic glare, said, "That's the last time you dog me out. I'm not gonna take your abuse anymore. You're a bully, and I've had it. You don't own me. You're not the boss of me. My life is too precious to waste on you." She yelled down the hall to the babysitter. "Serenity, we're leaving now. Help yourself to anything in the fridge. I'll only be gone a couple of hours. *He'll be gone for good.*"

"Have fun," the babysitter called.

Ruth glanced down the hall as she hid a sharp knife in her tiny beaded evening purse.

Candlelight danced on the vaulted ceiling of Crystal's peaceful lakeside loft.

Wild sounds of the rainforest played from her iPhone dock, creating a mellow mood. An electronic scent diffuser puffed, rotating a rainbow of colored lights. When her iPhone started to vibrate, Crystal rose from her lotus position and picked it up without looking to see who it was. "Crystal Clear," her voice intoned, conveying her usual business greeting.

"Hey, mamasita. Where you been hidin'? It's a silly question, right? I know exactly where you ran to, now I tracked you down."

Crystal's jaw dropped like a hooker's drawers. "Chase?" she mumbled, heart aflutter. "Why are you doing this? Leave me alone!"

"When you're alone, I'm lonely, *mija*. That won't never happen, girl. I can't never let you go."

Her finger twitched at the End Call button, hovering indecisively.

"Don't you dare hang up on me," Chase cautioned. "I'm not playin', girl."

Her eyes swept the room. *Was he watching her?* "Quit hounding me. What do you want?"

"You, baby girl. Same as always, kid."

"Get lost. You disgust me. Go away. I'm not getting caught in your trap again."

"That's what your friend said and look what she got."

"What are you talking about, what friend?" asked Crystal, stomach knotting.

"What friend do you think? Dear departed Darlene."

"Darlene...?" Crystal gasped and covered her mouth. "You—"

"Think I located you through an astrology hotline? Darlene dimed you out."

"But I begged her. She gave me her word," Crystal cried.

"That ho's word wasn't worth diddly, girl. How can you see all them auras and vibes and be blind as a bat to reality? That's what I love about you though. You're sweet and reliably gullible. You think the whole world is bright and gay. That's why you need me protecting you."

A watercolor stream of purple eyeliner and tears ran toward her chin. Chase found her again. He'd never stop. "You murdering slime. You killed Darlene? You did that just to get to me? Stay away from me, Chase Tortuga. Or I'll call the FBI. I mean it. I swear. I'll rat on you. Doesn't matter what happens after that. I'd rather rot in jail than let you slither back into my life again, you rotten one-man crime wave. I couldn't see who you were before, but I've got your number now. I'm not your shill. Not anymore. I won't cover for you one more time. You're not setting me up for another fall. You fooled me once, that's shame on you. You're not getting a chance to fool me twice. It's over. I'm out. I'm free. Let go." She lost her cool and wailed.

Tortuga was calm and clinical in his delivery when he addressed her again—his wayward mistress of five years—invoking his power over her. "It ain't your life no more, you hear? I own you, *Mami*, heart and soul. You're part of me. You're mine."

Travis was singing off-key in the shower while Zoey was emptying his pockets out.

Something was amiss.

The man Zoey trusted for three faithful years didn't take that New York business trip. He lied to her about it. Wherever he went, it wasn't there. Number one, he was gone too short a time to make a New York business run. Did he think she wouldn't realize that? Number two, it wasn't business or he'd have receipts to show for it. And three, she found no check-ins at his usual haunts near Gramercy, Fifth Avenue or Soho. She even called that spot in Greenwich Village where he loved the beds. There were other telltale signs as well. No New York-prefixed calls or texts in his cell or in his burner phone—the one he thought he hid from her in his trunk and was sure she knew nothing about. On top of all that, what she saw with her own two eyes put the lie to his "New York trip." He thought he was so damn slick and had no clue that she was slicker. Did he think she wouldn't find him out? Why did he lie and where did he go? More saliently, with whom?

She reached her slender fingers into the pockets of his golf outfit, that mellow-yellow atrocity he wore away, supposedly. His pockets always yielded clues. If he happened to catch her in the act, she'd say she was doing his laundry, but she needed to move fast anyway, to see what she could find. She searched his right pants pocket and came up with an oversize safety pin with a silver key attached to it. Why wasn't it on his key chain? The shower turned off and she nearly dropped the enigma on the floor. There was a scrap of folded paper pinioned to the silver key, and she hurriedly tried unfold it to see what it said before she got busted. The safety pin was strong and harder to open than she thought it'd be, and in her attempt, she broke her nail, but she finally got the paper loose without having to tear it off. The paper resembled a piece of origami, folded several times. She ran to a lamp beside the bed and opened it, holding it over the lampshade, moving it closer to the bulb and seeing it was blank.

"Hon," Travis said, bursting into the room, a towel wrapped around his waist.

She almost had a heart attack, and the paper flew onto the nightstand. It landed under the table lamp, in the light of its hundred-watt bulb.

"Love, have you seen my glasses? I had thought I left them on the sink, but I guess they're on the nightstand. I'm trying to read the contents of a shaving cream I'm ordering." Travis beelined for the bedstand, stopping to nuzzle in her neck. With a puzzled look, he nosed around.

"There!" she yelled a bit too loudly, pointing toward their teak highboy.

"Cool," he said. "You're a miracle worker. What would I do without you? I'll be out in a sec. I just need a quick shave." He donned the glasses, crossed the room.

When Travis went back in the bathroom, Zoey bent to grab the paper but withdrew her hand when something changed. Handwriting appeared before her eyes. It was almost like a magic trick. The print was tannish-brown. It must've been drawn with invisible ink. She remembered, from an art course she'd enrolled in at Art's studio, that invisible ink made from lemon juice could reappear on paper that got heated up somehow. She'd also seen that work with milk. She snatched the paper off the table, held it directly beneath the light bulb, saw a phone number materialize. *Who did it belong to?*

Travis began to sing again, so she hurried to look at the recent calls in his phone while he was occupied. The sixth one was a match. She tapped the number, held her breath, her gaze fixed on the bathroom door.

"Willy G," said a liquor-laced voice on the phone.

"Is… uh… is Sheila Mandrake there?" said Zoey, improvising.

"Nope, you got the wrong number, toots."

"Is it him?" a skeptical male voice said on the other end of the convo.

"Nah, it's some chick," the first voice said. "Who is this?"

Zoey hesitated, trying to suss out some background noise. "Is this 627-1358?"

"Who told ya to call?" the male voice asked, but the "chick" on the other end hung up.

At seven p.m., the gala was packed. Thanks to the sordid publicity, the crowd was overflowing. "It certainly isn't every day," said peppy anchor, Solstice Barnes, "that a well-known local artist turns up hanging in a gallery beside her paintings, murdered. It's like a horror movie plot. You couldn't make it up. Be sure to tune in to the live stream on our website, and on social follow hashtag #DeadDarlene."

Art set up the live stream and it proved to be a brilliant stroke. Video of the exhibit would not only show on the ballroom's stark-white walls, projected on a big screen, but art patrons all around the world could view the artists' works even though they were currently sequestered. Art had shot gallery videos before—for insurance purposes at the start and then to promote his exhibits—but once they got posted on social, they garnered many shares and likes. That's what gave him the idea this time. Since he couldn't display the original pieces, today he uploaded his Black Beauty clips and they instantly made a splash. Eager collectors blew up the gallery's phone lines, and the website crashed. He'd attracted international buyers to the gala virtually, and most of the watchers submitted bids. He had to buy more bandwidth. What once was a local event was becoming a viral art sensation. The fact that the paintings were evidence in the mysterious murder of Darlene was selling her pieces sight unseen, so why not start a bidding war on everything in the collection?

There were Darlene's sensuous pastiche nudes, Satin's vibrant "Innocentisms," Crystal's metaphysical landscapes, Zoey's fanciful book illustrations, and Ruth's homages to her spouse. Plus, in a marvelous stroke of luck, the air-conditioning kicked back in and prices really ballooned. Darlene's posthumous status commanded astonishing rates across the board. Phone offers pinged in from New York, Dubai, Los Angeles, Paris, London, Cairo, Rio and Beijing. The Internet offers spanned the globe, from the Côte d'Ivoire to Saint-Tropez to São Paulo and Hong Kong.

Profits exploded for Darlene's friends.

Satin's dubious offerings went for exponentially more than what they'd ever earned before, her outrageous beauty inflating their worth even more than Brick predicted. He and Satin were beaming, power-playing, radiating sex appeal, and making mad connections for his business and for hers.

In contrast, Ruth and Harper were a study in water and oil, the tension between them as taut as a canvas and mounting commensurate with her sales.

Zoey Wright was flitting from pillar to post, wide-eyed, darting among the crowd. She seemed to be looking for someone or something. Art could not determine what. When she wasn't clutching her boyfriend Travis's arm, she appeared to be hiding.

And then there was Crystal, who inexplicably showed up with a sleazeball who, fixated on her shapely legs, refused to shake hands with anyone. A devastatingly handsome Cuban, the man was decidedly déclassé, in Art's estimation anyway, nothing like Arthur's Cuban friends, who were rich and refined and dressed like models straight off runways in Milan. This guy looked like a felon, flaunting his Rolex, diamond cuff links, Gucci kicks, and way-too-shiny suit, effusing that air of conspicuous consumption denoting the nouveau riche, who, especially in South Florida, Art equated with drugs, illicit sex, and lurid human trafficking. Further, Art noted with great distress that Crystal looked preoccupied and listless. Why was that? She seemed to be out on her astral plane. She was acting antisocial. Normally vivacious, she looked overshadowed by a gloom, her normal glow and quirky extroversion imperceptible. She was a new age mystic. Was she sensing some bad vibes? Arthur sneezed. He desperately missed Darlene. The diva was sadly gone for good and nothing and no one could bring her back.

Was there no one Art could count on now?

Harriman cautioned his partner, "Stick to the plan. We capture him dead or alive."

"What a break," an anxious Nuñez said. "I can hardly believe we cornered him."

"Believe it, Nuñez," Harriman barked. "Get set to bust a bad guy."

The detectives sat in their unmarked car in the parking lot next to the packed hotel. A SWAT team was gathered across the street in a vacant foreclosure possessed by the Feds.

A bold and savvy forgery ring authorities tracked for two long years was holed up in the hotel where the auction was currently taking place, according to an informant. "This is a real high-profile bust," said rookie Nuñez. "Who's the source?"

"The best damn snitch I ever had. I pick up every clue she drops, and this one is a doozy. The suspect is the mastermind. Get him and we get all of them. He's in there. I can smell it. The cameras even caught him when he entered with his girl. His sheet is as long as a sermon, and we have him dead to rights. Video, shipping manifests, flight records, pix, the whole nine yards. Collectors he conned all over the world are ready and waiting to testify, and now we can tie him to murder one. Stick close, kid. You might learn some things."

"Let's do it!" came over the radio. "Move in, guys. Go, go, go!"

Harriman pushed the door open, whipped a gun out of his shoulder holster, crouched, took off across the street. "He'll never know what hit him."

Art shepherded Ruth's abusive husband, Harper, and Zoey's live-in boyfriend, Travis, into the men's room next to an empty ballroom down the hall, checking the urinals, peering under the stalls, and turning his cell phone off. Downing a handful of allergy meds, he informed his co-conspirators, "The Palm Beach Cheathams purchased the last of Darlene's fakes a week ago. They're having the piece appraised at their estate tomorrow morning. They're having the others we sold them taken a second look at too. You know what that means? More scrutiny. Shrewd appraisers inspecting the tiny details. I think they may be onto us. The auction drew attention. They clearly don't trust me anymore," said Arthur with a crackly voice, his forked tongue licking bone-dry lips.

"Get a grip," said Harper. "Think of the cash. There isn't one fake in here tonight." He whacked Art on the back. "Darlene was tops. They may suspect, but her work is undetectable."

"No forger is infallible," said Art, bending over the bathroom sink and pumping soap to wash his hands.

"Nobody's caught on yet," said Harper. "That should tell you something, man."

"It tells me we're on borrowed time. Yeah, up till now it's been all good, but it only takes one expert eye," said Travis, whipping out a vape. "And from my understanding, the Cheathams use Katz and my man could find fat in a celery stick. That chump will blow the whistle."

"I want out!" Art blurted, stomping his foot, loosening his bow tie, gasping for air.

"You got us into this," Harper reminded him. "Bait-and-switch was your idea. You took us out in the deep water, Art. Wise up and learn to swim."

"No way. Let's quit while we're ahead," said Travis, and he sucked his vape. "Zoey's suspicious, I can tell. I need her. I can't lose her, guys. That girl is the best thing in my life. I'm not gonna break her heart. And I won't do time for you two stiffs. I'm taking all the chances. You fools didn't see them killers in the limo like I did last night. Let's get out while we can."

"Run away while there's buckets of cash to be made?" said Harper. "Grow a set. I'll pin it on Ruth if the thing goes south, man. We don't have exposure."

"Oh no? That's easy for you to say. You're a family man. You're golden." Art turned and started toward the door. "Do it without me. I'm out of the loop."

Harper blew up like an IED. "You never turned down a dime before. You think you can leave me hanging just before this pays off big? What, are you too good for us?"

"Don't be absurd. That's not the point. Travis wants out too. A scam is not a long-term deal. I was getting the gallery on its feet, and you sold me a way to make big chips, but now it's way too dangerous. I'm on my feet. I'm moving on. It's not personal; it's how business goes."

"Well, it sure isn't how my business goes," said Harper. "I've got mouths to feed."

"Be reasonable. Darlene is dead. She sure didn't off *herself* like that." Art sneezed into his elbow, wiped his nose on his blush-pink cuff. "If I'd only kept my big mouth shut about how she could imitate the masters, she might be alive today. Who knows who knocked her off? The folks who did will track us when they find out that we sold her fakes and we're living off the money. Those fakes are in private collections, ticking time bombs ready to explode. I'm not waiting till they all blow up. And that could be tomorrow."

"Your slip is showing, Arthur," Harper gibed. "Yo, man up, dude."

"Art's right," uttered Travis. "It's out of control. Tortuga's got us in his grip."

"Chase Tortuga?" Arthur asked. "You're not serious. You're mixed up with him? That crime kingpin that Crystal ran away from? Are you crazy? Please don't tell me he's involved."

"How do you think we got this far?" Harper sneered at Art, advancing.

Arthur retreated. "Please, sweet spirit. Say this isn't real."

"We didn't intend to; it just happened," Travis explained. "A lucky break. When Crystal moved to Dreamland Cove, Tortuga sent his goons to bring her back. He has a thing for her. The goons didn't know where Crystal was, so they hired a crony in town to help them look. Turns out he'd banged Darlene."

"Wait. Hold on, you're losing me," said Art. "You both knew all this time?"

"What does it matter? We're in it now," said Harper. "You as much as us. Tortuga sent two weirdos gunning for Crystal. That's when we found out. They hooked up with the cop who shagged Darlene. Well, one of them anyway." Harper coughed and rolled his eyes.

"The guy is a cop? Are you kidding me?" said Arthur, slack-jawed, looking faint.

"The cop was connected in Florida, so they figured he'd help them find her fast. Find Crystal. But as fate would have it—"

"Stop right there. Not one more word. I mean it. I don't want to know," Art bade him, doubling over.

"It was a fluke, is what it was," Travis continued sheepishly. "Small world, that kind of thing. See, Tortuga is nuts for Crystal, but she eventually had to run from him. When he wanted her back and was chasing her down, he figured she'd do what she always did when she finally settled somewhere else. He decided she'd start off reading palms and selling landscape paintings. He told the two guys, and the guys told their friend the cop, who contacted his new gal pal—"

"That would be Darlene," Art reasoned.

"Yeah," said Travis ruefully. "The cop knew Darlene was involved with the local art scene. She was the perfect in. So he talked her into digging up leads by putting out feelers he could chase. And that's how Crystal met Darlene. Darlene found out that Crystal lived on the very same lake Darlene lived on in Dreamland Cove, and she dove in. It apparently gave her ideas because she went freelance on the cop, coaxing poor Crystal to join the Black Beauty Club to supposedly make some friends. Crystal knew nothing about it at first, but Darlene started putting the screws to her, playing all the angles."

"You know how Darlene played her games," said Harper, and he grabbed his crotch.

"Not me. That's how *you* rolled," said Art. "I keep mine in my pants. Darlene and I were strictly business. I respect women. They have souls… What else did you do behind my back?"

"Nothing. It was all Darlene. Darlene started blackmailing Crystal, threatening to tell Chase where she was. She thought Crystal was sitting on money she got from Tortuga, and she demanded it. It got out of control," said Travis. "Harper got greedy and messed things up."

"I made you guys a lot of cash." Harper clenched his fists. "I could've gone solo. I cut you in. So shut up and be grateful. It so happened that Darlene hipped me in pillow talk about the situ. About Crystal, Tortuga, and the cop. And yes, we were lovers. I admit. But, Art, don't act so innocent. You put ideas in Darlene's head. You were the one who ran around touting what top-notch work Darlene could do. About how she could be such a top-notch forger. How lovely her pastiches were." He mimicked Arthur's flourishes. "And how she could paint a masterpiece in any style or medium and make herself a fortune. Of course that got me interested. Who wouldn't tap a gold mine? When I found out Tortuga was looking for Crystal and he was a fence, I thought we—"

"That's not all he's into, Harper," Travis tossed in with disdain.

"Yeah, but I never got into that. It took me a while to catch on to it, and by then I couldn't walk away. You think you can bolt on a guy like Tortuga and live to tell the tale? No way. Darlene was terrified. She'd kept Tortuga to herself, and not only because of his bankroll. She had witnessed how deadly the dude could be. Tortuga would've done her in if he'd thought she'd squeal on him. But Crystal told Ruth, and Ruth told me. That's when it began to make sense to move. I saw I could get to Crystal's ex, Tortuga, to hawk Darlene's fakes to the money crowd. Old money. So I met with Tortuga behind her back. And Crystal's and Ruth's and your back, Art. You were the easiest of them all."

"I guess I was," Art figured, tugging his collar, sucking his teeth. "You wangled a deal with Tortuga in exchange for a piece of the action? Oh, I see. I should have seen it all along. All you needed was a patsy here in town to exhibit merchandise and authenticate the forgeries. And that's when you conscripted me."

"Precisely," Harper confessed with a grin. "We played you like a piano. We began by selling the fakes as investments to prospects from Brick's Facebook friends. Y'know, bigwigs who bought his spectacular homes. We figured they had dough. Poor Brick didn't have a clue, of course. Tortuga convinced us we'd make even more with our hands in a reputable gallery."

"What a chump I was." Art sneezed again.

"It didn't hurt your bank account," said Harper.

"You weren't the only sucker," Travis admitted with a frown. "For me, it was the timing. Business was down. I had Zoey to think of. Ladies like Zoey don't come cheap."

"Zoey's not that type," said Art. "She's not in it for your money."

"No, but my girl can have any man she wants, and she makes a good living. I couldn't come off like a loser, you dig? I needed to feel like a man for Zo, so when Harper approached me to back him up—"

"He jumped at the chance with both feet, Art. And own it. So did you."

"But why did you have to go so far?" Art asked.

"Because of Darlene. She wanted it all and she wanted it now. I was making grand theft dough," said Harper. "She gave me an ultimatum. Demanded I walk out on Ruth and the triplets, and when I refused—"

"You killed her," Art concluded.

"What are you, nuts?" said Harper. "Why in the world would I kill the golden goose?"

Arthur splashed cold water on his face and dried off with a paper towel. "Admit it."

"We see what you do to Ruth. You beat the mess out of your wife. You expect us to think you wouldn't hurt Darlene?" said Travis. "Tell the truth. Art's right. I might be a loser in some folks' eyes, but I'd never harm a woman. Any male who beats a female isn't a man or even a human being. My father taught me that before I knew my ABCs. If you didn't do it, who killed her, Harper? You must know who took her out."

"I'm betting you slept with Darlene till she was killed," Art said. "Perhaps that's why. Did you drive your wife to kill Darlene?"

"Why would you say a thing like that?" Harper took umbrage with feigned outrage. "You need to leave Ruth out of this. She doesn't have the guts. All right, we have problems," Harper conceded. "I know our marriage sucks, okay? But neither of us would kill Darlene. I swear on the triplets, I didn't kill her. I actually thought she loved me."

Arthur broke into a mirthless laugh. "Darlene? She only loved herself."

"Well, yeah, I know that now," said Harper. "After she painted that watercolor of all of us selling her forgeries, I knew she never cared at all. It was all just one big game to her. Anyone with half a brain could see exactly what we'd done if they saw her depiction of our crimes. You could pick every one of us out in a lineup if she put that painting out."

"Oh no," Arthur griped. "It could give us away? My heavens, where's the painting now?"

"We managed to buy it. I burned it up," said Travis. "It's a nonissue now."

"She threatened to put it on display tonight if I didn't drop Ruth for her," said Harper.

Arthur sneezed again. "I'm ruined. Totally, completely shot," he whined, bending over the sink to retch. "Buy it from whom? Darlene is dead."

"Don't worry. I called Tortuga," Harper admitted. "He got hold of it."

"You called that cutthroat?" Arthur asked. "Oh mercy. He approached Darlene?"

"He sent Willy G and Bounce to snatch it. Darlene wouldn't kick it up."

"Who the heck are Willy G and Bounce?" Art stammered.

"Wait," said Travis. "Hold up. You didn't tell me that. No wonder Darlene wound up dead."

"I was desperate. The broad wouldn't listen to reason," Harper declared disingenuously, his skin tone turned gunmetal gray. "There was no other way."

"They killed her. That's why Darlene's dead," Travis submitted, breathing hard. "Isn't it? That's what happened, right? They offed her to get that painting back. Oh man, this sucks. We're part of it." Travis paced the tile. "Let's go." He brandished a .45. "Harper, if you try to stop us, you're gonna get what you deserve. C'mon, Art. We're in the wind." He backed off with the gun.

Harper held up both his hands. "You're signing your life away, you fool. You don't know what you're doing."

Arthur, sneezing, followed Travis, skittering out to a fire exit. "Where are you going? Come with me," he said when Travis headed back.

"I have to go back for Zoey. She can't get mixed up in this," said Travis, sprinting toward the gala. "Head out, pal. I'll catch you later."

Pandemonium broke out in the ballroom. First came shouts, bloodcurdling screams, a boom and the sound of shattering glass.

A bullhorn blasted from outside. "You're surrounded, Tortuga! Surrender with your hands up! Now! Come out or we'll come in!"

Patrons in black tie fled like a bunch of hurricane evacuees, trampling each other and flooding the exits.

Tortuga screamed, "Come in and get me! *Culos,* try to take me down!"

A beat. The SWAT team swarmed the room.

More patrons swiftly evacuated except for a few who were trapped inside. They cowered under banquet tables, hid behind curtains, and ran along walls that were screening Black Beauty paintings.

Nuñez advanced and drew down on Tortuga. "Get down on the floor. Get down on the floor!" he commanded, training his weapon on Tortuga, who, cornered, grabbed Crystal and reached a hand into his tux.

"Don't do it. Stop, Tortuga!" Nuñez warned, assuming a shooting stance.

The last of the patrons, bolting from corners, panicked and scrambled for the doors.

Tortuga drew a gun and fired.

Nuñez, squatting, squeezed off shots he aimed right at Tortuga's chest.

Crystal's left arm began to bleed.

Tortuga grinned, and his gold tooth shone as he keeled over onto the hard tile floor.

"She's hit," Travis yelled as he entered the room.

"Where is he?" Zoey shouted. "Travis betrayed me for Darlene."

"Zoey, hand me back my knife," Ruth pleaded. "We can work this out."

"This is all his fault!" said Zoey, grabbing Ruth around the neck. "She stole from me to be with him." She backed Ruth through the parking lot.

"Stay still, Ruth, and you won't get hurt," she whispered in Ruth's ear. "I'm doing this to get away."

Harriman trained a gun on Zoey. "We won't harm you. Let her go."

"Please don't hurt me, Zoey. Please," Ruth begged. "Darlene betrayed me too."

"Drop the knife and let her go," said Harriman, reaching an arm toward Zoey, keeping his eye on the glint of the blade.

Ruth implored, "My babies need me. Zoey, don't hurt me. I'm your friend."

"Drop the knife," said Harriman, crabbing forward, backing Zoey off. "Let go of her. This is your final warning."

Zoey shrieked and jerked Ruth harder. Tears poured down her reddened cheeks. "I did it because she took my book. The text, my illustration files, the folder with my cover art. She came and stole it all. She was getting it published in her name. In Darlene Masters. Like she wrote it. Can you imagine? All that work. Darlene wanted everyone's everything. She ripped off my entire life!"

Harriman shouted, "Drop the knife!"

Fire trucks wailed to the parking lot. Ambulances. Paramedics.

Travis, one of the last to leave the ballroom, finally spotted Zoey standing next to Harper's car. Confused, he asked, "What's going on?"

Harriman ordered, "Back off. Now. Nothing to see here. Walk away."

"She's my girlfriend," Travis protested. "Zoey, what are you doing? Stop."

"Go away. It's over, Travis." Zoey babbled, "No more lies. I know you had an affair with her. I saw you in her house. I confronted her there and she denied it, but I knew the truth. She figured she could have you too. Why couldn't she leave us all in peace?" Bleary-eyed, she turned to Travis. "How could you do it? How could you screw her? I believed you loved me."

"I-I…" Travis stuttered, gaping. "Zoey," he begged. "Please give me the knife. Trust me, this is not the way. I'll help you, babe, I love you." He eased toward Zoey, arms outstretched. "I wasn't sleeping with Darlene. You've got it all wrong. I adore you, Zo."

"Don't lie to me. I saw you there."

"We…" Travis looked from Zoey to Ruth, and then he glared at Harriman, who actually was drooling, excited to fire at any non-white body that dared make a move.

Zoey went on with a vacant expression. "Darlene cracked up in my face. She told me I'd jumped to conclusions. But I saw you with my own two eyes. I believed in you, had faith in you. I dropped my trust issues and let down my guard. How could you help her rip me off? How could you let her have it all? You, and everything else I love."

"I didn't. I went there to get them back. Your drawings. Your book. Your flash drive. She told me when she took it. She had seen you backing up your files and swiped your thumb drive when you turned your back to serve her tea. She taunted me with it. She did it for fun. I broke in there to steal it back. She caught me; that was what you saw. I didn't want her. I love you, Zo."

But Zoey didn't hear his words. She was lost in a world of her own. "I had to kill her, don't you see? I didn't have a choice. She was not a nice person. Darlene was mean. She was a mean girl. Really, she was. She was awfully and terribly greedy too. Look what she did to poor Ruth and the triplets. Look how she tortured Crystal. She undermined Satin at every turn. She wasn't going to stop. She was planning to rip us all apart. She scheduled a book launch for *my* book, and she already had an editor. Not mine, a hotshot in New York. I couldn't let her do it."

Travis beseeched her, his arms outstretched. "Oh, Zoey, you don't understand."

"No, Travis, I don't understand," said Zoey, raising the knife to her throat.

Travis desperately lunged for the sharp-edged weapon.

Six loud shots rang out. Their withering peal echoed into the night and caused a car crash on the boulevard as Harriman's .357 Magnum fired a volley of bullets in an indiscriminate show of force. Travis's head exploded like a ripe melon shot from a cannon, his limp body collapsing in a heap of flesh that ricocheted off of Harper's car and tumbled to the asphalt.

Zoey, screaming bloody murder, turned Ruth loose and ran to him. "Oh, baby, please don't leave me. Please hang on. What have I done?"

In the aftermath of the horrid scene, Art confessed to everything. He copped the first plea in a series and was granted a get-out-of-jail-free card and a future in witness protection. He keeps a small stake in the gallery under his real name, which is Xander Smythe, and as a result of his testimony at trial when it came around, a judge threw the book at Tortuga's henchmen, Willy

G and Bounce. Since then, Art hasn't left his crib. Diagnosed with agoraphobia, a panic disorder, anxiety, and a plethora of allergies, he rarely if ever goes outside. An assistant remotely starts his car and has to pre-taste his groceries before Art consents to eat.

Harriman walked on the charge of excessive force for shooting Travis but got nailed with Willy G and Bounce for his part in selling forgeries, for inducing Darlene to crank out fakes, for taking a cut of every sale, and for shaking down local establishments. He's so popular with the prison crowd that he's lost both eyes and both his knees, eliminates via colostomy, can only handle liquid meals, and on the infrequent days his back allows him to actually sit upright, he's in a busted wheelchair. Remanded into the custody of the solitary confinement staff, he nonetheless does more dirt in prison than he did out on the street.

Details of Darlene's murder were so gross that most were never leaked, but according to Willy G and Bounce, they only pinned Darlene to the gallery wall after finding her dead. They insisted Tortuga was adamant that Darlene should pay a hefty price in order to keep his troops in line, so after they found her strangled, they staged the grisliest scene they could come up with, hoping to terrorize Harper, Art, and Travis, and they did. But the tired defense of finding her dead didn't jibe with their lengthy rap sheets, and the jury didn't buy it. Number one, they had bogus alibis that didn't account for the time of death, and though Zoey admitted she'd strangled Darlene with her own two hands in Darlene's house, there was also a noose around Darlene's neck—the pink nightgown—when she was found. Then too, the autopsy report revealed Darlene survived the strangling only to die of head wounds later on. Willy G and Bounce, though doing time, are launching an appeal.

Zoey remains locked up in a mental facility in Fort Myers. Her children's book got published in her name, but she's unaware of it and oblivious to its success. The publisher's marketing campaign made the most of the murder's publicity, but Zoey was too far gone when the book, entitled *Miss Wright and Mr. Wrong*, released at the top of the best-seller list and sold ten million copies.

Travis, having no family and sans Zoey, was buried alone.

Ruth's husband, Harper, did hard time for his role in the sale of the forgeries, his shady business practices, domestic abuse, and other charges, many of which he was proved to deserve. Ruth filed for divorce while he sat in jail and, citing his spousal batteries, gained full custody of the triplets. She sold their home in Dreamland Cove and moved with her kids to Paris, where her paintings go for hundreds of thousands of euros and are in demand.

Crystal, finally free of Tortuga, doesn't paint so much these days. She devotes her time to psychic readings. Her website, c4u.com, earns a modest yearly income, sharing her keen third eye with throngs of seekers all around the globe. To date, she's located kidnapped girls; a traitor; a serial killer; terrorist cells; and an active pedophile embedded in a nursery school. Nuñez got credit for all the busts. He firmly believes in Crystal's gift, and now the two are dating.

Brick anonymously purchased Satin's paintings at the silent auction, which went off without a hitch, artificially hyping the value of Satin's work by several hundred times, boosting her popular Innocentism and spawning a media darling. His fairly common art world gambit pushed her Instagram and TikTok channels to a top-ten slot. She and Brick moved on from Dreamland Cove to create Chicago landscapes in which Brick builds all-new, gun-free zones—nonviolent gated communities for low-income residents with kids. Brick and Satin live in the first one, and they named it Building Blocks.

The Black Beauty Sketchers and Painters Club meets quietly once a season. They gather at Zoey's mental facility, where they go unrecognized by Zoey, who has got the blues and can no longer paint the town red with them, or get green with envy, tickled pink, or filled with purple passion. She's too busy writing in gobbledygook—and sketching the late Darlene.

DUPPY LOVE

I WAS SEARCHING FOR something far from home.

And I chased it until it caught me.

I was rushing barefoot through sugarcane, its green stick figures waving above my head in an ancient island dance, bent on a balmy Caribbean breeze.

An opalescent, fat full moon cried midnight from the roaming skies as I hurried through the shadowed field, its tall canes beating my delicate torso, lush leaves thrashing my thin brown limbs. I panted in shallow gasps of sheer exhaustion, fear, and dread. Spine tingling, I dashed through the foreign terrain, pulse thrumming like a dundun drum. Before long, the sugarcane lifted away, dissolving like sweetener in hot tea, arising toward the heavens.

Poof! The high growth swept away, and I found myself in a clearing. I teetered at the edge of a vast expanse of aqua sea and thrashing waves that pounded toward the shore. The sensual seashore roared and surged, beckoning me from hundreds of feet below my shivering frame. A sheer, iridescent gossamer gown billowed softly in white poufs around me, sweeping the skin of my lithesome body, opening like a parachute. I smelled a whoosh of salty foam, heard the crash and hiss of surf, a roiling, smacking, rippling tide that teemed with starfish, seaweed, sharks, and sea anemones mating beneath cold depths of mysterious brine.

I floated off the cliff with sexy, silken-feathered wings.

Crystalline pink-and-silver sand sparkled beneath the ebb and flow of a watercolor Barbados horizon, dazzling even in the dark, and swells opened up like a giant conch shell, tempting me to wade inside. A wind caressed me, swept me up, hugged me to its gusting heart, rocking me to the calypso siren song in its eternal chest, ephemeral and comforting.

In the evening gloom, a cloud of gold dust swirled about me, glittering, blowing a meteor shower of glinting kisses into my awestruck eyes. I blinked, momentarily blinded.

When I opened my lids, I saw the sight.

I thought I spied a miracle. A sacrosanct Black angel. She flew into view with a glowing breadfruit, offering it on a beam of light. Her sweet smile soothed my weary soul. A brightly colored kite flew up between us, and I reached for it, wiggling my hungry fingers in its tail as it soared into astrospace. I grasped the angel, touched her hand, hovering over the water's edge. She turned into a fairy in ballet shoes on a milkshake cloud.

The sea rose up and swallowed me, its Poseidon presence dragging me into a silver dragon wave so huge it threatened to wash me away. I started to panic but found I could breathe underwater, and a peace took hold. But just as swiftly fright returned, a sense of my mortality, and undertow pulled at my ankles, leaving me sunken, choking, waterlogged. Oblivion overcame me as I began to believe I could not survive, that this would be the end of me. A violent tug toward the sea floor sapped my strength. I was about to drown.

I sank, sank, sank past seven sunken treasure ships with pirate booty, hoping for rescue from a source beyond my comprehension, praying to survive my whirlpool, vortex ride through silt and sand. As I sank, laughing clowns with bubble heads turned flips in an undersea carnival in a series of subterranean caves, blue pools, and cascading waterfalls that led farther toward the earth's magnetic iron metal core. As I journeyed, I chanced on prancing flowers, glimmering limestone rock formations, turtle sculptures, lizards, coral reefs, and a giant waving hand.

When at last I touched bottom, the sandy nether started to rock, quake, shift, and slide.

The earth's crust rumbled, cracked, and peeled. A gushing geyser of fiery-red and amber lava pierced the breach and shot me up beyond the beach to brightly twinkling stars.

I had that dream again last night. Once more, I woke up shivering, sweating, trembling, feeling isolated, mixed-up, lonely, caught up in a gripping psychic chain with broken links.

Lately, if I tried to sleep, I closed my eyes, but in exhaustion, the minute my head hit the pillow, a startling array of ghosts and goblins, ghouls, and other unsettled, disembodied spirits roamed my fitful world. They shot up out of muddy grave sites, sprang upright in satin coffins, zoomed at me in swirling mists. They appeared to be translucent, with their vacant, glowing eyes affixed, their bony fingers reaching out like spiderwebs from passageways, their skeletal remains out prowling for abandoned souls.

My dreams were animated films. The less I slept, the more they plagued me, wrapping me in anxious gloom. Relentless, they tumbled end over end in an endless stream of disjointed jumbles, showing me sundry scary sights. But this recurring dream was different. This was a prophetic portent providing supernatural glimpses that were wrought with terror. Ever since my childhood, many things revealed themselves to me before they happened. I could see the future. That's what was so troubling now.

At the end of the dream I had these days, I always wound up dead.

Imagine the concern that caused. Just think of the anguished, sleepless nights. That's why I decided—actually those who saw my swift decline asserted rather forcefully—that I should go to see someone. "A professional," they euphemized. "A therapist," they insisted. A shrink. *Oh great, it'd come to that.* I shrunk at the thought of my life spinning out of control in such a glaring fashion. Weight loss and insomnia. Long crying jags out in my car. Anxiety attacks. I'd begun to become low-functioning for the first time in my life. Almost everyone thought it was all my fault and failed to recognize the truth.

The fact was I was haunted.

I didn't need a therapist so much as I needed an exorcist, but no one was buying what I said, and it was so unfair. My family set me on this course. Unwittingly, but nonetheless. My mom, my daddy, Nana, and Aunt Treasure were responsible. It was them who came up with the old wives' tales that opened wounds from long ago and stirred our Bajan ancestors. But I was the only progeny alive who could hear without my ears. My sixth sense was a receiver and a transmitter I could not shut down. It landed me in therapy.

I wasn't ashamed to get some help. I was really excited to try it out.

Three of my Harvard alumni buds recommended a doctor they'd trusted when they were going through difficult times.

Harmony Reid, my bestie, had been seeing him for several years. She was a divorcée who was struggling to keep herself afloat in the manner to which she'd become accustomed by her baller ex, whom she adored. She fell into kleptomania, filching random stuff in department stores, due to a lack of impulse control and a lack of self-esteem. She said cognitive behavioral therapy got her back on track and it was due to Dr. Heedley. So when Salvador Sanchez, our good friend, hit the wall with a rampant sex addiction,

Harmony recommended Heedley's method, and it helped Sal too. Sal was a brilliant screenwriter I dated until he told too many lies. He was a serial dater and, though married since our brief affair, he failed to amply change his ways. And Chad Woo Chang, who's in my friend zone, simply went to Heedley in his search for work-life balance after burning out in his career, face-planting in his office. He quit and now seems happier.

Now I was on Borman Heedley's couch where the leather was making a scrunching sound when I sat or moved in any way.

Dr. Heedley ran a psychiatric spa, according to his brochure, for those who met with trauma or were deemed a danger to themselves or others. I was the former type.

Meeting with Heedley was a trip. He towered as tall as a brontosaurus, flashing a gnarly canine grin. His teeth were sharp and amber. Was he smiling for real or leering at me, sizing me up, trying to figure me out? Whatever, he looked too serpentine to become a beneficent force. He had me fill out a questionnaire, inquired about my overall health and my family's health in general, took my blood pressure, checked my lungs and ears and throat, and then got down to it.

"Are you comfortable lying on the couch?" he asked.

"Uh-huh, I guess I am," I answered. "Where do we start?"

"Anywhere you'd like to. We're here to help you grow. You've taken the first enormous step," he intoned in a singsong fashion.

"Now you pick at my scabs, rub salt in my wounds, lay open the quivering naked flesh protecting my vulnerability, and rifle through my psyche, right?"

Heedley chortled, stroked his beard. "Is that what you think I'm about to do?"

"I think you're going to try."

"And how do you feel about that, Willow?" Heedley probed. "Confiding in me."

"Like you'll be pulling a wisdom tooth."

"They only get pulled when they need to be."

"Or when the dentist wants some cash."

Heedley leaned toward me, elbows on his knees, hands under his chin. "Why have you come to see me, Willow?"

"That's a good question. I want… help."

"Well, as I said, we're here for you. What do you think I can help you with?"

"Please, Doctor, I don't play games. I'll get right to the point and just hope you'll hear me out before you diagnose. I'm not crazy. I'm just haunted. I have nighttime visitations… First off, Doc, do you believe in ghosts?"

"Willow," Heedley said in a condescending tone, "there's no such thing. But it doesn't matter what I think. It matters whether *you* believe and the impact it has on your mental health. That's the most important thing. Right now you appear to be suffering."

Oh really? I thought. Take a look in the mirror. You don't look so swell yourself. "Well, I wouldn't be here if I wasn't, right?"

"Suffering is a choice."

"People suffer from wars and hunger. They don't always have a choice."

"The same stimulus may elicit different feelings in different people. Our thoughts about our experiences define our quality of life. Perception is reality. It colors all we do. A starving person may have a better attitude about a famine than a wealthy person has about a feast."

"I get your point. We experience situations through the filter of perspective."

"We can choose our thoughts and exert dominion over our emotions. If we consciously process what comes in and interpret it responsibly, we live a life of happiness and freedom. Is that what you want? What are you thinking? Are you psychic? Is that what you're telling me?"

"I don't know if I'd put it quite like that. But there's more in the world than what we can perceive with just five senses. We see what we believe and not the other way around."

"I'm a scientist. Into demonstrable facts. I only believe what I can prove." He wriggled in his armchair. "Tell me what you think you see."

"Right now I see a psychiatrist more uncomfortable than he was when I arrived, but that's okay," I said. "We're different. Fine. I'm cool with that. Only, maybe your current belief system isn't infallible like you think it is. Maybe you ought to suspend your disbelief from time to time. You know, like you do when you go to the movies, a play, a ballet, or the opera. You tacitly agree you're going to accept another reality. That of a character, get my drift? I act for a living. Try it out. I'm a character, Dr. Heedley. Couldn't you plunge into my perspective? Stretch a bit to hear me out? Preconceived notions of real and not real are not realistic either."

"I hear you. Fair enough," said Heedley. "Only, I'm a therapist." He added a disclaimer. "I can empathize with patients' needs, not sympathize. That's different. I can understand your circumstances, feelings, and desires, but I can't decide to take them on. It would not be useful."

"No worries, Doc. I'm used to it. No one ever does."

"You see that as an issue," Heedley conjectured, tilting his head.

"It's isolating. I'm alone. Not lonely, just all by myself." He looked like he was listening hard, so I launched into my tale. "See, it was synchronicity. We were having my dad's big sister, my Aunt Treasure's, birthday party. Well, sort of. She was adopted. Nobody knows her actual date of birth. Our family always celebrates on the evening my grandparents brought her home. Aunt Vee was turning sixty, so we threw a birthday bash. We were whooping it up at my parents' house and everyone was having fun, but as the night wore on, the place was really in a mess. So I started to clean, and the older generation hit the veranda, chatting on the old porch swing and rockers while I washed the dishes. The windows were open, and I overheard."

"When did this take place?" asked Heedley, interrupting my train of thought and raking his mustache. He was eyeing me like a specimen he was growing in a petri dish.

"Oh, that was a couple of months ago, but it seems like ages now," I said.

"But you feel it's still affecting you?"

"I've been swept up in it ever since… My dad and Aunt Vee grew up in Barbados, a former English colony in the Caribbean."

"British West Indies. Yes."

"Uh-huh, but now they're citizens. One hundred percent American. But their mom, my nana, felt like a loyal subject of the Queen of England after 1966, when the island gained its independence. Nana maintained that heritage regardless of our ancestors being hauled there in the hulls of slave ships, treated as chattel, barely surviving the middle passage as they did. She was very light-skinned with long, straight hair, and I think she might've passed for white to get work for the sake of her kids at times… Nana comes to visit me," I confided, checking his reaction, gauging how much more to say.

"I see," said Heedley, drawing out the word like he'd had an epiphany. "Go on," he urged on the edge of his chair, fiddling with his facial hair. "Do you feel a special connection to her?"

"Yes. Because of the gift of sight. I inherited it from her."

"Why do you suppose you feel that way?"

"I *know* because she told me so. I've had it since I was little. I guess it's just our heritage. The West Indies has a big network of belief systems stemming from various cultures melded by colonialism, ranging from Christianity to Juju, Voodoo, Hindu, Rastafari, and a bunch of other sects that came to coexist. Crossover African-Spanish concepts. Many of them believe in communicating with the dead. With those who've passed to other planes."

"What do *you* believe?" asked Heedley.

"I believe in God. I was raised in the Presbyterian Church and attended a Lutheran school where teachers never taught those precepts. Except, of course, eternal life. I believe in Jesus's miracle resurrection from the tomb. I also believe that truth can be found in religions all around the world. When people worship a higher power of goodness, light, and love, I feel our oneness in the spirit… I saw a bumper sticker once: 'God is too big to fit into just one religion.' I like that idea. I say God is everywhere present all the time, and love transcends the grave. I try to see God in everyone, no matter what creed or color or whether they have any body at all."

"That indicates an open mind."

"I'm an artist. We have to have open minds. Creativity thrives in an open mind. Closed minds don't let in good ideas."

"Go on with your story," Heedley said. "What was it the old folks said that night?"

"Oh yeah. Right. That's what started it. Mom's side of the family traces back in the US for six generations. Daddy is second generation… Weird how imperialist nations pillage other countries all the time and then say 'Go back where you came from! We'll steal everything you have, including your culture and your freedom, but you're less than human in our eyes so you can't share our dream.'"

"Yes, amazing, isn't it? Causes many emotional, mental, and physical illnesses we see."

"Yeah, well, I can sure see why. Anyway, Dad, Aunt Treasure, and Mom are seniors, but they're really hip. They're cooler than lots of younger folks. They're into tech and everything. Aunt Tree says she's a recycled teen, and Facebook is my mom's best friend. While chewing the fat at the party, they happened to mention a genealogical site where they recently found a relative who brought up the family treasure."

"Family treasure?"

"Yeah, back home. Down in Barbados, a cousin revealed. Third cousin.

On my father's side. Daddy's ancestor on Nana's side supposedly buried it years ago, but no one ever found it."

"I can see why you're intrigued by that, but why is it causing you such distress?"

"Nana told me to find the treasure, that's why. She keeps telling me," I blurted. "Keeps me up at night. It's like she puts it all on me." A teardrop fell into my lap and spread in a pool on my leggings.

Dr. Heedley reached for a tissue box that was perched on the side of his rolltop desk and handed me a wad. "I see. You feel responsible."

"Of course. Wouldn't you? She says I am. She told me on her deathbed. She started the night of the party, and she's been harping on it ever since, egging me on from beyond the veil, coming to me in my sleep."

"So, your grandmother isn't—"

"Alive? Oh no. I thought you understood that part."

"Just trying to be clear."

"Right now, she can see us talking about her. I can feel her in this room."

The doctor's cell phone sang a tune, and Heedley jumped. "An hour."

"What? Already? That was fast. Time flies when you're having fun, I guess," I said and blew my nose. "The night of the party she passed away, and I can't get it out of my mind."

The doctor flinched reflexively. He rubbed one arm like he was cold, lifted a pad and scribbled something, rose, and headed for the door. "We'll speak more about your feelings for your grandmother at your next appointment. Here's a prescription to help you sleep." He handed me a paper. "Get it filled, and let's see how it works."

"It won't. I don't need it. I'll be fine. Polluting my body with drugs won't help."

"Sleep is essential to your health. Willow, lack of sleep can—"

"Yeah, I know. But I'm not taking it," I insisted, fleeing his office, drained.

"We need to decide on a treatment plan," he said as I scurried from the room.

I waved to his assistants on the fly, running down the historic office building's slippery granite stairs, mascara running down my jaw, Dr. Heedley calling after me. Why did I put on makeup just to visit a psychiatrist? It reminded me of my mother tidying up before housekeepers came.

That night, the dream came back again, recurring with a vengeance. Nana chided me as I tossed and turned inside a haunting twilight trance.

"Find it," she instructed. "We are the tree. The tree is we." She chanted, shaking me till I woke. In a sweat. With chills. Alone and shivering. Crying. Flailing in the dark.

We are the tree. The tree is we…

Maybe it was the cheap burrito and extrathick shake I gobbled down on the ride home in my SUV. Or maybe it was PMS from my period coming like gangbusters. Maybe it really was a mental disorder making my dreams seem real, but once the clock struck ten the following morning, I got gone. I bought a ticket out of town—to the island of my forebears.

"But, hon, it's the middle of pilot season," my agent, Sidney, reminded me. "You have that callback coming up, and they're calling you in for *The Pluto Code*, the new series by Cat Klone."

He was right, pilot season was finally on. Mid-January had arrived, when an actor could make a breakthrough in a new series if her luck prevailed. The time of year when TV producers, studios, cable networks, and the Big Three cast their talent and could alter people's lives. LA performers held their breath from now until the end of April or early May when opportunities shined their lights on many starlets' dreams. When a roller coaster ride of stress, hope, sudden success, or rejection spread through the body of every actor's work. Auditions, costume changes, new hairstyling, memorizing scripts, and combing the internet for gigs were top-of-the-list priorities. One had to be at fighting weight.

"A family emergency," I put forth, ignoring Sidney's acid tone. Slim, carrot-topped, and poker-faced, pushy and always in four-wheel drive, Sidney was a rep on steroids, pitching his clients relentlessly. Sid would sell ice to an Inuit and not hesitate to overcharge.

"They love you to pieces at *Kick Up a Storm*. They scheduled your screen test for *Hold Your Breath*. You musta gave 'em a heckuva read, kid. Sheila Downing blew the director, I hear, but after he saw you read, he withdrew her deal memo, forgot her name, deleted her number from his phone, and blocked her from his Twitter page. You, he calls 'Dazzling!' That ain't cheese. He didn't even balk at your number, and I pumped it up, believe you me. You stand to make big coin. The series is corny, but it's drama. You haven't done drama in two years. You don't wanna get stuck in sitcoms. It's your time, pet. Stick around."

"It's only three short weekdays, Sid. It's already Tuesday evening. I'll be back Monday morning, before you know. Before you can read the trades, okay?" I wasn't really asking.

"Have fun," he groaned. "Sure must be nice. Family emergency, my foot. Is the guy an A-lister at least? I can set you up with one, you know. Knight Hammond is champing at the bit."

"He chomps at everybody's bit."

"Maybe, but he's interested. I talked to him myself… Get your beauty sleep, kitten. Not that you need it. No limboing on the tabletops. Stay away from those Planter's Punch cocktails. Oh yeah, that's right, pet, you don't drink. Keep out of the sun, it's a skin killer. Wear a hat, and no hunky island studs. We don't need you getting your groove back right when you land the big one, get me?"

"I'm back Monday morning, hook or crook," I assured him. "Love you, Sid."

"Wish I was going," Harmony whined as she watched me pack my carry-on.

"I'll trade you this vacation for my nightmares."

"Nope, I have my own. Quincy is trying to get me back."

"At least you have a Quincy, 'kay? You had a once upon a time."

"I need another now. I'd have a bad dream every night to get what you'll experience. I'd do anything to squeeze into that teeny bikini you just packed. Those guys will be all over you. Not that they aren't always, but you're going to take that place by storm. You have to text me all the deets." Harmony was a singer, tall and puffy, shaped like a bowling pin, with braids as coarse as a hank of rope that hung down to her bubbly waist. She was half Black and half Mexican, one hundred percent go-getter, and I loved her like a sister.

"Yoohoo, Salt-N-Pepa," Chad Woo Chang said, entering unannounced. "You need to stop leaving your doors open, Willow. You're asking for trouble. It's self-care." Chad was a better friend than lover. Still, I felt a tingle in my tummy when he swaggered in and snatched my skimpy bathing suit. "Mm-mm, I bet you're fine in this. Maybe I ought to tag along."

Harmony stood and straight-armed him. "Dream on. You're not invited."

"You could use the tan though, bro," said Salvador, entering through my bedroom slider, punching Chad. "I bet you're glowing in the dark."

"See? I told you. Lock your doors," Chad chided. "Look what the cat dragged in. You need a man to have your back. You ought to take me on your trip."

"No, *I* need to go with you. Verity left and took the girls," said Sal.

"Poor baby. Aww," I moaned.

"That sucks," said Harmony. "Not for her. She should've left you sooner."

Chad asked, "She caught you in the act?"

Sal plopped down on my floral chaise. "No joke. They're gone. I'm not myself."

"Who are you, brutha, Spider-Man? A master of the universe?" Chad chuckled.

"You shouldn't have slept around!" I snapped before I caught myself.

"Get it together," Harmony scolded. "Work on your problem. You have kids. This could affect them all their lives. Be accountable for your actions."

"Don't everyone offer support at once," Sal whined. "It might go to my head."

Zipping my suitcase, I recanted. "Sorry. I shouldn't have said that, Sal."

"Why not? Just kick me while I'm down. It's a thing. I'm a punching bag."

I moved to squeeze him on the arm. "I'd love to attend your pity party, but I have a plane to catch," I said as I shooed my guests off the foot of my bed.

"Wait. Hold up, slow your roll," Chad said. "Say why you're going first. Like what's this 'duppy' thing you texted? 'Puppy' autocorrected, right? I thought you got a dog."

"No, it's a term West Indians use for a ghost or spirit. Duppy." I tugged my suitcase off the bed. "I'll tell you about it when I get back."

"Uh-oh," Sal carped. "That ain't good." He rendered his analysis. "A ghost is a manifestation of suppressed desire. Guilt or grief. Abandonment. Repressed emotion. You just suffered sudden loss. A grandmother dying so violently can cause great unexpected pain."

"Well, thank you, Sigmund frigging Freud," Harmony huffed. "She needed that. Did you ever consider she might be having psychic visions like she says?"

"Puh-leeze," said Salvador, waving a hand. "And I can channel Santa Claus."

"Don't laugh, you're starting to look like him," said Chad.

"They're just bad dreams," I lied.

"Willow, if you need my help—"

My cell phone interrupted Chad. I pressed my speaker button. The call was from my parents, who were bellowing farewell lyrics to the tune of the birthday song. "Bon voyage to you, bon voyage to you, bon voyage to our baby girl, bon voy-ah-ah-age to you!"

"Aunt Treasure sends her love as well," my father added at the end.

"I'm off to see the wizard," I said spritely.

Chad picked up my bag.

Dad issued me a warning. "You mind your p's and q's, okay? I don't want to have to hunt some rude dude down. You know I will. When you leave the States, the rules can change, especially for a pretty girl. Be careful. Keep an eye out, hear?"

"I'm taking my third eye in my purse," I quipped.

"Right on," said Daddy. "Remember to contact everyone on the list I emailed. Family ties are the most important bonds in life. I want them looking out for you."

"Dad, it's five days, it's not forever. I don't think I'll have the time."

"Remember to check your cell range when you get there, sweetheart. You'll need that. Check while you're waiting at customs. You don't want to wind up out of touch," Mom said. "Calls can be pricey there but, no matter the cost, call every day." She whispered as though a sinister spy was listening in and taking names.

"Did you get my itinerary, Mom?"

"It's printed. We have it right here by the phone."

"You can call us collect if you need to," Daddy offered.

"Sweetheart?" Mommy sniffled. "Don't let anything worry you, okay? Enjoy your trip. And come home safe. We're here for you. We love you more than words can say."

"We adore you, kiddo," Daddy said. "Stay safe and keep in touch."

"Nana is watching over," I assured my folks. "My angel guide."

"Of course she is," my daddy said. "And don't forget the map I drew."

"Blue skies and happy landings," bade my folks to me in unison.

The scene was breathtaking through the rosy lenses of the UV-blocker shades I wore with the cute wide-brimmed pink hat I bought at an airport shop by the taxi stand. After a truly idyllic ride, I arrived at my home away from home, the Cliffhanger Resort, an über-luxury beach locale perched true to its name high atop a cliff overlooking the Atlantic on the east coast of Barbados. My place was a spacious condo with three bedrooms and an awesome view. It was airy and clean and colorful, located in picturesque Bathsheba, a fishing village with rocky cliffs. Pristine white sands, lush woodlands, and a tropical rainforest welcomed me, and the warmth of the Bajan population radiated like the heat. *Bajan* was what the locals dubbed themselves down here in paradise, and they treated me kindly off the bat, seeming to sense a new prodigal child.

It was love at first sight for Barbados and me. I felt my heart belonged to it.

The Cliffhanger was more than I'd dream of for the hundred sixty-dollar Groupon rate on the app with a coupon code. During on-season. I was jazzed. My suite was European-style, formal and yet comfortable, furnished with hand-built solid Barbados mahogany furniture and floors. It was open to the ocean's salty, tantalizing sunlit breeze, with crafts by local artisans, a luxurious bed with a canopy, a charming bamboo ceiling fan, a sparkling private bath and hot tub, a wall of retracting bifold doors, and a wraparound balcony on the sand.

There was a nifty cell phone dock, big-screen TV, crammed minibar, and a pass to enter three restaurants, two beachside bars, a gym that would thrill an Olympic team, and a swimming pool shaped like Barbados. The room service menu looked insane. I was just six miles from the airport and twelve miles from Barbados's capital of Bridgetown, where the slick brochures from the lobby said there were theme parks, nature attractions, recreation spots, and shopping malls.

What settled me on the condo was its idyllic locale near Saint Joseph parish, the sector where my relatives and family jewels were said to be. I was picturing jewels, but the treasure could be gold, some kind of intangible, a currency, or a relic. Whatever it was, my family yearned for that and more, it seemed to me. Our lore was just a pretext. It was really connection we craved, not wealth. A link to our African diaspora, the rich tradition tugging us back to the land where we had roots. The treasure was a missing link to a past that showed our future.

I spent half the first day on a whirlwind tour of the one hundred sixty-six square miles of resplendent local vistas. Atlantic beach, wild surfer waves, and plush green vegetation.

I eagerly visited Tyrol Cot, the historic mansion and former home of Sir Grantley Adams, "the Father of Democracy," the first premier of Barbados. Nana was related to him, proud his blood ran through her veins. She was also related to white men we would never attend a reunion with. We shared DNA by them creeping in the night to oppress weary female slaves they forced their arrogant privilege on. Proud, innocent women they tore from a distant coast to sexually abuse, to use as free labor, to feather their nests, the Fathers of Stolen Lives.

According to island legend, Aunt Treasure was named for our family jackpot, and she spoke of Sir Grantley often, of the national hero he became because he fought for civil rights in the face of the British Empire's grip and strict governmental controls.

The government of Barbados was an oddly complex entity due to the acrid effects of colonization squeezing it for years. Its parliamentary democracy and constitutional monarchy were helmed by new King Charles III, who served as Head of State. Representing the King was a governor-general appointed by the prime minister. The prime minister was selected by the Parliament's majority. The PM appointed a Cabinet of Right Honorable Government Ministers who might or might not have been honorable, and a governor-general appointed the leader of the opposition. Barbados had thirty constituencies that voted for representatives. Thus, the House of Assembly had thirty members, the Senate twenty-one.

After Georgian Tyrol Cot, I zipped to the seat of government, its democratic parliament.

The prime minister chaired the cabinet there. A Black woman held the office. She was the first in the island's history, appointed in 2018. In the South Tower of the limestone Parliament buildings stood an antique clock that was circa 1885. It was built to replace an older clock that previously graced the Eastern Tower until that giant timepiece had to be razed because of unstable subsoil sinking it into the ground. In just ten years, it sank ten feet.

Then a light porch was built where the clock used to stand, the remaining budget for which erected a South Tower clock the islanders restored in 2011. It was stately, with seven-foot copper dials and a Gothic-style, fourteen-foot pendulum.

I mailed a postcard of it to Mom and Dad. *Wish you were here…*

I sort of did. But Bajan men were superfine. I was glad to be companionless in case I ran into Mr. Right. Though if Mr. Right showed up before I left, I might not want to go.

I moved on to another tourist spot, the Andromeda Botanical Gardens. It overlooked Trent Bay and featured orchids, heliconia, bougainvillea, palms, hibiscus, cactus plants, and other succulents of overwhelming beauty. The heady aromas and pollen in the glade stuffed up my nose.

Welshman Hall Gully was next on the list, a jungle with bananas, cloves, nutmegs, and luscious figs. The cool green oasis was part of a series of massive caves until a cave-in caused the collapse that forged the gully, home to the hijinks of native green monkeys, the naughtiest wildlife in the land. Bajan terrain could be turbulent, I mused as I thought of the cave-in, sinking clock, and stirring surf. The island was sinking, sliding, shifting like the landscape in my dreams.

I traded that thought for a taste of fine arts at the Gallery of Caribbean Art in Saint Peter to the north. Its artworks spanned the Caribbean. Its sculptures and photography lent a feast of bold expression.

I topped off the day with a chopper ride, a narrated tour that featured startling panoramic seascapes I was pleased to brain-record. An oscillating helicopter shuttled me and a lecherous male who smelled of mangos, raw fish, rum punch, sweat, and a tart and pungent aftershave over miles of sugarcane, sugar beets, coconuts, and nutritious yams. The plucky young pilot plied us with corny jokes and island expertise, extolling about producing sugar, molasses, and sweet Bajan rum. He told us how the Portuguese first came upon Barbados, and how British explorers settled there in 1627. And he spoke of the Bajan economy and how it's affected its population of two hundred eighty-eight thousand folks.

By the time the sunset painted rainbow colors in the western sky, my head was filled with calypso tunes and clues to the hidden meanings of the details in my flickering dreams. The cliff in my dreams, I observed through my Cliffhanger's window beyond the gossamer curtains hung between me and the water's edge. The underground cave I had dreamed of was identical to the Animal Flower Cave I roamed in a rented wet suit earlier in the day.

Also, in reality, there were seven sunken ships at the bottom of the sea off the coast of Barbados, laden with booty as yet to be mined. The kite in my dream represented an art form. Kite flying was a traditional springtime pastime in Barbados, particularly during Easter as young Garrison Savannah kite competitors came to show off skills. The erosive landslides and land turbulence in my dreams were mirrored everywhere. And the angel's breadfruit I beheld was a staple of the Bajan diet—baked, grilled, boiled, or fried into tasty breadfruit chips in restaurants and at street food stands I patronized. At dinner, I tasted its cream-colored center, felt its rough, green, bumpy skin.

I knew the sweet angel in my dream, the one that held the breadfruit too. She was Nana, evolved to a higher self, a heavenly form of the sturdy old lady from whom I learned courage, strength, big goals, living out loud on my purpose in life, and using my talents to change the world. I wondered if Salvador was right and what I perceived as a "duppy" was simply my wish to see my grandmother again or an agonizing sense of guilt because I wasn't there when she was robbed and brutally beaten to death. I realized my dreams bound Nana and me together, linked by loss and love. I wasn't going to give that up, no matter what I found down here.

It was dark when I left the restaurant, but I was so hyped with energy I convinced a loquacious cabby to take me shopping for some gifts. The outdoor mall was crowded and had an exhilarating buzz. I picked up a handmade ring for Mom; a duty-free, waterproof watch for Dad; earrings for Treasure; sandals for me; a cute raffia purse for Harmony; and T-shirts emblazoned with flying fish for Salvador and Chad. The same cabbie stopped to take me back. I thought that was auspicious. He chatted about the nightlife, wanted to drive me to some local clubs, and asked about my life at home as palm trees waved and floral perfume lingered in my nostrils. In the wake of my exciting day, I thanked him for his suggestions but I requested to go to the condo, where I could plan my treasure hunt.

When I got back to my swank hotel, I regretted leaving the locals as soon as I reached the driveway colonnade. I was alone and a tourist again, not the Bajan I fancied myself to be. I neither lived nor worked nor struggled to try to survive the island heat. I didn't play drums. I didn't teach school. I didn't sell fried breadfruit chips or demand equal pay in the Parliament, or help to rebuild after hurricanes. I didn't call Barbados "Bim" or eat apples while bathing in the sea, and most visitors at my hotel didn't look like me, like Bajans did. They came to relax or have a fling or hazard an exploit to write home about.

The concierge spotted me coming in and informed me of a package waiting for me at the teak front desk. I retrieved it from the hotel clerk and walked through the vaulted atrium, stepping out on a narrow breezeway and traversing it to the condo wing, my hairdo swirling on my head, my sundress billowing in the wind. Loud laughter exploded in the hall.

I was flooded with a wave of peace when I heard the roaring surf.

I placed my key card in the slot, spun the door lever, ventured in… and the haymaking fist of a masked intruder lurking in my fancy suite hauled off and knocked me out.

When I cracked my eyes open, the world was dark and spinning, and my jaw was locked. It felt like it had a gumball in it. My lips felt like dirigibles about to float up off my face. A gong reverberated in my skull to a pounding reggae beat. I heard Dr. Heedley ask me, "How do you feel about that, Willow?" I moaned as I tried to sit up, gripped by dizziness and nausea. My ribs screamed. I fell back again. I saw fuzzy blue streaks of moonlight. Dorothy wasn't in Kansas anymore. I took in the rented room but couldn't remember where I was. From the look of things, it wasn't housekeeping turning down the bed that did it.

The sofa and mattress were overturned. My trusty hard-shell carry-on was slashed to pieces, ripped apart, every bit of its contents scattered. The suite was ransacked big time, tossed like a salad, searched with a fine-tooth comb. An icy dart of fear shot through me, raising goose bumps on my arms. Who did this? What did they want from me? All my cash was in my money belt, along with two books of traveler's checks, each US dollar amount of which was worth two Bajan bucks. I was still wearing my jewelry—costume earrings and a heart-shaped ruby cross I wore on a dainty chain. I tried to take stock of what I brought, visually raking the tangled mess, unable to lift myself up off the floor, my motor skills underperforming. I felt sick. My mind was racing. I was lucky I hadn't been raped or killed.

What should I do? Should I call the front desk? They'd send someone to help me, right? But mightn't they want me to pay for the damage, or worse, would they get the cops involved? Who knew what trouble that might bring? The Bajan police could deduce that I was a mule and some-one came looking for drugs. Or maybe they'd figure I wasn't accosted, that I was an amoral tourist slut, one of those women who flew here for a tryst with an islander that went bad. They'd certainly asked me why I came, and I sure couldn't say to find treasure. They'd put me on the first plane out. Maybe I should be. I'd been attacked. Maybe more trouble was on the way. I was dazed. I felt compelled to flee. I couldn't worry Mom and Dad, but I had to tell somebody. Who cared about the treasure now? Well, Nana and everyone else in the fam.

Did someone get wind of why I came and try to get the jump on it?

Oh, if only Chad were here. He was the one I could always call. Chad was always there for me. With Chad, I was never on my own. But here in Barbados, all I had was a list of distant relatives who'd never laid eyes on me in the flesh and just knew me as my father's kid in the baby pictures Nana flashed back when I was an infant.

When I finally got up on my feet, I checked the locks, choked back my panic, breathed in deep, and steeled myself. I was grown. I was smart. I could handle this.

I was hesitant to turn on lights in case the intruder was on the beach outside my condo windows. Somebody knew I was traveling alone and decided to attack me. I shivered, scooped some ice cubes from a bucket, wrapped them in a towel, pressed them to my achy cheek, and sat in a corner hunkered down.

I required some kind of weapon. I removed a brass knob from a closet door with a knife that was left in the condo fridge in a dish with a couple of butter pats, dropped the knob into one of my running socks, and swung the heavy weight around. "I'll see you a knuckle sandwich and raise you two knobby knees if you come back," I growled. "I'll crack your skull."

I dragged a chair to the door, wedged it under the handle, and sat beside it, my eyes wide in the inky night, clutching my cell phone to my chest. I tried to come up with alternatives that didn't lead to pain or jail. Was the suite getting tossed a random act, an overseas hit like you saw on TV on a late-night real-life crime show? Or was someone aware why I was here? It seemed far-fetched but maybe not. What could a robber be looking for if not my jewelry or my cash?

The map! It occurred to me. It had value. It was the guide map Daddy drew that pointed the way to whatever was buried near his childhood home. Was it here?

I started to search for real.

I unzipped the small pocket in what was left of my suitcase and grew mortified.

The hand-drawn treasure map was gone!

Bam, bam, bam! came a knock at the door as I frantically searched around the bag.

Oh no, the intruder was back, I feared.

My heart pulsated. My mouth went dry. I felt weak. I thought I might faint. I scoured the rooms for the nearest exit, careful not to make a sound, gripping the doorknob in the sock. *Bam, bam, bam!* More threatening knocks. Maybe I ought to just scream bloody murder, but I had no guarantee who'd come, and I didn't know who to trust. The more people who knew, the less safe I'd be. I quietly peeked through the strange distortion of the front door fish-eye lens.

It was a woman. Tall and thin. Wearing a crisp peach uniform. Unmistakably disgruntled.

"Who is it?" My voice was sounding hoarse.

"Housekeepin'! I gwine home," she said in a Bajan accent, hands on her hips. "Wan sumting? Tow-elle? Mint? I cu' bring ya sum ice, y'noh, ar maebee a so-dah ar chips ar cookies. Need shampoo ar lotion? I bring dat." Against my better judgment, I relied on the strength of the thick door chain and pressed the handle, peeked outside.

"No, thanks," I said.

"Wa huppen here?" The housekeeper grimaced, pushing the door, eyeing my disheveled room. "Are ya crazy? Wa have ya done to da playce?"

"A man broke in and attacked me," I hissed, looking past her up the hall.

"Why ya didn't report it yet? Ya know de man? Ya slept wid he? Oh, I get it, ya married in the States."

"No. I'm frightened. I got hurt. I can barely stand."

"I see it. Someone click ya good," she uttered, finger to her lips. "Ya bleedin'. Wayt. Hold on. I come." She ran down to a cart like her hair was on fire, leaned over, reached into a bottom shelf, and hurried back, carrying a basket. I opened the door, and she slipped inside, inveigling me to lie down on the couch while she fashioned a poultice from herbs and a viscous liquid poured from a small brown vial. The concoction had a miasmic smell, but I was so glad for her ministrations I didn't let on that I noticed. To the poultice, she added dried flowers and leaves, and she wrapped it all up carefully, applying it to my forehead, speaking a pleasurable incantation. My pain dissolved like burning snow, and the swelling seemed to disappear, her homeopathic remedy working like a magic charm.

"Dey sometime rob de touriss here and hurt dey sistah women. What dey need is a chance for a honess jahb." She sucked her teeth in clear disgust. "But ya could only control yourself, y'noh, not no one else. Ya born, ya live, ya dah die, and sum-time tings gets kinda rough. But life goes on. Don't get distress." Her name was Windy. Windy Hart. And in a fantastic stroke of fate, she hailed from Saint Joseph near my family. She wasn't born or raised there, but she knew about the parish. Her husband had a business there. Windy was twenty-seven like me. She told me her bodybuilding husband owned a small gym where my people were from.

She related how that came to be. "He bulk up to protect ar home and he find out he were good at liftin', so he started to compete. He's champion of Barbados now." She poked out her chest, broke out a phone and swiped to a pic of a cute little boy. "Dis is our handsome eight-yare-ole, Leo the Lionhearted." The photo was of a child with a rust-colored Mohawk, holding two children's dumbbells high above his head.

"Wus dis 'ere?" she asked me, frowning, lifting what looked like a note off the dresser, handing it to me, eyebrows raised.

Its text was large, on a small, thin pad with the Cliffhanger logo printed in blue at the top in the shape of a flying fish. What resembled a child's handwriting scribble jumped right off the page. "It isn't yours. Stay out of it."

"Oh no, they're really after me," I said. "And I don't know who they are."

"Ya need to get out of here quick, miss," Misty said. "Dey ain' playin' around."

Call it survival instinct, kismet, acting experience, or no other choice, but ten minutes later, I followed my newfound friend, the virtual stranger, Windy Hart, clandestinely through a restaurant kitchen, dressed in her peach-colored uniform, watching her leave in my pale-pink dress, my curly dark hair in a hairnet, my meager possessions in a bucket. Something about the kind woman brought out a vestige of my trust. More than that, I was stranded and needed her.

We crossed the employee parking lot, piled into Windy's hot-pink Mini

Moke—a sort of convertible baby Jeep that didn't have any doors—and galumphed into the countryside.

The air in the middle of the night was bracing, pregnant with intoxicating scents from the tropical flowers and fruit-bearing trees we passed on unpaved roads. Thick growth closed in from every side. When I whipped off the hairnet, a breeze caressed my itchy scalp and sun-soaked skin. It made me feel alive and free. But I was unaware of the harrowing challenges waiting to waylay me and the trials that loomed ahead of me when the car ride came to an end on the next hairy leg of my adventure.

I shared most of my story with Windy on the ride through Saint Joseph in her car, omitting the tiny detail that it was treasure I was after. She invited me to stay with her and her family until I made other arrangements, arguing Bajans were friendly but reserved and I shouldn't let one bad experience keep me from having a wonderful time on another part of the island. I couldn't help but contemplate how a thief found out about the map, but I wasn't completely devoid of resources. I had Daddy's email with the list of family members I could call on in a pinch.

I resolved to make hay while the sun didn't shine the minute I got to Windy's house.

You'd have thought Windy's muscle-bound husband, Block, and their lovable Leo met wayward American strangers at their humble home at three o'clock in the morning on every weekday, such was the generosity, flexibility, and resourcefulness applied to the dangerous task of housing a victim on the run. But first I had to stay safe with them, and I wasn't sure I was.

I rode with Windy, Block, and Leo, guilty about deceiving them, saying I wanted to visit my great-grandmother's grave before I left on a seaplane later in the day. One could read by the moonlight overhead as Block stopped the chugging Mini Moke northeast of the outskirts of Coco Hill. We got out where a narrow trail ended in a rainforest miles from where they lived.

It was once a plantation, Treasure had claimed at Mom and Dad's before I left. It was owned by a titled Englishman, a drunken sot who was ruthless, cruel, and violent toward both friend and foe. He owned slaves—if you thought there was such a thing as owning another human being—and he had an insatiable appetite for slave girls, whom he routinely raped and left to raise mulattos he could then sell for exorbitant prices as they were physically fit and highly skilled. At the time, Barbados engaged in more trade than all other English colonies combined, and the Englishman thrived. But one enslaved son, after years of abuse, plotted a slave rebellion, killing the source of his suffering in the night, whereupon the not-so-nobleman's not-so-grieving widow left for England, selling the property, freeing the slaves, and taking her own son back to Europe, fleeing her husband's Black son when she auctioned off the land. The plantation was subdivided and parceled off to the highest bidders. It now consisted of family farms.

Nana, a descendant of the Englishman's slave wife and her son, was determined to share his largesse as a way of exacting a bit of revenge. Legend had it my distant grandmother was his fave. He fell in love with her—to the extent such men were capable—and in a ploy to prove his affection, the wealthy baron secretly set a king's ransom under a tree for her and the children she had borne for him. After he got shot and left for dead by the son he'd persecuted—the leader who later went on to bravely explore the Northwest Passage—the baron was forced to divulge the treasure's location with his dying breath. But his slaves were soon driven off the land by the threat of being enslaved again, and the treasure wasn't ever found.

Its supposed location was passed from father to son and mother to daughter as a rhyming fable over time until my several times grandmother dropped the ball when she got sick. Her duppy sometimes visited Nana's mother, my great-grandmother, to relay the whereabouts in dreams. Nana's mother pinpointed the fortune's locale for Nana, Nana was quick to tell Daddy where, and Daddy proceeded to draw a map and give the map to me. Daddy took it seriously, the first to do so in generations since the tale was told, and when Nana visited me and told me the treasure could fall in the wrong hands if it weren't found immediately, our urgency increased.

I still have another card to play, I thought, and it gave me confidence. Memorizing scripts and plays had honed my photographic memory into a vault for words and images. Studying Daddy's map cemented its charted landmarks in my head in what was almost total recall. No one could take the map from me. It was locked inside my mind.

Barbados, its tourist bureau said, was "21 miles long and a smile wide," with rich ecology.

This part of Saint Joseph's parish, Coffee Gully, was family stomping grounds for nearly a century of blood, sweat, tears, and immigration to New York. Like much of Barbados, it was dense with foliage where we were, and my comfort level plummeted, it seemed, with every step we took. I saw doubt in my companions' eyes, but still they went along with me, Windy clasping Leo's hand, Leo tracing his free hand over leaves, Block with a machete as we ventured off the beaten path north of Chimborazo Highway.

I followed my memory of the map under massive trees with jungle vines. I recalled my father drew them, and I recognized three giant rocks in a cluster, jumbo mushroom shapes that bordered an acacia tree in a triangle, east, due north, and south. My mouth fell open. My stomach clenched. "I think we're close," I told my comrades. "Let's head toward that—"

Something rustled. Something furtive. Something was scurrying through the bush. Somebody following? We stood still. Block crouched with the cleaver, slashed the air.

"Dad," said Leo. "What was that?"

Windy covered Leo's mouth, said "Sh." She whipped her head around.

I heard it again and perked my ears. "There it goes again," I whispered.

"Hide. It's making its way to us," said Block.

Out of nowhere, a troop of green monkeys appeared overhead in mahogany trees, chattering, scratching, jumping, baring their teeth to unnerve and intimidate us.

"Don't run. Put yar palms up. Back away," said Windy, shielding Leo. "Dere agitated now. Stay cool. Don't turn around, jus' back away. Don't look dem in de eye."

I did as I was told, and the monkeys ate tamarinds as we backed away and pressed farther into the rainforest, heading northward absent any trail. The sound of green monkeys faded, and I was able to breathe more deeply. About two hours later, we hustled through a mango grove and picked some fruit. While looking for a spot to sit and eat, we reached an open field and were awed by the girth of a baobab tree with a trunk so wide twenty people with outstretched arms couldn't match its circumference. It was the tree on the map, for sure. The Triple B tree, it was called. This had to be it. It blew our minds. I walked to its north, paced fifty steps, turned east a hundred paces. "Great grandma is buried somewhere near," I said as I took off toward the west.

"Dis might be someone's land," said Windy.

"I know," I agreed. "It definitely is."

"C'mon, we better get off it then," said Block. "I don't see any graveyard here."

"Wait," I pleaded. "Just a sec. She's buried near this giant tree. It's ours. My dad's and his sister's, I mean. My family actually owns this land. It was part of a slave plantation."

Their mouths dropped open as I moved.

I walked about fifty feet more to the west. And there it was. X marked the spot. An X literally marked the spot with a grouping of Pride of Barbados plants surrounded by mounds of creeping crab's eye vines, whose red-and-black seeds could be poisonous. Daddy and Treasure owned this land, deserted by the wayward dad they hadn't seen in fifty years. They bought it because of the family lore and intended to build a vacation home someday when they retired.

"I don't like it," said Block.

"I'll pay you a grand," I proposed without giving it any thought. "I mean it, I'll give you a thousand bucks."

"Leo, go play by those bush tea plants."

"But mama, I wanna hear this part."

"I gwine cuff ya. Do what I say, y'hear?"

"Ya make me miss everytin'," Leo protested, stomping off and kicking rocks.

"I'll send you another thousand when I get home. No questions asked," I bargained.

"Why?" Windy asked. "Are you up to no good? Is this why ya got attacked back dere?"

"I don't know, but I promise I'll pay. I will."

"Where's the cash?" said Block. "Do you have it here?"

I considered saying no but dug in my belt and pulled out my traveler's checks. "They're as good as cash. I'll sign them."

"What do I have to do?" asked Block, rank skepticism in his gaze.

"Just dig for the grave. That's all, just dig."

I paid half, and Block dug for three solid hours, slashing at the ground, employing his sharply honed machete. I took buckets of dirt he handed up and passed them over to Windy, who was amassing a great big pile of silt while Leo played in a plantain tree as though it was nothing unusual, his parents digging up the past.

Day broke, but we found nothing. No treasure except little Leo's finds—some feathers, a piece of a conga drum, a crusty red-footed tortoise shell and a fossil embedded in limestone. We trudged back to the sidelined Mini Moke and drove past grumpy island workers plugging along the road. We returned to their home disappointed and exhausted, and I took a nap. The couch was lumpy, but I dreamed. I dreamed and dreamed and dreamed and dreamed. Always the same dream, over and over. Even after I awoke.

I had to get out of there, clear my head, and touch base with something credible.

"Willow, sweetie, is that you?" cried Mom when I Zoomed home with my cell. "We've been frantic. They told us you trashed your suite. I had to remit a credit card."

"Where are you, baby? Are you okay?" Daddy bellowed.

"Mom, I'll pay you back."

"That isn't the point. Are you all right?"

"I'm fine," I reassured her. "I've had quite an adventure since I left."

"That's an understatement, don't you think?" said Daddy, sounding a little miffed. "First you don't even call to say you arrived, and the next thing we hear is you turned the place out."

"You don't have to stay there all five days if something happened, sweetheart. Who were you partying with last night?" Mom asked. "Did strangers trash the condo?"

"Kind of, Mom, but I'm all right."

"I'm sorry to say I told you so," said Daddy. "But I told you so. When Treasure and I saw the kite competition years ago, when we were kids, a kite lifted one kid off her feet and she never came back again. Are you trying to give us a heart attack?"

"Daddy, someone stole the map." I tried to sound calm, but it came out shrill.

Silence. "What?"

"I lost the map. Someone broke into my room and knocked me out.

I was unconscious. When I came around, I ran away. I went over to try to find the site, but there was nothing there."

"Hold on, baby," Mom said. "Someone attacked you? Do you know who it was?"

"That's how your suite got ransacked? Did you see him? What did he look like, baby?"

"Nothing. He took me by surprise."

"Somebody's at the door," Mom said. "Tell your father about it. I'll be right back."

Daddy's face took over the whole Zoom screen, their kitchen in the background. "What did the cops say? Did you call?"

The hairs on the back of my neck stood up. "Not yet, Dad. Who's that at the door?"

He flicked his hand, dismissive. "It's Treasure. She called us. She had a bad dream. She said she's coming over. You know what a drama queen she is." He gazed over his shoulder and held out the phone, but my mother didn't reappear. "What's taking the two of them so darn long? Is Treasure coming from Saturn?" He hollered, "Darling, get back on the phone. Come in, Tree. Willow's on the horn. You can tell us your story later." Dad clomped up the hall, and I saw their front door. "Where in the world did she—?"

"What'd you say, Daddy?"

"Where did she go? I don't see her. She's not on the porch or anywhere."

When Dad couldn't find Mom, he buzzed Aunt Treasure, who said she hadn't left home yet and didn't ring their doorbell. Unsettled, Daddy searched around for Mom. Her phone was on the hall console. Her purse was in the living room. She wouldn't just gallivant off in the middle of the convo we were having. Not after I told her about the assault. Before I could protest, Dad said he'd call back when he found out where Mom went. More upset than I was when I made the call, I looked down toward the beach, and I let it settle my nerves and ease my skittishness.

Lured by the gingery smell of a ma-and-pa grocery close to Windy's, I hastened to purchase three bags of food to contribute to the Hart household. I added a headscarf for Windy, a *Black Panther* frisbee for Leo to toss around, and a protein powder jar for Block called Bajan Manly Man. A short, cappuccino-skinned woman with a set of dazzling blue-white teeth and a booty the size of Jupiter was slumped by the side of the register, scratching her head, fixated on local news. She smiled as I approached but shook her head and looked down at the counter.

She was streaming a breaking news report on an iPad with a broken screen. The video showed a current rash of landslides, warning of more to come. "Don't be surprised," a reporter said, "if vine cuttings or seed yams you planted between cane crops wind up in your neighbor's harvest. Houses are slipping toward the sea. The island is on the move." I gasped. The land in Barbados was shifting. More reason to get out now, I thought. But that also gave me an idea.

As soon as I got back to Windy's house, I rushed to sketch another map, and I formed a better game plan too. I would execute it at nightfall— and this time I'd go alone.

When the sun set, utter darkness fell. I treated the Harts to a salt fish dinner, rented a car, bid the family goodbye, paid the remaining five hundred I'd promised, and stashed the bucket in the trunk. For the first time, it occurred to me that the box I'd picked up at the desk was gone, the package delivered yesterday. Someone took it unopened and had it now, and I didn't know what was in it. Furthermore, they ripped off Daddy's map, and they might have deciphered it like I did. Eventually they'd find the spot. I didn't want them to catch me digging up our family jewels.

I pulled the Jeep over behind thick brush miles farther than where Block had parked the Mini Moke when we came to search last night, and I tromped toward the excavation site that failed to yield the treasure. Hares, monkeys, mongooses, engorged tree frogs, and other creatures filled the night with noises foreign to my ears as I carried the shovel I'd purchased into the rainforest, trekking plantation land, climbing steep inclining slopes and precipitous hills that sapped my strength. I lost track of the time as my energy waned. Patches of ground began to bulge before me as I plodded through fresh mounds of dirt and mud. Long after I passed the ditch Block dug, the sod got even muddier, and I slipped and fell into a deep mud puddle, a sinkhole in front of a partial retaining wall that abutted trees that angled akimbo, leaning on a hill.

Slopes. Big bulges in the earth. Unstable trees. Fresh mud. Sinkholes. These were all signs of landslides Block and Windy informed me of earlier, describing how their doors and windows stuck, their plaster often cracked, and how broken asphalt, concrete, tile, and brick plagued landslide areas. This scary thought entered my mind as I desperately clawed my way out of the growing sinkhole, clinging to the roots of a slanting tree, pulling myself up using the shovel like a climber's spike, my tired body soaked with sludge as I grunted with the effort. I was hoping more mud didn't fill the hole before I could fight my way out of it. It almost felt like quicksand. It was right on the verge of swallowing me whole when five fingers pulled me out.

When I finally clambered from the hole, I flopped on my back and rubbed my eyes. I saw an apparition. But it wasn't a vision, it really occurred.

A canopy of age-old trees reached out its arbor arms to me. Long branches like human appendages issued from sculptures of people-like bodies and faces fashioned from soaring reddish wood.

One with an angel cleaved into its roots had pulled me from the sinkhole.

We are the tree. The tree is we.

The sight brought me to tears. It had to be the Nana tree. She was guiding me like I knew she would. She'd just saved me from a certain death. I was dreaming awake in real time now.

It was as if the trees were talking, bidding me to start to search. I sprang to my feet and walked the count. I paced the same steps as the night before, adhering to the map Dad drew. I turned north, paced off fifty steps, turned to the east and marked one hundred paces, then faced due west for fifty more. Renewed, away from the deadly sinkhole, I began to dig and dig.

Less than an hour later, the cutting edge of the shovel clanged against metal, and my pulse began to race. With muck lodged under my cuticles, I dug my manicured fingernails into the mire. And I saw a box. It was caked in layers of gunk, disguised in tarnish and patina. But it was preserved—a silver strongbox inlaid with an ornate painted copper royal English crest!

A clap of thunder rolled above me. Lightning bolts darted in neon streaks through the branches of the trees. I laughed as I bathed in a downpour, reveling in torrents of cool, refreshing rain. I rejoiced and danced a calypso jig in pools of water and squishy mud, my sandals sloshed, my outfit drenched, giving no thought to the fact that the box was too heavy to lift by myself. I believed I'd found the treasure chest and riches were hidden inside it. Giddy, I fantasized about the wonders the fortune could provide for our loved ones and for those in need. I didn't consider how hard it might be to cart the box back to the States. I just chopped at the dirt around the trunk, wedged the shovel under a corner of it, planted both feet on the handle of the shovel, jumping up and down and using my weight as a lever.

All of a sudden, I heard a disconcerting noise some yards away. It seemed to emit from the sinkhole. From its direction anyway. I heaved the shovel up out of the ditch, climbed out of the shallow end of it, and stalked toward the sinkhole, toting the shovel, thinking of feisty green monkeys and how I could gently fend them off. I waded through mud toward the gaping hole.

In midstride, a gnarled hand clamped my face. Its sandpaper fingers covered my nose and mouth and snatched my breath away. I twisted and turned. I wriggled and squirmed. I rammed the shovel backward. *Crack!* into my assailant's ribs. He squeezed me into a grizzly bear hug, growling like a tiger.

"Stop struggling or I'll break your arms."

Where did I hear that voice before?

He spun me around and punched my face.

My head whipsawed, and I heard a snap. I pitched backward, struggling to stay upright, arms flailing like a windmill. I wouldn't go down without a fight. I wasn't going down at all. If he thought he could steal my birthright, he would have to think again. I recovered and sped at him like a racecar, aimed my knee with all my might, and rammed it in his garbanzo beans. His shadow crumbled to the ground, and he kicked me so hard that I dropped on my butt. While he clutched his private parts and groaned, I groped for the shovel shaft and used it to get back on my feet. I hit him and hit him, harder and harder, drawing blood with every strike. He yelled my name, rolled toward me, caught my shoe and yanked my leg.

I scrambled away from him, right foot throbbing, torso riddled with stabbing pain. My ankle felt like he broke it off. He came after me, springing like a spider, forcing me down onto my back and grabbing me around my neck, pushing his full weight down on me, gripping my throat like pliers. I wheezed. I couldn't take in air. I saw stars, and my eyes began to close. I felt so close to death I prayed. He bore down on me, pushing his face in closer, grunting, and I bit his nose. Blood spurted from it like a garden hose. It doused my face and sprayed the ground.

My adrenaline surged. I groped wet grass. My fingers alit on a sharp-edged stone. I gripped it and smashed it into his head, gashing his temple, rolling from under him, hauling off to throw the rock. It hit him in the eye. He clutched his face with both hands, and I recovered the shovel and went at him harder, pummeling him over and over again, making him cringe to avoid the blows, kicking, stomping, forcing him backward toward the sinkhole, struggling with him at its slippery edge. As I felt myself sliding, I jumped away and clung to a leaning tree stump. I watched my adversary fall, the edge of the sinkhole caving in, mud piling down on top of him.

I ran like a gazelle. I knew, if he could, he'd be hot on my tail. I hauled toward the road without the strongbox, pumping and dashing as fast as I could, lamely limping on my ankle, stopping several times to rest. I hunched over, winded, nursing my rib pain, hiding in thick undergrowth, terrified of the man, the monkeys, and the night as I talked to the towering trees.

It rained. It stopped. It poured again. The wind blew like a hurricane.

An eon went by before I saw asphalt. I couldn't spot the rented Jeep. The ordeal wasn't over, I thought, unless I got to the car and vacated the island. I found out just how true that was.

Deep in the dark, I detected a buzz. I heard a loud vroom, saw a speeding scooter. Someone was whizzing directly at me, about to run me over. I swerved, but the biker bumped my hip bone, mowing me down without a glance, revving the scooter out of sight. I was flattened and couldn't get up this time. It took hours before I could rise again. A mongoose appeared and chattered at me, conducting a vigil by my side until I stumbled, limping, found the Jeep, and wrestled the keys from my pocket as I attempted to jump in the car.

The pursuer struck at that very moment, grabbed my left shoulder and spun me around. He was caked with mud and looked like an Orc escaping from *Lord of the Rings*. His fist ripped my top off with one quick snatch and left me to fight in my bra. I screamed and scratched and bit his wrist. The mongoose bit him on the leg and scampered off into the greenery. The man hopped, lost his balance, fell to his right, and broke a front tooth as he hit the ground.

I gunned the engine and took off. I checked the rearview mirror. The guy was already into a Mustang, ferociously lighting out after me. I floored it, but his car was faster. Soon he was veering in front of me, bumping my fender, sideswiping my Jeep. He was trying to run me off the road. I fishtailed into the oncoming lane and we raced a few miles side by side. I smelled his tires burning. A Mack truck approached us, closing on me, flashing its high beams, blaring its horn. It barreled head-on in opposing traffic, plowing straight at me at jet speed. I jerked the wheel. I held my breath. But at the last second before we crashed, instead of plowing into me, the truck skidded, sliding on rain-slick pavement, forcing my attacker into a ditch with a screech and a plume of sand. The Mustang flipped and overturned.

I didn't pass Go, collect $200, think of the silver strongbox, or so much as take a whiz until I'd reached Los Angeles. I was thrilled to see smog and the Hollywood sign.

But what happened back home gave me more of a jolt.

There were cop cars in my parents' driveway. I had to fight to get inside. Once in, I was grateful both Mom and Dad were there. Aunt Treasure wasn't. Aunt Tree's whereabouts were a mystery. She had never arrived at my parents' crib so they'd called to report her missing. And it turned out Mom got waylaid to a neighbor's by a cryptic note. She said the bell rang but nobody was there, just a slip of paper claiming I was waiting down the street. She ran down, and when I wasn't there, Aunt Tree said she was on her way but then she never made it. Her home was ransacked. Her dog was dead. Her car was found abandoned on the side of a road, burned to a crisp. Mom and Dad had a harrowing tale to tell of blood on the steps to Aunt Tree's porch.

I never saw Aunt Tree again.

Not in my waking hours.

I hosted a family gathering the following year when the smoke of our sorrow cleared and we could accept what had occurred, though I still felt guilt and grief.

When you lose a cherished loved one, your priorities tend to shift.

Death is an unpredictable source of sorrow, mystery, transformation, ardor and epiphany.

I'd seen Dr. Heedley for over six months. I felt horrid considering all that'd transpired that fraught week in Barbados. I wondered if I hadn't gone, would Aunt Treasure be alive today? That short vacation changed my life and that of many others. It took months before I could shake the feeling that someone was out there watching me, but I acted like nothing had happened. My support system grew and was stronger than ever, intuiting how much I needed it. And the joy of sharing my life—self-assured, surrounded by folks who loved me for who I was without judging what I did and loving me unconditionally, with all my faults and foibles, fears, neuroses, questions, dreams, and passions—struck me as immeasurable. I loved them all the more for this.

Who was it that said if you wind up with more than one friend when your journey ends in life, you've done better than most? Was it Emerson? By that standard, I was superblessed. I had Mom and Dad, Harmony, Salvador, Chad, and others who loved me and whom I loved with all my heart and soul. And not in that order, as it turned out. Chadwick was my one true love. We decided we missed each other too much while I was in Barbados.

It's funny how, when you least expect it, someone you've looked at for years without realizing he's the one comes into focus. Chad said he felt he lost me before he ever really had me, and I all of a sudden decoded what I never saw in him before. The glow of forever in his eyes. My soul mate, right in my own backyard. After all we shared and did together, all we had going between us that worked, we decided to let each other in and realized we belonged together.

What better choice for a mate than your dearest friend? It was a gift.

And speaking of gifts, one day one came. The day we announced our engagement, a package arrived with a picture postcard and a terroristic shock inside. In the parcel was a miniature of the silver box I'd found that night and abandoned on the island. I'd never disclosed the discovery. Not even to my mom and dad. I equated that box with a near-death experience. Therefore, I just let it go. I decided whatever fortune might be in it wasn't worth a life. Not mine. Not my parents's or Chad's. Not Windy's family's or Dad's cousins's. Aunt Treasure had paid the ultimate price for the legacy left to us by a fiend. I resolved to end his power there.

Only, suddenly it was rebounding now. Like the killer resurfacing from the sinkhole, taunting the daring new version of me. Couldn't the treasure remain in the past? Why wouldn't our history let us go? What was it, a fortune in silver or gold? Was it diamonds, blood rubies, ancient coins, the keys to a castle under the sea, crown jewels to be uncovered, what? Other families had finally recovered their family fortunes. *Why not us?*

At last, with Dr. Heedley's help, the dreams and Nana's voice were fading. Chad and I were steeped in love, looking forward to our marriage. And now this. It came to me out of the blue when I'd come to conclude Nana's soul was at peace. I'd landed a movie and TV show, but the little box snatched my peace away. It had to be what was in the stolen parcel in Barbados. It bore a Bajan postmark and came weeks before my wedding day. Empty, except for the threat it posed.

Why?

I tossed it in the closet. That's where all skeletons went to hide.

Our big day arrived with a cloud overhead, unseen by everyone but me.

The ceremony was a dream, and we threw a fun reception. When Harmony's band began to play, she sang a song she wrote for us, and we gathered to cut our wedding cake. I was ready to toss my bouquet. But a tremor was quaking inside my soul. Was that Bajan killer on the loose? Watching us, plotting a deadly deed? Who murdered Aunt Treasure, and why? And did they kill off Nana too? Was it interconnected, like family trees?

I kept the list of family names. Cousins. Uncles. Still alive. Some living on the island. I'd done research on all of them. Had one been in a car crash? Or was that a stranger out hunting the treasure, haunting my dreams, and tormenting our lives?

If so, he'll get more than he bargained for.

My husband and I, from the honeymoon suite of the ritziest spot on the island, are deep into a risky trek. Together. Searching high and low.

Where is the box and what's inside?

We think we've finally found a clue.

And if we can manage to stay alive, we'll unearth the truth tonight.